Also by Liane Brooks

DECOHERENCE

Time & Shadows
The Grey Room
Convergent Point

Heroes and Villains
Even Villains Fall in Love
Even Villains Go to the Movies
Even Villains Have Interns
Even Villains Play the Hero

Also by Liana Brooks

Time & Shadows
The Day Before
Convergence Point

Heroes and Villains
Even Villains Fall In Love
Even Villains Go to the Movies
Even Villains Have Interns
Even Villains Play the Hero

A BRIEF TIMELINE OF MODERN HISTORY

Prime Iteration

2029—The Asian Cold War ends with the assimilation of China into the Greater Asian Republic which includes parts of Old Russia, Mongolia, North and South Korea, Japan, China, Myanmar, Nepal, Bangladesh, Laos, Vietnam, Cambodia, and Thailand

2037—Borders close as tensions between the South African Union and the Commonwealth of South America battle for oil rights in the Southern Ocean

2039—Ellen Meeks, of Trinidad and Tobago, proposes the UN take on a more formal role as a legislative body

2044—Dr. Abdul Emir presents his graduate thesis about the iterations of time and designs the first model of the Mechanism for Iteration Alignment

2045—Samantha Rose is born in the United Northern Territories of America

2046—The UN consolidates into the World Council, the Congress of Earth, and the Court of Justice

2049—The last of the Amazon rain forest is cut down for housing space and access to oil reserves

2050—Overpopulation concerns push the Ruling Council to consider measures of eugenics

2051—Citizens deemed Suitable by the Ruling Council are moved to controlled cities, remaining areas are bombed under Project New Life

2055–2062—Widespread rebellion leads to worldwide population purges and the Undeclared War

2064—Dr. Abdul Emir is granted executive powers by the Ruling Council

2065—Year 1 of Progress

2069—The Prime Iteration loses dominance

2070—Decoherence expected

Iteration 2

2029—First human clone born

2037—Mexico, Panama, Costa Rica, Nicaragua, Honduras, El Salvador, Belize, and Guatemala sign the Central American Charter to form the Central American Territories

2043—The World Plague begins in China; an estimated 3 billion people die in the next six years

2044—First law requiring all clones to have a genetic marker passed in Canada

2045—First clone with a genetic marker is created in the United States of America under the direction of an international team

2050—Canada signs the United Charter with the Central American Territories to form the United Territories

2053—The United dollar becomes the standard currency in North America

DECOHERENCE

A Time & Shadows Mystery

LIANA BROOKS

HARPER
VOYAGER
IMPULSE

An Imprint of HarperCollinsPublishers

This is a work of fiction. Names, characters, places, and incidents are products of the author's imagination or are used fictitiously and are not to be construed as real. Any resemblance to actual events, locales, organizations, or persons, living or dead, is entirely coincidental.

DECOHERENCE. Copyright © 2016 by Liana Brooks. All rights reserved under International and Pan-American Copyright Conventions. By payment of the required fees, you have been granted the nonexclusive, nontransferable right to access and read the text of this e-book on-screen. No part of this text may be reproduced, transmitted, downloaded, decompiled, reverse-engineered, or stored in or introduced into any information storage and retrieval system, in any form or by any means, whether electronic or mechanical, now known or hereafter invented, without the express written permission of HarperCollins e-books.

EPub Edition SEPTEMBER 2016 ISBN: 9780062407696

Print Edition ISBN: 9780062407702

10 9 8 7 6 5 4 3 2 1

*To Sam. You earned your degree, and I wrote my book.
I guess we both finally found our Happily Ever After.*

2051—Citizens deemed Suitable by the Ruling Council are moved to controlled cities, remaining areas are bombed under Project New Life

2055–2062—Widespread rebellion leads to worldwide population purges and the Undeclared War

2064—Dr. Abdul Emir is granted executive powers by the Ruling Council

2065—Year 1 of Progress

2069—The Prime Iteration loses dominance

2070—Decoherence expected

Iteration 2

2029—First human clone born

2037—Mexico, Panama, Costa Rica, Nicaragua, Honduras, El Salvador, Belize, and Guatemala sign the Central American Charter to form the Central American Territories

2043—The World Plague begins in China; an estimated 3 billion people die in the next six years

2044—First law requiring all clones to have a genetic marker passed in Canada

2045—First clone with a genetic marker is created in the United States of America under the direction of an international team

2050—Canada signs the United Charter with the Central American Territories to form the United Territories

2053—The United dollar becomes the standard currency in North America

A BRIEF TIMELINE OF MODERN HISTORY

Prime Iteration

2029—The Asian Cold War ends with the assimilation of China into the Greater Asian Republic which includes parts of Old Russia, Mongolia, North and South Korea, Japan, China, Myanmar, Nepal, Bangladesh, Laos, Vietnam, Cambodia, and Thailand

2037—Borders close as tensions between the South African Union and the Commonwealth of South America battle for oil rights in the Southern Ocean

2039—Ellen Meeks, of Trinidad and Tobago, proposes the UN take on a more formal role as a legislative body

2044—Dr. Abdul Emir presents his graduate thesis about the iterations of time and designs the first model of the Mechanism for Iteration Alignment

2045—Samantha Rose is born in the United Northern Territories of America

2046—The UN consolidates into the World Council, the Congress of Earth, and the Court of Justice

2049—The last of the Amazon rain forest is cut down for housing space and access to oil reserves

2050—Overpopulation concerns push the Ruling Council to consider measures of eugenics

2057—European Recession cripples the world economy

2064—The United States of America votes to sign the United Charter

2065—The Commonwealth of North America is formed, and the first national elections are held in preparation for the writing of the North American Constitution

2069—Dr. Abdul Emir creates the first working time machine, a completion of his Grand Theory of Movement Through Time

2070—Sam Rose and Lynsey MacKenzie travel back in time to 2065, then move to Australia

CHAPTER 1

> *"Decoherence (n): a period of time when all iterations collapse and there is only one possible reality."*
>
> ~ excerpt from *Definitions of Time*
> by Emmanuela Pine, I1

Day 247
Year 5 of Progress
Capitol Spire
Main Continent
Iteration 17—Fan 1

. . . *three*. Rose stood and peered through the frosted, warped glass of the conference room as the speaker turned away. It didn't matter which iteration she was in, Emir was predictable. She had seven seconds to do a head count. She didn't need that long.

A quick head count was all it took to confirm that the einselected nodes she'd been sent to assassinate were where they belonged.

Every iteration had nodes, people or events that kept

that variation of human history from collapsing. Dr. Emir had created a machine that allowed people not only to move along their own timeline, but at critical convergence points, it allowed them to cross between realities. But the Mechanism for Iteration Alignment's greatest ability was the one that allowed Dr. Emir and Central Command to steer history by erasing futures they didn't want.

Rose knelt beside the door, did one final sweep for alarms, and nodded for her team to move in. It was her job to cross at convergence points, kill the nodes, and erase the futures that no one wanted.

One look at the version of herself watching this iteration's Emir with rapt fascination was enough to make her want to snip this future in the bud.

Chubby was the first thing that came to mind. Rose's doppelganger was enjoying being at the top of the social pyramid and probably gorging on whatever passed as a delicacy here. The squared bangs with a streak of riotous red only accented the corpulence and lack of self-control the inferior other had.

Even with a heavy wood door between them, Rose could hear that this iteration's Emir was hypothesizing things the MIA was never meant to do. Everyone with half a brain knew that decoherence didn't combine iterations, it crushed them. Only the true timeline, the Prime, would survive decoherence. Planning to welcome and integrate doppelgangers into the society was pure idiocy.

The techs sealing the door shut gave her the high sign.

Rose nodded to her hacker.

"Cameras locked. Security is deaf and blind, ma'am." Logan's voice was a soft whisper in her earpiece. He was a genius with computer systems, a fact that had saved him when they collapsed I-38 three years ago. "We have a fifteen-minute window."

"Hall cleared," reported Bennet. "Permission to move perimeter guard to the exit?"

Rose nodded. "Permission granted." She waved for the soldiers to move out. There could be no risk of failure. No chance for the errant nodes to escape, and no risk that her team would get killed here. Sending a node from the Prime was risky but sometimes required. Sending two nodes was something she and Dr. Emir had fought about more than once. She kept reminding him that he was risking the future of humanity.

The subject of argument rounded the corner wearing baggy coveralls that let him blend into I-17. Behind Donovan was Wagner, their intelligence asset, still sporting the ghastly blue-and-purple dye job that had allowed her to embed here for seventeen weeks. Emir had let Donovan jump ahead of the main demolition squad by over two hours to catch up with Wagner, a choice that still left Rose grinding her teeth.

Donovan shouldn't have needed two hours. They shouldn't have needed four months to find the information they needed.

Seventeen weeks was a disgrace.

Most iterations took days to infiltrate, but this one

had some truly outstanding cryptographers, who'd managed to hide the nodes for months. Wagner had brought a cryptographer home, a small gift for Central Command. Once the woman adjusted to life in the Prime, she'd be a very useful citizen.

Wagner nodded to Rose, stopping by her side.

Donovan walked past, going to check his soldier's work on the door. "Done." His expression was satisfied but cold. "This used to be my job."

"Then you won't have a problem setting the charges," Rose said. The nodes of this iteration were going down along with everyone in this high-rise. It was an unfortunate, and unavoidable, situation. Normally, she did her best to keep the death toll to a minimum. Although it was rare for a non-nodal person to retain memories of their alternative selves from other iterations, there was a strong correlation between mass violence in demolished iterations and psychological trauma of the citizens in the Prime.

Which meant an event like this would cause a worldwide ripple of anxiety. No one would sleep easy tonight. Tomorrow, everyone would be on edge, a little more jittery, a little closer to crossing lines they would never normally cross.

Central Command had prepared for that before she'd left for the mission. There were extra guards scheduled for duty tomorrow, and next to her bed there was a little green pill that would ensure she didn't dream of being torn to pieces by a bomb.

She knew, though, that most people wouldn't be so lucky.

If the price of safety was only a few bad dreams, it was worth it.

"Charges set," Donovan reported. "We have six minutes to exit this iteration."

Rose activated her comm unit. "Strike team, move out."

Donovan took point, leading the team through the octagonal building toward their portal home. Wagner took rear guard. If someone came up behind them, Wagner would stall them.

"Entering the secured area." Donovan's low voice grated on her sensibilities. It should have been Senturi running point with her. But a lucky shot by a sniper had put her second-in-command on the reserve roster, leaving her to run a major mission with the Donovan's JV team instead.

They tromped like a herd of elephants. Two of them couldn't keep their weapons high, the muzzles of the guns slipping downward to aim at the floor every time they turned a corner. Not a single one had even glanced upward yet, a lesson her team had learned the hard way several years ago.

Or had it been longer than that?

Her personal timeline was such a knot of traveling that even the computers programmed to track agents' movements had trouble keeping up with hers. The chronometer on her arm said she was close to thirty-two, but her birthday wasn't quite twenty-five years past.

"Contact." Wagner's voice came in terse and tight, like an electric shock against the spine.

Rose held her fist up to stop the team. She was willing to sacrifice herself for the cause—and losing operatives was part of the harsh reality she lived—but she didn't want to waste their lives if Wagner could talk them out of a situation.

"Good afternoon," she heard Wagner say through the earpiece. "Line code 671-59-60. Here's my ID—"

Two heavy thuds followed.

"Threat neutralized," Wagner reported. "But there will be more coming."

That's one way to talk through an obstacle, Rose thought. "Secure the jump room," she ordered. The overhead lights flickered and died. That was not in the plan. "Wagner, explain."

"Brownouts, Commander. This iteration has reached peak energy crisis. They lost the offshore oil rigs two years ago, and now every building is subject to temporary electric shortages."

Fear fired under her skin like liquid lightning. "The machine?"

"On a priority generator," Wagner said.

"The meeting will break early," Donovan said.

Rose closed her eyes, mentally cursing Donovan for speaking out of turn. A few slow breaths, and she was able to respond in an even tone. "The room was sealed. If they try to leave, they can't." If Donovan had as much brain as he did testosterone, he would have realized that himself. Sadly, being a node had nothing to do with intelligence and everything to do with charisma. The more influence and power a person had, the more likely they were to make a future-altering choice and become a node. Somehow, despite having the brains of a flea and the social grace of a concussed sloth, Donovan was a node.

"They may stay anyway," Wagner said. "The brownouts usually don't last more than a few minutes before the generators for the capitol building turn on."

"Ma'am?" That was Logan.

"Speak."

"They'll regain the security feeds when the generators kick in."

There was a snort from someone in the darkness, then, "The building will be rubble in ninety seconds."

"Thank you, Donovan," Rose said tersely. "Everyone, move to the control room. Operations team, I want that portal at full travel capacity in twenty-five seconds." It was an impossible order to fulfill, but they'd scramble. It took sixty-five seconds to walk from the sealed conference room to the jump room. Every second scraped against her skin like a knife blade. *This is not how I die. This is not where I end.*

Donovan cleared the control room with a spray of fire, and the techs programmed the coordinates for home into the machine. The portal glowed, first a menacing purple, then a cool blue, then the warm, fiery white that meant safety.

"Everyone in!" Rose ordered, counting heads as her soldiers moved past.

A shot rang out. "Contact in the hall."

Five more to go. Four. Three. "Come on, Wagner, move it!" The membrane of the portal shivered, taking on a cooler tone as the hole in the space-time continuum healed. Arctic blue streaks appeared like fissures. "Wagner!"

Rose gave it a half second more before she stepped through, unable to wait any longer.

There was a disorienting moment of complete sensory deprivation, a weightless moment in the place of nothingness, then her feet landed on the concrete floor of the control room of the Prime.

CHAPTER 2

> *"In theory, the probability fan is infinite. In practice, Prime is limited to a finite number of iterations that are closely related to the true reality in some way. When the nearest fan closes, another fan opens. From this we can extrapolate all possible futures and pasts. With that knowledge, we control time."*
>
> ~ excerpt from Lectures On the Movement of Time by Dr. Abdul Emir I1–2074

Day 159/365
Year 5 of Progress
(June 8, 2069)
Central Command
Third Continent
Prime Reality

"Twelve," a controller shouted out. "We are losing portal integrity."

Rose held her breath though she'd never let the fear show. The blue lines seeped across the portal, an insidious poison. *Come on, Wagner. Move!*

MOVE.

There was the sound of someone sucking in their breath behind her. "We're losing it . . . Portal closed."

Monitors beeped around the room in the frustrated silence. Rose closed her eyes. Tried to remember how Wagner had looked in her final moments before she'd been erased. Dark brown hair bleached in strips and dyed electric blue and plum purple, both fading. Pale, full lips on a lean face and green eyes. *Young.* Rose opened her eyes. That's what she remembered; Wagner looked young.

She sighed, barely acknowledging the thought that she felt old. There was a time and a place for weakness, and this wasn't it.

She pivoted around to face the techs behind the controls. "Did Wagner try to get through?"

"Yes, ma'am," one round-faced man answered. "She landed in 2050 by the old calendar."

"Date?"

"November 21."

"Iteration?"

There was a sound of furious typing. "Ours, ma'am. We've matched her with a vagrant Jane Doe buried in a mass grave that year. Cause of death was believed to be disease and malnutrition."

Rose clasped her hands behind her back to control the shaking. Adrenaline was no longer her friend. "Send condolences to her family. There will be a closed-casket memorial."

"Yes, ma'am." Two quick movements, and her lieutenant was nothing more than a name on the list of fallen soldiers. "Ma'am, Dr. Emir wishes to see you immediately in his office on this level."

"I'm sure he does. Tell him I'm on my—"

"No need." Emir's voice behind her made all her muscles tense. They'd killed each other too many times in too many variations of history for her to be comfortable in his presence.

It took no small measure of control for to lock her emotions away, but by the time she turned, though, a polite smile was pasted on her face. "Sir."

"An excellently run mission, Commander. Four iterations collapsed with that one. Fan 2 has dropped into Fan 1's position. There are over a hundred iterations there. By morning, the weaker ones will have collapsed, and by this time tomorrow, we'll have information on all of them." He smiled, the all-seeing king, with the universe at his command.

"We lost a soldier," she reported, the words tasting sour in her mouth. Wagner had been one of their best intelligence operatives.

"A non-nodal grunt," Emir said with a wave of his hand. He always did that. Like a magician's trick, he waved his hand, and another life was erased. "Some lives must be sacrificed to save humanity. Some pain must be endured, so we can make progress."

Saying Wagner had been a good soldier was useless. Emir understood physics, not people—but it wasn't a misunderstanding Rose could afford to just pass without comment.

"We lost a highly versatile intelligence operative who had visited over fifty different iterations. We have no one on tap with that kind of experience or aptitude. It will take years to bring a replacement up through the ranks. Attrition of talent will kill us if we aren't careful."

Even as she said it, she knew it might be a mistake, and she quickly snapped her mouth shut, locking down her emotions. This was a public room, and Emir wouldn't forgive dissent. Node though she was, Control knew ways to keep a person alive long past the point of wishing for death. She wasn't going to get herself arrested for treason over something like this.

A bushy white eyebrow twitched up on Emir's face. "We have a large pool of talent, Commander."

"Yes, sir." Her tone was as neutral as the flat paint on the beige walls of the room.

He smiled benevolently. "It does you credit that you are concerned about the loss of one life, Commander. Take the rest of the day off. Spend a few hours meditating on the good you've done. And then consider the stakes. Decoherence is only a few short months away. Our survival is worth any loss."

"Yes, sir. Which leads me to another point, sir, if I can have a private moment with you." She glared at the room. Her team hurried away, while the techs suddenly became engrossed in their monitors.

Emir stepped closer with a grimace and a sigh. "Yes, Commander? What thorn did you collect from your last trip through the briar patch?"

"It's Donovan," she said quietly, so no one could overhear. "Sending two nodes into a collapsing iteration was a risky move. He took point when he should have been on rear guard. It could have been he who failed to get through the portal."

Another magician's wave. "He needs training, and this matter should have been easily handled. Central Command did not anticipate this kind of resistance from I-17. As for his taking point?" Emir shrugged. "You had more than enough time to prepare your team. I recommend you put them through a few more training drills, so Donovan learns his place."

Emir wasn't listening. Again.

"Sir, *all* these missions are high-risk. As you mentioned, this close to decoherence, we can't afford any kind of mishaps. I don't want to take another node with me again. Ever."

"Donovan is your replacement should the unforeseeable happen. Prime needs you to have a backup, and he specifically requested more mission time."

"With Senturi, who is as experienced as I am and not a node." Rose shook her head. "Sir, if we lose two nodes during a collapsing mission, Prime will suffer."

"A Warrior Node is easier to replace than a Paladin." Emir's smug smile said he'd considered this argument and already found a way to beat her. "Would you like Donovan to take over your team?"

"No, sir."

"Then I suggest you find a way to stay alive." His smile held no warmth.

Rose saluted. "Yes, sir." She left the room as fast as decency allowed.

Survival was all that mattered. Especially now with decoherence rushing toward them like a brush fire.

The quest to keep the Prime Iteration intact through that rough ride had driven Wagner to dye her hair, move to a foreign iteration, and risk everything. *Lose* everything.

Rose would do the same if that's what it took.

She checked to make sure the locker room was empty, locked the door behind her, and stripped off the hateful coverall. A boiling, hot shower wouldn't make her feel clean enough, but it was a step forward. To wash off the dust and sweat of the fallen timeline . . . to wash away the memories. To wash off the scent of fear and desperation and humiliation in front of Emir.

Her missions had grown increasingly risky.

Early on, it had been rare to have an agent injured, let alone lost. Now they were suffering injuries on nearly every mission.

Team Two, led by Captain Raza Lin, hadn't returned from a collapsed iteration last week. They'd gone in, and it had taken thirty-two hours for the iteration to collapse. There was no way of knowing how they suffered, but only catastrophic failure could have caused the delay. Those had been good agents.

Rose leaned back against the black tile of the shower, letting the icy water pelt her as it warmed up. As long as she knew that the end was in sight, she could survive.

And decoherence was definitely coming.

Which meant all the iterations would collapse as the universe flat lined. For one brief moment, there would be no other possibilities. No doppelgangers. No alternate timelines. Only after that life-shattering stutter could the universe breathe again. Expansion would open the doors of exploration, and her teams would go back to plundering the intelligence/academic/research wealth of other iterations.

All she had to do was ensure that her iteration retained its position as Prime until then.

The water heated up, and she tried to let those thoughts drift away from her like the steam filling up the stall.

If only it were that easy.

CHAPTER 3

> *Each operative wears a personal chronometer on all missions. This measures our actual, rather than apparent, life span. If I leave at 1630 for a mission and return at 1631 local time, have I only aged a minute? No, I've lived during the time I was away, even if it is now a closed pocket of time. I've lived nearly eleven years outside of the normal timeline, but I've aged very little since our first foray into foreign iterations. Why? Science has yet to tell us.*
>
> ~ private conversation with Agent 5
> of the Ministry of Defense

Tuesday October 29, 2069
Cannonvale, Queensland
Australia
Iteration 2

"Have a good night," Todd said, as Sam clocked out of Wild Blue, the dive shop where she worked as part of her immigration agreement with the nation of Australia.

She gave the boss a little wave. "Night."

It was barely three thirty, but there was no one in town to sell to. The only open hotel had no guests registered, and all the staff had been sent home at noon. Sam had helped Todd finish inventory, packed up a few dive souvenirs for online customers, and now there was nothing left to do. Airlie Beach was a ghost town in the wake of a plague scare.

A few drunk university students came home queasy, and now the whole town was holding their breath and hoping it wouldn't mean another quarantine and evacuation like they'd experienced at the height of the Yellow Plague.

Sam knew with 97 percent certainty that a new plague wasn't around the corner, with a 3 percent allowance for iterational drift, a phrase she and Mac had made up to describe the minor changes between this run through history and their first trip through 2069, when they had lived in the Commonwealth of North America.

Tossing her purse into the passenger seat of the car, she rolled down the windows and let the ocean breeze sweep away the oven-hot air. Australia was beautiful, ridiculously charming at times . . . and always way too hot for a girl born in Toronto.

Not that she wanted six months of winter or anything, but sometimes she wished she could shiver without stepping into the grocery store's deep freeze.

Her phone beeped as she turned north, heading toward Cannonvale and home. She slowed at a stop sign and looked around. If she'd been in the Commonwealth's Southwest, a tumbleweed would have rolled across the street. Zombie movies had more life.

Putting the car into park, she checked her phone, expecting a message from Mac about a missing ingredient for tonight's dinner, or a request for her to get dog food for their mastiff, Bosco.

Instead of a text, though, her phone pulled up a navy blue screen with the Commonwealth Bureau of Investigation seal in the top left corner and a file number she didn't immediately recognize.

Case-756581530263

The notice wasn't strictly illegal. Technically—and she'd be the first to admit it was a very broad technicality—she was a district agent for the CBI. Time travel and the multiverse were the stuff of science fiction when she'd first gone to the bureau academy, and they had never gotten around to writing rules about agents who went back in time to stay like she had.

With a frown, she tossed the phone into the passenger seat and tried to remember her old case files. Case-756581530263 . . .

And then it clicked.

Jane Doe.

The phone clattered between the seat and the door as she took a turn too fast and kept accelerating. No one was supposed to open those files. The events that had reshaped Alabama District 3 in the summer of 2069 were classified top secret need-to-know. Elected officials didn't even get read in on it unless it was a matter of national security, which it wouldn't be until late February, 2070.

She crested the hill of the empty road, the tires squealing and smoking in protest as she hit the brakes hard before she destroyed the car door.

Her husband's head poked above the fence, curious but ready.

If she came home driving like the very hounds of hell were chasing her, she knew Mac would be ready to either talk her into quitting her job, or to make dinner, or to grab the very illegal shotgun from the family armory and go shoot some hounds.

"Sam? Sweetie?" He stepped in the back door as she slammed the front door closed.

In the back of her mind, she registered the sweat glistening on his bronzed chest and the extra dog fur and bubbles on his arms. It was Bosco's bath day. But she shook her head and went straight for the computer.

Mac grabbed a hand towel from the kitchen and followed her quietly.

"Is the IP signal still bouncing?"

"Always," Mac said. He pulled out a chair and sat beside her at the kitchen table. "Want to fill me in?"

Sam pulled out her laptop and started typing in passwords more from muscle memory than actual memory. Her old codes got her to the bureau website, because they were the current codes a younger version of herself used every day at work.

Growling in frustration, she pushed the laptop toward him. "Get me in."

"So, we're angry and hacking into the bureau website. Did . . . wait. This is District 3 in Alabama. Your younger self isn't there."

"I know, but I got an alert. Someone's trying to access Jane Doe's files, and I need to know why. This isn't right." She ground her teeth as two sets of memories beat against each other. "This didn't happen last time."

"It's not that alarming," Mac said calmly as he typed, rooting through the bureau's back alleys to access forgotten entrances in the code. "It makes sense that Agent Parker is looking through his predecessor's old cases. It's not like either of us had time to train him before we left."

Sam crossed her arms, almost hugging herself with fear. "He's had months. Why now?"

"Maybe he's a slow reader." Mac stopped typing and smiled. "In."

"Thank you!" She pulled the laptop back and started flipping through Parker's computer history. "He caught a murder case."

"In Alabama District 3?" Mac sounded amused. "Who got murdered, the mayor's dog?"

"A woman. She hasn't been identified yet. Had a name tag from a diner on the edge of the district, though. ELISSA. So we should have an ID by tomorrow."

"*Parker* will have an ID," Mac corrected her. "You and I are not getting involved. We agreed."

She shot him a glare that bounced right off him. "*You* agreed," she muttered.

"Chasing after our younger selves only risks mucking up history."

"This isn't our younger selves. This is two agents helping a fellow agent."

"From across the globe."

"Like armchair detectives."

"Except it's illegal."

"I'm only looking," Sam said. "Okay, here it is. He looked for similar murders in the district and pulled up a description of Jane Doe filed by the first patroller on scene. I knew we missed something in that cover-up!"

Mac leaned over to look at Parker's notes. "Did he find anything?"

"Similar phenotype and superficial murder weapon. They were both abused."

"Jane was professionally tortured." Mac had done the autopsy, and she knew he'd been thorough because he'd redone everything once he'd identified Jane Doe as Sam Rose, CBI junior agent and his work partner.

He leaned over and kissed her cheek. "Sam, the tide's coming in soon. The surfing should be good. Or swimming. Using Parker's access code to look at his files is a breach of etiquette if nothing else."

Sam tilted her head, point acknowledged but not conceded. "Parker never checks his log-ins anyway. It's not like he'll ever notice. He's a lazy prat."

"Did you ever check your log-ins and keystrokes when you were in Alabama?"

She snickered because neither of them had. Things had been easier there, or maybe simply a different kind of difficult. Her worldview had been narrower. There was the CBI and Commonwealth government who were Right, and there were the lawbreakers who were ever so obviously Wrong.

Time changed that. Really, time *travel* changed that. Suddenly, the playground of Commonwealth laws that defined her space seemed like a kindergarten classroom. Iterations, einselected nodes, and changing histories didn't fit within the boundaries of law. So she'd stepped outside—outside the law and outside of time. Mac had followed.

Mac lifted the printed files from another case. She knew what he saw. Jane Doe: age twenty-nine, height sixty-six inches, hair dark brown, eyes dark brown, cause of death . . . inconclusive.

"We never found her killer," Sam said. "There weren't even suspects."

"When we found her, we couldn't risk naming her or finding suspects." Mac sighed, a little frown on his face.

Sam shared his expression. "I always felt I failed her. Me."

"Not you," Mac said vehemently. "Never you. She's like the one in Florida: a variation, from another iteration. She got caught in the temporal cross fire, or murdered and dumped on purpose, who knows. But it's not the real you."

Mac brushed his lips across hers, just a little rough, but oh so loving. "I won't let anything hurt you."

Sam shook her head. "You don't know that."

He tugged the folder away from her. "Yes, I do. Because there's one thing no other Sam in the multiverse has: me. I won't let anyone hurt you. I won't let anyone take you away. You have me. You have Bosco. You have training. Even if Emir shows up with his goon squad, there is nothing they'll be able to do. So, let it go. You're letting the worry of a potential maybe take all the fun out of summer."

With a sigh, she leaned back in her wooden chair. "I just . . ."

"Worry," Mac finished for her. "I know. It's part of your charm. But today, the sea is beautiful, you are beautiful, and we shouldn't waste our time worrying about what might happen."

She agreed they should enjoy the day. But letting go of the Jane Doe case wasn't going to happen. The fact that she'd never found the killer nagged at her like a thorn in her toe, a constant reminder that she had failed. Still . . .

Bosco clambered through the doggie door and stomped across the tile floor, leaving large, wet paw prints.

Sam automatically reached out to pet him. "Did mean ol' Mac make you run, puppy? Did he make you run all around the beach?"

"Don't let him fool you," Mac said. "He's mad at me because I wouldn't let him eat a seagull, not because I dragged him out to run with me." He closed the folder. "Time to do something else."

Her eyes wandered over his bare chest, bronzed by the sun and honed from a return to his Ranger-style training regimes. He was nothing like that pale, bloated, drug-addled man she'd met so long ago. Now he leaned over her, hazel eyes gleaming.

"I suppose you have some activity in mind?" Sam teased. She knew exactly what he had in mind . . . and had to admit she was starting to think in that direction, too.

It helped that he was so very good at it.

"Pigeon Island looks nice today. Maybe we should go kayaking, then come home and grill some ribs. And then . . ." He bent so his nose touched hers. "Kayaks are so much better than corpses."

She bit her lip. "Well . . ."

"Warm water. Beautiful sunshine. Maybe see a dolphin."

"Or a sea snake." Australia balanced out its otherworldly beauty with a lineup of the world's most dangerous animals.

Mac stole another kiss. "Nothing is going to bite you."

"Oh?" She pouted. "But what if I wanted you to nibble, just a little?" She ran a hand down his arm, enjoying the tension of the muscles and the smile that only appeared when she reached for him. "You know, I don't think we should go kayaking in the middle of the day, though—too much sun. So maybe we can start with the 'and then' . . ." She lifted an eyebrow in question. Not that Mac would ever say no, but it was fun to flirt.

"Bosco, *bien di*," Mac ordered in Vietnamese.

The dog looked at them, then tromped out of the

dining room to flop on his giant cushion in the main living area.

"Poor, neglected puppy," Sam said with a fake pout.

"Poor, neglected husband," Mac countered. "I spent nearly two hours away from you."

"And I missed you."

"Yeah?"

"Yeah."

"Prove it."

She gave him a little push. "Race you to the shower."

CHAPTER 4

> *"Who am I? What am I? Why am I? True peace comes from knowing that the answer to all three can change with a breath."*
>
> ~ excerpt from the *Oneness of Being*
> by Oaza Moun I1—2072

Day 160/365
Year 5 of Progress
(June 9, 2069)
Central Command
Third Continent
Prime Reality

There was a knock on the solid door of the mediation room, a sound that rasped against her soul. Rose snapped her eyes open to the sight of the brown-and-green air recyclers molded and painted to look like trees. "Yes? Come in."

The "leaves" didn't flutter like frightened butterflies as the door opened with a gasp of cold air from the hall. These leaves were metal, far too heavy to ever fly.

"Commander Rose?" the quiet voice behind her was Donovan's.

"Yes?" She stayed in half lotus, right leg folded atop her left knee, and closed her eyes again. She would keep her eyes closed, her senses locked, until she found the sight of the recyclers less offensive. "Is there an emergency?" she prompted, when Donovan didn't say anything.

There was a rustling sound to her left as he sat down on the cement boulder smoothed into the shape of a rounded chair. "I need advice."

"From me?"

"From anyone." His sigh was heavy.

It made her skin crawl. Donovan always had. He was a large man with the precise physical control of a sniper, but he always seemed a hair's breadth from diving into some unseen abyss.

Even his psych profile had a red flag for obsessive behavior. Then again, so did hers. But while she made every effort to keep herself neutral and emotionally distanced, so she wasn't tempted by obsession, Donovan openly courted the madness. The man was one bad day away from sending Emir an engraved invitation to replace him. Although—of course—Donovan didn't see it that way.

And right now, she was ready to help him with the engraving.

More fidgety noises from Donovan. "You were very

generous at Wagner's memorial service. I didn't think you liked her that much."

"I had no opinion on her," Rose said. Which was true enough. She was good at keeping her opinions to herself. "She did her duty and sacrificed herself for the good of humanity. I respect anyone who makes that choice."

"She died for fake trees." Donovan's growl bought her attention.

Opening her eyes, Rose glared across the reclaimed-plastic lawn and clinking minirecyclers with petals painted an obscenely bright pink. "I wouldn't complain, if I were you. Maybe you didn't take the time to review the census data of that iteration, but I did. You don't exist there, not as an adult. Your other-self died in infancy because his father had an undiagnosed mental health issue that resulted in uncontrolled rage."

"So what?"

"Wagner died so you could live."

Donovan crossed his arms. "Is that supposed to reassure me?"

"Is there any reason it wouldn't?"

He stood, booted feet crushing a minirecycler with his careless behavior. "Emir is locking me out. Telling me less and less every day. He's paranoid, and I'm worried he's growing delusional. I want to know the endgame."

Rose found herself glaring at the crumpled metal flower. There should have been a scent released. She was certain she'd read that somewhere. *"The flower re-*

leases the sweetest perfume when crushed." It was probably from a motivational poster, but that was irrelevant.

The techs need to fix that—add a pocket of scent that would evaporate whenever someone stepped on a minirecycler.

Donovan's pacing brought him in front of her, scant inches from the reach of her foot if she lashed out with a kick. "Are you listening?"

"Yes," she said, suppressing the sigh she felt. "Emir is hyperaware of the possibilities going into a decoherence event. Including the possibility that *someone*"—she gave him a significant look—"might betray him. There are rumors about the Ruling Council's having ideas above its station. Central Command isn't as popular as it was in the early years of Progress. People who openly voice doubts in the path of history aren't being given a chance to steer it."

Their eyes met, and she could see the rage sizzling off him. If looks could kill . . .

"I am loyal to Central Command."

"You need to be loyal to *Emir*. Everyone else can be replaced. You and I, we're nodes, but he can always train more. Workers? He'll let them die by the thousands if that's what he thinks is required. The elite hiding on their island? After decoherence, they'll all be gone. You don't need to be in the inner circle to see that. Emir doesn't like being challenged."

"Has he calculated a date yet?"

She shrugged and turned away. "Less than a year is the rumor, but I don't think he has an exact date. What you're seeing from him is fear. He can't pinpoint which event will trigger decoherence. It makes him nervous."

"Emir? Scared of the future?" Donovan snorted with amusement, but his eyes stayed cold. "I thought he trusted his machine."

"He does. He fears what he can't control. That fear leads to distrust of us."

"The soldiers?" His shoulders rolled back as his chin lifted. The soldiers were his, their honor was his honor and name.

Rose shook her head, half at his blind pride and to assuage his concerns. "Emir fears the nodes. One misstep from us could topple everything. We are the ones who can deviate. That's why he doesn't confide in you. He doesn't want to put power in our hands that he doesn't have himself."

His lips curled in a sneer. "But he tells you everything?"

"Emir tells me nothing. I'm the Paladin. My skill is understanding people. I watch. I see. Remember, I was recruited by Emir before Progress began. He may have forgotten those early days, but I haven't. That's why he has my loyalty. Because he picked me when everyone else discarded me like trash." The hunger for acceptance burned through her like a cold fire, turning her veins to ice and her spine to steel.

"I don't see how we could change anything." But she could hear in Donovan's voice that he wanted to. That scared her almost as much as it probably scared Emir.

"None of us know how." She unfolded her legs and stood, carefully staying out of reach of Donovan's long arms. He had a tendency to gesticulate wildly when upset, and his expression was already stormy. "We never know what choice matters and which ones change nothing but our mood."

Donovan watched her like a drowning man looked for the safety of the shore. "Then how do we do this? There's no preparation. One day I was in training, getting my team ready for a night mission in the badlands, and this man showed up. I was pulled out of my unit, given a big, empty bedroom, and told I'm a node. You handle it. How?"

"I'm not afraid."

"Of what?"

"Of anything. Fear is always an irrational emotion. People fear spiders, bats, dark closets, and creaking hinges. None of those can hurt them, but do you know how many requests the Ministry of Defense sees daily asking Central Command to obliterate all future iterations that might contain arachnids?"

"Humans are not a rational species," Donovan observed, his shoulders untensing.

Rose nodded in agreement. "But still the dominant one. It's our job to keep it that way." She stepped back, dusting imaginary specks off her loose, black gi pants. "If you need nothing further, Captain, I need to get ready to teach this afternoon's combatives class."

He folded his arms across his chest. "One more question. What end state is Emir steering us toward?"

She hoped her loose hair covered the telltale fluttering of her pulse in her neck. Fear was irrational . . .

except when it wasn't. "There is a plan, and it is need-to-know." That was a direct lie told with a straight face and even tone. A familiar lie she'd been repeating for years.

The truth was that the jump teams were pruning other iterations ruthlessly. Emir wasn't steering so much as he was mercilessly destroying every iteration he saw. His endgame was to be the only game left.

It was getting out of hand. Emir wouldn't ever admit to a mistake, though, so they kept pushing forward into the darkest unknown. All she could do was maintain a balance until decoherence leveled the playing field, and she could safely redirect Emir's manic energy.

"You shouldn't worry about it," she told Donovan in her blandest voice. "The future will be ideal."

Maybe it was the blandness of her tone, or the intentional emptiness of her expression, but something triggered him. His nostrils flared as his shoulders rose to his ears.

Donovan swung his arm wide. "Ideal? *Ideal?* Do you even hear yourself? You're sitting in a room with metal and plastic plants pretending it's a garden because the air outside this building is so toxic it is corroding the walls! Rations were cut again this week. Too many mouths and not enough food."

"Fewer deaths," Rose countered, holding her own fury in check. "Fewer accidents. No one is jobless. No one is hungry."

"No one is free," Donovan said with a guttural

sound in his throat. "No one is creating. No one is thriving."

"Humans as a species are too apt to make poor choices. This way is better. Safety always means sacrificing some freedom. Selfish instinctual mandates are pushed aside for the safety of the whole. You know this, Donovan. You went through the same schooling regime I did. Emir's program, the MIA—it's keeping you safe. It's protecting you from your own stupidity."

He pivoted on his heel, hands balled into angry fists.

"If you won't accept that, try this: During decoherence, there is only one possible future. There no more infinity, only the binary of survive or die. Only the Prime iteration survives to become the seed of the new expansion. We're the starting point of infinity."

Donovan stopped and stared at a wall.

"Take a walk," Rose said. "Cool off. And think about it: Would you rather be alive, or would you rather have a tree?"

His eyes were bitter when he turned. "I want both."

Rose shook her head. "That was never an option."

CHAPTER 5

> *"The future is endless, our souls eternal, so while there is a sunny day, let me rest in your arms and dream of our forever love."*
>
> ~ excerpt from the poem *Eros Eternia*
> by Deyan Yanes I5—2073

Wednesday October 30, 2069
Cannonvale, Queensland
Australia
Iteration 2

The door to the back porch opened and closed, bringing the scent of the ocean, Australian summers, coconut-scented sun lotion, and wet dog. Sam waved without looking up. "How's the beach?"

"Almost as beautiful as you," Mac said. He laid a hot kiss on her neck. "What's with the papers? I thought inventory at the shop was last week."

Sam raised a shoulder and dropped it. "This is a side project."

"Rose, your badge is showing."

That made Sam turn. She'd cut off her old surname, and it had felt like chopping off her hair after a bad breakup: cathartic. There was nothing from her family or life before Mac that she wanted. He'd argued—rather predictably—that having two MacKenzies would confuse everything. Especially since she persisted in calling him Mac instead of his first name, Linsey, like his mother had; or Eric, his middle name that his army friends used.

He called her Rose only when he really needed her attention.

"My badge is not showing."

"That's a Commonwealth case file you're giving a death glare to."

"So? It's not like I hacked into their computers. I logged in with a valid code. They practically granted me permission."

Mac shook his head—she would have never used this kind of circuitous logic before they'd met. "We *just* agreed not to worry about this. Remember—*yesterday*."

"I'm not looking up the Jane Doe case," Sam protested. "This is completely different."

He crowded her, trying to persuade her to ditch the autopsy files to go play with him.

Sam nudged him with her shoulder. "Go play fetch with Bosco, he's got too much energy."

"I don't want to play fetch with the dog," he teased. He pulled a chair up next to her. "What's the case?"

"Agent Parker has more information on the woman

found in District 3." she said. "It was right on the district line, so District 4 probably caught the case the first time. At least, that's what I'm hoping. There would have been no reason for either of us to know about it, and there's no way to check." A fact she hated more than she could say.

Mac sighed in defeat. "I'm not going to convince you to let this go, am I?"

"Nope."

"You still planning on making dinner?"

"Grilled shrimp and lime sorbet sound good?"

"Sounds like heaven." He sighed. "Sam?"

"Hmm?" The silence condemned her. She looked up into his worried eyes. "I am not obsessing. I swear, this isn't even about Jane."

"You kind of are." His body language invited her to lean on him, to trust him. She always had. "I just want you to be happy."

Sam closed her eyes, leaned against him for a moment, breathing in the scent of coconut suntan lotion and the beach. "I'm living in paradise with the most perfect man alive. I am happy."

"But not really." A strong arm wrapped around her, cradling her. "You're bored."

"Well..." That she couldn't deny. "Working twenty hours a week at an empty surf shop is kind of dull." She sat up, aware of Mac's lingering hand on her shoulder. "This is just a hobby. Like reading a murder mystery."

Mac raised an eyebrow skeptically.

"I promise, by the time you're done wearing out

Bosco, I'll be ready to put this up. It's not a difficult case. Once Agent Parker finds the victim's boyfriend, he'll have it wrapped up by dinnertime."

"All right. I'll go finish up outside. Try not to break Parker's brain."

"No promises," Sam said as she opened Parker's e-mails. The new senior agent in Alabama District 3 hadn't done much work on the case. And something about it was niggling at her. She couldn't put her finger on it yet, but something she'd seen when she skimmed Parker's case notes had kicked her survival senses into overdrive. She just had to find it again.

Twenty-three-year-old Elissa Morez was attacked late Monday evening. She'd bled to death behind the Dumpster for the restaurant where she worked and hadn't been noticed until Tuesday morning. That was frustrating—if someone had noticed her missing earlier, she might have gotten to a hospital and lived.

Of course, if it was domestic violence, then the lack of notification made sense.

Sam clicked through the notes Parker had taken. Elissa lived alone in an apartment on the edge of District 3. She was taking online classes for a master's in business, running a small custom-art company from her home, and waiting tables three nights a week to make ends meet. No significant other or spouse mentioned, which killed Sam's original theory.

Elissa's family lived outside Mobile. Phone records showed two or three calls a month home, but it didn't look like any of them had traveled to visit her, and there was no history of domestic violence on record. On paper, Elissa's life looked almost idyllic.

Pulling out her data pad, Sam started scribbling down ideas. An irate customer, a junkie—although those were rare in District 3. It could have been a random passerby, but that didn't make sense. Murders were rarely crimes of opportunity unless there was a serial killer, and that seemed unlikely.

But she was curious . . .

Sam pulled up the list of recent crimes in District 3. Elissa's death was the only unsolved case on record. The younger other-Sam who worked Melody Chimes's case had closed it with the same steps Sam had used the first time around. Mac had warned her to stay out of it, but Sam had allowed herself some judicious stalking to make sure their time-twins stayed on the right path to a happily-ever-after relationship.

She shook worries about her other-self out of her head and widened the computer search, looking for recent assaults in the neighboring districts. By the time Mac came in, showered and dressed for dinner, she had a color-coded map spread across the dining table.

"So, is this a no to cooking dinner?" Mac asked as he pulled out a chair, flipped it backward, and sat down.

"I'll cook," Sam said, only half hearing him. She placed another blue dot on the map.

Mac made a clucking sound. "So . . . want to fill me in, love? This little armchair investigation looks a lot less hypothetical than I was hoping for."

"I found a string of murders possibly related to

the Elissa Morez case Agent Parker found. Red marks are where the bodies were found. Yellow was the last known location. Blue is the home of record." The map covered western Georgia, the whole of Alabama, and the two bodies found in the Florida panhandle. "I'm trying to figure out who the first victim was."

"Um, wouldn't that be the first body found chronologically?"

Sam shot him a frustrated glare. "Yes, smarty pants, it would be if they'd all been found at the same stage of decomposition."

"What about a timeline based on when they were reported missing." He tipped the chair so he could have a better view. "How do you know the victims are related? Do we have a nifty ritual killer?"

"Nifty ritual killer?" Sam asked in disbelief. "You watch too many bad TV shows. No, I'm linking the cases based on phenotype and cause of death. All are Hispanic, or Hispanic-looking women, ages twenty through twenty-six, long black hair, dark eyes, and all were beaten to death. There are no signs of a weapon's being used. This guy likes to punch."

Mac's eyes narrowed as he caught the scent of prey. "You have a suspect."

Bosco, their long-tailed South African Mastiff, wiggled past her legs, jostling everything on the table, to sit between his two favorite humans.

Sam reached down to scratch behind the dog's ear before he lay down. "I'm guessing the killer is male. Call it gut instinct right now. I don't have evidence, but for a single person to deal this much damage, they need to have considerable mass behind their blows. Statistically, serial killers who favor physical attacks are male. Women usually use something subtle, like poison. But, you know, it could be a woman, or a nonbinary person. I'm open-minded."

"I'm sure the killer appreciates that," Mac said with a grin. Sam punched him in the shoulder— none too lightly. "Ow!"

"You deserved it."

"Fine," he said, rubbing his shoulder. "Do you think the killer is stalking his victims?"

She shook her head. "If he is, he's really good. None of them filed a complaint with the police, had a restraining order against anyone, or even seemed to tell anyone they felt uncomfortable. There's no business connection between any of them. They're from different religions, different political parties, use different forms of social media. I can't find one place where they would have overlapped."

Mac grimaced. "Which is why no one else is looking at this as a serial killer case."

"Right. The range is broad. But, statistically, what are the chances that all these victims would die the same way and look so similar?"

Mac's forehead wrinkled in a frown. "In that part of the Commonwealth? A good 60 percent of the female population is Latina. The age range is a little specific, I'd expect some older or younger outliers, but the body type is average. Average height. Average weight. Statistically, a majority skin and hair color combination."

Sam raised a dubious eyebrow. "You don't think any of them look a little like me?"

He fanned the flatpics out and shook his head. "Aside from the obvious skin tone, no. The noses are different. The eye shape is different." He glanced sideways at her. "How much trouble will I be in if I admit that, statistically, you're average? I mean, I love you and know you're one in several billion, but . . ." He trailed off with a shrug.

Sam rolled her eyes with a huff. "Are you saying I'm paranoid?"

"Maybe, but I'd never say that was a bad thing." He kissed her temple. "Any ideas on how the killer is covering this large an area? Businesses maybe?"

"I looked. There's no commonality."

"Not enough." She pushed away from the table in frustration. "There's a connection here. I know that. The same bones broken. The style of bruising. Like . . . there's a rhythm?" She stood up, trying to figure how the attacker might have come at the girls. "Come here."

Mac stood up and held his arms open. "Okay."

"You're coming after a smaller opponent, what's your first move?" Mac had been a US Army Ranger before the Commonwealth formed, and he'd trained in a variety of fighting styles.

He shrugged. "Why am I attacking them?" He moved behind her, held one arm over her head and one by her chin. "If I need a quick kill and the person is much smaller, I snap their neck unless I can use a weapon."

"Right. A splat gun would be better if you want to immobilize someone."

Mac stepped in front of her again. "You're sure this isn't a ritual of some kind? Initiation? Hazing? There are still gangs that use a group beating to welcome new recruits."

Sam shook her head. "The bruises are uniform across the bodies. Same size handprints. Same size boot tread."

"Did you find out what kind of boots? That could give us something."

"No. It's not coming up on any of the databases." She tried taking a step toward him and a step back, trying to imagine how the killer caught the victims.

Mac held his hands up as if to choke her. "Defensive wounds?"

"On some of them. Blood and skin under the fingernails, but that's not flagging anything in the system, either." She put an arm up to block. "How would this work?"

"Him knocking a victim down? Hit them hard right away?" He faked a punch that missed her nose by a good six inches.

She leaned back anyway, slowly staging the crime.

"Are you assuming he doesn't know them?" Mac asked. "That changes how I would attack someone."

"Right, if you knew them, it would be easier to strangle them, but you don't choke someone, then beat them, do you? Unless you had a personal grudge, you don't attack a dead body."

"So they're attacked first? All the bruises are antemortem?"

"A majority, yeah." She nodded and motioned for him to throw another mock punch. "You swing."

Mac shook his head. "I corner you first." He marched up to her so their toes touched. "A stranger does this, you back up."

She stepped back. "Right, the killer is big. Physically imposing."

"The killer encroaches on the victim's personal space, then they punch." He backed her into a corner and held his fist near her face. "Now what?"

"I drop, curl up." Sam moved down.

"And then the killer starts kicking." Mac mimed the motion. "Where were the victims found?"

"They were all killed in public places while alone or isolated. Work, school campus, bus stop . . . oh, no, the teacher was killed at home."

"All places with corners, trees, walls. The killer is controlling the environment. Picking the hunting grounds." He held a hand out to help her up.

Sam stood and made a note. "Controlling the environment, picking his targets, but which comes first?"

Mac nodded as he thought. "No victims found in cars?"

"Or in parking garages. Which is odd. That would be a good place to corner someone." She sat back in her chair, resting her chin on her hand.

"There is steam rising from your head," Mac said as he rubbed her shoulders. "Stop thinking so hard. We don't need to solve this tonight."

"But—"

"But what? Even if we solve this, how are we going to tell anyone?"

"Anonymous email?" she said hopefully.

He leaned close to her ear. "Sam?"

"Hmmm?"

"You are not getting paid for this."

"But . . ."

"And it's after nine."

Her shoulders slumped. "I bet you're hungry."

"Mmmhmmm." His lips brushed the sensitive skin of her neck. "Come on, sweetheart. Let it go for a few hours. You know that cases don't get solved overnight. This is real life. Someone has to go knock on doors, pound the ground, sort through personal effects. Eventually, a link will appear if there is one. No crime is perfect. But sitting here and getting upset won't speed up the process."

Sam let him tug her away from the computer. "You're right. You're perfect." She squeezed his hand in thanks. "Do you still want shrimp?"

"We have leftovers from yesterday." He kissed her, long and slow.

When she opened her eyes again, Mac was smiling. "You said I was perfect."

Sam laughed. "You already knew you were the most perfect man alive."

"Did I tell you that you were perfect? Because, you are."

"Does that make us the perfect couple?" She was

going to kiss him again, but Bosco wiggled in between. She shot the dog an angry look.

"Want me to heat up the spaghetti from last night?" Mac asked as he kissed her temple and nudged the dog away with his foot.

"Not really," she admitted. She smiled. "I'd rather strip you naked."

"Oh?"

"You still have energy left? Or is it too late?"

Mac picked her up and spun her around. "It's never too late for us."

CHAPTER 6

"Of all the possibilities I've seen, only the future remains a mystery."

~ excerpt from the private journal Agent 5
of the Ministry of Defense I1—2063

Day 186/365
Year 5 of Progress
(July 5, 2069)
Central Command
Third Continent
Prime Reality

Lockers rattled and the building shook as Donovan's team jumped through time. The MIA was getting a workout this week. Futures were fracturing as the world government argued. Jump teams sent to ensure the future of humanity were leaving on an almost hourly basis, reacting to the splintered paths of probability.

Rose slammed her locker shut, avoiding the mirrored, chrome surface and the wraith's face she knew she'd see there. Lack of sleep was catching up with her. That, and the constant barrage of the war with time. She tugged her thinning hair into a tight ponytail and shoved away the memory of thick black waves curling over a face fat from luxurious living.

In other iterations, she was a pampered diva, a politician, a police officer, and a motivational speaker. She'd watched her other-selves from a sniper scope and pulled the trigger without hesitation every time. Those Samanthas were a lie, the person she would be if she were willing to trade fame and luxury for the future of humanity.

Not even an option.

Metal rasped against metal as the MIA warmed up again. In the far corner, a locker painted matte black popped open.

With a curse, Rose crossed the room, then crossed herself. She believed in no god, unless feverish devotion to the math equations of time counted as a religion, but the motion of her hands touching forehead, heart, and shoulders was grounding.

The Locker of Doom rattled, the engraved plaque with the warning never to store anything here and the number 666 swung loose. Rose caught the plaque, rehung it, and glanced inside.

Silky black curls damp with blood obscured the face of a woman wearing a lacy canary-yellow camisole. She'd been folded in thirds, legs tucked up close to her chest, and placed in the locker. This was exactly the sick sort of joke that she didn't have time for.

Automatically, her hand went to the comm unit hooked on her belt, then she hesitated. There was no one to call. Emir had ordered the police force out of Central Command four months earlier. The military police loyal to Central Command weren't equipped to handle an investigation, and they weren't allowed in the building anyway.

The closest thing to a detective who was available were the forensic techs who worked with the infiltration teams exploring new iterations.

Rose knelt, anticipating the first round of questions: Who was she, and where was she from? Brushing aside the hair so she could see the girl's face, she tried to match the deceased with anyone she'd ever seen. Elegant lines of a thin, aristocratic nose and high cheekbones—one cracked by the force of a blow—with skin the color of dark sandstone, and all unfamiliar. The woman could have been any of the millions of women in the world with the dominant genes for darker coloring. Smeared black eyeliner and gold eye shadow gave her away as a stranger, a victim from another timeline. There was no makeup in the Prime. Little wastes, that's what they were . . . paints and colors and brushes that served no purpose and squandered workers' time.

Emir would never authorize a tech to investigate. There was too much at risk right now and too good a chance that the dead woman had come from a now-vanished iteration.

Rose closed Locker 666, shoving it shut and checking the lock. The murdered girl didn't belong here. Didn't belong to her.

Yet she felt the dreaded tug of curiosity and guilt. She was the Paladin, after all, a node who held the future together simply by existing. Paladins were meant to be champions who could see past the surface to the potential of a person. It sounded strangely unscientific the first time Dr. Emir had explained her role in the world. Math and physics she understood. Gravity was the same anywhere (or anywhen) on the planet. But intuition?

Her fingers lingered on the lock.

Intuition said this wasn't just an anomalous murder victim who had been picked up by the MIA's oft-generated temporal cyclones. She wouldn't have been able to explain why she felt it, but this felt intentional.

She'd been on the team that had calculated where the temporal cyclones could appear in Prime, and all of those were sealed with black pillars. Their work had taken the bulk of a year because the calculations required working with complex equations. For someone else to do the math and find an unguarded touchpoint was unlikely, but the Locker of Doom had its name for a reason. Every so often, the temporal waves shifted just right, and everything in Locker 666 was pulled into another iteration.

Usually, the temporal cyclones brought back odd things. A lost sock, a patch of grass, a set of unfortunate koi from someone's pond. To the best of her knowledge, a temporal cyclone had never brought in a body. It wasn't impossible, of course. Her team had used the anomalies to infiltrate well-guarded iterations before, then made every effort to prevent intruders from using the same manner of ingress.

She bit her thumbnail and looked back at the locker. Somewhere among in her infiltration gear she had a fingerprinting kit. No one would raise an eyebrow if she searched the massive database stocked with information from thousands of variations of history.

The building shook again, and as the locker rattled, the sound hollowed. Without looking, Rose knew the girl had been swept away, another piece of flotsam in the ocean of time. Her body perfectly hidden from all authority. Taken by time, and with her, time took Rose's chance to make a different decision.

She stood, studying the locker until she saw what her intuition had picked up before her conscious mind acknowledged it: blood drops on the outside of the locker. Jane Doe had been outside Locker 666. Child of another time though she was, Jane Doe had been here. Possibly even killed here.

She grabbed her travel kit from her locker and pulled out an evidence bag for the blood sample. Central Command probably didn't have the woman's files, so there was unlikely to be a way to look for a genetic match, but it didn't matter. Even when a timeline was destroyed, there were echoes.

Every crime left a trace.

Swabbing the sample, she cleaned the floor with a frown and marched out of the locker room. No one looking would see a change in her behavior, but it was there as she watched the techs run past. She saw the morass of humanity swirling around her and watched for the killer who hid in the crowd.

CHAPTER 7

> *"Only a law that treats everyone as equals has a right to be called a law at all."*
>
> ~ excerpt from a speech by Mississippi
> Governor Chantrell Norin I2—2051

Thursday October 31, 2069
Florida District 18
Commonwealth of North America
Iteration 2

"And this," Dr. Runiker said with a ringmaster's flourish as he pulled the sheet off the body, "is another kind of corpse."

"Looks Latina to me," said one of the students with a laugh.

"Looks hot," whispered his friend in a voice that made Ivy take a large sidestep away from the university biology students.

They were on an anatomy trip for class credit. She was there on a goodwill tour because no one else from the New Smyrna Police Department wanted to drive four hours. The fact that she was a Shadow—a government-owned clone freed from her master because of her gene donor's sudden death—meant she was low person on the totem pole. It didn't matter that in January she'd be a legally recognized human being—it was easier to remember that until then, she was just another corporate bot. She didn't let it faze her, though. *Better a grunt than property.*

So here she was, unhappy about the babysitting assignment but knowing it could be worse. She looked at the bruised corpse, trying to guess what made it special.

Runiker waggled feathered eyebrows. "What makes this body unique?" he asked the crowd as if echoing Ivy's thoughts. "What makes her different than all the others."

"Type of death?" one of the girls asked. She had a red kitten heels and a look that said I Am Going To Be Your Boss Someday. Very Type-A—and exactly the kind of person who would hate Ivy for existing.

Because clones like her took up valuable jobs. Or so the opposition argued. Ivy worked at the police station, and she'd never seen anyone offer to take her jobs, whether it was sorting through garbage looking for evidence or cleaning the drunk tank. Seemed to her that she was doing five jobs for a meager paycheck that went straight to her caseworker. But what did she know.

I'm just a Shadow.

Her pen bent in her fist.

"Wrong," Runiker said. "This woman was beaten, probably in a case of domestic violence. Next guess?"

"Importance of the victim?" a baby-faced boy asked.

Runiker pointed to him. "Close."

"Identity?" Ivy said.

The doctor looked at her for the first time.

Ivy pointed to the corpse's feet. "No toe tag. She hasn't been identified, or if she has, her family is paying to keep her identity secret."

Runiker inclined his head. "Thank you, er, is it Officer?"

"Officer Clemens, New Smyrna PD. And this lady is a Jane Doe." Pride crept into her voice. She was solar at her job, better than good. She'd never been credited, and never allowed to work alone, but she was made with good genes, and she was doing more with her brain than her gene donor had ever considered trying. Although she didn't like to dwell on that thought. Her gene donor had died before she'd reached adulthood, and it was a little unfair to judge the child based on what Ivy had dug up on her parents.

Runiker clapped his hands. "Very good. All right— who knows the procedure for handling an unknown body?" He held up a finger. "Don't help them, Officer. The students need to learn this." There was a twist on the way he said students that made it sound like he meant to say humans.

Ivy buried the thought as another overreaction on her part. Her paperwork was all labeled SHADOW and even the most forward-thinking people wound up having some innate bias against her clone status. Even if he'd meant the insult, there was nothing she could do, not for sixty-one more days. When the Caye Law went into effect January 1, she'd be legally recognized as a human being. Until then, she was an oddity. A rich man's insurance against the untimely demise of his daughter. Subhuman.

A college student wearing a Violent Violets shirt under her knee-length blue lab coat raised a hand. "We should check the missing person's database first."

"No, but good guess," said Runiker.

"Facial recognition for legal ID?" another student asked.

"No."

"Fingerprints?" an exasperated voice asked from the back of the room. It was getting close to lunchtime, and the pampered children were losing their patience.

They'd never make it in the real world as doctors. Emergencies didn't care if you were hungry, or tired, or having a bad hair day. When the sirens screamed, you either could do your job hungry and tired, or you let someone get hurt because you failed. Ivy had never needed to learn that the hard way. This was her second chance at life, and her first chance to be more than an organ factory.

Runiker must have noticed his audience's impatience because he sighed. "Quick clone test first. If this is a clone, what do we do?"

"Toss it in with the rest of the trash!" said the boy who'd commented on the corpse's physical attractiveness.

Ivy scribbled his name down. That kid was either going to therapy or become a serial killer before the decade was out. And it never hurt to have her suspects lined up early.

She raised her hand. "As of January, even a clone will warrant a full investigation. Right now, most cities have a policy of checking out who damaged a clone. They can only be charged with littering"—a fact that made her furious— "but someone willing to kill a clone will often escalate to murdering humans. It's not like you can tell the difference without a gene test."

Runiker nodded. "Excellent. Thank you, Officer." He checked his watch. "We will adjourn for two hours, so everyone can find some food. The cafeteria upstairs is open, and there is a shopping plaza down the street, where several food trucks park. I recommend the tacos. We'll resume at eleven thirty to watch an autopsy."

Ivy stepped aside as the college students hurried away.

Runiker pulled the sheet over the dead woman's face and stripped his gloves off. "You support clone rights? That can't be good for career advancement in a small town. I'd think that, at least publicly, you'd support the Higgins Proposal. The whole 'sentient but lesser' idea that clones aren't fully humans. Only publicly, of course. I'm sure very few clones who support Higgins's movement actually believe they're lesser."

"I'm a clone," Ivy said with a shrug. "And a good cop. I can't support Higgins without underperforming so the rest of my department looks good. If I do that, nothing will get done. One day, the police department will have to decide if they want to promote talent or bigotry." By the time they got around to that, Ivy hoped to be gone. The Caye Law, and Agent Rose, meant she didn't need to settle for a second-rate police department in a small town. There were better things in store for her.

She nodded to the dead woman. "Who's handling this case?"

"No one right now. She's from Tampa, and the CBI is still debating who has jurisdiction."

"She really doesn't have any ID?" Ivy asked before realizing that's not what he'd said. "She has a clone marker?"

"No clone marker," Runiker said. "But no ID, no matching fingerprints, no gene match on file. She's a ghost."

"An illegal immigrant?" In Florida? "How?" She understood people crossing from Brazil into Panama on the Commonwealth's southern border, but Florida? The nearest foreign nation was across an ocean.

Runiker shrugged. "Could be an illegal immigrant, could be a black-market clone, could be a kid raised off the grid by antigovernment types. Not everyone wanted to join the Commonwealth. Especially not down here in the South."

"Yeah." She'd heard all about that in August, when her personal hero was put through a public trial. CBI Agent Rose was the only clone working for the Commonwealth Bureau of Investigation, and she was everything Ivy aspired to be. When Agent Rose's district had been charged with corruption, the local news stations had accused her of everything from being in an incestuous relationship with her estranged father to plotting the murder of her senior agent. They'd buried the part of the story where the senior agent had plotted to undo the Commonwealth because he didn't want women of color taking his job.

They were good at burying things like that.

With a gloved hand, she lifted the sheet and peeked at the woman again. "She looks like she was going to a party. Look at the clothes." The girl had done her makeup, dressed up like she owned the world, and now here she was, unnamed, in the morgue.

"I noticed," Runiker said. "I'm not completely unsympathetic, you understand, but I can't do anything until the CBI releases her into the morgue's custody."

"Would you mind sending me a copy of the autopsy if you get to do it?"

"Why?"

Ivy shrugged. "To read, I guess. I'm going to be a full officer in January. I might catch a case like this, help the CBI or something." Like apply to the CBI and handle the case all on her own. "I figure I'll do better if I have something to study."

"You read autopsies?"

She nodded.

"That's morbid. Even for me. And I'm a medical examiner!" Runiker shook his head. "But . . . whatever

I guess. Sure, if I do the autopsy, I'll slip you a copy. As long as it's not classified. But don't expect anything. This lab is probably not going to be handling the case. They have their own people. I get the ones from obvious accidents and the hospital."

"That's fine," Ivy said. She replaced the sheet. "It's not a big deal."

Runiker smiled. "Lunchtime?"

"Right. Thank you for your patience."

"No problem." He grinned sheepishly. "It's just that the line at the taco truck is long, and if you don't get there early, they run out of jicama." He held the door to the locker room for her.

Ivy stashed her coat and lab shoes and switched to sensible sneakers before grabbing the tiny purse that had her walking-around money and her city-issued ID.

A noise in the morgue made her turn around. "Dr. Runiker?"

She pushed the door open. The lights were off, and no one said anything. Frowning, she let the heavy door swing closed until only a sliver of vision remained. She held still until the lights in the locker room shut off from lack of movement.

It was pitch-black in the morgue, but it took her eyes a minute to adjust to the gloom. Someone was there. Tall, built like a club bouncer, and digging through the boxes of the victim's personal belongings.

She watched in silence as he pawed through several drawers before grabbing what he wanted and running off down the long hall to the loading docks.

Ivy pushed the door open, turned the lights on, and pulled on a latex glove before checking the drawer. It belonged to Jane Doe.

Someone had stolen her clothes.

Fuming at her own stupidity, Ivy wondered how she would explain to Dr. Runiker that someone knew who Jane Doe was. After all, who but someone who knew her would come and steal her clothes?

CHAPTER 8

> *"With age comes the choice: betray yourself, or betray your people. A person cannot serve their interests and the interest of the state at the same time."*
>
> ~ excerpt from *Broken and Betrayed: The True Story of the Last Soldier* by B. E. Contrite I1—2070

Date Unknown
Magdelia Corporation Housing
Sequence 6—Unit 27
Main Continent
Iteration 11—Fan 1

Hot blood flowed over Donovan's hand as he sliced his other self's throat with clinical dispatch. The body fell to the floor with a thud, the arterial spray caught on Donovan's clothes and hand instead of ruining the room. It was a selfish action. He wanted to look at this iteration's life one more time. Soak in the essence of another reality. Capture the memories of this Donovan for himself.

"Donovan?" a woman's voice called cheerfully as he heard a door open. Quick footsteps, then a beautiful woman with red hair stepped into the archway between the living space and the front door. Sunlight made her glow like an angel.

For a moment, she glowed. Her eyes alight with love. Her smile inviting, and sincere. She stretched out her arms . . . and stopped.

Too late, she noticed his blood-soaked uniform, the knife in his hand, her beloved lying dead at his feet. Love turned to fear. She screamed.

She was still screaming when Donovan walked into the backyard and crossed through the portal, leaving the iteration to shatter around the broken woman.

He knew that there would be a sleeping pill next to his bed when he returned to Prime. And he knew with the same certainty that he wouldn't be taking it. He wanted to savor this Donovan's death. The man had looked at the pictures on the wall as he died. His last thoughts had been of the beautiful woman.

And now Donovan would have them for himself.

CHAPTER 9

> *"There is no shame quite like the one you feel when you look on what you could have been and realize only your own pride caused you to fail. I could have had so much more, but I thought I was invincible. I thought I was above it all. Now, look how I have fallen."*
>
> ~ **excerpt from Memoir of the Fallen Man by A. N. Otra 13—2064**

Day 186/365
Year 5 of Progress
(July 5, 2069)
Central Command
Third Continent
Prime Reality

Donovan tossed his Kevlar vest across the room so it clattered against the metal chair. It was an efficient alarm clock.

In his hospital bed, Senturi stirred, opened an eye, then winced. "What do you want?"

"To fragging talk. What else?" He rubbed a his thumbnail where a bit of his other self's blood remained.

"Do you know what time it is?"

"Doesn't matter." Donovan leaned against the window overlooking a dark plaza and darker apartment windows. The government was cutting back on electric wastage with another set of rolling blackouts. "Time isn't real."

"Not this again." Senturi swore and pushed himself up into a sitting position. "Why do you do this to me? I don't need to be your Father Confessor or whatever those people were in that backwater iteration you were stuck in."

"They were priests," Donovan said. "They talked about death. I liked them."

"You would."

A shadow of a nurse passing by cut through the weak yellow light spilling through the frosted glass of the hospital room's door. Donovan waited patiently. Always patiently. He checked the window again, scanning the opposing rooftops for the telltale glint of a sniper's rifle. "I did another run."

"I know," Senturi said. "I still get the briefings." He sighed. "Is this about Wagner?"

"No, she was grist for the mill. Emir sent me back. Alone. To a little sprig of an iteration. They had trees. The one where Wagner dies had an arboretum." Donovan's leg bounced involuntarily. A dangerous tic. It was getting worse. He was losing control with every jump. Splintering. He locked himself down and turned to Senturi. "Trees. Gardens. Plants I'd never even heard of."

Senturi shook his head and shrugged. "So?"

"There are people going hungry here. We can't produce enough food. We're growing algae to maintain oxygen levels because we strip-mined the Amazon rain forest."

"Again—so?"

"So how is *this* the better iteration? How is this the better path for us?" He remembered the red-haired woman, with wide green eyes and a sprinkling of cinnamon freckles across her nose.

Senturi shook his head. "I told you not to think like that. You can't question. That's how agents lose their minds. You stare at yourself from behind a gun too many times, and you start wondering if the right person came through the portal."

"So what's the answer?" Donovan's voice cracked, breaking with a need he couldn't verbalize. Begging for reassurance. He could feel himself tearing between duty and desire.

"The answer is: That arboretum was going to lead to failure. They had trees. That doesn't mean they had stable leaders. That doesn't mean they were safe. We are months away from the decoherence event, and it is our job to make sure that the time collapse doesn't knock humanity back to the Stone Age. We've dodged so many missteps, narrowly escaped extinction, and you want to question that?"

The woman's smile was all he could think about. "I saw pictures of my other self. He had a home. A lover. Maybe a wife. He was happy." An idea tickled the edge of his brain. The first whisperings of a plan. A way to escape.

There would be . . . consequences. Fatalities.

"Well," Senturi said, "if you left the capital more often, you'd see people smiling around here, too. Not near Rose or Emir, but there are happy people. I've seen them."

Donovan paced to the corner of the room, eyeing the dark night outside as he weighed how many lives he could justify as acceptable losses in this silent war. "That's the other thing. Rose . . . her head's all wrong." She supported Emir with a pathological madness.

"Her head's wrong in every iteration," Senturi said. "Ignore Rose. I have her under control."

Donovan turned his attention to the pale man sitting in the bed, sizing him up and weighing his worth. "You've got nothing under control, including your own body. You're broken. Emir is ready to use you for parts."

Senturi's lips pressed into a thin, grim line. "Emir knows what I'm doing. I keep the peace in the old corporation families. He doesn't have the head for politics, and Rose doesn't have the *cojones*. The Council listens to me. The Chief Minister of Defense is my cousin. Rose's father has debts owing to my family that he couldn't pay in three lifetimes. The only thing Emir fears more than death is a loss of control. He thinks he's manipulating the Council, but he's not. The Council is in control."

Which meant that Senturi was a fool, too.

Donovan turned away, recalculating. "Manipulation, lies, and mind games. It's how the whole damn world works."

The other man stretched, putting his hands behind his head. "As long as it keeps working."

Donovan drew in a long breath. "How much longer?" He needed time. To win Emir's trust, to find the perfect place, to find his red-haired woman . . .

"Decoherence should occur before March of next year. The iterations will flatline. Violence might spike for a week or two, then it gets better. We can let the probability fan run out, and when it hits the right point—"

"We move," Donovan said. Senturi's plan would push the Council into power, remove the iron grip of Central Command choking humanity, and replace Emir with someone more acceptable. Senturi thought he had a chance of taking over. Donovan thought Senturi had an excellent chance of being found dead with a knife in his back.

"Emir and Rose are out. You and I are in. The Council will accept me as a full member, and you'll be my right-hand man."

Donovan nodded. That wasn't going to happen, but Senturi's quest for power fitted nicely into his own plans. He waved to Senturi and grabbed his vest. "I need to take a walk."

"Do that," Senturi said. "And get some sleep, too. You look like hell."

Donovan didn't bother saying that was because

they lived in hell. They both knew the truth. Prime was stable because it was the lowest common denominator, the worst of all possible worlds.

Somewhere, there was an iteration where he was a good man. Or at least pretended to be. Either way, in this iteration, he wasn't, and he knew he didn't deserve a good man's life. But he'd take it anyway. Like a knife flashing in the dark, he'd carve himself into a better world and have everything the other iterations promised that he could only dream about now. Because one thing was clear:

He'd rather die with having had even a taste of happiness than survive only to remain in this misery.

Rose waited until the third shift before she left the relative safety of her room for the medical labs three floors below. While she technically was Emir's second-in-command and had the right to go anywhere, she was wary of what lurked in the shadows. Central Command had once been a large, multibranched quasi-military establishment with research, and training, and layers of protective red tape. Over the past two years, Emir had streamlined it.

The first cut, she hadn't noticed. Her team was ordered by Central Command to go to a new iteration that had spawned its own fan. The world had been virtually identical to Prime. It wasn't until months later that her habit of browsing data from old files had shown the single difference: a life. In the iteration she'd destroyed, Councillor Ibrahim Mesar survived what was considered an accidental encounter with a nut he was allergic to.

In the Prime, Counselor Mesar had not survived.

She took the stairs, not the lifts, down three flights, and opened a door with a broken lock that she'd neglected to mention to maintenance.

After the councillor's death, she'd started paying better attention to what was happening. The budget cuts that didn't look quite right. Little things like mortality rates and population counts not adding up kept her up at night. She noticed the changes between worlds, and a madness in Emir's eyes that she prayed was a reflection of her own paranoia. When Emir had announced they were within two years of a decoherence event six months ago, the changes had moved from large to reckless.

It was noticeable when she walked into the nearly empty lab. In a huge space that easily could have housed over a hundred people, there were only two research teams of six. Stations sat dark and vacant. There should have been programs running to extrapolate data collected from the other iterations to improve life here in Prime. Emir had ordered them all shut off six weeks ago. She took a deep breath when she realized her hand was shaking.

"Commander Rose?" A man with wispy black hair and gold, wire-rimmed glasses stood, hands fiddling with something is his lab-coat pocket.

"It's Dr. Basch, isn't it?" She smiled because she knew it would make him more likely to help her, and she hated herself for knowing that. She hated herself for choosing to manipulate someone. But it had to be done. Needs must.

The man nodded, his bangs falling over his glasses. "Yes, Commander. Thank you for remembering me."

"I read your work on the new species of edible algae," she said, not adding that she'd read it less than an hour ago as she researched her own people to prep for this mission in the same way she prepped to destroy a timeline. "I was wondering if you could help me with something."

"Of course, Commander!" Basch practically glowed. The poor fool thought being noticed by her was a good thing.

If he only knew that everyone she focused on died, he'd know he should run in fear. But there really was nowhere safe for him to run. The towers where the civilians lived were actively decaying. The air outside was unbreathable. There was no safe place on Earth but here, at the right hand of the devil.

Basch's smile wilted under her examination, unaware of her inner thoughts. "Do you want to discuss this later, Commander?"

Rose shook off her melancholy. "No, now is good. I have a sample I need tested." She took the evidence vial with the swab of blood from Locker 666 from her pocket. "It's probably nothing, which is why I didn't put a security alert out, but I found blood during a routine sweep of the command tower. I need to know who it belongs to so I can check the medical log and make sure they received the appropriate attention."

Basch lifted the sample to eye level with a little frown. "Was this all you found?"

"Yes."

"If it was by the gyms, it was probably just a nosebleed, those have been common since the new training regime started. I'm told the thirty-seventh form is very tricky to learn."

"It is," Rose said. So far only she and Donovan had mastered it.

Basch nodded. "I can have this for you by my next shift tomorrow."

"Are you working on something more important?"

"Only the samples Captain Donovan brought in. They were on the training floor, too. I think he's trying to find out who didn't clean up after their session."

Her smile was calculated and flawlessly warm. "Great minds think alike. It's good to know I'm not the only one who noticed this. But, please, don't share the results. I'll let Captain Donovan handle the soldiers in his own way. There's no reason to give him another target if I can pull them to the side and give them a quick reminder."

"You're so much nicer than he is," Basch said with the openness of someone who wanted to be eliminated by Central Command's Internal Intelligence Division. The IID frowned on people's having favorites. Anyone with a power base was a threat to Emir, and IID was Emir's guard dog.

"Thank you for your service," Rose said, stepping back. "I'll come by tomorrow to collect the results."

"I look forward to it. Sleep well, Commander."

"Good evening, Doctor." Her smile never wavered, but her hands were shaking when she reached the stairwell. Her walk was nearly a run by the time she reached the floor where her room was tucked in a corner away from everyone else. The door closed behind her with a silent, solemn click before the panic attack swallowed her whole. She let the dread run over her, consume her. Felt the tears heat her cheeks and burn the cuts on her dry lips.

I am a force for good in humanity, a guiding light to the lost, a voice of hope for the hopeless. I believe in humanity and the greatness of the individual. I am the Paladin. That had been her pledge. When she'd left the UN intelligence to work for Central Command, she'd come because she knew with a rock-solid certainty that she was the Paladin, that she could change the future for the better.

The MIA was meant to be the answer to everything. The end of wars, famines, destruction, and senseless hate. Every tragedy could be averted by simply removing the iteration where it happened.

And she had failed humanity. Everyone who looked to her as their guiding light was stumbling into darkness because her blind faith in Emir meant she hadn't seen this coming. She hadn't seen his madness. Hadn't understood until it was far, far too late.

The dead girl in the locker had been a wakeup call.

Tomorrow, she would go and drag the future back into place. She would be the Paladin and make things right.

CHAPTER 10

> *"Everyone wants to believe they're special, that their choices matter and that they are truly unique. We tried applying that human fallacy to time and failed, spectacularly, to understand the truth."*
>
> ~ Dr. M. Vensula, head of the National Center for Time Fluctuation Studies I4—2071

Friday November 29, 2069
Cannonvale, Queensland
Australia
Iteration 2

Mac rubbed Bosco's ears in meditative circles as he contemplated the contents of the fridge. Five years married to a woman who could be a gourmet chef—and was playing one on a dinner cruise tonight—and he still couldn't seem to find a meal when he needed one.

Bosco stepped forward to nudge a block of aged cheddar cheese with his nose.

"You're a cheese fiend, Bosco." At the word "cheese," Bosco's rump hit the floor with an echoing thump. "You are not getting cheese."

Bosco's tongue hung out.

Mac shook his head and reached for a half-finished hoagie. He wanted a proper dinner, but he'd stayed late up at the single hotel still open on Airlie Beach where he worked as a local guide. It was his stupid fat mouth that got Sam a job helping out on the cruise. He should have kept silent when Wendy asked if anyone could fill in for the other chef who'd gone up to Townsville to be with her sister, who was in labor.

Never volunteer.

He was a former US Army Ranger, and he'd volunteered. The sergeant in him was deeply disappointed.

Sandwich in hand, he wandered back to the dining room, where Sam's latest case was spread over everything like an encroaching coral. He'd been trying to stay out of it. Someone had told him years ago that spouses needed their own hobbies, but . . .

He took a bite of his sandwich and sat down to see how Agent Parker was doing.

Poor guy. Sam hadn't even had time to train her replacement before she was swept away by the CBI and given a promotion to keep her from telling anyone what they'd found.

His assignment to Chicago had been more of the same.

Parker had identified four victims so far: Elissa Morez, Jane Doe, Amanda Leyvas, and Carolina

Avalos. And there was an e-mail from Florida District 20, south of Lake City, Florida: Leigh Locklear, a nineteen-year-old massage therapist who had moved to Tampa to work for a cruise line. That made no sense. She fit the phenotype the killer preferred, but Tampa? That was just too far away from anything. And she didn't have a car.

So how did she get from Tampa to Lake City?

Mac was mapping trucking routes when Sam walked in. "Hi."

"What are you doing up?" She looked a little frazzled, her usually neat hair escaping from her bun and her white work shirt stained with something yellow. "Do you know what time it is?"

"Not really, no." He smiled. "How was the trip?"

"Wendy paid me double when I told her I was never coming back." She dropped her bag by the table and sat down. "I'm still never going back again. I spent more time trying to keep a drunk tourist from grabbing my butt than I did cooking."

Mac raised an eyebrow. He knew better than to storm off and coldcock a tourist, but if Sam wanted it, the man would be in a body bag by sunup.

"It's fine, Mac," Sam said, clearly seeing the murderous look in his eye. "I did the thumb hold you showed me, and told him if he didn't leave me alone, I'd feed him to the sharks. He spent the rest of the cruise hiding in a guest room."

He smiled. "Good."

"So, what are you doing?"

"Digging through the CBI travel database to see if any trucker visited all these areas."

"And?" She sat down beside him.

"Nothing. I don't think the killer was using the main travel routes."

She pillowed her arms on the table and laid her head down. "So . . . what? There's no connecting the victims. I've tried every angle I can think of. There's no rhyme or reason for why these victims were picked."

"Except for the physical similarities," he said.

"Yeah. But it's so superficial!" She sat up, and he saw a familiar look of annoyance. The criminals were doing it WRONG by golly, and his beautiful wife wasn't having it. She paused. "What? You're grinning."

"I was just thinking of what would happen if you ever turned to a life of crime." It would be glorious watching her storm across a continent beating henchmen into line.

"I wouldn't do that!"

"You might want to consider it as a future career option. You'd make an amazing crime boss."

"I'd tell everyone to follow the law."

"Crime boss, politician, they're so similar. Plus, we'd get henchmen."

Sam giggled. "Henchmen? And wait—*we*?"

"I'm your loyal second-in-command."

She hit his shoulder. "All right. Did you find anything helpful?"

He turned the map so she could see. "Amanda Leyvas, lived in rural Alabama and worked as a middle school teacher. She didn't come back to school after spring break. When her coworker went to check on her, they found her body lying next to her car, dead and cold. The police found nothing. There was a speed trap less than a mile from her house in both directions. Leyvas hadn't left her house since midweek, and no other cars went past in the coroner's window during the time of death."

Sam frowned. "Did they question the person who found her?"

"A sixty-two-year-old woman with bad hips and a bandaged hand because she burned it baking cookies for her class. Mrs. Amil was not listed as a suspect."

"Yeah, I can see why. The ME reported her being extra cold?" Sam raised an eyebrow.

"Not rapid postmortem cooling as far as I can tell." Mac said. "A late-season cold front swept through, and her windows and door were still open. I flagged it because it's the first home invasion although it doesn't look like it had anything to do with a robbery. But she's the first one who wasn't killed or dumped in a public place."

Sam nodded slowly. "A change of pattern usually means an outside pressure, or something similar. What was she near? A rest stop maybe? Truck weight station? It would fit the target-of-opportunity theory."

"There were no tire tracks in her yard, but her house is near public land, so there's a place to park a few miles away . . ." They both came to the same thought at the same time. "Hiking trails."

"Private home on the edge of public land." Sam's smile was fierce. She stood and sorted through the file before handing the datpad to Mac. "There it is in the crime scene photos, see? She hung her laundry out to dry, and you can see a footpath in the background. See the dirt trail?"

"So the killer is walking, sees a woman hanging her laundry . . . and attacks her?"

"Suggesting the killer picks victims before locations. And, possibly, that this phenotype is triggering uncontrollable rage."

"That's not sane."

"Killing usually isn't," Sam said, taking the datpad back. "But it's a lead. Everyone who hikes has to sign in and carry a trail tag. If a trail tag is still missing when the park closes at sundown, the park rangers are alerted and go out to find the missing hiker."

It was Mac's turn to smile. "Tracking means GPS, and a GPS means there is a time and location of the hiker. That would give us a list of suspects, if nothing else."

"As long as they checked into the ranger station at the parking lot," Sam said, trying to temper their expectations.

"How close is the next parking area?"

She sat and pulled up the public land files on her computer. "Thirty miles. It's on the other side of the wood. Still, someone could have parked along the side of the road."

"And not have been noticed? Do you know how

many poacher cams are lining the public lands these days?"

She made a face of disgust. "Not enough. I don't suppose she had a convenient ex in the picture, did she? A lot of serial killers get their start obsessing over one person, either killing them first or killing surrogates as they work up the nerve to kill the person they really hate. If there's a break in the pattern here, it could mean she was the targeted victim all along, and the killer was practicing on the others."

"Amanda . . ." Mac pulled the right screen up and shook his head. "No boyfriend, no family in North America. Her parents live in Panama, but she worked her way north by teaching at various schools. According to her profile on PlusWe—you remember that? The online friend maker site?"

"I remember not using it," Sam said.

"Yeah, well, Amanda posted every few hours, if not more often. She liked hiking, had a tiny organic garden, washed her clothes in a vintage spin machine that came with the house, and she was planning to move to Detroit at the end of the school year."

Sam shrugged. "Sounds annoying, and I bet the school wasn't happy, but that's not a motive. Did she have any PlusWe friends in town who might have been at her house when she died."

"Not a one. That's why she said she was moving. Most of her online friends live up in the Great Lakes region. But she did post a picture of herself hanging the laundry out, so we have an approximate time of death, which will help once Parker gets the forest rangers to give him the park data."

He pulled up a collage of the crime scene photos. "There is something else, though. I was looking over the crime scene photos, and none of the women were found where they died. Some of the investigators noticed, but not all of them. But I looked, and there's not enough blood at any of the spots they were found. Amanda Leyvas's house was immaculate. There's no blood inside or out."

"You'd expect blood if she were killed at home." Sam sat close and leaned over to look at the crime scene photos. "These look almost like movie sets." She drummed her fingers on the table. "Can we—"

"No."

"You didn't even—"

"You were going to ask if we could go to the Commonwealth."

She put on her Catholic Schoolgirl Smile. "We could use a vacation."

"We could. But that's not a vacation. That's trying to enter a foreign country illegally."

"But Mac." She batted her eyes.

Mac kissed her nose. "No. Find a murder in Australia to solve."

She groaned and leaned away.

"One of us has to be the sane one who puts their foot down. Otherwise, we'd be running all over the world trying to fix all the problems out there."

"And that's would be a bad thing why?"

"Do you want to own the world?" Mac asked, only half joking.

She grumbled something about, "Not the worst idea," under her breath.

"Let's get some sleep. The Davis boys are taking a boat out early for dives, and that means the shop will be in complete disarray. It'll be easier to cope with if you haven't spent all night awake worrying about this."

Sam crossed her arms. "Can't we do anything? Send someone in? Get some information?" She nibbled on her bottom lip. "Mac, how much does a private detective cost?"

He took her hand and pulled her away from the table. "We'll look into it. Tomorrow."

She wrapped her arms around his torso and snuggled in close. "What would I do without you?"

Mac looked down at the love of his life and kissed her head. "You'll never have to find out."

CHAPTER 11

"Nothing changes faster than the future."

~ excerpt from *A Brief Summary of Time*
by Dr. Henry Troom I4—2065

> Day 187/365
> Year 5 of Progress
> (July 6, 2069)
> Central Command
> Third Continent
> Prime Reality

Rose moved around the quiet command room, trying to find the files compiled from the latest MIA runs. The lights were at 30 percent, mimicking night and discouraging anyone from lingering after their shift was over. She was alone with the soft hum of data collection interrupted only by the occasional chirp of a computer spitting out data.

Sixteen iterations had been demolished in the past twenty hours. There was no rhyme or reason that she could see, but she was searching. At the moment, she had six computers running. Five were collating data and comparing the recently destroyed timelines in a hunt for a pattern. The sixth was scrolling through the information collected from a thousand iterations in the search for Dana Cardenas, the woman in the yellow shirt Rose had found in Locker 666.

Dr. Basch had given her the name but couldn't place the adult Cardenas in any one iteration. Which was very odd. Every iteration they'd made contact with had a file. But Basch's research had only pulled up Cardenas because she was from Prime. She'd died at age six during a bombing of her city, and her DNA was on file.

One by one, the computers turned up zero results. It was improbable that Emir was operating without a reason. Even with decoherence looming, the other iterations didn't present a threat. They'd all self-destruct when the iterational fan collapsed in that one moment where the only possible future became Prime's future. When all other options ceased to be viable, when some earth-shattering catastrophe hit and only Prime had the answer, the other iterations would vanish.

Collecting the information made sense. Pruning certain radical futures made sense. But this current surge in missions was senseless to her.

With a quiet sigh, she went to each computer, erasing her search history and wiping the stations clean of any genetic evidence. She was supposed to be on duty watching the MIA in case there was an unexpected intrusion, not hacking into the system to run unapproved searches.

Cleaning everything up brought her a sense of peace. For a moment, she could pretend that everything was going well and enjoy the sense of awe she felt standing here.

This was the very center of the universe. Prime was the master control, the heartbeat of the universe.

Rose's fingers brushed across the synthapaper scrolls that showed the constant sine wave of time. With training, she'd learned to read each dip of the iterations.

Here, the birth of an einselected node.

There, the tragic outcome of an event that crushed a million iterations and left only four struggling forward.

The future had a unique brilliance. During the times of expansion, all of time looked like a rainbow fracturing into infinite color. Now the lines of possibility were thickening, collapsing. Decoherence was drowning the rainbow in brutal black.

Quietly, the machine drew the newest line. Tomorrow shifted into view.

Prime appeared as a thin black line at the base of the sine wave. The scroll rolled out, and the black line surged up like a wave, following the possibilities of the lesser iterations. Hour by hour, ink drop by ink drop, the future appeared. She held her breath as the wave crested and crashed down, back to where it belonged at the baseline.

For a moment the whole universe held its breath.

Prime sank, and sank, and plateaued as a rogue iteration shot past it.

Heartbeat stuttering with an unpleasant rush of fear, Rose watched another iteration take Prime's place. Another line touched the baseline and took dominance.

Someone was stealing her future.

Rose went to the communications board and dialed a number she thought she'd never need to use.

After a moment, the screen shimmered as the stern visage of Emir appeared.

"Dr. Emir, my apologies for calling at this late hour, there's been a mishap here at the command center."

He raised a bushy white eyebrow. "A mishap? A flood perhaps? Did you run out of synthapaper? You're a commander. You are supposed to be able to handle these things on your own."

Rose bristled at his tone, furious and fearful. "There is a problem with the machine, sir." She only barely managed to keep her tone respectful.

"The MIA?"

"No, sir. The reader attached to the MIA. The probability fan, crashed and Prime didn't take the Prime position again. It must have a glitch."

"Impossible." Emir sneered. "The machine is infallible."

"If that is the case, sir, then we have lost our place as the dominant iteration."

"Impossible!"

"Then the machine is broken. Sir."

Emir's scowl burned through the screen. "Call the techs. I'll be there in twenty minutes."

Rose slapped on her Kevlar vest with more force then was strictly required. Under the blue-tinted glow of the lights, she found herself trying to avoid catching her reflection in the polished chrome of the lockers. Afraid she'd no longer see the pride and righteous fury that she needed. Afraid that she'd look into her own eyes and see confirmation that, somewhere, she'd made a wrong choice. *This was an impossible situation. Untenable. Utterly ridiculous.*

The silent room became an echo chamber of memories. From her first mission as a freshly minted lieutenant shaking with excitement at the idea of going to a different timeline, to a seasoned veteran, shaking with exhaustion from the years she'd spent in the pursuit of maintaining their Primacy. Now she wondered if all those choices had been right. There had been a few tiny, unauthorized changes to ensure that Samantha Rose got the promotion, to ensure that the stars aligned for her and her alone.

All of those choices haunted her. Begged her to question if that was why Prime was no longer truly the Prime. If her selfishness had doomed all of them to a horrible fate.

The locker room door snapped open with a metallic clatter. "Do you know what hour it is?" Cornelius Senturi, her second-in-command, asked as he opened the locker next to hers.

"I see the surgeon was unable to fix your lack of discipline," Rose said, but there was no bite to her words. She was glad the emergency had pulled in Senturi instead of Donovan. Despite Emir's assurances, the thought of having two nodes out of the iteration made her want to vomit.

"It's three in the morning," Senturi grumbled.

"Time is irrelevant." The response was almost automatic now. Everyone in Central Command knew time was an illusion. And the illusion was running out.

Senturi gave her a put-upon look. "Sleep isn't an illusion. I'm supposed to be healing. Why are we going *now*? This can wait until I've had my beauty rest."

Rose didn't even bother turning to watch him strip. Senturi fishing for compliments was as common as the ticking of a second hand. "No amount of sleep is going to make you pretty, Senturi."

"If time is ours to control, we can wait to run this op until after breakfast. That's all I'm saying."

She tugged her boots on. "Time slipped."

"What?" Senturi demanded, pushing her shoulder so she was forced to turn. He glared at her with pale eyes and an ugly sneer that very few ever saw. "Time slipped? What's that even supposed to mean?"

"We are currently not the prime iteration. Someone else has taken over."

"Impossible."

"Improbable," Rose corrected calmly. "There wouldn't be a possibility fan if things were impossible." Her hand shook a little as she thought about it.

Somewhere out there was the far edge of the fan. A world where she existed, but was so foreign as to be completely alien, and they were going there.

This wasn't a matter of small-change iterations where the wrong politician was elected to the World Council—they were going to a place where there was no World Council. No Central Command. No Ministry of Defense. Nothing she knew existed on the far edge of the fan.

Too late, she realized Senturi was scrutinizing her. She stared back. "What?"

"Commander, is this a drill?" For the first time in his life, he looked serious.

She lifted her chin. "Does it matter? If you can't perform correctly on a drill, you won't do your job in the field. Suit up and meet me in the jump room. I'm taking Bennet in the field, but you'll be needed no matter what."

"What about Donovan?"

She grabbed her travel kit from her locker, slammed the door shut, and waited for the gene lock to cycle closed. "This is not a situation we can afford to risk two nodes on. If something goes wrong, Donovan needs to stay here."

"This doesn't sound like a drill, ma'am."

"Then maybe this will be your first bad hair day." With a small, cynical smile, she walked out of the room, leaving Senturi to admire the chiseled perfection of his reflection . . . even with the confused look on his face. It felt good to rattle his cage, and safer keeping the Council off guard. The longer they were kept in the dark, the more time she had to put everything back together.

Under her breath, she hummed the tune to Humpty Dumpty. *All the king's horses and all the king's men.*

The jump room was really three rooms built in concentric circles focused on the time portal. The core was dark still, lit only by the sullen, purple glow of the closed portal that rippled with lazy waves. The secondary circle should have had data screens brightening the place like noon on a clear summer day, but today there was nothing. A sick feeling in the pit of her stomach made her blood colder than a time jump.

"Commander Rose." Dr. Emir waved to her from the far side of the room.

She walked through the outer layer, where techs in pale mint-green scrubs and masks carefully prepared for every eventuality. An agent could step through the portal and be in an operating room in under ninety seconds if needed. *Which has been necessary more and more often.* "Doctor."

"I traced the aberrant iteration to the outer edge of the fan."

"Let me guess, dinosaurs and cavemen?"

It was a joke, but Emir treated her to a withering glare. "One would think that after committing such an egregious error, you would be do your best to perform as a professional. Your levity is not welcome. Nor are your sloppy mistakes."

"My mistakes?" Practice kept her tone from rising

or from blood flushing her cheeks an unsightly red. He didn't know what she'd done in those other iterations. No one knew. So he could only be blaming her for the machine readings that were beyond her control. "Don't put the blame for this fiasco on my doorstep. We both know I'm not the one who's made a mistake." It was so close to what she wanted to say and still so far away.

"The machine and my science are infallible," Emir said curtly.

"Your MIA and your science aren't being questioned." Only his motivations, but she kept that to herself because she had a healthy sense of self-preservation and a desire to live to see old age. Facts were facts, and the one fact that could never be forgotten was that Emir was the one who chose who lived and died. "But this isn't an iteration where my team was sent in and failed. This is . . ." The word IMPOSSIBLE bubbled up in her mind. "Unheard of."

"Nevertheless," Emir said. "It will be your fault in a few short hours. Unless your team manages to topple the iteration."

Senturi walked in, dressed in the team's black uniform and trailing the other seven members of their jump crew behind him.

Rose motioned for them to go into the second tier for briefing.

Senturi glanced at the dark ring and crossed over to her and Emir. "Where's the data for this launch?" he asked.

Her mouth twisted into a bitter scowl. "There is

none. We have no operatives there. No safe house. Not even local identities." She looked at Emir and hoped he read her silent fear. They were taking a huge risk sending her in first. It was a calculated risk, no one had more experiences on the far side of the MIA portal than her, but she'd only gone in blind once before. Her knee still ached some days because of that mission.

Emir ignored her with practiced arrogance. "It's an inconsequential iteration on the far side of the third fan. There were never enough variations of it to justify exploration."

"So why is it taking precedence?" Rose demanded, furious at this little nothing-timeline. There were *rules*. The prime iteration was always the one with the most variations branching off it, like the trunk of a tree. A healthy tree had many branches and deep roots. A weak tree had a few spindly branches and shallow roots.

A terrifying thought gripped her. *They call us Gardeners. Was it possible? Could we have pruned away too many branches?*

No. Logic asserted itself, stuffing her fearful fantasies back down to her subconscious psyche.

Senturi was studying her again. "Commander?"

She shook her head. "Your orders, sir?"

"Three-man strike team," Emir said.

She nodded. "Senturi, have your team on standby in case we need an extraction."

"Aye, ma'am."

Emir's eyes flared with cold fury. "Rose, go find out why these parasites are stealing our future."

CHAPTER 12

> *"Individual choice is the driving force of history. No movement, philosophy, or law can ever replace the individual as the fulcrum point of change."*
>
> ~ excerpt from *Thoughts on History* by Levin Duprey

Tuesday December 3, 2069
Florida District 8
Commonwealth of North America
Iteration 2

"Clemens!"

Ivy skidded to a halt two feet from the front door of the precinct. She'd worked a twelve-hour shift, and the ice-cream truck was pulling away. If this was a mutt run to chase missing mugs from the break room, she would . . . well . . . she'd suck it up and do her job because she had no choice. But she'd be thinking about physical violence the whole time.

The ice-cream truck pulled away, playing Evinna

Madier's hit single "Summertime Beach Waves," and with it went her orange creamsicle push pop. The highlight of her day for $3.75. She'd have to run two blocks to catch it.

With a sigh, she turned around. "Yes?"

"I got something for you," said Tom Wall, the overnight officer in charge. "Just came in."

Her shoulders slumped. "Missing dog? Lost skateboard? What is it?"

The older man smiled sympathetically. Wall was one of the few decent people on the force. It was going to suck manatee balls when he moved to Boca in two weeks.

"This is good, promise. There's a murder case from up north. The ME sent the autopsy over and asked if you'd look it over." He held out a datpad.

Ivy's eyes went wide. "Really?" No one had ever asked for her help on a major case. She'd tagged along, even managed to help once or twice, but this was unprecedented.

"I skimmed it, and then double-checked the send code. It came from the CBI ME's office." He raised an eyebrow. "What'd you get up to when you went to that exchange conference?"

She shook her head. "Nothing. I just asked a few questions about a Jane Doe they had. It wasn't a big case." But maybe Runiker had sent it out of sympathy. If Jane was a clone, no one else was going to care about who killed her.

Wall looked at her. "You sure that was it?"

"Yes!" She paused. His tone was all wrong. "Why?"

"There's multiple case files in there–including one from Alabama, where a teacher was found dead in her kitchen. The CBI is putting together a serial killer case up there."

She stared at the datpad. "Really?" This was the biggest case she'd ever worked on. Ever even been asked to think about. This was so much better than stolen cars with disabled trackers!

"Cool your chill, Clemens. You get to look at the file, that's all. Chief isn't going to let you go up north to actually work on it."

"Of course." She tried not to sound disappointed. "Still . . ."

"Still, it's a step forward," Wall agreed. "Sorry I made you miss your ice cream."

"It's okay." She flashed him a smile. "Have a good evening, sir."

"Stay out of trouble, Clemens," he said with a wave as he headed back to the bullpen.

"Yes, sir."

She walked to her car in the fading evening twilight, only half seeing the world around her. Ocean breezes and museum-worthy sunsets happened 350 days out of every 365.

Serial killers were rare.

Her car was a late-model Firebright Racer that the city had taken in a drug bust, bright orange with a dented door panel and the backseat stripped out. It was ugly and didn't drive great, but it was all she had. There was a chance it might even transfer in January to become her official property. Until then, she drove it like an old lady creeping toward church on a Sunday morning because the supply officer would charge her for every scratch. Come January, when she could run her own bank account instead of having it go straight to a caseworker, and have 95 percent docked for expenses, she was going to save. In a few years, things were going to be different.

Once she reached the studio efficiency apartment, she raced upstairs. There was leftover oatmeal in the fridge for dinner, but what she really wanted were her binders.

When she'd first started working for the department, they'd cleaned out old cases, and she'd wound up liberating a few case binders in her first act of rebellion against her oppressors. Even if their oppression was limited to treating her like a thing to be bought or sold and didn't actually involve whips, chains, or genuine oppression. But that wasn't the point.

The point was she had nearly seventy years' worth of case files that would help her find patterns the CBI might miss.

It probably wouldn't break the case. And she doubted they'd listen to her if she found anything, but she could try.

Laying the cases on the floor in a rainbow around her, she leaned against the metal frame of her bed and turned on the datpad. The very first note was a scrawl reading, "Where were the crimes committed? Find the crime scene. LM"

She started reading the files, hunting for the crime scene and answers for the CBI.

CHAPTER 13

"We measure time in minutes, but lifetimes in memories."

~ **excerpt from the *Oneness of Being*
by Oaza Moun I1—2072**

Date Unknown
Location Unknown
Rogue Iteration

Nothingness bloomed into life. Green, was Rose's first thought. There was green everywhere. An unforgivable number of fruitless trees and bushes with no visible purpose. She sucked in the air and all but gagged as it stuck in her throat, thick enough to chew.

Behind her, Bennet started coughing. "Mercy and life, where are we?"

"The coordinates place us less than a klick from the main facility in this iteration." Logan sneezed. "Ma'am, there seems to be some sort of contagion in this city. The air is—" Her words were choked off by a wet cough.

"Masks on," Rose ordered. She hated wearing gas masks, but already her eyes were swelling shut in response to whatever poison this iteration allowed to float around. Over the years, she'd seen some bad places. Smog-filled cities. Towers eroding from acidic clouds of pollution. This was something else entirely.

With her mask filtering everything, she fought for breath and scanned the area. "Did we land in an arboretum?"

"No, ma'am." Logan's voice was tinny, distorted by the breath mask. "It seems we landed in an open field with vegetation?"

"Is that a question or a statement?" Rose demanded angrily. She didn't need to look over to know Logan was gulping down fear. "Never mind. Fan out. Let's establish a perimeter."

Times like this she wished she believed in a god so she could blaspheme just a bit. This iteration was the stuff of nightmares. Vines with little spikes hung everywhere, grabbing at her pant legs and threatening to rip the exposed skin of her forearms. Strange things ran along the tree branches, chittering and shaking the trees. Something in the distance made the sound of a broken buzz saw starting to scream. It sounded uncomfortably organic.

Sweat formed on the edge of her mask and dripped down her neck.

"What is that smell?" Bennet asked.

"Your mask," Rose said, tallying what paperwork she would need to do to get filter replacements after this mission. Bennet coughed. From the corner of her eye, Rose saw him remove his mask to shake it. "Problems?"

Bennet nodded. "There's a smell getting into my mask. Past the filters." He coughed, sneezed, and shook his head. "This place is toxic."

"Then aren't you glad it isn't going to be your permanent home?" The original mission parameters included embedding Bennet here as an intelligence asset, but she'd written that off the agenda after her first breath. There were limits to the torture she'd make her soldiers endure. Already, the damp heat of this place was soaking through her shirt and making it cling. After this, a cold shower would be a welcome relief.

"Ma'am, I have the target building in sight."

"Thank you, Bennet." Rose triangulated on her soldier's position and moved through the dense foliage, cursing plants in general and this unknown genus in particular.

Logan stepped up beside her, pulling dangling vines off her pants.

"We aren't supposed to leave a trail."

"It was them or me, ma'am," Logan said. "I wasn't going to let the plant win."

Bennet motioned for them to join him. "Are you sure about the coordinates, Logan?"

"You want to check my math?" she shot back.

Rose held a hand up for silence. From their spot on the tree line, it was easy to see why Bennet was confused. This wasn't Central Command. In front of them, a small hill led to a green expanse of lawn, with picnic benches in a three-sided courtyard, and a small building that couldn't have more than two floors at best. It hardly looked like the seat of a world power or the home to the most powerful weapon in human history. "Do you have any life readings?"

Logan scanned the building. "Two, on the far side of the building."

"No perimeter guard?" Bennet scoffed. "What are they doing?"

"It could be a trap," Logan said.

Rose checked her digital display for the local time. "It's Oh-five-fifteen—no one's at work yet."

"That's no excuse for lax security," Bennet said.

Logan shifted on her feet. "Ma'am, is it possible they could have moved the machine? We sent the probe in twelve hours ago. In the early days, Dr. Emir had a floating lab that moved from location to location to prevent just this kind of attack."

"It's possible," Rose admitted though she hated the idea.

If the machine was in a floating lab, they would need to leave someone behind to gather intelligence. It was possible Emir would even order *her* back to stay here. Not many of the others had her deep-cover training or her language skills. It wasn't always a good thing to be the best. "Let's check the building. Once we know what's going on, we can report back. Making plans without proper intelligence is how you lose wars, not win them."

She glanced at Bennet. "Time to the next portal alignment?"

"Sixty-seven minutes, ma'am."

Rose nodded. "Make it snappy and keep it quiet."

Logan went first, half running, half skipping down the hill until she skidded to a stop near a metal utility door. Bennet followed as Rose took a covering position. Both her soldiers were non-nodal, expendable.

Logan signaled that everything was safe, and Rose moved down the hill with as much dignity as possible. If she returned with grass stains on her pants, she'd never hear the end of it. "How's it look?"

"Basic security," Logan reported. "I have the cameras on a loop. There's a key and a number pad for the lock. Do you want me to blow them or pick them?"

"Explosions draw attention, and this is just an information-gathering foray," Rose said. "Keep it quiet."

"Yes, ma'am." Logan bent over the lock as Bennet surveyed the perimeter.

"Problems?"

"It's just weird, ma'am." He shrugged. "Nothing about this is natural. There's no sky-cleaners, no major city in view, nothing that looks like home."

She wished she could take off the air mask and wipe the sweat from her face. "All iterations are different."

"Not this different. This is . . . where did we diverge from this? If this is one change in history, what was it that did this?" Bennet asked.

"It could have been a population control measure,"

Logan said, popping up as the door opened. "Thirty years ago, the government vetoed a law that would have resulted in millions of deaths and a limit to the number of children allowed to live. No disabled persons would have been left alive. Life-limiting illnesses like asthma would have resulted in immediate termination of the individual. We voted it down." There was a note of smug pride in her voice. "Maybe they didn't."

Rose pulled her gloves on and pulled the door wide. "Nice theory. Let's prove it one way or another."

They leapfrogged down the hall, taking refuge in empty alcoves and scanning for trouble. The halls were disquietingly empty.

Logan raised her hand. "This is the machine room." The door swung open at her touch. "The lock's broken."

Bennet swore.

Rose pressed her lips against the plastic of her air filter. Fear, and the pressing certainty of death, chilled her despite the heat of this abominable place. "Stop playing tourist, kids. Get in the room. Get what we need. Get out. Bennet, time?"

"Fifty-nine minutes, ma'am."

"More than enough time." There was always time enough to die. She led the way into the room beyond the door. It was situated like a stadium with risers. Someone had marked out concentric rings on the floor with tape, but otherwise there was an air of haphazard slipshoddiness that made her uneasy. Like looking at a faked painting—it was almost correct, but some indefinable something was off.

"Accessing the computers," Logan said. "They have no encryption."

Not a good sign. Emir was a careful man in every iteration. "Bennet, sweep the room."

"Yes, ma'am."

The lights turned on, revealing a strange box at the center of the taped circles. It looked . . . "Logan, check our date again."

"Day 193, year five. We made a lateral jump."

"This is one of the original prototypes of the machine," Rose said, the enormity of the thought almost making her laugh. "That's why this isn't working. This machine is barely functional. It's . . . it's . . . an antique!"

Bennet stopped beside her. "That explains what we saw outside. This iteration must be decades behind us. There's no protection because no one knows what this is yet." He laughed.

Rose eyed the machine with a frown. "That doesn't explain everything. The trees. The sounds. The poison in the air."

"I've accessed this iteration's main information hub," Logan said. "We should have enough data to identify the deciding nodal event that turned this iteration into what it is."

Knowing the change point of history would help at least.

"Forty minutes," Bennet reported. "We should get out of here." He poked at the machine, and the blue dial fell off, cracking as it hit the cement.

"Good job leaving no trace," Logan said sarcastically.

"There will be replacements here," Rose said. "Logan, get out of the system and erase your tracks. Bennet, start rummaging in the drawers. This is Emir's lab, so it will be well stocked."

It took them two minutes to find another dial, green this time, and for Logan to erase any evidence of their presence. Rose secured the utility door behind them as they heard a strange motorized vehicle pull up near the building. People were coming to work. "Back to the trees." The blighted, benighted trees.

Once she got home, she promised herself an extra ration of soap in the shower. She'd need it to wash away the stench of this place.

CHAPTER 14

> *"The human body is exceptionally adaptable, the human mind even more so. An individual can be made to accept almost any circumstance if the one who controls their environment is careful."*
>
> ~ personal study notes found in the margin of the textbook *Principles of Rule* by Anton Fiarro 16-2062

Day 188/365
Year 5 of Progress
(July 7, 2069)
Central Command
Third Continent
Prime Reality

Breathing in the recycled air of home, Rose felt the stiffness in her muscles finally ease up. Chow tonight was a simple grain salad with parsley, peppers, and diced chicken. It wasn't particularly savory or inspiring, but it was nutritionally balanced and . . . she poked at the quinoa as she fumbled for an adjective. Homey?

Reassuring? *Safe*. That's what it was: The salad was safe.

Familiar as the recycled air or the hum of the generators outside.

Soothing as the steady flow of encrypted data across her console.

This all felt right. Deep down in her bones, Rose knew this was how life was meant to be. This was the safest path for humanity. The true line of time and history. Every time she stepped away from it, things felt jagged, like rolling across a floor of broken glass.

She took another bite of her supper as she scrolled through the data from the iteration they had stumbled through. The major change point in history seemed to have been a world plague. In the Prime, political tension had kept the borders closed. In the other iteration, peace talks had allowed for free travel and the death of billions.

Ironically, the worldwide tragedy meant that there were more resources available, including the awful forest she'd been forced to walk through. Trees, land, food, jobs . . . the other iteration didn't need population control because they had an embarrassment of riches. All fairly well distributed by the local governments.

Rose tried to imagine living like that, having a house rather than a barrack room with a shared mess hall and a communal shower like she had until she'd reached the rank of commander. Or vacation time to go climbing in mountains where the land wasn't irradiated by war. It was nearly impossible to picture.

Her eyes watered at the thought of more trees giving off poisonous fumes.

With a shake of her head, she went back to reading the reports. There had to be a reason the Plague Iteration had gained dominance. And it wasn't because of the plague or the trees. She'd seen iterations that were spiraling toward universal extinction. Those were easy to deal with, and they'd always been on the far reaches of the probability fan.

She flicked through the files. Sorting out the primitive work the Plague Iteration Emir had done. She saw that he had identified a few nodes—hypothetically at least.

Her door chimed, and Dr. Emir entered.

Rose stood. "Sir? Is there a problem?"

"Nothing significant," he said as he circled his hand, gesturing for her to sit back down. "I came to ask for your impressions of the new iteration."

"It's an unpalatable, backward hell, sir. Years behind us in terms of development and with significant nodal shifts. I'm not sure how we're connected."

Emir nodded and paced the three-step space between her wall locker and her bed.

"It will make removing the nodes difficult, sir," Rose said, the problem had plagued her on the way home. "It's unlikely they'll congregate in any one place, not this early in the development of the MIA." She hesitated a moment before plunging onward. "Sir, our theories—"

Emir's sharp glare cut her off.

"I thought," she said, carefully rewording her sentence, "nodes were nearly static across all iterations.

History-changing events are very rare. The nodal people are all individuals of a certain age at the time of nodal events, who have the personality traits that drive them to seek change and who score high as influencers for their spheres."

Another spear of a glare hit her.

"I may have misunderstood, sir, but this shift doesn't . . ." She couldn't say the rest. Her tongue wouldn't move. The air wasn't in her lungs. Some baser instinct and drive for self-preservation locked her up. "I just don't understand the situation, sir."

"That is painfully obvious, Commander," Emir said in a tone of deep disapproval. "After all these years of training, I would have hoped you had a better grasp of the basic mechanics that hold the universe together. What is the one thing that gives our iteration precedence over all others?"

"Nodes, sir." The answer was a rote one she'd learned when she'd first been pulled from military intelligence to work for Dr. Emir. "But we have the nodes but no longer have precedence."

Making a sound of disgust, Emir shook his head. "Were you subjected to brain trauma on your last mission? You sound like a child! Think of what you've said. Think." It was an order.

Rose took a deep breath. "The answer is that Prime has fewer nodes than the other iteration—but that simply isn't possible, sir. We have all the nodes. All of them. At this stage in the evolution of history, the other—"

Emir held his hand up for silence.

"Sir?"

He sat on the edge of her bunk, look[ed] weak.

A frail body, ravaged by age and the lack of p[roper nutri]tion. It was moments like this, when his iron wil[l faltered,] Emir looked almost vulnerable. It affected Ros[e the same] way a change in the gravitational constant of th[e universe] would affect the orbit of the Earth. She wobbled.

Emir took a deep breath, inhaling the rec[ycled air] to fuel the savage fire that burned in his ey[es when] he looked up. His voice was utterly calm as he [asked,] "What did you think of Donovan's behavior [on] your last mission with him?"

Rose stilled, aware that this could very easi[ly be] a trap. "I found him to be an acceptable soldier." [She] struggled to remember any variation. "He follow[ed] orders as well as he ever does. Fulfilled his missio[n.] I don't believe Wagner's death was his fault." Eve[n] though he should have taken the rearguard, she found she couldn't be angry at him for living. Her carefully won control faltered, and she frowned. "I'm sorry, sir, I noticed no abnormalities. Should I have?"

"Perhaps." Emir stood again.

Rose stood as well. "Do you suspect him of something, sir?"

"Not of anything unseemly, but he is not filling Peterson's place well."

"Captain Peterson was an exceptional man. There aren't many who could compare to him, and I don't think we can fault Donovan for not being Peterson. He need to be. He only needs to hold the loyalty of [sol]diers so he can influence them."

"[B]ut we have lost preeminence. That can only [mean] we have lost a node. You and I are here, un[chan]ged. The ones who cannot serve on the front lines [are u]nder careful watch in IID safe houses. That only [leav]es one possible traitor to our cause." Emir waved [his] hand with a little gesture, indicating the futility of [life] and the downfall of fidelity.

"Sir, with all due respect, I cannot support calling [D]onovan a traitor unless I have evidence. If I accuse [hi]m publicly, I will lose the respect of the soldiers [u]nder my command." So would Emir, but mentioning [t]hat would result in the deaths of those soldiers.

"With all the respect you are due, Commander, it is not the soldiers you should be worried about." Emir looked disappointed with her. "Donovan leans heavily on Senturi. Perhaps too heavily, considering how reliant Senturi is on his masters in the Council."

"That is a leash I've long suggested we sever."

"Indeed."

Rose nodded, feeling her heart slow as the storm of Emir's wrath turned away from her. "I will see to the matter, sir. Undermine him, if that's what you want. Or cut him loose entirely. We have . . . fail-safes." Information left over from her days in military intelligence when the United Nations still held control of the world. Even before she'd met Emir, she knew that one day she'd want enough blackmail to insulate herself from the ever-changing political winds.

"We'll watch, for now. The Prime is too fragile for me to want to push. But . . ." He trailed off and raised a bushy white eyebrow. "If it is necessary?"

"The fail-safe can be activated and run its course in under an hour, sir."

His second eyebrow went up. "Dear me, Commander. What on Earth did you find about poor Senturi?"

She smiled cruelly. "Enough."

"I would warn you to be careful, Commander."

"I always am, sir."

"Nevertheless, if Donovan has lost faith in our cause, it won't be me he attacks, and it won't be here in your sanctuary where he wages war. You are running another mission in two days. Are you prepared to risk a knife in your back?"

"Every mission carries a risk of failure, sir, and I am always prepared for betrayal."

He stood. "You are our Paladin. I must rely on your intuition in these matters. Do you trust Donovan."

Her blood crystallized with icy realization. "No, sir. I never have. But that doesn't mean he isn't the node. We shouldn't act against him."

"Nevertheless," Emir said. "We should watch. Your mission as of this minute is to find me a new Warrior Node at all cost. If Donovan comes into his own, very well. He's an obedient soldier, and I won't waste him. But I won't allow his weaknesses to hold Prime back when decoherence is approaching."

Which made her wonder what he would do to *her* if he suspected she wasn't properly performing as a node.

CHAPTER 15

"Your voice adorns another sky, but I will always hear it, and my feet will find you again."

~ excerpt from *A Hidden Road*
by Meiko Orui I1—2073

Wednesday December 4, 2069
Cannonvale, Queensland
Australia
Iteration 2

Moonlight spilled across a white quilt, the shadows of palm fronds danced in silhouette as Mac came to awareness. Beside him there was sound of soft breathing and the heat of Sam's body as she slept. Their room was filled with familiar scents: the lavender of the laundry soap, the honest smell of clean sweat, the smell of Bosco the dog, and a hint of garlic wafting down the hall from the kitchen.

Eyeing the open door, Mac slid his hand down the side of the mattress and retrieved the military-issue gun he'd smuggled out of the Americas six years earlier. Every night, the door was locked.

Bosco slept on the cool tiles in front of the door, 180 pounds of heavily muscled mastiff who had been trained to attack on command. Mac slept between Sam and the bulletproof glass they'd installed. Carefully planted shrubbery made sure no sniper was getting a clean shot, and the reinforced walls had been the final step to turning the bedroom into a bunker.

But something in the darkness disturbed him. A scent or a sound out of place that woke a sixth sense and brought him into battle mode. Hairs on the back of his neck stood up as he silently stood and crossed the carpeted bedroom floor to survey the hall. Bosco was nowhere in sight.

Logic said that Bosco, despite his training, might be wandering the house. Maybe the dog had wanted to pee and gone out his doggy door. Maybe a kangaroo was sleeping on the other side of the fence, and Bosco had gone to plan his next battle with the monsters of Australia.

The problem with "maybe" was that Mac knew the other maybes meant terror teams might have infiltrated the house. This might be the night they found Sam. This might be the night the war began.

"Captain MacKenzie?" The calm voice was so familiar it startled him. But Sam was back in the bedroom...

He turned the corner to the kitchen with his gun up, safety off. "You are not welcome here."

Shadows played across the woman's face. Black hair was pulled back into a tight bun. Her face was thinner than Sam's, the features more pronounced. Without needing an X-ray, Mac was confident there were signs of a healed fracture on her left ankle.

She stepped away from the counter with a cold, cruel smile. A twisted parody of the woman he loved.

"Where's my dog?" If this other-Sam had killed Bosco, she'd be fish food by dawn. His Sam wouldn't even question the blood on the tiles.

"Sleeping outside," the woman said. "I locked his doggy door. He whined a little, but I suspect he'll live."

Mac kept his gun trained on her chest. "Excellent. You're now free to leave the way you came. We don't want anything to do with you. Not now. Not ever. Go back, and tell Emir to stay on his side of history."

She tilted her head to the side in a waggling shake that was equal parts familiar and foreign. "I wish it were that simple, Captain. I really do."

"I never made captain," Mac said. "You're in the wrong iteration. Leave. This is my last warning."

She stepped toward him, making herself an easy target. "I choose to believe that it is you in the wrong iteration. You are Captain Linsey Eric MacKenzie of the 23rd Home Regiment. Einselected designation: Warrior. We need you, Captain."

In one quick motion, she grabbed his wrist with a cool, clawlike hand. He felt something sticky, then felt the ground fall away, then he knew nothing at all.

CHAPTER 16

> "They who dream of conquered nations are but fools,
> but they that conquer themselves are mighty."
>
> ~ from the teaching of Soyala Méihuà I4—2067

Day 189/365
Year 5 of Progress
(July 8, 2069)
Central Command
Third Continent
Prime Reality

Sirens blared, bringing the base to high alert. Donovan stood by the outer door, the scent of rust and desperation palpable, but no gates dropped down. He pulled his uniform jacket on and ran for the stairs. Where had he been?

Where should he have been?

Senturi hadn't asked him to do the security sweeps on the lower levels. Didn't even trust him with that job. Rose might accept running, but Emir?

Better if he wasn't found near the stairs at all.

He hit the bottom living level, where the ghosts of shops remained as a promise of better days ahead. Tree-shaped abominations glistened in the darkness like an invasive, oleaginous vermin choking out the place of true autotrophs. The planning committee said this would be a promenade, a place for free commerce, shopping, entertainment, and socialization. Donovan didn't think they knew what those words meant.

The brown commbox secured at his hip squeaked. Wincing at the technical reprimand, he punched in the code to reset the box to the Command frequency.

"Repeat, Captain Donovan, Soldier, sound off." The frazzled voice was edgy with panic, and unfamiliar.

He unclipped the box. "Donovan, 21505. Present."

"Location?" The voice asked.

"Living-area stairwell." Paranoia whispered he shouldn't divulge his true location. Seventeen months ago, Rose's team had used the exact same method to trap a missing node in an iteration scheduled for demolition. He lifted the box back to his ear. "Comm check?"

"Lieutenant Shelle Sonand, authentication code: cloudberry." That made Lieutenant Sonand Central Command Intelligence.

"Authentication confirmed. Where should I go, Lieutenant?"

There was a longer pause than required, and when the commbox turned back on, there were several voices in the background. "Captain, repeat request?"

Donovan swore. He'd missed a code early on. Now

he was on the hot list no matter what he did. "I wanted to know if I was required in the war room, but I'll report to my squad's designated area." That would get him a mark for insubordination and possibly some of Emir's sideways censure, but nothing more.

It took him ten minutes and two guesses to find his squad in one of the small communal rooms designed to be team-building recreation areas. To the best of his knowledge, the only time his squad had all been there together was when they'd painted a new shade of beige on the walls.

"Captain Donovan." Commander Eriant wasn't regular army, like Donovan, but Command Fleet with prior service in UN Intelligence, like Rose, and he looked the part. His black uniform was pressed to a shine, with chrome buttons embellished with the adder-and-mongoose insignia of IID. "You're late."

"I was meditating," Donovan said.

The adder checked his tablet. "The meditation room log has no record of you entering today."

"There are other places to meditate. The promenade is quiet this time of day." The damning words slipped out before he could stop himself. "I wanted to walk."

Commander Eriant took this at face value. "Very well. Please be seated."

Donovan took his seat on the edge of the semicircle the squad had formed. Red plastic chairs with aluminum legs and matching tables . . . what had they called it? The Aluminum Wasteland? No, the Aluminum Desert. Private Torman had joked about painting a cactus against the sand-covered walls.

Now no one was joking.

The private in question was studying his boots. The others were looking anywhere but at Donovan and Eriant. Only the E5s and up maintained the facade of being relaxed.

Sergeant Coughlin's personal techpiece chimed.

Commander Eriant spun as if he'd been hit up his fat-lipped head. "What is that?"

"Duty reminder, sir," Coughlin said.

"A reminder?" The commander sneered. "Disciplined individuals fall into a routine."

"I know, sir," Coughlin said without a trace of rancor. "I switched shifts yesterday, and I'm trying to get into the new rhythm. This is helping me out."

Eriant's nose twitched, probably because Coughlin had given the right answer, and Eriant couldn't put him on report.

Quick boot steps heralded the arrival of Commander Rose. She looked in, eyes wide. "Captain Donovan?"

There was only a second, but he saw the flash of relief there. The quickly hidden look that said she'd found someone to blame.

He stood. "Commander?"

"You're needed in the war room."

Donovan followed Rose to where Emir waited, along with the other jump team leaders—Senturi included—and Atlee Brost, director of internal security. Brost couldn't be happy about IID's intrusion. It was a weakness in Central Command Donovan could exploit.

Brost frowned at his arrival. "Captain, you were late reporting to your rally point."

"I took the stairs."

Rose shot him an angry frown, but he knew that when she turned around, her face would be placid as the fake lake in the city's central dome. When he thought about it, fake was a very good word for Rose. And Central Command. They were shells, and in a few days, they would crumble into ash.

Donovan took his position at the fourth monitor from the left—a plush, half-egg chair with computer console and a constantly updating data stream from any live missions. He'd planned more deaths from that chair than he could count. Now the screens were dark. The chair's overhead light was dim. It was either restful or coffin-like, he supposed; it all depended on your point of view.

Emir did his trademark hand waggle, which meant there was information that didn't matter in the grand design, and he was going to let someone else deal with the humdrum details of things much like he handled questions about vanishing rations or tainted water. "Proceed, Brost, proceed."

"Thank you, Doctor." Brost's chest puffed with self-importance. "Security did a random sweep of personal locator beacons at 0719 this morning and found an anomaly. Are any of you familiar with a tech named Laura Para? She works on the air systems in this building."

Most of those assembled shook their heads.

A tertiary team leader raised his hand. "I've seen her, sir. She was handling the repairs to our training room air conditioning. The heat wouldn't turn off. Is there a possible security breach?"

"Miss Para is dead," Brost said, his eyes narrowing. "I will need you and your team to proceed to the adjacent room to talk with my people."

The team leader's back went stiff. "Sir, I know where my people were all day."

"I am not suggesting the killer is here," Brost said in the same tone Macbeth had used to humbly take his leave of Duncan before stabbing him. "We'll start by establishing a timeline for Miss Para. Please, if you'd move in, the sooner this is handled, the better."

The team leader reached for his commbox as he walked out, an unhappy look on his face.

"How was Miss Para killed?" Rose asked.

Brost stared at her for a moment. He'd probably never met someone as arrogant as Commander Rose before. "How does that matter?"

"Answer the question."

Brost turned to Emir for support and found none there. "I . . . she was beaten," Brost said finally. "Slammed into a wall or pushed down the stairs, and then kicked repeatedly."

Rose wasn't the only one suddenly looking at people's boots.

"Standard issue footwear?" she asked.

was a weakness in Central Command Donovan could exploit.

Brost frowned at his arrival. "Captain, you were late reporting to your rally point."

"I took the stairs."

Rose shot him an angry frown, but he knew that when she turned around, her face would be placid as the fake lake in the city's central dome. When he thought about it, fake was a very good word for Rose. And Central Command. They were shells, and in a few days, they would crumble into ash.

Donovan took his position at the fourth monitor from the left—a plush, half-egg chair with computer console and a constantly updating data stream from any live missions. He'd planned more deaths from that chair than he could count. Now the screens were dark. The chair's overhead light was dim. It was either restful or coffin-like, he supposed; it all depended on your point of view.

Emir did his trademark hand waggle, which meant there was information that didn't matter in the grand design, and he was going to let someone else deal with the humdrum details of things much like he handled questions about vanishing rations or tainted water. "Proceed, Brost, proceed."

"Thank you, Doctor." Brost's chest puffed with self-importance. "Security did a random sweep of personal locator beacons at 0719 this morning and found an anomaly. Are any of you familiar with a tech named Laura Para? She works on the air systems in this building."

Most of those assembled shook their heads.

A tertiary team leader raised his hand. "I've seen her, sir. She was handling the repairs to our training room air conditioning. The heat wouldn't turn off. Is there a possible security breach?"

"Miss Para is dead," Brost said, his eyes narrowing. "I will need you and your team to proceed to the adjacent room to talk with my people."

The team leader's back went stiff. "Sir, I know where my people were all day."

"I am not suggesting the killer is here," Brost said in the same tone Macbeth had used to humbly take his leave of Duncan before stabbing him. "We'll start by establishing a timeline for Miss Para. Please, if you'd move in, the sooner this is handled, the better."

The team leader reached for his commbox as he walked out, an unhappy look on his face.

"How was Miss Para killed?" Rose asked.

Brost stared at her for a moment. He'd probably never met someone as arrogant as Commander Rose before. "How does that matter?"

"Answer the question."

Brost turned to Emir for support and found none there. "I . . . she was beaten," Brost said finally. "Slammed into a wall or pushed down the stairs, and then kicked repeatedly."

Rose wasn't the only one suddenly looking at people's boots.

"Standard issue footwear?" she asked.

"I . . ." Brost cleared his throat. "My team has yet to determine that."

"Dr. Emir?" Of course Rose went over security's head. "Permission to follow the case? If this is an intrusion from another iteration, my team is best equipped to handle the matter."

"It is most likely an internal matter. No need to concern IID at this time," Brost said quickly. Perhaps a shade too quickly. Emir could scent weakness like a shark smelling blood in the water.

One more gear was about to be snapped off the machine. Donovan hid a twitch of a smile by rubbing his chin.

Emir turned to Brost with a look of cold fury. "Of course it's an internal matter! Rose, are you suggesting our perimeter has been breached."

She shrugged off his rage with a casual nonchalance too perfect to be real. "It has happened."

"Not in years," Emir said, his mouth tightening into a thin line. "Every transfer is documented."

"Except at the anomaly points."

Donovan was grateful he was in a chair. The existence of the temporal cyclone touchpoints in Prime was a hotly debated subject. Central Command officially denied their existence, but the Ruling Council would pay good money for that information. There were over a half dozen people in the room. Including Senturi, who was already on the Council payroll.

Having Rose confirm it openly was . . . not good.

Especially for his long-term plans. He'd have to take that into consideration. If nothing else, working for Emir had made him adaptable. Everything here could be twisted to his advantage

Emir made his dithering hand-waggle motion again. "All blocked. All cordoned off. Brost, see to this matter. Rose will offer her assistance and her teams. They are, after all, expert killers."

Her hands started shaking as soon as she was certain she was alone. Rose stopped, practicing the calming breaths she'd learned as a child. Barely eleven, destined for war, she'd sat in a pale gray room as hidden lights slowly changed color behind translucent panels and learned to control herself. Training had taught her how to slow her heartbeat, hide the panic growing in her body, even keep her mind clean of the poisonous whispers of doubt. It took ten seconds, then she was herself again.

One more deep breath, then she continued down the dimly lit hall. The low ceiling was testament to the afterthought this floor was. Squished between the control levels and the main living areas, the Floor of Boxes was just that: eight-by-eight-by-eight-foot cubes created when the control areas were expanded with new ductwork and two floors were sacrificed. Technically, her rank gave her a living suite in the main area closer to the food court, but she'd declined it in favor of the tiny triad of rooms she'd claimed so she could have a measure of privacy. The living-quarter walls were thin and the halls crowded. Every once in a while, she wanted to be where the people weren't.

Her door was unmarked, indistinguishable from the neighboring ingresses in every way. The anonymity gave her an added measure of safety. Looking over her shoulder out of paranoid habit, she typed in the fifteen-digit lock code to her room and stepped inside. Her kidnapped node sat sulking on the far side of the room.

"I apologize for the delay," Rose said, her voice frosted-metal cold. "There was a minor disturbance that required my attention."

"You have sirens and a lockdown for a minor disturbance?" MacKenzie asked. He was seated on the floor, arms and legs crossed, and his expression gave her no sympathy. "What do you do in a real emergency?"

Rose smiled, pride warming her chest. "We have no emergencies. Our future is set. By controlling the other iterations, we ensure a smooth progression from day to day."

"So why does this look like a military gulag in North Korea?"

She tilted her head to the side. "I'm not familiar with that term."

"This looks like a prison camp. Locks on the doors. No windows. No clearly marked exits. I didn't get to see many people, but I'd say you're one wrong turn from a coup."

She sucked in her cheeks. Soldier Nodes were not

usually lauded for their intelligence. It would be nice to work with someone who could think their way out of a wet paper bag, but not right now. "Habitats are not safe to leave," Rose said. "The air outside is toxic. You can walk outside, but you won't get far. And there will be no burial. The acid rain will wash you away before anyone knows you're gone."

He stood, unfolding and stretching as if she needed the reminder how physically imposing he was. "I'm so glad you brought me to this little piece of paradise, Jane. It's charming."

She stiffened her spine. "My name is Commander Samantha Lynn Rose."

"The only Sam Rose I know is my wife: former CBI Agent Sam Rose, now MacKenzie. You aren't her."

"I'm her original," Rose argued, as her heart drummed with anger. "I'm what she can only aspire to be."

"That'd be a serious step down for Sam." For all his smiles and relaxed posture, MacKenzie's eyes were cold.

She shook her head. This was going all wrong. MacKenzie was a soldier, he was supposed to understand survival and the need to adapt. He just needed time, she counseled herself. And she needed him so she could buy time to stabilize the iterations. "I'm not arguing with you," she said. "You have the understanding of an infant. In a year, if you want to hold this discussion, I'll consider you qualified to have this debate."

His sharp smile said he thought she was wrong.

Rose turned away and hit the unlock code for her dresser, hyperaware of the man in her room.

"Would you like me to leave?" MacKenzie asked, his arms still folded across his chest.

"If my clothes make you uncomfortable, turn around. I have no intention of showering or changing in front of you. But I accept the mental limitations that were imposed on you by a backward iteration." A place that smelled of salt, flowers, and strange foods in the kitchen she'd found him in. It was alien as the surface of the moon. She pulled the dresser open and lifted a silky, canary-yellow camisole off her uniforms. It hung as limply as the dead woman it belonged to.

There was a suppressed cough from behind her.

"You have a comment?"

"Is that blood?"

"Yes." Cold, dried blood that spread like across the shirt in rivers of death.

"Is that your shirt?"

She hoped the look she gave MacKenzie conveyed how truly stupid she thought he was. "No."

"Then, as much as I hate myself for saying this, put that down before you contaminate the evidence any more." He sighed, then wrinkled his nose. "Sam would laugh if she saw me right now. That woman . . ." For the briefest moment, a smile flitted across his face. "My badge is showing."

Rose looked him up and down. He was still wearing the same clothes she'd found him in, long, black sleep pants and a gray shirt, with an unseemly stain on the bottom left corner. There was no badge, tattoo, or identity card. A sudden change in his mental stability was not what she needed. "What are you talking about?"

MacKenzie pointed to the shirt. "That belongs to a murder victim."

"Yes, a young female in her late teens or early twenties."

"Did you kill her?" MacKenzie asked in a slow, almost patronizing voice.

"Certainly not." Rose lifted her chin. "I only make authorized terminations of einselected nodes who need to be removed to collapse an unwanted iteration."

"Do you know who killed the woman?" MacKenzie asked in the same tone as if she hadn't said anything.

"Of course not."

"Then you are currently smearing your holier-than-thou DNA all over evidence."

She stared down at the shirt and tried to adjust her brain to think like the primitive man MacKenzie so obviously was. "You want to find out who killed her?"

"Yes, after I find out who she was and report the death to the proper authorities, the killer will need to be found, put on trial, and dealt with in the manner appropriate to the current laws."

Understanding crept over her like a winter sunrise clawing its way through the mountains and clouds. "You think this should be investigated?"

"Yes, of course I do. A woman is dead—that's grounds for investigation in every iteration I've heard of."

"But she's not from our iteration." Rose held up the

shirt. "This color doesn't come from here! She's not one of us. Would you investigate the murder of a body that came in from another iteration?" She shook her head with a wry chuckle. "It's . . . you're not laughing." They stared at each other for an uncomfortable moment. "You're serious?"

MacKenzie nodded. "My specialty is forensic medicine. I solve murders all the time. Two cases I know for sure were from another iteration: Jane Doe and Juanita Doe. Juanita was Captain Samantha Rose from the Federated States of Mexico. Her killer is a man named Nialls Gant. He's in jail." Mac stopped and shook his head. "No—he *will* be in jail in spring of 2070."

Rose shook her head. "I'm not concerned about finding a stranger's killer." She held the bloody shirt up. "I'm concerned with finding out who put a dead woman's clothes in my locked room."

CHAPTER 17

"Day by day, memory by memory, mistake by mistake we built a life of love and dreams and forgiveness."

~ excerpt from *Love, Lies, and Happiness* by Erin Li I2—2076

Thursday December 5, 2069
Cannonvale, Queensland
Australia
Iteration 2

A gray mist of soft rain swathed the house like a familiar blanket. Sam stretched, peeking out the window as fat teardrops fell from the clouds. This was orange-juice-eggs-and-bacon rain—rain meant for cuddling or reading books. This was the rain meant for cartoon mice with heart-shaped noses and daisies for umbrellas. The shops would be empty of tourists today. A sad, still end to the week.

"Mac?" Her voice echoed down the tiled hall. Neither Mac nor Bosco was in the kitchen. The stove sat cold, the curtains closed. A chill premonition of danger crawled up her spine.

From the back door, she heard Bosco whimper, the sorrowful whine of a puppy in the rain.

Shaking off her nerves, Sam went and opened the door. "Hey, love . . ." Her sentence trailed off as a soaking-wet Bosco stepped into the kitchen and shook off. There was no way Mac would have left the dog out in the rain long enough to get that wet. A lump of fear formed in her throat. "Hey, Bos. Where's Mac? Where's your other human?"

Bosco shook again, then walked over and flopped onto his oversized mat with a grumble.

Sam went back to the bedroom. Mac's phone was still on his nightstand. His keys were in the hall, and his car was in the double-wide garage. She checked for his gun under the mattress and found nothing.

Tight jawed, she grabbed her CBI-issued splat gun from the bedroom closet and stepped into the armory-turned-office that they'd set up a few years ago. Originally, it was intended to be the nursery, with pale blue walls and glass hot air balloons hanging near the window to catch the light. After the miscarriage, she hadn't been able to walk past it without crying, and Mac had decided to turn it into a fortress.

Metal plating in the walls, rows of weapons and currency, and several sets of identity papers from around the world for both of them. While he turned it into a bunker, she'd read physics papers about time travel and other theories aloud. They'd made contingency plans. Talked about what they'd do if Emir came for her, or for both of them. The idea that Emir would only target Mac had never crossed her mind.

Now she flipped on the computer and pulled up the security-camera footage from around the house. It had seemed like overkill at the time. Cannonvale was hardly a bustling hive of crime, and between Mac's Ranger training and Bosco's loyal bulk, she'd felt perfectly safe.

The black-and-white image on the screen came on, the cameras tripped and turned on by movement in the kitchen. Sam crossed her arms. The face on the screen was familiar . . . thin, too bony to be healthy, but still hers.

She had seen this woman once before, in Alabama, when an Emir from another timeline insisted she come home with him. They'd stood face-to-face for seconds before Sam bolted for safety, but the woman's burning hate and contempt was seared into Sam's mind.

Bosco nudged her knee and whined.

Out of habit, she petted him, rubbing his ear like a lucky penny. "Want to go on a trip, Bosco?"

His ears perked up, and his heavy tail thrummed with excitement.

"Car ride?"

Bosco's bark made the grating of the gun case rumble in response.

"Good boy. Let's go pack. We have to fetch Mac."

CHAPTER 18

> *"One day I woke up and realized I would never wake up again. I would never sleep again. This was the day time would end."*
>
> ~ excerpt from "Final Thoughts on Decoherence"
> Dr. M. Vensula, head of the National Center
> for Time Fluctuation Studies—I4—2069

Day 190/365
Year 5 of Progress
(July 9, 2069)
Central Command
Third Continent
Prime Reality

History was divided into epochs. The whole world chopped into easy-to-define chunks with tidy labels. Mac's personal epochs were Home, Army, Disaster, Sam. He'd have to sit and do the math to figure out how many years had been lost to the ambush in Afghanistan and the resulting depression and addiction to sleeping pills. It hadn't mattered after Sam came into his life. Scientists sometimes tossed around the phrase Extinction Level Event, and that's what Sam was: his own personal ELE.

Sam was perfect.

Everything that had been missing in his life, Sam offered. Now, trying to sort through data on the tiny datpad left to him by Sam's evil twin in a room that smelled of gun cleaner and despair, he realized Sam was probably half of his brain, too. He couldn't describe her absence like a hole in his heart or a lost limb. Those were cutesy phrases that were far too weak to explain what he felt. It was like half of himself was missing. He needed her here to talk to, to toss ideas around with, to . . . be.

Every minute that ticked by on the clock was one where Sam was alone without him. She could protect herself. He'd made sure she could, above and beyond the training she'd received in the CBI. But they both knew Sam wouldn't pick up a gun unless it was a matter of absolute last resort. She wouldn't hurt someone unless there was no other choice.

She'd probably even sit down and weigh the risks of altering some hypothetical timeline before doing anything about his absence.

He looked up at his broken reflection in the metal wall of the evil twin's room. Yeah, Sam would come for him. Or wait for him. She'd think of something. That's why he'd married a woman who was smarter than he was, so she could come rescue him. Right?

Right.

"Why can't I print these?" he whined at the empty room. His voice echoed in the cloying silence. "I need my murder wall and my maps. This is ridiculous." Borderline impossible. The datpad required him to see the big picture in his head, keep track of everything with no visual aid, and that was making his gray matter melt. There had to be some way to do this . . .

Several hours later, the evil Sam walked through the door, and he had the pleasure of watching her jaw drop.

"What did you do to the walls?"

"I used them as whiteboards," Mac said around the pen cap he was chewing on. "Found the pen in the closet next to the first-aid kit. Don't worry," he added as he took the cap out, "it washes off. You'll be able to get your security deposit."

"I won't be able to pass inspections, though." She stared incredulously at the walls, walked, and smeared the ink.

"How are you going to pass inspection with me here anyway?" He shook his head. "By the way, that is my timeline of the crime that you're erasing, thank you very much. Stop destroying evidence." Worst cop he'd ever seen. And that included Marrins, his former Senior Agent who had kidnapped Sam and tried to change history so the Commonwealth never united. He frowned at the evil Sam. She really did look like Jane Doe from Alabama.

Awful as it sounded, he hoped she *was* Jane Doe

from Alabama. The possibility that it might be his Sam that died was too much for him to contemplate. He couldn't lose Sam without losing himself.

"This is not how things are done here."

"Sam would approve."

She stilled. "Again, I must insist you stop using the awful shortened name on me. You can call me either Commander, or Rose, or Commander Rose."

"I meant the real Sam would approve."

"We are identical," Jane said with a little foot stomp that, in real Sam at least, meant she was dangerously tired. "We are genetically identical. Our life histories ran parallel. The differences between us are minimal."

"The difference between you two is everything." He didn't want to get into it because it made him angry. All day he'd been pushing it back, trying not to think about what had happened to him. His voice was arctic cold when he said, "In every way that matters, you are not Sam MacKenzie. You don't think like her. You don't act like her. In every way, she has you beat."

Jane crossed her arms. "You love her."

"There was never a question about that. I love her. She loves me. We love being together."

"If you loved another Samantha, you can learn to tolerate me. In a few years, you'll see, you'll have forgotten her entirely."

"Not going to happen."

She threw her arms in the air in frustration. "Why are you so stubborn?"

"My mamma said it came from my dad's side."

The words were flippant, but the glare accompanying them would have made anyone who knew him back off. Jane's lack of reaction only underscored how alien she was.

"I am Samantha Rose."

"You're a pale imitation. The cheap, knockoff copy sold at marked-up prices to dumb tourists, but you're no Sam. Sam would never, ever rip apart someone's world for her own selfish reasons. She wouldn't kill anyone, not even if her life was in danger. I know because I've been the one pulling her out of scrapes before. You can be whatever you want, but you'll never be my wife or the real Sam."

Jane stalked around the room, angrily glaring at him, the walls, even her shoes at one point. "Fine. It's obvious I can't make you see reason."

"You're not presenting reason. You dragged me to this hellhole and told me that if I stay, this will be the future. No Sam, no trees, no beaches, no food . . . you do realize the nightmare you've created here? You abducted me. You presented me to Emir like your pet. You have me confined to this room like a prisoner of war. This is not my first time behind enemy lines. I got out once. I can get out again."

She rolled her eyes. "You have this all wrong. I am trying to help you. You have to understand, this iteration may seem less than desirable at times, but it isn't hurtling toward humanity's extinction at breakneck speeds; yours is. There is only one way through decoherence, and that is for the Prime to hold the line so whatever disaster is coming to obliterate humanity, someone survives. We're it. We're the only ones who can survive."

Mac lifted an eyebrow. "You sure about that?"

"Yes!" The word snapped like a whip.

Yet she wasn't sure at all. It showed in the crinkles around her eyes, the tiny frown lines by her lips, in the sleepless shadows under her eyes.

She wasn't sure—she was scared.

And she looked just enough like Sam that he wanted to reach out and pull her close, protect her. He turned back to the scribbles on the wall. Advice columnists wouldn't even have ideas on how not to feel an emotional pull from a wife's other-self. Words of prayer tugged at his lips but stayed a silent petition to the heavens.

Let me get home to Sam.

He didn't bother promising God anything—they both knew there was a long walk between him and heaven—but if he could get home to Sam, maybe he would at least consider checking a map for directions.

Her voice cut through the thickening silence. "I have a proposal."

"You apologize for kidnapping me and return me to my home? Fine. I accept."

She ignored him. "Before your arrival, I found a dead woman in a locker that is a known anomaly point. It's created by the MIA, and usually controlled, and because I knew the dead woman was from another iteration, I let the matter go."

Mac glared at her.

"There was a blood sample, but it belonged to Donovan, whose locker is right next to the anomaly point. He was scratched during hand-to-hand training, so it was a dead end. The woman was pulled through another anomaly, so I let it go. But someone went, found her, and took her clothes to leave in my room as a warning. Help me find the person who left them, and I'll let you go back to your iteration. It won't do you any good. You'll cease to exist when the decoherence event arrives, but it's what you want. I don't have a habit of saving fools from their own stupidity."

There was a catch there. It might have been an outright lie. Still, it was a chance—the only one he had right now—so Mac nodded. "Fine. Quick question, what did the victim look like?"

Jane wrinkled her nose and shrugged. "I don't know. Average height, above average weight for the Prime, but probably normal for other places, she was just a young woman. Like everyone."

"Brown hair, brown eyes, dark tan skin?" Mac guessed.

Jane frowned. "Yes."

"Want to see what I have?"

Jane eyed the walls with suspicion.

"There have been murders here in Prime. All those sirens yesterday. You have access to the personnel files, so I looked up the phenotypes, and I have a theory. These murders and one I investigated several years ago are connected. Agent Parker, who hopefully will never have the misfortune of meeting you, connected the case to a new string of murders.

"If I'm right, you are the Jane Doe Sam and I found in Alabama. We buried you, and we know what the murder weapon was, and we know Emir's machine was used to dump your body, just like the victim in the yellow shirt was dumped using Emir's machine. We never found the killer—there wasn't enough evidence—and we had reasons not to pursue the case."

Jane nodded slowly. "So what do you want to do?"

"I'm going to find out who killed you."

CHAPTER 19

> *"What courage it takes to leave the shore, to venture to lands unknown. In the swollen wave and stormy sky, the restless heart finds home."*
>
> ~ excerpt from *A Wild Sea* by Laya Zaffre I2—2036

Friday December 6, 2069
Sydney, New South Wales
Australia
Iteration 2

"Smell that, Bosco? Dead fish and rotting gull flesh." Sam took a deep breath of briny, polluted air and smiled. "That's the smell of an escape hatch."

Bosco sat by her feet and watched the bustling docks with the disbelieving look of a dog whose definition of abuse prior to this moment was running out of kibble. He turned to her with a mournful expression in his big black eyes. As if to say, "We left home for this?"

Really, it was unfair. Mastiffs weren't water dogs,

and Bosco wasn't fond of dead fish, but she wasn't leaving him behind while she chased shadows.

She scratched his ear, rubbing the silky, short fur between her fingertips as she searched for the cargo vessel she wanted. "There we are, *The Piper*, pride of someone's fleet I'm sure. Bosco, đên đây."

He stood obediently and followed Sam past the forklifts and cargo containers.

They walked to the foot of the gangplank for a trans-Pacific cargo vessel already stacked high with anonymous and rusting containers in a variety of colors.

A broad-nosed man with a clipboard frowned at her. "Can I help you?"

"I'm looking for Captain Hanshi of *The Piper*," Sam said. "I'm one of your passengers."

The man sucked air through a gap between his front teeth. "You sure, lady? This isn't our usual run. We're headed to Los Angeles in the Commonwealth. Maybe you got the date wrong."

"Pretty sure I didn't," Sam said. "Is the captain here? I'd like to sort it out with him."

The man looked at her, then down at Bosco, before looking over his shoulder at the ship. "It's just I've got thirty more containers to load before the tide changes, and . . ."

"How about I go find the captain myself. He should be up near the helm, right?"

"Up the gangplank, turn left at the green container with stars, then up the stairs," the man said. "And don't tell him I sent you."

"I don't even know your name," Sam said with a smile she knew wasn't as friendly as it should have been. She'd lost the skill to smile without making it threatening over the years. Mac didn't seem to mind, though, and his opinion was the only one that mattered.

She slapped her thigh, and Bosco trotted up the gangplank beside her. He stopped once, as a wave from a passing cruise liner rocked the boat, but other than the disapproving look he gave her, he registered no further complaints.

The ship deck was a maze of containers that looked like the scene from an old dystopian movie. At any minute, she half expected a zombie or a teched-up cyborg with cables dangling from her eye to jump out. Sounds echoed oddly, distorting the voices of the crew members shouting from the depths of the stacks and amplifying the sounds of the engines churning water or dumping ballast or doing whatever it was they did in port.

Her knowledge of ships this size was limited to what she'd picked up from retired captains and crew who visited Airlie Beach on holiday. Kayaks she could handle. Sailboats weren't bad as long as they were small, and Mac wasn't trying to convince her to sail around the coast of Australia. This ship was something else—a behemoth, a titan, a Mt. Everest when all she'd ever climbed were rolling hills.

Bosco stopped to pee on a green container with faded yellow stars, and they continued through the maze. Up metal stairs welded to a tower, and onward to blue skies and screaming gulls.

"*Ngôi*." Sam held her hand in a fist, and Bosco's rump hit the deck with military discipline. She knocked on the rounded door in front of her. "Captain Hanshi?"

The door swung open to reveal the rounded, suntanned face of a man only slightly taller than Sam. He frowned slightly at her, then saw Bosco, and his eyes went wide in alarm. "What in the hells is that?"

"A mastiff," Sam said. She snapped her fingers, signaling for Bosco to scoot closer to her. "He doesn't bite anyone. Not unless I tell him to."

The man sniffed and rubbed a finger under his nose. "Yeah? Looks like a man-eater."

"Only when I'm too lazy to hide the bodies myself. Are you Captain Hanshi?"

"I am. Are you the mystery lady who called me up last night?"

Sam shrugged. "Probably. But that depends on how many late-night calls you get from beautiful women."

Hanshi smiled and laughed. "Come on in. He, ah, won't do anything . . . will he?" he asked as he watched Bosco.

"He goes toilet on command, so unless you know the Vietnamese phrase for telling him to do his business, you're fine."

"I know some Vietnamese," Hanshi said, "but I'll stick to English."

He opened the door wider and invited them into a small cockpit lined with computers and buttons Sam didn't even think of pushing.

"Why Vietnamese?" he asked.

Sam shook her head. "It was one of the few languages no one in the neighborhood knew. We were going to use German or French, but I didn't want a high school kid to walk past the house and order him to jump the fence on accident."

"Fair enough," Hanshi said. He sighed, looked at Bosco one more time, then turned his attention to Sam. "So, you want to go to the Commonwealth."

"That's the plan."

"I know I mentioned this to the broker you spoke to, but that's impossible. For any amount of money."

Sam smiled, she'd anticipated that response. "Not to a Commonwealth citizen." She reached into her back pocket and pulled out the old Commonwealth passport she'd been carrying around for a lot longer than the 2068 stamp suggested.

Hanshi raised an eyebrow in doubt. "And what is a Commonwealth citizen doing in Australia? The border's been closed for years."

"I work for the CBI, and anything else I tell you would put you at risk of being exposed to extreme government scrutiny." As far as she knew, that was a lie. The Commonwealth's interest is the South Pacific was strictly commercial; fabric and trade goods were welcome, people were not.

Most of the Commonwealth's leaders didn't have

the same obsessive intelligence-gathering drive as some of its predecessor countries, but Hanshi was a man operating on the edge of legality. He wasn't a Commonwealth citizen, but he was doing trade with them. Theoretically operating out of Sydney, but she knew his ship was flying a flag from Greece and making undocumented runs to China.

In short, he was exactly the kind of man who couldn't risk the Commonwealth's attention.

Sam snapped her passport shut with a smile. "I know you take passengers sometimes."

"On shorter trips," Hanshi said. "A quick run between Darwin and Indonesia. Tourists who want the experience and a chance to go the places the big cruise ships don't. From here to the Americas, it's not a short trip."

"You average twenty-four days, don't you?" Sam asked. When Mac had suggested traveling by cargo ship to get back to the Commonwealth, she'd put it at the bottom of the contingency list. God had created planes for a reason, or at least inspired Joe Sutter to design the Boeing planes used worldwide. But all the other plans had involved going back to the Commonwealth together, on their own terms, after making contact with someone in the CBI who could understand the situation.

Now she was alone, and the only person who could help her was scheduled to die in fourteen weeks. Not that she was counting. Or hoping.

She didn't want Troom to die. *Again*. She rubbed her

head and tried to focus. It was getting harder. Memories from the years she'd lived colliding with memories she knew were currently forming. The human mind wasn't meant for time travel, and the English language wasn't meant to describe it.

Hanshi tapped his foot. "My average rate for a passenger is eleven thousand. In advance."

"I'll give you twenty, and we can haggle over your tip in Los Angeles," Sam said.

The captain looked at Bosco. "Is he, ah, coming with?"

"Don't worry, we can share a cabin."

Bosco let his tongue hang out.

"I have his kibble and my gear waiting on the dock," Sam said. "All I need is a ride back home. I'll stay out of your way. Bosco here will handle my security and make sure no one accidentally winds up in my bunk. With a little luck, in a month, you'll be wealthy, and I'll be back home, where I can give my boss the swift kick in the pants he so rightly deserves for abandoning me out here."

The captain waggled his head back and forth with a little dithering sigh. "Half now, half at the dock. To show I'm a loyal patriot."

"You're not from the Commonwealth."

"Doesn't mean I'm not a patriot," Hanshi said. "But the dog, he doesn't go in the galley. The cook would have a fit."

"Bosco will stay in my cabin except for his walks. I promise. You won't even know we're here."

"Somehow I doubt that," he said, but held his hand out to shake on it.

CHAPTER 20

> *"Every time we think we fully understand the mechanics of the machine, something changes. It is operating with a mathematics we do not yet comprehend."*
>
> ~ **Dr. Abdul Emir, Prime—2069**

Day 191/365
Year 5 of Progress
(July 10, 2069)
Central Command
Third Continent
Prime Reality

Rose pulled her hair back, stabbing pins into the severe bun with sharp, angry jabs. The woman looking at her from the mirror looked placid, but Rose could feel the turmoil roiling inside. Her breathing was even; her thoughts were not. Quickening her steps, she went to the small living area, where the kidnapped node was curled in the corner, sleeping. He looked like what he was: a vagabond from another place. She could only hope he wasn't as useless as he appeared.

"Wake up," she ordered, throwing light body armor and a coverall at his feet. "We have a meeting in twelve minutes."

One eye opened with a baleful glare. "Twelve?"

"I was given short notice." Donovan's doing, no doubt. Last night, he'd made a formal complaint about her living arrangements. Laura Para's death could have been ignored, swept under the rug for "morale purposes," but now a civilian from one of the other towers had been found dead in a passage connecting the command tower to the less important living domes. Central Command was scrambling to gain control, Brost was blustering around like he owned the place, and Senturi was smiling far too much for her to be happy.

Donovan had suggested that Rose was unsafe living alone. That it would be better for her to bunk with some of the female techs. It was a logical argument, calculated to make her look weak without Donovan's risking an outright attack.

If Emir or Donovan found out about MacKenzie on their own, it wouldn't look good.

"Hurry!" she shouted, as he staggered to a standing position. "How do you stand being this out of shape?"

He raised an eyebrow. "I'm in shape, but I need more than forty minutes of sleep to operate effectively."

"Just get dressed." She paced by the door as she waited for him, burning the nervous energy now, so she could appear calm when she faced down Emir.

The odds were in her favor. Emir liked her for some inconceivable reason. He thought she agreed with his schemes, not quite realizing that her driving goal was always self-preservation and the preservation of humanity. It was a nervous tic she couldn't suppress. She needed to protect people, even if it meant defying Emir or taking him out.

MacKenzie stepped out of the washroom, looking clean if not well-groomed.

"You need a haircut."

He ran a hand through his short hair. "I'll be sure to go to the barber the next time I'm out."

Always with a little joke. She unlocked the door. "Dr. Emir is the leader of this iteration. You will speak only when spoken to. You will not question him. You will show him the respect he is due, or you will die."

"Is he as crazy here as he is in other iterations?" MacKenzie asked, as they walked down the hallway.

Rose paused and took a deep breath. "No iteration of Emir is insane. Your inability to understand his genius reflects poorly on you, not him."

"He's a mass murderer with sadistic tendencies. It has nothing to do with IQ. It's his personality that's flawed. Maybe his genes."

She pivoted, refusing to listen. "Don't talk. I need to keep you alive."

He shrugged and followed her the rest of the way in silence.

They drew curious looks from passing technicians, but no one said anything. This was her domain as much as Emir's. People feared him, but they respected her, and that could be just as important in terms of intimidation. Everyone knew who she was. Their Paladin. Their shield against the dangerous future. Their advocate against time and human failings.

Pressing her hand against the lock pad, she opened the door to the conference room. It was cooler than the halls. The air was fresher and the fabric on the chairs a better quality. This was where the nodes met, and Emir maintained it with a sense of understated luxury the rest of Central Command was not afforded.

Emir sat at the head of the long wooden table, the king on his throne. "Commander Rose and . . . a bodyguard? Is this your answer to Donovan's concerns? I'm surprised you acknowledged them."

"I didn't." Because giving Donovan any ammunition against her would allow him to take her down, scoop her out of Central Command, and have her imprisoned like the other nodes if he didn't have her killed outright. She couldn't prove it yet, but Donovan was up to something. He was too calm, too focused, and spending too much time with Senturi. It was time to throw a wrench in Donovan's plans.

"Dr. Emir, may I present Captain Linsey MacKenzie."

Emir shook his head with a little frown. "I'm not familiar with the name. Is he important?"

"Only at home," MacKenzie quipped.

Rose glared at him behind Emir's back. "He was the original Soldier Node before his untimely demise in the final days of the War of Peace." Thirteen decades of fighting had paved the way for the world government and Emir's meteoric rise to power. Thirteen decades, and several billion lives. "I brought him here to stabilize our iteration until decoherence."

Emir steepled his fingers in front of his chin. "A new node?"

"Donovan has been acting impulsively, even recklessly. We discussed this, and both agreed that the only way we could have lost our position as Prime was if we had lost a node. Donovan is clearly the broken link. Captain MacKenzie will allow us to regain preeminence." Rose kept her face calm. Not a muscle moved, and her pulse didn't leap, but inside she felt the familiar surge of joyful victory.

Emir was going to let her have this.

He looked at MacKenzie skeptically. "Where did you find him? I sincerely hope you didn't entangle our own past to bring him here. Have you been trained as a solider?"

MacKenzie stared Emir down. "I have. I've also been trained in surgical medicine, forensic medicine, investigation, and physics."

Rose wanted to slap him. He'd issued a blatant challenge, and only the thick layers of ego insulating Emir from reality were keeping MacKenzie's execution from being ordered.

She rushed to retake control of the conversation. "Sir, I took him out of the iteration that was trying to take our position as Prime. You'll notice that since his arrival, the two iterations are running parallel. The theory of Einselected Maximums seems to be holding true."

It was a risky statement, skirting close to the possibility of insulting Emir's theory without actually questioning it—but she had to press now; it was the only way to survive. "We've never been able to mature two einselected nodes of the same designation before. I know several of your students posited that such a buildup would result in a temporal instability."

What she didn't bring up was the fact that the ones who had posited that the iterations with the most options going forward would survive had been found dead within the hour. Directly contradicting Emir's scientific discoveries was suicide.

"Their theory was that having several variations of the same individual gathered in the same space will cause instability and mental anguish," Emir corrected, his goatee framing a patronizing smirk. "Very few people are able to handle the dissonance of seeing another version of themselves."

Rose nodded. "It can be disconcerting at first, sir." Inside, though, she was excited: He was going to say yes. She could practically see him writing MacKenzie into his plans, plotting how to turn this twist to his benefit. "MacKenzie won't have that problem as his other-self is already dead."

Emir stood, fingertips resting lightly on the table. "Very well, Rose. You may keep your experiment. Find him housing and a uniform. Get him into training. His nodal set never does well with forced inactivity."

"Thank you for allowing this, sir." She bowed her head to hide the first hint of a smug smile. She'd won.

Emir cleared his throat. "After he is settled, Commander, we need to talk about how you were able to bring him here. I know there was no authorized mission to that iteration."

Now she smiled openly. "I'm grateful you asked, sir. I've found some unexplained temporal anomalies. New ones. Possibly caused by the spiral pattern of our interactions with the other strong iteration. It's creating security risks."

He raised a bushy white eyebrow. "The dead women?"

"Almost certainly related. The killer is either using the anomalies to enter our territory or as a means of disposing of the bodies." The civilian who had died the day before was seen on video only. When the techs had gone to the remote area to retrieve the corpse, they'd found blood but nothing else. "Tightening security needs to be a top priority in the coming weeks. Before we lose someone else or gain someone we don't want."

Emir turned to MacKenzie. "You said you had experience with investigation?"

"Yes," MacKenzie said.

"Yes, sir," Rose corrected him sharply. "You'll have to forgive him, Doctor, he wasn't living in a rigid environment when I found him."

MacKenzie glowered at her. "No, I was living at home with my wife and dog."

"A dog?" Emir chuckled. "What a waste of resources! Why would you expend energy on keeping a creature that does nothing but drools? Oh, you poor boy, we've saved you just in time!" He reached for MacKenzie's shoulder, and MacKenzie pulled away.

"Maybe you'll have a chance to meet my dog, sir." MacKenzie put a special emphasis on the title. "You'd be amazed what animals can be trained to do where I come from. You might find you like dogs after all."

Emir shook his head, too wrapped up in his own narcissism to realize what MacKenzie was doing. "Yes. Of course. A dog in the Prime. They went extinct when, Commander?"

"Nearly a decade ago, sir." She didn't dare look to see MacKenzie's reaction.

"Well, such is the loss of our times. The sacrifices we make." Emir smiled at MacKenzie. "If you get lonely, let me know. I'll see if we can find a stuffed bear for you from the nursery. Dogs!" He laughed to himself as he walked out.

Rose looked at MacKenzie's fists, clenched and white-knuckled. "Let him go," she ordered.

MacKenzie glared at her. "He is who you choose to follow?"

"No." Honesty was the only way forward. "Not for some time now. He's . . . I don't know what's wrong with him."

"He's an insane megalomaniac," MacKenzie said. "You know how I know? Normal people don't try to control the future."

"Oh, of course they do!" Rose slammed the door shut, so their conversation wouldn't drift into the hallways. "Everyone tries to control the future. We plan things in advance, we have preventative medicine. We have habits simply because it reduces the amount of choice-related stress in our lives. Everyone wants to control the future; Emir just happens to be better at it."

MacKenzie shook his head. "Habits aren't healthy. They become addictions. They box us in. If life doesn't give you a few surprises, you wind up living in your head, and reality evaporates."

"Maybe that's what happened to Emir," Rose said. "To all of us. We have our routines and our carefully plotted life, but we're simply pieces in a computer. Interchangeable and replaceable."

MacKenzie nodded.

"But we are still the only future humanity has. I realize how much you must abhor the thought."

"I really don't think you do."

She ignored his protest. "When decoherence comes, it will destroy humanity. Not a few thousand people, or a few million, or a continent. Everyone dies in decoherence." She had to make him see how real the risk was.

He leaned closer. "So stop the decoherence from happening."

Rose stared at him. "That's impossible."

"Why?"

She frowned in confusion. "Because it is?"

"Citation needed, Jane. Unless you have scientific evidence that decoherence can't be stopped, you're going about this all wrong. You shouldn't be trying to ensure one iteration survives, you should be trying to find a way for all of them to survive."

Her throat went dry. "But, if that were possible, we . . . we'd be doing that already. Central Command would . . ." She licked her lips. "They would . . ."

MacKenzie raised an eyebrow. "You can't say it, so you don't believe it."

She shook her head. "I don't know. I'm sure there's research on the matter. We can look it up. But you do realize how difficult what you're suggesting is. Decoherence is a huge force, you can't hold up a hand and expect it to stop for you."

"An object in motion will stay in motion unless acted upon by an equal and opposite force. Physics 101. Time is in motion, it is moving forward, and that means it has more momentum than decoherence. All we need to do is remove the equal and opposite force."

CHAPTER 21

> *"Under a star-shattered sky, wrapped in the tempest's embrace; here I find solace. Here I find grace."*
>
> ~ excerpt from *A Wild Sea*
> by Laya Zaffre I2—2036

Tuesday December 31, 2069
California District 21
Los Angeles
Commonwealth of North America
Iteration 2

Sam leaned against her pillows, knocking the toes of her boots together as *The Piper* rolled in the waves. They were less than five miles from shore, but until Captain Hanshi gave her the all clear sign, she was cut off from the Commonwealth by a metal hull and some very polluted water.

Bosco rested his head on the bed and looked at her mournfully.

"Sorry," she said, scratching his ear. "We can't play fetch today."

He heard FETCH and not CAN'T. His tail thrummed with hope. Playing fetch on the desk meant chasing balls while the crewmen scrambled for cover. They looked on, taking bets on how long the string of drool hanging from Bosco's mouth would get.

It could get very boring in the middle of the ocean while the weather was fair.

She sighed and rolled on her side. This was the easy part. After she got onshore, things would get complicated. There were enough cash and IDs in her bag to get her a rental car. A plane would be better, but half the airports did facial and fingerprint scans. They'd let her through, but CBI Agent Rose would be tagged in the system, and there would be questions.

A yellow light in the corner of the room, tucked between the door and the wall, flashed for the first time since the trip began.

Sam sat up. "Looks like we're coming into port."

The faint sound of a siren echoed outside. Not one of the ship's warning bells but another ship.

She licked her lips. Hitting the intership comm, she called the deck. "Captain Hanshi?"

"This is not a good time," the captain responded. "We are being surrounded."

"Pirates? In port?" Impossible.

"Coast Guard," Captain Hanshi said in a clipped, angry voice. "We're being escorted out of the port."

"What?"

"I'm very sorry. I'll refund your money." The comm line cut off as Hanshi answered the Coast Guard's hail.

Sam looked at Bosco. "Want to go for a walk?" She pulled her tennis shoes on, clipped Melody's truncheon to her belt, and grabbed her bugout bag. The rest of her luggage would have to stay. Clothes could be replaced. IDs and money couldn't.

The halls outside were an ant's nest of men rushing to their posts, sealing doors, and tidying away stills in case the Coast Guard decided they wanted to have an inspection. Hanshi was turning *The Piper* around in LA Harbor.

Bosco followed Sam to the deck.

The lights of LA were less than a mile away. Fireworks were going off, celebrating the New Year, and a light fog made the light of the Coast Guard ships bounce in an odd way. Refracting and throwing up shadows where they didn't belong.

"Miss." One of the crewmen grabbed her elbow. "You need to get belowdecks."

Sam turned, recognizing Jon from Malaysia. "I . . . right." She forced a smile. "How bad is the water here?"

Jon frowned. "What? We're not drinking it. Get belowdecks before the Coast Guard spots the dog. The captain is still trying to talk our way in. But, they see the dog, that's illegal animal smuggling."

Sam patted Bosco's head. "Sorry. I'll go."

Jon nodded and hurried off. *The Piper* was a well-run ship. She couldn't guess what the Coast Guard was using as a reason to turn them away. But she'd played the games of Commonwealth politics enough to know that it could be as simple as someone's having a bad day and wanting to throw their weight around. There could be another plague scare. Or maybe they'd heard about the incident in Airlie Beach.

"Bosco, *theo*," she ordered in Vietnamese. Bosco obediently fell into line behind her, following as she weaved through the stacks of containers to the edge of the deck. "This is going to suck," Sam said as she looked down at the dark water. *The Piper* was moving slowly, drifting on prior momentum rather than running her motors. But the Coast Guard was circling, four small ships herding the larger vessel back toward the open sea. She gripped the iron rail and looked down.

Bosco whined.

"It's okay. We've swum farther. Remember the day on the sailboat? This will be just like that. We jump in. We swim. No problems." She was lying to herself and the dog, which was possibly a new personal low. But every minute she hesitated, the shore of California drifted farther away.

She jumped.

Cold Pacific water pulled her under. Her feet tangled in only heaven knew what. Lungs burning, she kicked off her shoes and swam up toward the light. Everything around her was darkness. She looked up and saw Bosco's silhouette against *The Piper*'s lights. "Bosco, *nhảy xuông*!"

He whined, disappeared for a moment, then arched over the railing to splash down a few feet away. The cold water panicked him, and Bosco started flailing.

Sam grabbed him under the forelegs, but he was

writhing. "Bosco, *dùng lại*. Stop. Calm down. *Dùng lại*."

His paw clawed at the straps of her backpack and pulled her under.

She fought to get back to the surface, but the bag slipped. It was the money or the dog.

She let the bag sink and pulled Bosco's forelegs over her shoulders as she kicked for shore. A quarter mile into the swim, Bosco climbed off her and began swimming alongside. A big, happy doggy smile on his face.

Sam frowned at him. "Now you like the water?" She snorted out seawater that washed up her nose with a wave. "See? Just like the sailboat." Rolling onto her back, she kept swimming.

Larger waves rolled off *The Piper*'s wake as Hanshi turned on the engines. Before she reached the shore, one of the Coast Guard boats caught up with *The Piper* and she watched as a ladder was dropped. Unless someone had seen Bosco go overboard, no one had an idea where she was. The Coast Guard might find her luggage, but Hanshi could lie about that. Jon had seen her above deck. In time, she trusted the crew would figure out what happened.

Her hand hit rock, and Sam rolled again, clambering up so she stood with the waves ripping around her knees. "Welcome to California."

Barefoot, sopping wet, and stinking of sewage, Sam walked along the shore to the curious looks of the latenight revelers. *The Piper* had been too far out for anyone to notice which craft she was likely to have jumped off, but there were going to be people tomorrow morning checking the news feeds to see if some heiress had fallen off one of the luxury yachts that dotted the coast like fireflies. All she could hope for was that the alcohol would fuzz their memories enough that they didn't remember details.

"This is a shout-out to everyone looking for a better year in 2070!" a voice roared up ahead. "This song's for you!"

Sam looked at the lights and the banner that read KJAM NEW YEAR'S EVE BATHHOUSE BASH. The word "bath" sounded promising, and parties meant food. Maybe she could find a dry T-shirt, too. "Come on, Bosco." His leash had been in the backpack, but he wasn't wandering. As long as they didn't meet any overzealous cops, she felt safe. Her brain finally woke up, and she smiled down at Bosco. "Have I told you today that I love you?"

Bosco looked up at her and woofed as they walked up to the party.

Over the speakers, the lyrics to "Beachwave Romance" by Brandi and the Dawls threatened to ruin everyone's hearing.

"You're like a riptide," Sam mumbled along, hips moving in time to the music. "A riptide to my heart. Pull me down. Pull me down. Pull down."

Someone wearing an offensively bright pink shirt turned. He was sloshed. Reeking of cheap beer and sweat. "Hey! I like this song!"

"Yeah, me too," Sam said. "Do you know if anyone here is not drunk?"

The guy shook his head. "Maybe the dudes in black." He started bobbing his head to the beat of the music and wandered into the thickest part of the crowd.

Sam scanned the sidelines until she found three muscly black men with black shirts that said SECURITY. With a smile, she grabbed Bosco's collar and pulled him toward the guards. "Hey, how are you guys? Happy New Year!" She shot them her best please-tourist-buy-my-overpriced-trash smile. "Can you help me?"

A heavily built man with his head shaved frowned at her. "You find a lost dog?"

"No," Sam said. "This is my puppy. He got loose, and I ran after him without his leash. Or my shoes." She grimaced and nodded down at her sandy feet. "The fireworks spooked him, and he went straight through my screen door and down the beach. Do you have, like, a lanyard or a rope or anything I can put on him to walk him home?"

The security guard blinked. "Yeah. Sure. The radio station has a bunch of stuff they're giving out tonight. Want some flip-flops?"

"That would be amazing." Sam upped her smile.

Bosco barked, and the guy jumped about a foot off the ground.

"That dog's big enough to start a tsunami. Where'd you get him?"

"He's a rescue," Sam said, petting Bosco so he would calm down. "He's friendly, but he's loud."

"Yeah." The guy nodded his head to the side. "This way. I'm Dante."

"Sam," Sam said.

"You got a weird accent," Dante said.

Sam smiled. "I was born up north. In Toronto. I came down here to get away from the snow."

Dante nodded along with the music as the DJ switched to "Flare and Burn" by the Brute Beats. "I used to live in Portland."

"What's it like up there?"

"Rainy." Dante led her behind the speakers to rows of boxes filled with T-shirts, flip-flops, beer cozies, and key lanyards that flashed neon rainbow. "Have at it. Anything you want."

"You won't get in trouble?"

"Nah, perks of being security. I'm allowed to give solar ladies like you whatever I want. You run into trouble, you give Dante a call." He flashed her the two-fingered peace sign and went back to watch the partiers.

Sam rummaged until she found a T-shirt that would fit. It was the same bright pink the drunk had been wearing, but it smelled clean. Next to the boxes, there was an arctic-blue duffel with the words CABRILLO MARINE AQUARIUM. She stuffed two more shirts, a second pair of flip-flops, and a handful of the flashing lanyards in. After all, Dante had said she could take what she needed, and any change of clothes was good.

It took a few minutes to tie enough lanyards together to make a leash with a decent length, but Bosco accepted the new, hair-thin restraint with amiable animal grace.

Clicking her tongue, she led him away from the party toward the public showers. Fireworks were going off in the west, and while the onlookers oohed and aahed, Sam watched the beach blankets for unattended shorts. She found a long white swimsuit cover sitting alone in the sand; it wasn't too thin and would work after she rinsed the sand off. Closer to the showers, she found a pair of tan capris that were only a size too big and a light blue skirt, both sitting under a sign that said LOST AND FOUND.

"One more thing to discuss next time I remember to go to confession," she told Bosco as she shook off the clothes and stuffed them in her purloined bag. They rinsed off as best they could in the tepid showers with the water pressure of a light drizzle. Bosco shook himself off. She changed into the shorts and one of the pink T-shirts and stuffed her salt-hardened jeans into the bag. "Okay, Bos. Where to?"

Bosco looked up at her with mild mastiff alarm.

"We need a car. I'm thinking . . . city impound?" If LA was like San Diego, the impound lot had cars that had been sitting there for decades. All she had to do was get one and get it out of the lot without anyone's asking for an ID or an explanation. "Sure. No problem. We can do this."

Mac, where are you when I really need a rescue?

CHAPTER 22

> *"One of the great traditions of war is to turn one's enemies into one's assets."*
>
> ~ **General Levi Dankir speaking to the graduating class of Antwood University I3-2056**

Day 199/365
Year 5 of Progress
(July 18, 2069)
Central Command
Third Continent
Prime Reality

A stack of thin, paper-sized plastic pages dropped beside Mac's hand.

"That's everything we have." The man who went by only the name Donovan sat down in the chair across the table from Mac with a glare. "Do you really think you can solve a murder like this?"

Mac picked up one of the ultralight datpads with a grimace. "For me, it's a five-year-old cold case. And, no,

I'm not likely to be able to solve it without the rest of the data." He flipped through the files. "Where are the other case files?"

Donovan shook his head. "There aren't any."

"If Sam was right about the serial killer, there are at least four more victims you don't have files on. I thought your people had everything."

"We do, from the point of time where the two iterations converged." Donovan held up a hand. "The iterations are acting abnormally because of the upcoming decoherence event. Instead of running parallel and bumping, we're spiraling around each other. Twisting and tangling like a storm system. It's making everything difficult. Usually, we operate with some form of linear time on the other side of the portal. Right now, going through could land you anywhere at any time."

Mac rubbed his forehead as he sorted it out. "So even though it's early January there, it's not in this iteration?"

"Unless my team collapses your iteration at an earlier date, there exists an early January in your iteration. We just can't find it."

"My wife's going to kill me," Mac muttered. This wasn't taking three hours to get groceries because he'd stopped to fix someone's flat tire. Sam had to be beside herself with worry right now. "I could wind up back home before I'm kidnapped." That wouldn't go over well. At all.

He'd probably shoot himself if he ran into himself . . . that sentence shouldn't have made sense, but it did.

"I wouldn't worry about it." Donovan smirked. "You're never leaving."

"Commander Rose has promised she'll let me leave when this investigation is finished." Even as he said it, though, Mac studied the other man. He was very similar to the man who'd traveled with Nialls Gant to kill Sam before they moved to Australia. Tall, muscular, hardened by a lifetime of brutality that had scraped the light from his eyes and left him as flat and cold as any killer Mac had ever seen.

A physical fight between them would result in at least one bruised rib even if Mac fought dirty. Donovan held himself like a person who knew how to fight, and the cruel smile twisting on his lips was no comfort.

And a seed of doubt crept in.

"Do you doubt your commander's integrity?" Mac asked.

"Rose would never allow anything to jeopardize our truth, the real timeline of humanity. The best you'll get from her is an offer to bring your girlfriend over."

"Wife," Mac corrected. "She's my wife." Even if traveling back in time meant the wedding was still several months away. "And she wouldn't like it here. Your food is terrible."

Donovan shrugged in acknowledgment. He looked at the stack of files. "Can I help?"

Mac sighed. "Have you ever investigated a murder before?"

"No."

Figured. "I'm going to read through all of these and looks for details I missed. Foreign objects listed in the autopsy, traces of chemicals that are unusual, fingerprints on the belongings of the victims that don't belong to the victim. I also need to look for similarities. The killer chose these women for a reason."

Donovan grabbed one of the files and turned it so he could read. "Don't they all look the same? Maybe that's the link."

"It's *a* link," Mac agreed. "But most killers have a pattern for choosing their victims. Serial killers can't go on a dating site and filter out victims that don't look right." He stopped. "Well, that's a lie. They can do that. I worked a case in Chicago where one did. But the method for picking each of the victims was the same. Dating site, bars, grocery stores, biking trails, car sales lots; the killer is a predator. Predators go back to where they know they can find prey."

"So the more times the killer has a successful kill from a method, the more he repeats it?"

Mac nodded. "Usually, yes. If the killer were being completely random in his victim selection, we'd see a wider range of victims. They'd probably be isolated to a single area. Instead, we have a roving killer who targets these women for their looks."

"Maybe they're useless?" Donovan suggested, tossing the file back on the table with a shrug. "Unwanted women. Working women? What do you call them in your iteration?"

Mac frowned in confusion. "Are you suggesting

they're sex workers? Homeless? I'm not sure what you mean, actually."

"Some people aren't as valuable to society," Donovan said with an arching hand gesture. "People who no one cares about?"

"I'm a bureau agent, and my field is forensic medicine. There's no insignificant death or person." He glared down at the files, fighting the desire to get up and run away.

Deep down, he knew the type of people Donovan meant—he'd been one. Isolated and overlooked. He'd cut off contact from his family, avoided making any friendships, drowned out his common sense and worries with ever increasing doses of sleeping pills. Until Sam pulled him out of the abyss of depression, he'd been taunting death. Welcoming it, even.

Mac shook his head again. "If you aren't going to help, please leave. I'd like to get this done sooner rather than later."

Donovan shrugged and left Mac to himself. Once the door closed, Mac looked around, then sighed. There was nothing else he could do but sit in the room with the files, so he did. Reading through the details over and over, scant though they were.

The only thing that stuck out was the fingerprint on Jane Doe's body. *His* fingerprint.

Drugs had created a hazy bubble around him the morning Jane came to the morgue. He remembered a few colors, the red of Sam's lips, and the green of the grass, and the cloying smell of antiseptics masking the sickly-sweet scent of death. He'd probably forgotten to put his gloves on before wheeling her into the lab.

Probably.

Donovan was smiling, which was enough to make Rose nervous. Senturi was avoiding her eyes. The whole team was working hard to pretend they didn't know each other.

The air on her arms prickled, a primitive alert system that backed up what she was already sensing. Something was going to go horribly wrong today. She'd felt the same way the morning before they'd lost Wagner. The same gut-churning sensation had nauseated her the day Senturi was shot.

Now the awareness was an itch impossible to scratch. It grated against her nerves, heightened all her senses until the faint scent of deodorant and clean sweat became overwhelming.

Senturi finally made eye contact. "You doing okay, Commander?"

She gave him a tight nod. "How's your shoulder?"

"The doctor gave me the all clear two days ago. It's a little sore, and I'd like to avoid getting shot again, but I'm fine."

She looked at the members of her team, trying to find some clue to what was about to happen.

Senturi frowned at her. "Problems?"

"No. Just . . . too large a team, maybe. We can do this detonation with half the people. There's no security to worry about." She finished tightening her gear and headed for the jump room. The lights were too bright. The air too cold.

"Commander Rose!" Emir's voice cut through the noise.

Her emotions froze into a cold steel shield. Turning, placid smile in place, she nodded to him. "Sir." With alarm, she noted the bulge of a bulletproof vest under his suit.

"I'm coming with you," Emir announced. "On a slight delay, of course."

"I have to protest," she said as politely as she could. What she wanted to do was shout *"Are you crazy?"* A civil war would erupt if Emir went missing. They were already on the edge of one. The world government was splintering already. Only fear of Emir's pruning them from the future kept the peace right now.

"Sir, we do not have enough control in this iteration to ensure your safety."

"I'll keep Captain Donovan with me," Emir said in a placating voice. He wasn't going to change his mind—not that she expected him to.

And Donovan would see this as a sign of favor. The poor fool. He didn't realize how close he was to being collateral damage.

"How far from our arrival point will that place you?" she asked

"The iterations are frayed at this convergence point. It almost looks like a node is trying to form."

Rose shook her head. "There's no nodal event on

this date. Not in the history of any of the iterations we've been to."

He smiled, eyebrows raising. "I know. Isn't it exciting? I wonder what we're creating."

Dread of uncertainty filled her. She didn't dare voice her question: *What if we aren't the ones creating the node? What if someone else, on the dark side of history, was changing everything?*

She shivered. Life would be so much better once they'd collapsed the rogue iteration. They'd go, destroy the nodes, destroy the MIA, and move on. She'd spend some of her very limited company credits to buy a hot meal.

By tomorrow, it would all be over.

Donovan stood at Emir's right hand, surveying the busy kingdom of the control room. Techs in scrubs, agents in jump gear, and Emir in his power suit . . . there was a fluid nature to it. What was the natural spiral found in nautilus shells called? A golden ratio or Fibonacci or pi? The math of time was the same. At the center, there was always a central point on which everything else turned. Emir fancied himself to be that axis. Donovan knew better.

He caressed the tiny bumps on the butt of his gun as Commander Rose prepared her team. Black hair framed the stretched copper skin on her bony face. Oh, how he dreamt of this day. Of finally taking her down, beating her into the dirt, where she belonged.

Her black eyes caught his look, and he smiled. There was fear in her eyes. She knew she was hunted. Knew with some animal instinct that he was coming for her.

It didn't change anything—in old nature videos he'd seen that the gazelles saw the lions before they attacked, too, but they went down nonetheless.

The jump sequence began, and Rose's team moved in to secure the building. Senturi looked up, and Donovan nodded. The traitor would do his job.

Emir clapped his hands as the portal closed. "Thirteen minutes until our entry. Are you ready, Captain?"

"Always, sir."

A tech scurried across the room and handed Emir a datpad. "Excellent. Absolutely excellent. Come along, Donovan." Emir handed the pad back to the tech and walked down to the portal. "Begin the jump sequence."

"Sir?"

"We've made contact of sorts with the other iteration."

Donovan could have wrung that man's scrawny neck. "Sir?" He kept the reproach and disapproval out of his voice, but only barely. "This is not part of the agenda." Emir was going to ruin everything. The man simply delighted in making his life difficult. He was going to frag up everything to what, feed his manic ego some more?

Emir waved his hand with a tut-tutting noise that drove Donovan to the edge of rage. "One of our people intercepted a communique from a man named Marrins. He's trying to blackmail my other-self." He chuckled with self-indulgent cruelness.

"I can't imagine that matters, sir. The iteration will cease to exist in a matter of hours." And Rose would be obliterated with it. A tragic accident. He'd wear the black armband, give an appropriately joyless speech at her memorial, and move on without a trace of guilt.

It was her fault, after all. She'd brought them an extra node to ensure this iteration's stability. And MacKenzie was easy enough to get along with. A big, stupid fellow who would follow Donovan anywhere he led.

Emir patted his arm. "Indulge me, Captain. It has been a long time since I was able to safely explore all the worlds the Prime touched. I'm curious."

"Yes, sir." Donovan hid his anger well. He was nothing if not adaptable. He'd let Emir wander, it would give another layer of verisimilitude to Rose's coming "accident."

CHAPTER 23

"Why are stars seen as romantic? They're forever alone, doomed to destroy anything that comes too close."

~ excerpt from *Serenade of the Quiet Heart* by Jaylee Dini I2—2027

Wednesday January 1, 2070
California District 21
Los Angeles
Commonwealth of North America
Iteration 2

Hunger woke Sam. Not the mild pangs she associated with sleeping in but a gnawing, bone-biting hunger like she'd never had before. Sixteen hours without food. She'd never gone that long without something. She rubbed her fingers on Bosco's ear. "I am not going to survive on the street."

Which meant doing something drastic. The buses wouldn't let her bring Bosco, there was no one in the Commonwealth to call, and her cash was at the bottom of the harbor. Eyeing the aquarium duffel bag, she mentally calculated how much selling the T-shirts would get her. Enough for breakfast and something for Bosco. But not enough to get her a car.

Bosco whined, stretching at the end of the lanyards that had finally quit flashing a little before dawn.

She stood up and stretched. Sleeping behind the bushes next to the DMV had seemed like the safest choice last night, but now it seemed like a bad idea. There were lines of people, a crowded parking lot, and across the street a police substation with its own impound lot. She'd thought everyone would have closed for the holiday, but apparently not. A beat-up brown car pulled up in front of the impound delivery gate, and the driver hopped out.

"Oh . . ." She looked at Bosco. A story from her past bubbled up from under the demands of hunger and the fog of frustration. Ruthie Reid, the Polynesian rugby goddess from the Academy, kept a mailing loop of craziest stories. Sam had never contributed, but before Troom's death, Mac's meteoric reentry into her life, and the decision to jump back in time, Ruthie had told her about the wonders of the new volunteer program. The police and the CBI were understaffed on the West Coast, so some brilliant mind in HR had decided to farm menial work out to volunteers. Sometimes clones, but usually college students who could use the hours for credits at the government-funded colleges.

The volunteer program ended when a carjacking

ring started posing as drivers. They showed up, volunteered to park the car, and drove it to a chop shop across district lines before anyone was the wiser. It had taken months to sort things out, and the CBI had never recovered all the cars.

Bosco whined.

"Yeah, this is fine." She watched the volunteer take the paperwork from the impound's front desk and drive into the parking lot. "Let's go find breakfast. I probably have something we can sell." Searching through the duffel, she didn't see anything the pawnshop down the street might want until she checked the pockets of the jeans she'd jumped off The Piper in. There was an Aussie ten-dollar bill, and a bill worth 1000 rupiah. Both worthless in the Commonwealth, but they might have value to a collector.

Whistling, she led Bosco down the street. He lapped up a bit of a puddle left by the sprinklers, peed on the gates of the DMV, and let his tongue hang out as she pushed open the door of the pawnshop.

"Hey!" the man behind the counter shouted. "No pets allowed."

"He's my comfort animal," Sam said without missing a beat. "I was assaulted." She looked him in the eye to see if he'd squirm. He did. "Bosco makes it so I don't have panic attacks."

The man grimaced. "Fine, but if he ruins anything, you bought it. Hurry up."

"I'm here to sell, not buy," Sam said, holding up the bills. "We're moving grandpa to a nursing home, and

I'm in charge of cleaning out his old things. Grandpa said I should shred these, but I figured I'd check and see if they were collectible."

With a disappointed look, the man slid the bills across the glass counter. "Australian? And, what's this?"

"Indonesian," Sam said, pointing to the rupiah.

"Where's Indonesia?"

"Ah, it used to be a group of islands north of Australia. I think it's part of the South Asian Union now. Like I said, older than fossils." She smiled.

He shook his head and pushed the bills back. "I don't sell currency, lady. I don't even take cash. But there's a coin shop two blocks away. Go north, second left. It's Art's Coins and Collectables. I can't promise he'll pay anything, but he's the only one around here who might unless you want to go to the valley."

"Nah, Art's will be fine." Her stomach growled.

The guy looked at her. "There's a deli down the street that does a good breakfast."

"I'm not really hungry," Sam lied.

"There's nothing healthy about skipping meals," he said. "My granny died of doing that. Kept starving herself to lose weight, and her bone density was awful. Here"—he rummaged behind the counter and handed her a card with a flower and a handful of almonds on it—"that's the number of my dietician. She's very patient. Very affordable. Give her a call, tell her Paul sent you, and she'll give you a free consult. With a little mindful eating, you can make a whole lifestyle change."

"A lifestyle change?" Sam nodded in confusion. "Of course. What a wonderful idea. I'll call her. Paul, you said. Good. Thank you, Paul." When she was back on the street, she looked down at Bosco. "Do I look like I need to diet?"

He grumbled. "No. I didn't think so either. I can run a six-minute mile. I paddleboard. I parkour. I eat healthy!" she shouted loud enough to draw worried glances from customers leaving the DMV. She waved and walked down to Art's. He bought both bills for four hundred—enough to buy used sneakers at the thrift shop next door and breakfast for both her and Bosco, with enough left over for meals throughout the week.

After finding a pet store and a good leash, she and Bosco circled back to the DMV. It was three in the afternoon, people were shouting, people were sweating, the lot was filled to capacity. In other words, it was perfect chaos.

Sam waited until the manager walked out back to evaluate the chaos before she attacked. Smiling, she walked into the arctic cool of the air-conditioned building. The bell overhead rang, and the clerk sneezed.

"No dogs!"

"Oh, he's a comfort animal," Sam said. "And I'll just be here a minute. Someone said you need one of the cars moved to the other impound? I'm with the volunteers . . ."

The harried clerk sagged with relief. "Oh, thank you! We have been calling for hours. Someone said something about orientation today, and all the volunteers were busy?"

Sam shook her head. "I used to live down in San Diego, and I did the training down there. I told them I wouldn't mind helping while I was up here visiting my grandpa." She nodded, then looked at the ground and counted to ten. Pressing her lips together, she let the stress and fear of the last month show when she looked back up. "He's not . . . he's not okay. And his memory . . ." She shook her head and covered her mouth. "He probably only has a few weeks. This sounds so selfish. It's just, when I'm there, all I do is cry. I need to get out for a few hours. Pretty please, can I help?"

"Yes," the clerk said with a sympathetic smile. "That would be perfect. Ah . . . what are you comfortable driving?"

Asking for something that was fuel-efficient and nondescript might raise a few red flags. "Well, if there's anything flashy, I'd love to drive a Sunburst."

"No," the clerk said. "We have pickups, a food truck, an ice-cream truck that was used for selling drugs, and a bunch of midrange cars."

"In that case, I'll take anything with working air conditioning," Sam said.

The clerk looked through the computer. "An Alexian Gemini, dark blue, everything works but it's been here for five months and needs to be driven before it goes bad. Did you give the chief your paperwork?"

"Mmmhmm, outside," Sam lied, earning her another five Hail Marys. It was getting easier every time. At this point, her next confession would take over an hour, and penance would take a few days of constant prayer. "He said I should check in with you. Where am I delivering this one?"

"Long Beach is full. Bellflower is near capacity. Do you think you could go to Bell Gardens? I know it's halfway to Vegas, but they have an empty lot since the auction was last week."

Pretending to worry, Sam hemmed and hawed. Finally, she shrugged. "I guess. Does it need fuel?"

The clerk grabbed the keys and a fuel card. "Take it to any station around here. They'll do a quick road check and make sure the water battery is running right."

"I thought all the cars out here were on solar-capture cells?"

"They're supposed to be," the clerk said. "This one is from Oregon. We're lucky it doesn't run on goat cheese."

Sam laughed obligingly at the joke, took the keys, and all but skipped out the door. A friendly nod to the chief, fifteen minutes getting the car checked, and she was on the highway.

Bosco sat in the front seat, scaring drivers as they passed.

"Don't drool on the upholstery," she told him. "This is genuine leather. And I'm pretty sure this is quartz decorating the steering column. We're going to Vegas and selling this to the first shady dealer we find." It was one of the advantages of grunt work at the CBI—she knew which rocks to flip over to find slime in every district in the Commonwealth. All she had to do was change her MO. Instead of watching the slime and arresting them when the big gangs were broken down, she'd make them work for her. And do so while staying under the radar and getting to Florida District 8 before Henry Troom blew himself to Kingdom Come.

CHAPTER 24

> "The night was wild. The mountains echoed the thunder's refrain: here are the forgotten, the children of pain."
>
> ~ excerpt from *A Wild Sea* by Laya Zaffre 12-2036

Monday January 6, 2070
Florida District 8
Commonwealth of North America
Iteration 2

The Basilwood Apartments were exactly as soul-suckingly mundane as she remembered. The synthetic wood and lacy fringe were no better than her first trip through 2070. Possibly worse now that she had the condos of Airlie Beach to compare it to. Dry January grass added a level of despondency because the rain wasn't there yet.

In a few weeks, the grass would be green, the birds would be nesting . . . and this place would be crawling with CBI agents looking for a clue of what would become a double homicide.

Sitting in the car outside Henry Troom's apartment, she wiggled her wedding band off. It wasn't the same black-opal-and-diamond engagement ring Mac had originally proposed to her with. That was safely tucked away in a safety-deposit box in Cannonvale, waiting for her return. This was the black metal, non-reflective ring Mac had given her last year on their anniversary. He'd called it a Field Ring . . . a sniper's ring. Meant to be combat-ready because no light would bounce off it. On the inside was inscribed Mac's favorite quote: *Decisions Determine Destiny—T. S. Monson.*

Four lives were riding on her choice today. Five, if she counted Mac's.

"That's the problem, isn't it?" she muttered under her breath. "Do I want to save Mac more than I want to save Troom, Nealie, Donovan, and that other Sam?"

Bosco licked her face.

"I already did this once. I made the choice to have Troom build the machine before. So maybe it's inevitable. Maybe I don't have a choice at all."

It was a terrifying thought.

With a heavy sigh, she rolled down the car windows. "Stay here," she ordered Bosco as she locked the door. Then, reluctantly, she climbed the steps to Apartment 12B. She knocked.

Fake gunfire rattled around her head with the echoes of déjà vu. Her ears strained to catch the music of the video game. It wasn't Wars of Wars, the beat was too arrhythmic for that. Whatever it was, it clearly had the attention of the player more than her knocking. She knocked again—louder this time—and inside she caught the unmistakable curse of Devon Bradet.

Staying here to save Henry and Nealie meant saving Bradet, too. That definitely put a point in the let-them-all-die column. Bradet had an uncanny ability to drive her crazy.

The door swung open, and Bradet swung into its place. He leaned against the doorframe, face thinner than she remembered and brown hair greasier. "What?"

"No comment about my stunning good looks?"

With exhausted, sunken eyes, he gave her a quick once-over. "Not my type. What?"

"I'm here to talk to Henry Troom?"

Bradet stood up, looking like a startled possum caught in the headlights. "I already talked to Officer Clemens and her boss. I didn't know what he was doing."

An unnatural chill dug into Sam's bones. "Where's Henry?"

"In jail!" Bradet shouted. "Right where the murdering bastard ought to be."

The door slammed in her face before Sam could think of a reply. She turned and walked back to the car in a daze. Henry had never gone to jail. He'd never had any trouble with the law.

Bosco licked her face.

Time passed as she sat there, staring at the steering wheel and trying to find sense in the disaster of her life. Like a life raft tossed up on the stormy waves, her mind caught hold of one word: *Clemens*.

Did he mean Ivy Clemens?

She looked at Bosco. "How do I disguise myself from someone who has a poster of me in her apartment?"

The dog licked her face.

"I think it's going to take more than makeup," Sam said as she patted Bosco's head. "But that's a good place to start."

The smell of bleach made Sam wrinkle her nose every five seconds, and her new contacts didn't just itch, they looked ridiculously fake. She'd asked the technician at the salon for a "California Look" and wound up looking like a tourist from Sydney with bottle-blond hair, Day-Glo-blue eyes, and shimmery bronzer smeared across her already bronzed skin. If anyone asked, she had the name of a great tanning salon on speed dial.

She tossed a stick of bright pink bubble gum in her mouth. Bosco crouched in the seat next to her, whimpering.

"It's temporary," she promised. "Just until I can get out of here. The absolute last thing I need is Clemens realizing I'm here, and in the CBI office downtown." The clone had worshipped Sam when they'd first met. Which, she realized, with the familiar snake-pit feel of time travel biting into her, wasn't going to happen for another month at the earliest.

Ivy wouldn't approach the CBI until she found Nealie's body on the shore.

Traveling like this felt like free fall.

Because it dawned on her that if she just saved Nealie, Ivy wouldn't ever meet Young Sam. If Ivy and Sam never met, Sam would never give her a recommendation for the CBI Academy. It all came down to what the cost of a life was.

And it wasn't a question she was prepared to answer.

Thoughts still turning upside down and inside out, she parked under a spreading oak tree in the corner of the Smyrna precinct building. She clipped Bosco into his harness, hung a Working Dog vest over him, and strutted into the building like she owned the place. *Saint Michael and Saint George, forgive me the lies I'm about to tell.* The automatic doors swung open, and the scent of cheap soap, sweat, and recycled air flowed out into the street.

Sam blew a bubble of bright pink gum.

The rookie sitting at the front desk was young enough that his eyes focused on her tight red crop top, not the baton at her hip or fake badge in her hand.

"Hiya, cutie." Sam leaned against the counter to give rookie a good view of her cleavage. "I'm here to talk to whoever's running the Lexie Muñoz case." At the time Sam had left California, twenty-three-year-old Lexie had been the latest victim.

"Um . . ." The rookie blinked, looked at Bosco, then finally at her face. "Who are you?"

"Private investigator Lexie's daddy hired to make sure the case wasn't buried. Strictly helpful stuff." She pulled a sheath of folded papers from the ten-dollar knockoff purse she'd bought from a boardwalk vendor and prayed no one actually wanted to investigate anything. The ID she was waving was real enough if no one did a computer check, but the papers were ones she'd grabbed from some college students promoting a sidewalk art fair. Even a boob-blinded rookie would know those weren't real.

The rookie grimaced. "I don't know if the chief would really want . . ."

Sam held up her hands and gave him her most innocent smile. "I'm not here to step on toes or steal a collar. I just brought some details. List of Lexie's friends down here. Her family. Her ex. Her drug dealer . . ." She let that carrot dangle. "I don't even need to ride along, but maybe you have someone in the department who can help me make my hourly wage here, right? A Shadow or someone in the doghouse. I sit, I chat with them, I bill Daddy Muñoz eight hundred an hour. Easy money."

He wasn't budging.

Sam leaned closer, pushing her breasts together a little more. "Maybe it could be you? I bet I'd make you look real good. Or real happy." She winked.

He jumped like he'd been bit. "I . . . ah . . . right. Let me talk to someone."

She watched him run through the series of locked doors and the metal detector like the devils of hell were on his heels. "Must be a Baptist," she told Bosco. "Want to bet he confesses to sinful thoughts when he sees his pastor next?"

Bosco lay down on the cool tile floor without even a tail wag.

"Yeah, you're right, I don't think Baptists have confession, either." Though she needed it right now. Not that she'd practiced Catholicism much since she lost the baby, but at times like this, she missed washing away the guilt. Mac always argued that a few prayers weren't real repentance if you went and did the same thing the next week, but she figured God understood. Sure, this was a lie, but if it freed an innocent man and brought a killer to justice, surely God would forgive a little sin.

Wouldn't He?

With a sigh, she peeked over at the desk. "Rookie was playing Downtown Race Fire on the computer," she informed Bosco, as if the dog cared. "Left his post, left the computer open . . ."

She eyed the doors and wondered if she had enough time to log into the system for a quick peek before someone with authority to arrest her showed up. *Probably not.* "Why do I get the feeling that the rookie will be looking for a new job next week if his superiors ever find out about this?"

The rookie turned the corner, with Ivy Clemens hot on his heels. Ivy looked different than Sam remembered her. Paler, perhaps, less radiant. Ivy had always seemed to burn from within with a radioactive personality that threatened to overwhelm everyone she met. This Ivy looked beaten, sallow . . . dying.

Sam reached for Bosco, her fingers itching to touch

someone for comfort. Bosco obligingly stood up and leaned against her leg. He was the first thing Ivy noticed.

"That's a really big dog."

"About 180 pounds," Sam said, thankful for an easy opening gambit. "He can pull more than five hundred pounds on the sand track next to our house."

Ivy stepped forward as the rookie retreated behind his desk, probably planning to fake work until they left.

"Markum here says you came out from California?"

"Yup," Sam said.

"You're a long way from the West Coast," Ivy said. "What brings you here?"

"Lexie Muñoz. Her parents aren't happy with the pace of the case, and they have money. They sent me with some details and some cash to help move things along."

"I'm sorry you made the trip. The killer was arrested yesterday."

"Henry Troom?" Sam pretended she was amused with the thought. "I bet you a milk shake he's not the killer."

Now she had Ivy's full attention. Green eyes, brittle and biting as sea glass studied her. "What did you say your name was?"

"Rose." *Damn it!* "MacKenzie. Rose MacKenzie. My mother had a thing for Highlanders. You should have seen her e-reader when I was a kid. I peeked once, and boy can I tell you that my senior trip to Scotland was a serious disappointment after that. Not a muscle-bound, kilt-clad lover to be found." Her cheeks heated as the lies tumbled off her tongue. If Mac ever found out about this conversation, she would never hear the end of it. Although, Mac in a kilt was an idea worth considering.

"But you managed to marry a MacKenzie anyway." Ivy's smile held the baleful envy of someone who had heard of a prize but thought they could never touch it. "Did he wear a kilt to the wedding?"

"He wore flip-flops and swim trunks," Sam said. Bosco had been their ring bearer. Mac had promised that one day, when the timelines aligned, they'd have a real church wedding. The jury was still out about whose church it would be. "But he's not here." She twisted the wedding band.

The more she thought about Mac, the more it hurt.

She realized then that she'd decided what she was here to do without meaning to. Mac was more important than Nealie, Ivy, or even herself.

She had to get Mac back, at any cost.

If she couldn't get Henry out legally, she'd ruin her younger self by breaking him out illegally. But that was a measure of last resort.

But . . . she was now sure it was a measure she was willing to take if her other options failed.

Which meant she had to make this work.

Sam tossed her newly blonded hair and hit Ivy with a megawatt smile she'd perfected for winning commissions from tourists. "So, how about you and I hunker down, talk shop, find a killer, and we all go home happy?"

Ivy glanced sideways at the rookie, who was doing an excellent job of pretending they didn't exist. "Troom is in jail for the murder. That will need to be enough for your clients. The department doesn't have the manpower needed to chase hunches."

"What about you?" Sam's voice almost cracked. She was ready to beg.

Ivy's chin lifted, and a hint of the fire Sam knew flashed in her angry eyes. "I'm a clone. I'm no help to anyone."

"That's not true. You could be a big help to me."

All the muscles in Ivy's face tightened with fury. "Thank you for stopping by, Miss MacKenzie. I'll be sure someone hears about your theories. We'll call you if there's any interest in pursuing the leads you brought." She turned and stomped off without even asking for Sam's number.

The rookie hunched over his computer, trying to avoid being noticed.

Sam rolled her eyes. By hook or by crook . . . she'd find a way.

Sam sat on the trunk of her car with the loop of Bosco's leash hanging off her wrist. He had a bowl of water, she'd had four chocolate ice cream bars shaped like dolphins, and Ivy Clemens still hadn't left work for the night. "Bosco, we've got a problem."

Bosco's tail thumped on the parking lot.

"Where are we staying tonight?"

He didn't have an answer.

Neither did she, which was worse. She was reacting to everything. Chasing down Mac like a bloodhound with a sense of direction and purpose, but no long-term plan for self-preservation. She didn't have a credit card to use at a motel, and it wasn't like she could sleep on a friend's couch until she found an apartment. She had an irrational urge to call Brileigh and ask for help. Except Bri was nosey as an Italian grandma, and she knew that Sam had an apartment here. Sneaking into that apartment was out of the question, though.

Bosco stretched, his butt going skyward as his front legs reached out.

"The yoga feel good, puppy?"

He hung his tongue out in response.

"Yeah. I could use a few sun salutes, too." Maybe meditation would help her gain some focus. Move her away from this place of panic. It felt like her heart rate hadn't dropped in a month.

"You know what? There's a yoga place south of here," she told Bosco with a speculative smile. A farm down south of Titusville run by a family who opened their home to anyone who wanted to drop by and help in the garden. They wouldn't want her ID or money. She'd probably even be able to convince them to let her trade cooking for the garden work. "How do you feel about watching some goats this week?"

If Bosco was going to answer with one of his expressive doggy looks, he didn't have a chance to. Sam was distracted by the sunlight flaring off the precinct door as Ivy Clemens walked out.

Sam smiled for real for the first time in weeks. "Come on, puppy. Look cute. One of us has to convince Ivy to play ball with us."

At the word "ball," Bosco jumped to his feet, tail wagging.

With a slight tug at the leash, Sam led him across the parking lot to corner poor Officer Clemens. "Hey."

Ivy froze beside her car, eyes wide with fear, lips puckered as if she'd just bit a lemon.

"We didn't seem to hit it off earlier."

"I told you the case was closed."

Sam leaned on the roof of Ivy's car, arms pillowed under her chin. "You think Troom killed Lexie."

"Because he did."

"Did he kill the other nine girls?"

Ivy had yet to learn how to hide her emotions. She stepped back, shock written in every moment. "What other girls?"

"When I started looking into Lexie's case, I found nine other victims. All physically similar. All killed in the same way. I'm thinking serial killer."

"You should take the information to the CBI. I have no jurisdiction. We didn't even make the arrest. The CBI handled the murder with cooperation from the police in District 7."

Bugger all. There were so many reasons she could not go to the CBI. Especially since her younger self was still dealing with the shadow of the accusation that she was a clone. Sam wrinkled her nose. "You know, the CBI . . . they're . . . how should I put this? They're a little dull. A little too by-the-book for my style of fact-finding."

Ivy squared her shoulders. "The bureau is one of the finest organizations in our country. They do so much more than they ever receive credit for."

Saints and angels! "Yup, great people. Just not super-helpful."

"Have you talked to them?" Ivy asked accusingly.

"I did." It was only a half lie. She'd sent several anonymous tips to Agent Parker before Mac disappeared. "The agent I spoke with wasn't cooperative."

"Have you tried Agent Rose here in District 8?"

If her hands hadn't been busy holding the leash as she leaned on the car, they would have been fists. "Not yet. But!" Sam cut Ivy off before the other woman could object. "I don't have enough evidence for her yet. If Agent Parker in Alabama wouldn't listen to me, I doubt an agent here in a busy district would. And the victim was found in another district. They'd bounce me around."

"So why are you here?"

"I would like to work with the police to verify that Henry Troom is the killer. Or find the real one if they're still out there."

Ivy shook her head. "No one is going to help you with that."

"What about you?" Sam stretched and smiled.

"Wouldn't that be a feather in your cap? The underrated officer bringing a serial killer to justice and helping the CBI. It'll look good on your record."

Ivy's eyes closed in frustration. Sam knew what the officer wanted her to understand, and she was being obtuse on purpose. Clones were legally people, but like all bigotry that had been codified into law, it was hard to convince people that clones were equal human beings. Ivy was struggling with years of being a slave to the police department. She'd been handed the worst jobs, received the least credit, and treated like the department gofer for too long. She didn't think she could help, and she didn't want to be anyone's fetch-girl.

"Listen, I'm not wrong about this. There's not a large risk."

Ivy sighed in defeat. "Define large risk."

"We'll find the killer. I can all but guarantee that. The only risk is the killer might find us first. It happens, only once or twice to me, but look at this way: I'm the one with the bull's-eye on my back. You should be perfectly safe."

Her laugh was bitter and humorless. "Safe? I can't even fight back in self-defense."

"That's why we take Bosco," Sam said. "In Florida, he's allowed to eat people in self-defense."

Bosco whined helpfully.

"Don't let his tough-guy act fool you. He's fierce," Sam said.

Ivy shook her head, and her shoulder slumped. "I'll think about it. Where are you staying?"

"Tickseed Meadow off Manatee Lane," Sam said. "It's south of Titusville."

"Tickseed?"

"It was once the state flower. Saw that in the brochure." Nearly six years ago now. Somehow, it had stuck. "Their number is in public records. Call me if you're willing to help."

Ivy looked down at Bosco and shrugged. "Yeah. Sure. I'll think about it."

"That's all I'm asking," Sam said.

She watched Ivy drive off, and her smile failed. "I really hope this works."

CHAPTER 25

> *"Even when you have the ability to walk through time, you still live only one day at a time."*
>
> ~ a private conversation with Agent 5—I1—2078

Tuesday January 7, 2070
Florida District 8
Commonwealth of North America
Iteration 2

"Rosie? Oh, Rose! Oh, hello, puppy. What a sweet puppikins."

Sam opened one eye and peered out from under the duvet. Her face had been swallowed by the most wonderful, butter-soft pillow in the world on a bed curtained by vines. This Eden was idyllic. Also, noisy. Her fingers clenched over the butt of the truncheon as she oriented herself.

"Rosie?" A magpie of a woman wearing a fluttery, multicolored caftan hovered just out of reach. Wild daisies were braided into her fading red hair. "Rose?"

Sam gave up on the idea of going back to sleep and rolled over. "Yes?"

"I'm so sorry to wake you. Anyone with half a third eye can tell you need to rejuvenate and realign your chakras, but there's an Officer Clemens on the phone. She's most insistent, dear. Would you like me to tell her to leave you alone? You have rights, you know. Our Davin is a lawyer. Still licensed, too. Very popular with the nudists."

"Did she say what it was about?"

"Nope!" The woman could make even that sound cheerful.

"Okay—can you check?"

"Of course!" The woman hurried away, leaving Sam to contemplate the vines hanging from the ceiling in macramé nests. Mac would hate this place. Sam could see herself enjoying it for a week or so before the novelty of living in a fairy garden wore off. As soon as someone asked her to sew her own clothes, she'd be gone.

For now, it wasn't so bad.

"Oh, Rosie!" The woman bustled back in with a big smile. "She says it's about a corpse, dear. Did you kill someone?"

Sam groaned. "No. I'm trying to find a killer. The police thought he was in jail. I was playing a hunch he wasn't." She rolled out of bed and stretched. "Is Ivy still on the phone?"

"Is that Officer Clemens?"

"Yes . . ." Her memory for names failed her.

"Maribel," the woman said kindly. "Maribel Moonchild First Breath Ocean Peace Starchild Jensen."

At least they kept a family name.

"Jensen is the name of mother's favorite actor," Maribel said, as if reading Sam's mind, "goddess rest her soul. A sweet woman, my mother. Not a vegan, but we can't all be perfect." Maribel beamed at her. "You look delightful this morning, Rose. Rose Dewdrop Honey Sun, that should be your name."

Sam nodded because disagreeing would have only prolonged the painful conversation. "Sure. Why not? Where's the phone?"

"Third door on the left. Just hit the gong when you're done. It clears the negative vibrations from the room." Maribel took off again, knees bent and arms swinging, but somehow her scuffed-slipper-clad feet never left the bamboo floor. It was an odd little walk for an odd little woman.

Amused, Sam tugged the borrowed plum bathrobe tight and walked into the study. Tickweed Meadow had an honest-to-goodness vintage phone complete with tangled cord attached to the wall. "Hello?" Sam said as she lifted the heavy phone to her ear. "Ivy?"

"Miss MacKenzie?"

"That's still me," Sam said. "Although they're planning a naming ceremony this evening, and if Maribel gets her way, I'll be Dewdrop Honey Sun."

Ivy's horrified silence was delightful.

Everything was delightful this morning. It made her wonder what exactly had been in the tea at dinner.

Sam made a mental note to drink water before leaving. "You still there, Officer Clemens?"

"I . . . yes. Sorry. I wasn't sure if you were joking or not."

"I was. Maribel probably isn't. But if you have news on the case, I'll probably be working late tonight. What happened?"

"We found a body right on the district line. It's in the morgue while everyone argues jurisdiction, and I thought you might want to look."

"I'd love to!" Sam said with a little bit too much enthusiasm. Ivy was going to start thinking she was a real mental case. "Where can I meet you?"

"District 6. The medical examiner is Lawrence Dom. I should be there before you, but if I'm not, I called ahead, so he knows you're coming. He's a little . . . weird," Ivy said apologetically. "He's very particular about where everything is. You should be fine as long as you don't touch anything."

"Got it," Sam said. "I'll be on the road in a few minutes."

"Do you want directions?"

Sam winced and lied. "Yes! Thank you. I'm not at the top of my game first thing in the morning." She listened as Ivy gave her the directions and repeated the street names back as if she were writing them down. As long as Ivy didn't ask to see the written material, she'd be fine. After hanging up, she sighed and let reality set back in.

She had three changes of clothes, no real ID, and a

giant mastiff who couldn't come in the morgue or be left in the car. She hit the gong.

It didn't seem to fix her problems.

Maribel's frizzy red nest of hair appeared in the doorway. "Rosie? Are you done? Is your friend all right?"

"She's fine. I'm going to drive up and go help her with this." Sam tugged at her braided, far-too-blond hair. "Can Bosco stay here today? Chase the chickens or something for you?"

"Oh, of course! Dogs have very healing souls. Especially him. There's so much wisdom in his eyes."

Sam narrowed her eyes. "Now you're pulling my leg."

Maribel shrugged, and an impish smile appeared. "Well, people say cats are healing. Why not dogs? I like them better than cats anyway."

Sam laughed. "I knew I liked you for a reason."

"Do you have time for breakfast before you go?"

"No, probably not. I need to get to the morgue in District 6."

"Oh." Her wrinkled face sagged into the most despondent frown. "It isn't anyone you know, is it?"

"No." Sam shook her head. "It shouldn't be. But I need to get there and help Officer Clemens find the perpetrator before it happens again."

"I'll pack you a goodie bag. Do you think Officer Clemens would like some dandelion cookies? They're very nourishing."

"I don't know her that well, but she might. Who

says no to free cookies?" She paused. "Wait, is there any of that spinach salad left over from dinner?"

"Of course! I'll put together a little lunch for you."

"You're the best," Sam said. She rushed to back to the nursery-turned-bedroom, changed, and was out the door with a cooler full of nourishing goodies in under twenty minutes.

The labs in District 6 made Sam sick with envy. A gleaming chrome-and-glass edifice to science surged from the white sidewalks like a temple to research. There was even a fountain. She hadn't been able to get a full-time medical examiner, and Petrilli had a fountain.

That was unfair.

She parked the rental in the back of the lot and walked in, with her hair hanging loose and wavy. From the Tickweed Meadow's communal closet she'd grabbed a pair of bright, Mediterranean-blue pants that hung loose on her hips, some short black, faux-leather boots, a white tube top, and a white crop-top jacket. With a few tasteful pieces of costume jewelry she'd grabbed at the flea market on the side of the road, she looked exactly like a trashy California PI from a movie.

Even she was startled by her reflection in the mirrored glass of the lobby. The look was Not Her in so many ways. But that was the point. She'd met Lawrence Dom once, very early in her move to Florida, and she didn't want to risk a run-in with Petrilli. If either of them recognized her, she'd be the one in the detention center explaining things. There was no way it would end well.

The doors swung open automatically, inviting her to step out of the pleasant Florida plaza into a sterile, ultramodern lobby that looked eerily familiar. She'd bet a milk shake and a side of fries the architect for the District 6 labs was the same person who had drawn up the plans for N-V Nova Laboratories in Alabama.

A bright silver half dome rolled past. It took her a moment to realize it was the latest model of cleaning bots. She'd seen the ads before, but District 8 had never been on the list for the upgrades.

Feo Petrilli really was a lucky dog.

"Rose MacKenzie here to see Dr. Dom, please." She held up a fake ID with her thumb over the fine details as she approached the security desk.

The guard was a middle-aged woman who reminded Sam of her old landlady, Miss Azalea. Except Miss Azalea smiled and cooked fried chicken, and this woman looked like she'd been sucking lemons for the past six hours. "Are you expected?"

"Yes, ma'am." A hint of Southern twang slipped out. Sam prayed the women wouldn't think she was being rude.

The guard sighed and handed over a datpad. "Sign in here."

Sam scribbled some loops in place and handed it back with a smile.

"This is your name?"

"Mmmhmm."

"There are letters in there?" The woman had missed her true calling. The nuns at St. Agnes would have welcomed her with open arms.

Sam pretended to inspect the signature with interest. "Right there's an R and that's an M."

"That M doesn't quit."

"Neither do I." Sam winked at her.

The guard rolled her eyes. "Fourth door down the green corridor. Follow the tiles. Hit the buzzer when you get there and smile for the camera. I'll unlock the door from here."

Following green agate tiles to the eastern wing, Sam buzzed in and stepped through the doorway into the memorable *Eau de Morgue*. The fug was something she'd tried to scrub from her brain, but, like the procedure for securing a crime scene, it just wouldn't leave. Her heels clomped on the hard floor, the sound echoing down the whitewalled hall and warping on its return.

When the door behind her opened, she spun.

"Miss MacKenzie?" Ivy stood in the doorway, frozen.

Sam forced a smile. "Sorry, you startled me. Morgues always give me the creeps. All alone . . . I thought maybe one of the corpses wanted to go out for a donut."

Ivy chuckled nervously as if she wasn't entirely sure Sam was joking, or how she was supposed to handle the situation if she wasn't. "District 6 has some of the best facilities in the state. The precinct considers ourselves lucky that we get to work with them."

"It's lovely if modern architecture is your thing." Sam waited for Ivy to catch up, then followed her down the hall to the ME's office. "I prefer some greenery. Fresh plants or a fish tank maybe. Something alive."

"I think it's a very practical design." Ivy stopped in front of Dom's door. "Have you ever seen a corpse before?"

"Several," Sam said. Two of them had been Sams from other iterations. *Hopefully* other iterations. There was still an uncomfortable question mark over Jane Doe's origin. "I'll let you know if I have a problem."

Even Ivy's smile was apologetic. "Last time I was here was with Detective Monroe, and she had morning sickness. The formaldehyde did her in. I didn't want to . . . you don't have anything like that, do you?"

"Not in several years," Sam said, biting back the bitter sorrow.

She pretended not to note as Ivy's eyes dipped to her abdomen. "Oh. You have—"

"No." Sam cut her off. "I miscarried. I don't like pineapple. My first kiss was in college. Are you done prying into my personal life? Can we get to work now?"

Ivy shrunk in on herself, and Sam silently cursed her own temper.

"I'm sorry. That was curt of me. It's a touchy subject." Sam held her hands up in apology. "Can we, please, move on?"

Ivy quickly nodded and opened the door, but Sam noticed how she stepped away. It was like kicking a puppy, it really was. Ivy had opened up to her—would open up to her—before Sam had slipped back in time and moved to Australia. She knew what was going on, how hard Ivy fought to be seen as human.

A mutinous voice in Sam's head muttered that getting snapped at was human, too. She wished Mac were with her. He was good at tag-teaming these situations. Playing the gormless medic with big, hazel eyes and a sad smile while she did her job as the by-the-book agent. People trusted Mac. She just made them angry.

"Dr. Dom," Ivy said to the room at large. "Doctor? It's Officer Clemens from New Smyrna."

A chubby man with a gleaming bald head wheeled across the room in an oversized office chair. "Officer Clemens! And visitor. They sent me the visitor's signature, but I couldn't read this." Narrowed eyes glared up at Sam accusingly. "With handwriting like that, you better have a Ph.D. Who are you?"

"Call me MacKenzie," Sam said, holding out her hand.

Dom shuddered. "Eww. No. I have spent too much time studying the wealth of biology growing on human flesh." He looked away in disgust and took a moment to recover. After making a gagging face, he said, "I'd say please come in, but we all know I don't really want that. But, come in anyway. There's not much to see."

"Have you identified her yet?" Ivy asked.

"One of my assistants is running the dental work now. Very unusual amalgam."

A red flag went up in Sam's mind. "Can I make a guess about her physical description?" Sam asked. "Female, Latina, long black hair, beaten-in face, just over average height, below average weight, and under thirty?"

The ME turned his chair to look at her with focused interest. "Do you want to guess the lotto numbers next?"

"Miss MacKenzie was hired by Lexie Muñoz's family to ensure her killer comes to justice," Ivy said. "She thinks that Lexie was possibly murdered by a serial killer."

"If this girl fits the pattern, she's number ten," Sam said.

Dom grimaced. "I was under the impression this was a very open-and-shut domestic abuse case. Find the boyfriend, find the liquor, and the case would be closed."

Sam shrugged. "That's what we thought about the other cases. So far, all the victims have been single. But anything is possible."

"But not likely," the ME grumbled. He kicked off the floor, sending his chair sailing into the next room. "This way! Our Jane Doe is in here."

Sam walked in and stared at the corpse, who wore a set of loose, navy coveralls with the patches torn off. She pulled on gloves and touched the suit. "Any idea whose uniform this is? One of the garbage companies or something?"

"No tags, no patches. Once I get her on the table, I can

check the other tags, see if there's anything that gives us a pointer, but right now, they're just clothes. You can buy coveralls like that at half a dozen stores around here."

The fabric felt strange through her gloved fingertips, like it wasn't quite the right thickness or weight. "How long has she been dead?"

"Hard to tell," said Dom. "Her body's colder than it should be for where we found her, so I'm guessing she was moved."

"Where was she found?" Ivy asked.

"In Carroll Park. A patrol officer discovered her along the jogging track," Dom said. "There are footprints, but nothing to indicate a struggle."

"And there's not enough blood and her body is the wrong temperature, and there's a circular breakage pattern on her bones that's very unusual," Sam said. Mac needed to be here. They might as well label this girl Jane Three. If the facial reconstruction pulled up her own face again, Sam was going to vomit out of sheer anger. "Skip that. What's the murder weapon?" She looked over at the silent Dom. "No guesses?"

"You seem very well informed about this case."

"I've seen a few like this before."

Ivy frowned. "I haven't, and I checked the records. Even the police database."

"Some of them were very, very classified records," Sam said. "If you have enough money, you can make sure your loved one's death isn't fodder for the media doom-and-gloom machines." She pointed to Jane Three. "Murder weapon?"

"My guess is fists and boots."

"Just like the others."

Ivy groaned. "Troom has an alibi."

"Don't get ahead of yourself," Sam cautioned. "We still need to tie this victim to the others. Unless we can put all of them together with one person, we'll need to find a weapon, or trace material, or something. Otherwise, we have no case." And Henry Troom stayed in jail. She looked at Dom again. "You said boots. Did you get a make or style? Manufacturer imprint? Please, I'm begging, tell me it's a rare doeskin boot hand-stitched on one remote farm in north Georgia or something. That would do so much to speed this case along."

"Well, um, first, it's a partial imprint," Dom said. "We matched the bruising to the ridges of a boot, but not one that's on the regular databases."

"Any links to other cases?"

"One," Dom said. "A locked case from Alabama District 3 last summer. I put in a request to have the files opened." He held up a datpad for Sam to look at.

The temperature of the room dropped a few hundred Kelvin.

"Do you think they'll open the record?" Ivy asked.

Sam shook her head no as Dom said, "Yes."

He scowled at her. "I have top secret clearance. I assure you, if they let you look at it, they'll let me."

"If I did see something," Sam said as she thumbed through the information, "it wouldn't have been through official channels. Wait, what's this? Grease on her hands and under her nails? I don't see an analysis of that listed."

"There isn't one yet," Dom said. "My tech brought back some data that were just impossible."

"How?" Ivy asked.

"She said the grease had high levels of polychlorinated biphenyl. You can't even find those in trace amounts in Florida unless she worked on antique machines. Even then, it's odd. We're recalibrating the machines and doing a secondary test. We should have a better reading by tomorrow."

Ivy's and Sam's eyes met. Ivy looked worried.

"It'll be soon enough," Sam said. After all, what's the absolute worst that could happen, someone else could die? It wasn't like Mac could get any further away. He was lost in time. Kidnapped by—probably—the dead woman whose autopsy she was holding. At least she hoped it was Jane's autopsy and not hers.

She rubbed her head, trying to knock the anxiety loose. Being two breaths away from a panic attack wasn't going to help anything. "Okay. I guess Clemens and I will hit the park. See if anyone knew her or if we can find anyone in the uniform she was wearing. Doc, can I give you my number, get a phone call if you have information?"

"Do you have clearance?" His button nose twitched in the air like a sanctimonious rabbit from a kid's cartoon.

She pulled a pad of paper from her purse and scribbled her number under the contact information for

Tickweed Meadow. "Call me. Or I can hack in, check the files, and leave your screensaver set to the kind of pictures that will get your clearance revoked while they drag you to jail."

His thin eyebrows went up. "You wouldn't."

"Your security code is 046471. You drive a white Delion Breeze, the 2064 model, and the left-rear taillight has been out for over a month. You eat rice bowls for lunch every day and two burgers from Swing n' Snack for dinner." Sam leaned down to look him in the eye. "Would you like me to keep going?"

"H-how do you know this."

She smiled. "I know people. I know things. It's my job." And she had a very good memory for obscure details. The first time she'd met Dom, he'd been enthusiastically showing her around while covertly trying to determine if she was a clone. His password was close enough to her old gym locker combination that she wasn't likely to forget it.

"Is there a leak in the CBI?" He sounded genuinely worried.

Her smile gave nothing away. "Maybe. Or maybe I have better clearance than you think. Do you want to play chicken and see who gets fired first?"

His Adam's apple bobbed as he choked back fear. "No. I don't think that's necessary. I'll keep Officer Clemens informed. Degrees of separation and all."

"Scapegoats and plausible deniability." Sam nodded and smacked Ivy's shoulder. "Come on, let's get to the park before the good citizens trample our evidence. Dom will call when he has more."

Ivy hurried after Sam's long steps. "Where did you get all of that? I . . . I can't be your scapegoat."

"You won't," Sam promised, only now realizing how it must have sounded: Break the rules, blame the clone, and dance away without consequence. "I have some friends in the CBI, and this isn't my first case working with them. That's kind of why I don't want to work with them if you catch my drift?" She hoped Ivy did because she was still assembling the lie in her head.

But Ivy shook her head. "Are they mad at you?"

"You ever met Feo Petrilli?" Sam asked. "Tall guy, handsome in an Italian Stallion sort of way? Likes to flirt?"

The pink tinge on Ivy's cheeks told Sam all she needed to know.

"Yeah, he and I . . . yeah." Sam looked at the floor and mentally apologized to Petrilli. "If I can, I want to avoid him this trip."

Ivy nodded. "I can understand that. He's never been bad to me or anything, it's just . . . has he ever met a woman he didn't make a play for?"

"Not that I know of," Sam said. "Let's get to the park. I want to see the grounds before we do anything else." Because Jane Three wasn't the first unidentified woman to drop out of a cloudless sky into Sam's life. She just hoped Jane Three was the last.

Ivy watched Miss MacKenzie circle the crime scene twice without comment. On the third lap, she lost patience. "Are you looking for something in particular?"

The other woman shrugged. "Do you see anything that indicates this is a crime scene?"

"The police tape?" Ivy suggested, but since Miss MacKenzie had invited her to enter the crime scene with a look, she stepped forward. The grass was watered by the city sprinkler system, but the drought-dry earth had greedily drunk every sip of moisture down, leaving the jogging path dry, and the green grass was limp.

Miss MacKenzie stepped across the tape and stood beside her. "If this is where she died, what would we see?"

"Blood?"

"Broken grass. Broken branches. Scuff marks. Mud. If someone dragged her here, there would be drag marks. Maybe even some impressions in the ground."

"It's a dump site, not the original crime scene," Ivy agreed. "We knew that already. So what do we do?"

"We widen our search. No one comes from nowhere."

"Clones do," Ivy muttered.

Miss MacKenzie gave her a sharp look. "You came from a lab, yes, but there was a twisted sort of love behind it."

"Not for me."

"Yeah? Well, take it from someone whose biological parents dropped her off at a boarding school at age four, clones aren't the only ones who get forgotten."

"You were loved."

"Not really," she said, as they walked down the path.

"I was a gimmick for my mother's career. As soon as she got what she needed from me, she dropped me. It happens." She didn't seem bothered by the admission.

Ivy frowned. "There are no security cameras out here."

"Either the victim came to the park on her own and was murdered somewhere out here, or her killer brought her here. Somewhere, there is a sign of one of those two events."

"Why here?" Ivy asked, looking around at the trees. "This is a community park, part city-owned and part paid for by user fees and donors. It's well lit, heavily used, patrolled by an off-duty officer. I know the people who patrol here. They come to walk the trail to get their workout in and get paid extra to do it in uniform. It's one of the worst places to dump a body I can think of."

Miss MacKenzie nodded in agreement. "Which suggests two things. What are they?"

"Is this a class?"

"It's mentoring," she said as she brushed a leaf aside to look at the underside. "Come on. Play along."

Ivy rolled her eyes and tried to think. She'd audited psychology classes but never had to use them in the field. The CBI took murders. The local PD handled the rest, but all she ever did was ride along. "Maybe the killer wanted her to be found. A, 'Look at me! I'm here!' sort of taunt to the police?"

"Or because the killer threatened the victim before and now wanted to prove they'd won something. It's common enough with stalkers and domestic abuse." Miss MacKenzie pointed at something that was little more than a rabbit trail. "Thoughts?"

"It looks used, but there's deer here, wild pigs, stray dogs."

"Still." Miss MacKenzie started walking, following the trail of scuffed earth and broken bushes. "The other reason the killer might have left the body here is because they aren't familiar with the area. The park is next to wildlife land, isn't it?"

"Tomoka and Tiger Bay are just north of here. And there's South Tomoka to the east."

"And there's I-95 running from Miami to New York, I-4 headed inland, and 92. All major roads with plenty of traffic. Around here, if you don't know better, you can turn off the highway and think you're in the middle of nowhere. If the killer is transient, and they have to be if all these murders are connected, then they could have turned off anywhere, taken an access road."

"And failed to notice the lamps and paved trail?" Ivy asked skeptically. "Criminals aren't that dumb."

"Yes they are. Especially if they're intoxicated, on drugs or the buzz of killing." Miss MacKenzie stopped as the trail at a gopher tortoise hole. "I hate this. I hate having nothing. Ten crime scenes, and all I have is a psych profile, and a dodgy one at that."

Ivy led the way back to the main trail. "You know what we wouldn't find a trace of? Wheel marks. If I were going to drag a body somewhere, it's not like I'd throw them over my shoulder and jog out here. We're over a mile from the main parking lot."

Miss MacKenzie raised an eyebrow. "But lamps mean someone needs to get a maintenance truck in."

"Which means an access road," Ivy said. "There's an access point about three hundred meters this way."

The path curved, and there was an open space under several aging oaks. There was a rest area with a bench, a flower bed, and several chin-up bars next to a plaque with the name of the donor. Ivy smiled. "Look at the sandbox. Someone was feeling zen on their workout this morning." They'd gone and drawn perfect concentric circles in the sand. They'd even gone and trampled down some of the grass.

The beauty was somewhat marred by what looked like a drunk's unfortunate encounter with the petunias.

Miss MacKenzie's face twisted in disgust and fury.

"They're just annuals," Ivy said. "Flowers like that, they're ripped out and replanted in a month."

But she wasn't looking at the flowers. She was glaring at the sand art as if it had pulled her hair, stabbed her kitten, and stolen her car.

"Ma'am?"

She held up a hand and stalked into the grass. "A gun," she said reaching between some tree roots and pulling out a dark gray weapon. She sniffed it and nodded. "I bet I know what murder this belongs to, too."

Ivy shook her head in confusion. "The victim wasn't shot, she was beaten. I mean, we need to take it in, but it's not related to our murder."

"Oh, it is. The killer was carrying this but didn't use it. What does that say about them?" Miss MacKenzie demanded.

Ivy hesitated. "They had a weapon, but they used their fists? That seems angry to me."

"Me too," she agreed. "And angry people make mistakes."

Ivy took an evidence bag from her pocket and held it out.

Miss MacKenzie chuckled. "It's not part of the murder, and it won't help the investigation." She tossed the weapon up in her hand.

"You said it belonged to another crime."

"It's a hunch."

"Worth testing the ballistics."

Miss MacKenzie shook her head. "Not really." She waved a hand at Ivy's protest. "It's complicated, and the case this might belong to is out of my jurisdiction. If I bring it in, things will get complicated."

"Out of your . . ." Ivy's eyes narrowed. "I thought you were private sector. You don't have jurisdiction."

Her smile was sad and amused all at once. "Yes. That's a good thought. Run with it." She tossed the gun in her hand again. "It's not too heavy, either. Do you want it?"

"I can't have a gun."

"You can't legally purchase a projectile weapon or own a long list of guns. I promise, this one isn't made by any of those manufacturers, and I'm not selling it." She opened the chamber. "It is missing a bullet, though. How are you at metalworking?"

"What?"

"You won't be able to find bullets for this gun anywhere in the Commonwealth." Miss MacKenzie held it out to her. "If you learn to make your own bullets and always wear gloves when you load it and clean it, you should be fine."

She stared at the strange weapon. "What do you mean you can't find ammunition for it in the Commonwealth? Where does it come from? Where do *you* come from?"

Miss MacKenzie didn't answer right away. As Ivy grew impatient, Sam held up a hand. "Hold on, I'm trying to think of an honest answer that won't significantly shorten your life."

"Because you'll need to kill me if you tell me? That's a bit trite."

"I don't kill people," she said. "I drive them mad and arrest them. Or I arrest them and drive them mad. Sometimes the order gets switched up. Either way, they live. But there are people who will kill to protect certain secrets, or to own them. Since I'm not in the habit of endangering people without a reason, let's try this: You might need this, and I'm basing that off a hunch."

She blinked. "A hunch?"

Miss MacKenzie winced. " For now, until I can confirm a few details with an expert, yes, it's a hunch. This looks exactly like a gun that I saw on a prior case. The owner was . . . let's say private military. The kind of group everyone likes to pretend doesn't exist in the Commonwealth. They manufacture the guns and the bullets. You won't find it anywhere on any registry or sold by any company. Which makes it the perfect, untraceable weapon."

Ivy shook her head. "No, the CBI wouldn't let that happen."

"Even the CBI has cases they'd rather not solve," Miss MacKenzie said. "Now, can we get out of here? This place is giving me the creeps."

"I don't understand why you're scared of circles on the ground."

"I hope you never understand," Sam said. "I really do. And I hope my hunch is wrong." But she knew it wasn't.

The detention center wasn't much different than it had been when the reforms kicked in after the Commonwealth united. It wasn't supposed to be a prison but a rehab center for individuals addicted to antisocial behavior; however, the million-dollar landscaping only gussied up the surface. Inside there were cellblocks, neon-green prison jumpsuits, and hard-eyed men looking Sam over like she was a piece of meat. In training, she'd been told not to make eye contact, that it encouraged reckless behavior.

Today, she made eye contact, and the criminals were the ones who looked away in fear.

A woman was waiting inside a prison advocate room with a white plaque stuck on the door that read FAMILY THERAPY ROOM. Her escort opened the door and returned to his desk.

Sam nodded at the woman. "You're Dr. Mallory?"

"Yes, Mr. Troom's rehab facilitator for first-stage therapy. I'm afraid we aren't having much luck breaking the denial cycle. It's holding him back." Mallory had the look of a perky cheerleader: bright pink lipstick, eye shadow a few shades darker than her suntanned skin painted to elaborate the arch of her eyes, and hair curled and shellacked in defiance of the humidity outside.

Sam supposed she didn't look much different right now. "Have you considered that Dr. Troom might not be guilty?"

"Everyone is guilty of something," Mallory said. "A person may not be here long, but if he isn't guilty of murder, there are other things he can confess to that will put him on the road to a healthy, happy, productive future." Her smile never faded, and it didn't reach her eyes.

Sam smiled in kind. "What are you guilty of?"

Dr. Mallory's smile shattered, and, for a moment, Sam saw rage. It was quickly covered by a smirk worthy of any high school student. "Trying to rattle me, Agent?"

"Do I need to?" Sam asked.

Guards arrived at the lock, with Henry between them.

Mallory looked over her shoulder and back. "I will leave you alone for the private conference the CBI has requested, but I must remind you that you are required by law to give us any relevant information that would help us put Mr. Troom on the path of rehabilitation."

"I am aware, and I will comply," Sam said. Her

smile sharpened. "First step: Call him by his title and respect his intelligence. He earned his degree."

The therapist's lips puckered like she'd bitten a lemon, and her heels rapped against the cement floor with quick, angry steps as she exited.

Henry's guards let him in as Mallory left the room, locking the outer door behind her. His smile was genuine, then he laughed. "Your hair looks awful."

"I know. It's for a case."

Henry shook his head. "Nice job with Dr. Mallory. You have a talent for driving smart people crazy. Dr. Emir had that look on his face every time you talked to him."

"Really? I didn't actually mean to antagonize him." She took a seat in the plastic chair across the table from an identical one the prison had provided for Henry. "How are you doing?"

He shrugged. "Solitary confinement and the accusation of being an antisocial element at risk for suicide, with a prescription medicine to fix my delusions."

"Hmmm. Are you suicidal or delusional?" Sam asked.

"I know you're required to report this to the therapists, but I'll say it anyway. I'm feeling homicidal. Low-key. I'm not an advocate for violence, but the pills make me violently ill, and they can't erase what happened last summer."

Sam frowned. "They have your files from the N-V Nova Labs case? That's not supposed to be available for civilians."

"They don't have the whole thing. They called around and got ahold of my cousin, who told them I was into weird stuff although that's probably not the term he used. He's a crackle addict, legalized and non-addictive LSD for the gezes who can't get their lives together. He lives in Alabama District 12 on disability and has a prescription for the pills. I saw him in September. Got drunk."

"You talked?"

"Not about specifics. I didn't know any. But I told him what I'd heard. What'd they'd done. It was a near-death experience!" He crossed his arms. "I didn't kill Lexie Muñoz if that's what you wanted to know."

Sam shook her head. "I already know you didn't. But I need details. And your alibi."

His eyes narrowed into a mulish look. "Agent Rose, is this really necessary? Can't you just, I don't know, do a DNA test or something? Rule me out as a suspect?"

"You took Lexie to the beach party. Multiple people saw you walk onto the beach with her and leave with her. You were the last one to see her alive, so start there."

Henry squinched his eyes shut, then shook his head. "Son of a—" He bit off the curse. "Are we friends?"

Sam raised an eyebrow. "Friends? Is this relevant?"

"You saved my life. Twice, by my count. You know what I've been through. It's not like I can talk to anyone else about this . . ." He gave her a pleading look.

"Henry, I don't know what you're asking."

"Just . . . don't make fun of me, okay?"

"Okay."

"Bradet invited me to the party. The station had a thing going on . . . have you met Bradet?"

Sam tried to hide the wince that came with those memories. "Yeah."

"He's solar wind. Wild and fun, and all the girls want him."

Which spoke to the poor taste of the girls going to these parties. Every time Sam had talked to Bradet, she'd felt the need to wash.

"I thought if I went to the party maybe some of his magic would rub off on me. Girls don't like geeks, you know? I start talking about work, and their eyes glaze over."

"Try talking to smarter women," Sam said.

Henry blushed and looked at the table. "Lexie was solar. I mean, hotter than the sun, solar. She's triplicate, the whole package. She was working on a math degree at the college, she's from a good family, she had a body that was just . . ." His hands curved in the air and dropped as he tried to describe her. "It wasn't love, but I thought we were having a good time. We went to the beach to get away from the noise and talk about her thesis paper, which sounded really promising for a master's student, and she said she was thirsty. So I went back up to the bar."

Anger suffused his face, creasing it. He wasn't seeing Sam anymore, but that night. "I came back with sangrias, and she was with some guy. Tall, handsome, surfer tight with a military haircut and muscles." Henry shook his head. "She was having fun."

"It could have been small talk," Sam said.

Henry looked her in the eye. "They weren't talking."

"Oh."

"Yeah. Bradet had already seen me. He'd winked at me when I walked out with Lexie. Gave me the high sign when I got the drinks. If I went back in, I was going to be humiliated. So I figured I'd walk down the beach a bit and loop around, get to the parking lot, and make a quiet escape. Bradet usually goes home with a girl, so it wouldn't matter. I could lie about it, and he'd leave me alone."

Sam rubbed the bridge of her nose. "I feel like there's a piece missing here. I get the male ego, trust me—married life teaches a woman these things. But why not tell the cops? Someone saw Lexie leave, and it wasn't with you, that's a mistake."

Henry rolled his eyes to the side and bit his lip.

"What aren't you telling me?"

He put his hands over his face and rested his elbows on the table. "This could end my career. I haven't been at the think tank a month. It's paradise, you know? Like being the kid in a candy store."

Sam shook her head. "Not that big a fan of candy."

"Makeup shop?"

"No."

"Gun store?"

"Me?" Sam gave him a disappointed look. "I like fresh produce, running shoes, and my truncheon."

He sighed. "Fine, you have your healthy ways, and I

have physics. And the think tank lets me do work without writing grants, without answering to committees, without teaching. I can request anything. I can try crazy things and fail because I don't need to show results to anyone for years. Do you know how wonderful that is? This is the golden apple of science."

"Isn't the golden apple the one that started the Trojan War?"

He nodded. "Yeah. People would kill for the slot I got. I'm only there because I'm Emir's protégé, and his posthumously published papers were very well received. They're on particle wave physics and advanced communication between the planet and orbital satellites, but it has wonderful applications for the space industry." He paused, and a little smile crept onto his face. "He wrote those papers years ago. Erased most of them, but I had copies since I had worked with him in grad school. I did some of the math, nothing major. After he died, the lab wanted to publish something, and it wasn't like we could let his current research get out. I thought it was a nice memorial."

Sam tapped the table. "Back to the night Lexie died?"

He closed his eyes. "If anyone finds out the truth, I'll lose my place at the think tank."

"If I don't find anything, you'll be here for murder for years. Eating the horrible pills and still not working at the think tank."

"I went home with someone!" Henry shouted.

Sam shook her head in confusion. "So? Who could

you possibly go home with . . ." Her imagination caught up with her tongue. "She is over eighteen, or he, right?"

Henry glared at her. "She's twenty-three, five years younger than I. And she's a protestor." He looked at the floor like he'd just confessed to some lewd form of bestiality.

"I don't get it," Sam admitted.

"Her name's Krystal, with a kay. She protests government oversight and waste."

Sam shook her head. "Still not seeing a problem."

"She's on a government watch list for antinationalistic behavior."

"Like Marrins?"

"No!" Henry sounded horrified. "As an undergrad, she was part of a modernist group pushing to reopen various habitats for human use."

"Are those the anti-ecoterrorist types?"

"Oh! No. She's not with them, she was petitioning to open up various preserves for recreational activity. Camping, kayaking, that sort of thing. She's really into outdoorsy things and . . ." He shut his eyes tight. "We had a thing, before I graduated. Not anything formal, but kind of an open relationship. N-V Nova Labs told me I couldn't work there if I was associated with anyone who couldn't pass a background check. Krystal was chill with it. There were other guys, I spent too much time in the lab, it wasn't a big deal."

"Except she followed you here?"

"She came to see some guys who live in the swamps.

There's a protest coming up, and she's out here rallying troops or something." He shrugged. "I was going to leave, and I didn't even know she was at the party. Lexie was kissing this beach guy, then there's Krystal."

"The perfect rebound."

"She likes sangria. We finished our drinks in maybe ten minutes, then headed for the car."

Sam took out her notepad. "This Krystal, dark hair, about five-five?"

Henry nodded. "She doesn't look like Lexie, but at a distance after a few drinks? I guess they look alike."

"You left together?"

"Yeah. Maybe, thirty minutes after I left Lexie? She was still on the beach talking to the guy when I left."

"Do you remember anything else? Anything odd?"

Henry stared into the distance for a minute. "It was a bit serendipitous running into Krystal again. But, no. The party was noisy, people were laughing, listening to bad music, drinking. It was a beach party. The weather was nice. Warm I guess—that probably caused the heat lightning."

Sam raised an eyebrow as a sense of certainty settled over her. "Heat lightning? In January? When the party had heat lamps in every corner?"

Henry frowned. "I guess that was a little odd. I was wearing my slacks and a sweater, so I guess I didn't think about it. The pavilion on the boardwalk was hot, but it wasn't really warm, I guess." He frowned.

Sam pulled up her notes. "It was fifty-six that night.

It was the tail end of the cold snap." She closed her notebook.

"Does that help?" Henry asked.

"It confirms something I suspected and gives me the murder weapon."

"Lightning isn't what killed Lexie," he said. "They made me look at the crime scene photos. She . . . they . . ." He shook his head and looked away.

Sam grimaced in sympathy. "Did you see any concentric rings in the sand, or was the area too trampled."

Henry frowned at her. "What?"

"Concentric rings," Sam said slowly. "Were they there?"

"Like the rings from . . ." He shook his head. "No. That's not what happened. Lexie was beaten to death by someone. Not me, but someone."

"There's no blood on the beach. Witnesses saw you leave the party, but if you left with Krystal—whose full name and address you will be giving me—then no one saw Lexie leave the beach. She didn't die there. She was dumped there. I think I know how. With Krystal as your alibi, you'll be cleared of charges. And then we'll talk about the rings."

"Agent Rose," Henry said quietly, "what you're cryptically suggesting is impossible. The device in question was destroyed."

Sam looked him dead in the eye and let him see what had driven the other inmates to look away. "Tell me right here, right now, that you didn't make another one. Look me in the eye and say it."

He looked at his hands.

"Exactly. You tried to reconstruct the device. How unstable is it?"

Henry jerked back in surprise. "How . . . ?"

"Just be honest with me, Henry. We are friends, after all."

"It's okay, but the charge is weak. I need a better battery. I didn't . . . I didn't put anyone at risk. I swear it. I know what it did to Matt and Miss Chimes, so I took it out in the desert."

She frowned.

"I went to Colorado to see a friend at the School of Mines before I moved down here. I took the machine out to the sand dunes. Middle of winter, the wind and cold, it was abandoned. It turns on, but there's not enough energy to get the portal to accelerate properly. It fizzed, and there were some weird little dust storms. Almost like an energy pulse but at a distance. Subportals maybe, but I don't know. I'm missing some of the original components, and there's no way I can find a replacement for the core you smashed. Thanks for that, by the way."

"I had a very good reason for smashing it," Sam said. "Not that it worked like I planned, because if it had, Lexie would be alive, and you'd be at work right now." She pushed her pen and paper to Henry. "Give me a way to contact Krystal, please."

He slid the notebook toward himself and froze. "Are you sure about this?"

"Do it, Henry."

Obediently, he wrote down the name and address.

"I'll get this wrapped up and get in touch with you." She stood. "Don't call the CBI office, though. If you do, I won't remember this conversation, and it will be awkward all around."

"What do you mean you won't remember this conversation?" Henry demanded. "Agent Rose?"

She held up her left hand. "Agent MacKenzie, now."

"Congratulations on the engagement?"

"Marriage." She studied her ring. "We're getting married before the year's out, and we've been married five years already.

"Isn't time funny like that?"

CHAPTER 26

> *"A time cyclone, or uncontrolled time portal, is created during a moment of convergence or expansion when multiple iterations pass through one another's probability fans. Calculating these events is difficult, and controlling them currently not within the scope of our abilities."*
>
> ~ memo to senior members of the
> Ministry of Defense—I1—2067

Thursday July 4, 2069
Alabama District 3
Commonwealth of North America
Rogue Iteration

Stars and cicadas were the first things Rose noticed as she passed through the portal into the rogue iteration. Moonlight illuminated the wooded glen and the portal's ringed imprint in the grass without giving the verdant foliage a chance to shine. The vivid green leaves were a muted shade of near black that blended with the bruising blues and purples of the rest of the landscape.

Rose did a visual sweep with night-vision goggles and signaled for her team to move forward.

Senturi hit the door first. "Locked."

She motioned for him to keep his mouth shut and unlock it. A light blipped in the corner as he touched the door. The first reconnaissance team hadn't found a hidden security system, but if someone had gotten sloppy... The treacherous memory of the broken dial demanded attention.

It was such a slight change, green to blue. Emir would have dismissed it as an office prank if he'd noticed it at all. Surely, this iteration's Emir would be no different.

Senturi pushed the door open, and red lights flared in the hall.

"Fan out, control the exits." Everyone moved but Senturi. "Problems?" This was not the time for him to remember he was a spoiled child coddled by a mother in the world's Ruling Council.

"Someone needs to go into the building," Senturi said. "I should go."

"I will. I've been there before and know the layout. Get back to the drop site and wait for Emir."

She pulled her face mask on and stormed into the eerily silent hall, flooded in red. As a child, she'd read a horror story about a house with bleeding walls. This was that building. Cold and silent as a tomb, red light dripping from above, boots echoing on the tile. This is what it felt like to storm the gates of death.

The faint murmur of a voice intruded on the silence.

She hurried forward, trying to locate the sound. It came from the office, muffled by a wall.

"I am telling you, Agent Marrins, the alarms are going off, and everything is in danger." It was Emir's voice, but worried, harried. This was the Emir from the other iteration.

Rose jiggled the door handle and found it locked. She leaned in to listen.

There was a prolonged pause. "Once again, Agent, I must remind you of the vital importance of secrecy." A breath. "You . . . I . . . ugh! I am developing a machine that will change the course of humanity. Make the world a better place."

That was debatable.

The other Emir made a squelching sound of frustration. "Agent Marrins? Agent . . . insufferable imbecile." Something made a crunching sound, probably a plastic of some kind, possibly the comm line.

Rose smiled. This would be the easiest detonation she'd ever done. Shoot Emir now, and the whole iteration would crumble to dust.

The other Emir began to pace.

A melody played, then . . . "Agent Rose, this is Emir. You must come to the lab. Now! You must come now!" His footsteps stopped. "Agent Rose, you must come to the lab. You owe me that much. My life is in danger. They are coming for me. If I don't give them what they want, they will kill me. They know it works now. I can't stall any longer."

She sighed. "Why must you make your life difficult?" Rose asked the man who couldn't hear her. Of course they were coming to kill him. What other possible outcome could there be?

"My machine!" Emir said. "You told them it works. You showed them it works."

Rose's hand clenched on her gun, thumb hovering over the safety. Usually it took only moments for an iteration to collapse, but if there was someone else continuing Emir's work, he could—theoretically—be replaced. They didn't have the other nodes collected. Without letting this iteration progress, they couldn't even find the other nodes.

Coming back to this nightmare wasn't on her wish list, so she waited. They might need the name of his collaborators later.

A thought whispered in her mind: If Emir could be replaced here, he could be replaced elsewhere.

"Agent Rose!"

She startled, half expecting to see Emir standing in front of her. But he was still on the comm. Talking to her other self, she realized. Not that it mattered, but she'd rather not kill herself again. It gave her a headache.

"Please, I beg of you. Come to the lab tonight. Bring your partner, bring Altin, bring anyone, but come. Save me!" There was a pause that grew into the silence of rejection. A shuddering sob tore through the stillness of the red-soaked lab. It was the cry of the prisoner facing execution.

That would haunt her.

It was so out of character for Emir—for the true Emir, or any of the others she'd encountered—that she *knew* this iteration was truly different. And that meant it had to be eliminated.

It was easier to take out the other nodes without giving them warning. She did everything she could to make sure they didn't suffer. Now . . . she flipped the safety off, pulled her goggles on, and aimed for the heat-bright outline of the cowering Dr. Emir.

"Commander Rose?" Donovan's voice crackled in her ear.

She flipped the safety back on and touched her commlink to turn it on. "Yes?" she demanded through gritted teeth.

"Pull back. On Emir's orders."

In his office, Emir pushed away from his chair and stumbled toward the door.

Rose shook her head. "I have the target node in sight. Confirm orders to withdraw." Donovan could play games if he wanted, but she wasn't going to.

Emir was poking something on the wall. A keypad, probably. In less than a minute, he'd leave his lab and come face-to-face with reality.

"Order confirmed," the real Emir said over the comm. "Pull back to the tree line, Commander. I have something special planned for this meddlesome *other* of mine."

Donovan, you fool. She replied with a clipped, "Yes, sir." Swinging her gun onto her shoulder Rose pulled her goggles off and ran down the hall as the other Emir stepped out. She waited in the shadows by the back door until she heard his footsteps fade away in the direction of the building's main entrance. Quietly opening the door, she stepped into the darkness and ran for the rendezvous point as a siren's wail screamed in the distant darkness.

"Where are we going, sir?" Donovan asked, as the portal spun faster, changing from purple to white.

"We're going to answer a call," Emir said as he stepped through the portal, a comtech and Donovan following after.

They arrived in an empty field with drought-dry grasses and copses of trees huddling in clumps along the moonlit horizon.

Emir waved his hand at the tech. "Start the call on the scheduled time. Donovan, watch the portal. We'll be transitioning back momentarily."

Swallowing a growl of dry irritation, Donovan spat out a, "Yes, sir."

In his growing impatience to escape Prime, he'd forgotten why he worked hard to get along with Senturi and Rose in the first place. A single person couldn't keep Emir in check. His ego was bigger than any one person, and his tendency to create convoluted schemes only made life more difficult for everyone around him.

With Senturi busily spinning his own webs and Rose lost to her latest doomed project, he was the sole proprietor of Emir's sanity. And it seemed he'd misplaced it in his rush to line everything up.

"Sir?" The tech looked up. "The original call just ended."

Emir held out his hand. "Put it on the open comm."

"Yes, sir." The tech sat cross-legged in the long grass, ignoring the plague of midnight insects, and tapped industriously at his computer screen. "Connecting now, sir."

An unnatural ringing of a flat bell tone cut into the night air.

"What?" a surly male voice demanded.

"Agent Marrins?" Emir asked with a voice of silk as he smiled.

Donovan looked away. He knew that expression. It meant that Emir had found a new form of torture to inflict and a new victim to practice his cruelty on.

"Emir, is this you again? I told you to shut your mouth and let me sleep." The man had just signed his death warrant.

Emir chuckled. "I am the Emir. Not the one you spoke to previously, but the original. You should feel honored."

"Really?" Marrins asked. "'Cause all I feel right now is a strong urge to punch you. Do you know what time it is?"

"Time for a change, Agent Marrins. I'm sure you know this world desperately needs one. History has betrayed you."

There was a speculative pause, filled by the whirring of grasshopper wings and the saw of cicadas. "What are you going on about, Emir?"

"I understand you have problems with the way the government is currently being run?"

Donovan flicked away a beetle with a glowing back.

"What are you suggesting?" Marrins asked.

"A simple trade," Emir said. "You remove an inconvenience from my life, and I give you the keys to staging your revolution."

"Can't have a revolution now. It's too late."

"No, not now," Emir agreed. "But think what you could do if you had the knowledge of these past years when your nation was voting to keep their independence or give it away."

Donovan frowned over his shoulder at Emir. He couldn't honestly be suggesting this iteration move further away from the history of Prime. The vote for government control was an einselected node. It had to happen. He took a deep breath and reminded himself that this iteration had a future that could be counted in hours, not years. Even Emir couldn't frag it up that bad.

"That's what your kooky machine is?" Marrins asked. "A time machine?"

"Something like that," Emir said with a lethal smile. "Not as crude as you might imagine, but very similar."

"What do you want done?"

"Come to the labs," Emir said. "And shoot the man you know as Emir."

Marrins huffed; it might have been amusement or annoyance, Donovan couldn't tell.

"You realize I'm an agent of the Commonwealth Bureau of Investigation, and you've just asked me to commit a federal crime? That's not going to look good on your record, Mr. Emir." Marrins dragged the name out so it became a slur.

"It's your choice, Agent Marrins. Would you like to continue living in the Commonwealth, or would you like your United States back?"

"You already know what I want," Marrins said. "I'll be there in twenty minutes."

Donovan bent over to check the faux-Emir's pulse. "Dead."

"The bullet hole between the eyes should have been enough," Emir said as he stepped over and looked at his discarded other self. "What a horrible little man."

"This whole iteration is awful," Donovan said. The colors were too bright, the noises too strange. Even the bright crimson blood seemed to glow like fire in the light of the orange sunrise.

The only thing everyone seemed to agree on was that this iteration needed to end.

Then the Prime would shift again, and he already had the new Prime picked out. It wasn't as radically different as this place, but not too similar to the current situation, either. Senturi had found it on one of his runs, took a bullet in the shoulder to protect it, and was using the anomalies to jump between the two and maintain the Shadow Prime. Acting like a node in defiance of all of Emir's expectations.

Emir sighed. "Let's leave before this iteration causes us another headache."

Donovan looked down the rolling hill to the building and the white police car pulling out of the parking lot. One thing still bothered him. "Sir, why did you tell him that you could change his history?"

"Because ten minutes from now, he'll cease to exist."

"You set a date to meet again."

Emir shrugged and started walking into the trees.

"I could have done this," Donovan persisted. The rogue iteration had to fall to make room for the Shadow Prime. His plan was running on a tight timetable. Emir's ego couldn't be allowed to destroy his future. The red-haired woman was there. Senturi had seen her. She was waiting for Donovan.

"You could have," Emir agreed. "Rose, Senturi, Bennet—any of you could have disposed of this Emir. But the other nodes weren't here. There is a chance, however slight, that this iteration may continue for a day or two. With luck, we'll never need to worry about this place again. If we do, we now have an asset here. He won't dare tell anyone about us, not with his precious *country* at stake." Emir put so much contempt into the word that Donovan grimaced.

That needed to change. Emir thought he ran the world, and he did it with no thought to anyone else. When Donovan's plan came to fruition, Emir would be a footnote, not the headline, of history.

Up ahead, a soft glow between two trees signaled the portal was opening. Donovan stepped over a branch broken by their intrusion and checked his locator. Only he, Emir, and Rose were still in this iteration.

"Everyone else is gone?" Emir asked.

Donovan looked at Rose's location, nearly fifty meters away in a thicket that obscured her from Emir's view. It was time for step one. "All clear, sir. I'm reading no other signals." He shut off the volume on his comm just as Rose pinged him.

Emir stepped through the portal with a happy smile.

Rose pinged again, demanding an update with the flashing yellow light on his comm.

He could picture her, eyes widening with fear and confusion as she realized the portal location had changed. She hadn't known about the second jump or the new calculations. He'd planned to have Senturi take her out here, leave her corpse to rot in the woods while this iteration imploded, but this was better. More satisfying.

She moved, starting to walk into view as the portal dimmed.

Donovan stood there for a moment, waiting for the light of the portal to turn navy. At the last possible moment, he called her name, "Rose!"

She turned. The look of horror on her face was everything he'd ever wanted. The stupid, witch. She was the means to her own downfall. She had brought MacKenzie to her world, replaced herself, and made all of this possible.

Donovan stepped through the portal and watched it snap shut on her betrayed and anguished face.

CHAPTER 27

Day 200/365
Year 5 of Progress
(July 19, 2069)
Central Command
Third Continent
Prime Reality

Mac watched Emir pace the floor. He'd counted the returning assassins twice with a look of frustration. Now they both watched as the portal darkened to an abyssal blue and faded into black.

"Everyone out!" Emir roared.

The soldiers and techs fled as Emir glared at their retreat.

Mac stood his ground. If he'd understood half of Jane's notes, they were going to his iteration. Back to July of 2069, which was a long way from home in many ways, but he could make it work. The guards had kept him locked in the observation room when the portal was open. They'd been polite about it, of course. Offered him a meal that made his stomach clench in disgust and tepid water that tasted of poor filtration. Now they were gone. He opened the door and walked into the jump room.

Emir glowered. "I told everyone to leave."

"They did," Mac said. "But it's obvious even to an outsider that something went wrong. You're missing three people."

"Yes. Commander Rose, Captain Donovan, and Mr. Senturi. I can live without Senturi, but the other two I need back." Emir crossed his arms and regarded the closed portal. "This is unfortunate timing."

"Yeah," Mac said. "Everyone likes the battle cry, 'Today is a good day to die.' But the truth is there's never a good day to die." He tapped the top of one of the computers. "I could get them back for you."

Emir turned to him. "What?"

"You want your people back. I was trained to extract soldiers from behind enemy lines. It seems to me that we could help each other out."

Emir snorted in dismissal. "I'm to trust you? You must be intelligent enough to realize how unlikely that is."

"Your people are in July 2069 in Alabama. I want to go back to December 2069 in Australia. You may not realize how far a walk that is, but I do. So I figure we can make a trade. Let me retrieve Jane and Donovan for you, then you can send me back to the moment after your commander abducted me. We all walk away happy."

"That would be suicide."

"For me or you?" Mac asked.

Emir's face was frustratingly placid. "The decoherence is coming. You would return only to die."

"We only have your word for this," Mac said. "It seems to me you can't even pinpoint how to pick the arrival date in an iteration. If you can't do that, how could you possibly calculate decoherence?"

"No one can calculate an exact timetable like that." Emir waved his hand, dismissing the problem. "I've worked on the problem for years with no success."

"No success *here* you mean." Mac twisted the knife into Emir's ego. "The Emir in the Federated States of Mexico figured it out. I didn't meet him, but I met some killers who used his machine. They had interesting things to say. In their timeline, the portal is used for vacations. You can jump back to watch your own wedding. Or go watch your parents meet. Sappy things like that."

"Impossible!" Emir turned, eyes blazing with fury. "That sort of thing isn't possible. If it were, I would be the first to know. This iteration is the base for all others. The bedrock of humanity."

Mac shook his head. "And you base that on what? Your ability to kill other people better than someone else?"

"That is the basis of evolution." Emir lifted his chin with pride.

Mac shrugged. "Survival of the fittest. People always get that concept wrong. It's not survival of the strongest, it's survival of those who pass on the most genes. If an animal doesn't reproduce, it isn't genetically fit according to biologists. Same thing happens to cultures. If you don't create, if there's no art, music, or architecture, the culture doesn't just go extinct, it is forgotten entirely. I imagine it's the same thing with iterations. Except you've been busy killing every seedling." He rapped the computer with his knuckles once more for emphasis. "What happens when there are no more branches of history spawned by your iteration, Emir? Do you think that's what causes decoherence? Because I do."

He looked at the portal. "If you want your people back, let me know. I'm willing to trade their futures for mine. Better hurry, though. You leave Jane and Donovan out there together too long, and you're not going to get anything back but corpses."

CHAPTER 28

> *"Do you value Humanity as a whole, or simply your own humanity? To put the whole above the one requires a sacrifice of individual humanity. If that is the requirement, can your course of action truly be for the betterment of all?"*
>
> ~ excerpt from the *Oneness of Being*
> by Oaza Moun I1—2072

Saturday January 11, 2070
Florida District 8
Commonwealth of North America
Iteration 2

Ivy's phone started ringing way earlier than it should have on a Saturday when she wasn't scheduled to work. Glaring at it, she rolled over, pulling her pillow over her head. The phone kept ringing. After ten minutes, she gave in and picked up. "I am not on duty!"

"Sorry, were you still sleeping?" Miss MacKenzie sounded worried but excited.

Ivy propped herself up on an elbow and looked at the poster of Agent Rose on her wall, mentally willing her idol to give her strength to deal with the crazed Californian. "Do you know what time it is?"

"A little after six. Maribel woke me up for dawn yoga."

Ivy sighed. "I'm a clone. I can't arrest anyone. Even for inflicting yoga on you at dawn." Which sounded like it contravened a few international torture agreements.

Miss MacKenzie laughed. "I don't need you to arrest anyone, probably. I was just calling to see if you wanted to come grill a suspect with me."

"Grill a suspect?"

"Would you feel better if I said I was going to talk to a nice bomb maker?"

Ivy sat up. "What?"

"She makes seed bombs. Her name is Krystal. And she was with Henry Troom the night Lexie was murdered." Even across the phone, Ivy could hear the smug smile. "Can I pick you up at eight?"

"Sure," Ivy said. That gave her another a hundred and twelve minutes to sleep. Five to shower. Two to gulp down a breakfast smoothie. By the time Miss MacKenzie arrived, she was as cheerful as she was legally obligated to be on a Saturday morning.

A sense of dread drove Sam to go slightly above the speed limit. In her own car, back when she'd had a car in the Commonwealth, she'd paid for a fast-lane pass that let her drive ten to fifteen miles above the posted limit. Now, every time she went three miles over the limit, the car blared a warning and slowed down of its own accord. It was a health hazard. Especially if she ever had five minutes alone with the engineer to express her opinion.

Ivy sat beside her reviewing the notes from the interview with Henry. "Why didn't he just admit he left with someone else?"

"One, because he drove after drinking. And, two, because Krystal isn't the kind of person a nice scientist with a government grant is supposed to spend time with. Technically, the Commonwealth can't forbid this kind of contact, but rumors are enough to ruin careers."

"Wouldn't murder be worse?"

"Only if someone could find evidence that he didn't commit the murder, and let's face it, no one is looking for that evidence."

"The CBI is."

"Yeah? Which agent?" It hadn't rolled across Sam's desk. She'd checked her younger self's files. Agent Petrilli didn't have it. In fact, as far as she could tell, no one was handling the case. She took a left off the highway and headed inland, looking for a side road Henry swore would lead to Krystal's current residence.

Ivy made a little confused noise.

Sam glanced over at her. "What?"

"Nothing." Ivy shook her head and reshuffled the paperwork.

"That didn't sound like nothing. Did you recognize someone?"

Ivy slumped. "This is going to sound ridiculous."

"I did yoga at five A.M. with the sound of mosquitoes buzzing in my ears. Trust me. I can handle whatever you've got."

Ivy pulled out a picture of a pretty Latina woman wearing a bright, canary-yellow party top. "This is Lexie Muñoz."

"Taken at the party before Henry showed up," Sam said. "It's a good color on her."

"I've seen her before."

"What, at the police station, around town? Were you friends?" She'd prefer having Ivy along as an expert witness, but investigating the death of a friend was always hard. "Why didn't you say something when you heard her name? I wouldn't have dragged you into this if I knew."

Ivy sighed and stared straight ahead. "I saw her at the morgue."

"On the day she was murdered?" Sam asked hopefully. "I know they say they didn't have the body, but maybe she's just mislabeled and waiting. Or cremated. I hope she wasn't cremated yet."

"It was in October," Ivy said quietly. "I went to do a morgue tour in District 18. There was a woman there, beaten to death, with no identity. Dr. Runiker was in charge of the tour. We talked about why she was dressed up so beautifully. It was a very pretty top. It looked expensive."

"Oh." Sam bit her lip and stared at the empty road

ahead. Dead before dying. Mac probably had a cute phrase for that, too.

"It gets worse," Ivy said. "Someone stole the woman's clothes."

Silently, Sam breathed a sigh of relief. "So, you saw the clothes before but not the woman? That might actually be a good clue. Maybe the killer is in retail. Working one of the shops where the blouse was made, possibly?"

Ivy shook her head, red hair flashing in and out of Sam's peripheral view as she did. "Her face was . . . was only badly beaten on one side. Do you know what this means?"

"Yes," Sam admitted.

"It means one of them is a clone!" Ivy exploded. "If the first girl is the clone, it's not so bad. But if the one Henry left was a clone? It'll set back clone rights a decade at least. People aren't happy about the Caye Law as it is. If this comes out, I might as well hand in my badge and go pick up trash on the roadside. I'll never get to be human!"

"You are human," Sam argued. Her GPS flashed, and she took the turn to Krystal's house. "There's more than one explanation here."

"Like what?"

"Genetic drift? Twins? Cousins? You don't need to be a clone to look like someone. Besides, you're basing this assumption on a memory that's three months old and a picture taken at a party with weird lighting. A good makeup artist can make you look like anyone.

Maybe Lexie isn't the same person as you found in the morgue. Maybe there's another explanation."

"Why would anyone dress to look like a dead woman?"

Sam parked the car beside an old trailer with faded purple sheets hanging in the windows as curtains. "That's a very good question," she said. "After we talk to Krystal, we'll try to answer it."

CHAPTER 29

> *"People will fight for many things over the course of their lives. It hardly matters. If you want to know who they really are, ask what they will not live without."*
>
> ~ private conversation with Agent 5
> of the Ministry of Defense

*Day 202/365
(July 21, 2069)
Village of Missingham
Shadow Prime*

A gentle summer breeze ruffled the feathery, gen-engineered grass of the Shadow Prime. Donovan reached down and ran his hand over it, feeling the difference from the sharp blades in the hellish rogue iteration. This was soft, almost fuzzy, like touching a cloud.

Senturi walked up the hill toward him, smiling. "What do you think?"

"It feels real." Not quite right, but solid.

"There's no known nodes here," Senturi said. "They diverged from the Primes when pacifists won the vote, and Emir never came to power. He's here, but working out of a basement lab. Everyone thinks he's mad."

The corner of Donovan's lip twitched up in a smile. "Have you found a way for us to move the soldiers in?"

"Not all of us. Not yet." Senturi licked his lips and looked away. Lying. "They have a sort of urban legend about a group of radicals who went underground and started building a secret army years ago."

"We're that army?" Donovan shook his head. "I don't want more violence. There needs to be an end to it."

Senturi nodded. "We're escapees. When I first met the locals, I slipped, told them I worked for a military organization. They filled in the rest. It will be so easy!" He smiled. "We'll be the heroes. The coddled, protected lost boys. I have names for all of us."

"We have names."

"Now we have the names of the dead. Children who went missing before the world wars ended. They're dead, but we can still have their lives. We can have their families, their place in society. It'll be perfect."

Donovan ran a hand over his arm. He'd been itching since going to the rogue iteration. Something in the air there made him crazy. "Rose isn't returning to Prime."

"Good," Senturi said. "She'd only ruin this."

"She wouldn't know how," Donovan said. "There's

no one for her to murder. No way for this iteration to collapse." Which is what made it so perfect. The low population could withstand an influx. There were plenty of resources to go around. "What about the leadership? How do we control things?"

Senturi shrugged. "Everything is done by democratic vote. No one here had real leadership skills. They're all a bit docile, to be honest. Very calm." The way he said it made it a warning.

"Drugs or genes?"

"Indoctrination, I think. No one gets angry here. When you argue with them, they agree. If you try to provoke them, they ignore you. If someone did take over, they'd make good slaves. Very amenable to whatever you suggest. But it hardly seems worth the effort. Why fight them? They don't resist."

"They need us," Donovan said. "Need us to keep them safe." He wondered if this was how Rose felt every time she was asked to decide humanity's fate. Did she feel like she was soaring? Rushing to the sky with the whole world held in the balance?

He walked over to a tree with white bark and yellow leaves with frosty-white tips. "Do you have the evacuation list ready?"

"The first wave of soldiers can be here in three hours." Senturi crouched. "You do realize there is a payment needed."

Donovan nodded. "What does the Ruling Council want?"

"Power. Always power. They already know what

the conditions are like in the Shadow Prime. It will be easy for them to walk in here and take control."

"They'll make a pet of Emir," Donovan guessed.

Senturi shrugged. "He needs to be controlled. You know that. This is how things are. The Council gets to control the population, and we get to live here unchallenged. You'll have everything you want." Senturi patted his arm.

Donovan nodded. "I know." Lifting a pair of binoculars, he scanned the streets of the nearest village, looking for a woman with bright red hair who walked along the dirt road from her home, where she'd had lunch, to a shop each day. He'd seen her before. Soon, he promised her.

Soon, I'll spend all day with you.

The villagers hurried from their homes to the shops, but the red-haired woman was missing.

"She's not there," Senturi said.

Donovan turned to him with a frown.

Senturi smiled apologetically. "I had to show the Council what was available here. We need weapons, soldiers who will obey us."

"We had both already."

"You think you did, but I don't trust anyone who was raised in Emir's shadow. We needed the Council's troops. Soldiers trained to ignore Emir."

"Where is the woman?"

"In the Prime," Senturi said with a shrug. "She's a very striking woman. Very agreeable."

There was something in the way he said that that made Donovan's throat tighten.

"Don't take it personally," the other man advised. "This is simply politics. Here or in the Prime, there's always going to be someone whose needs are greater than your wants. And the Council needed a sign. Call it a partial payment."

Donovan pivoted, driving his fist into Senturi's jaw and stunning the other man. Senturi dropped to the ground, dazed. Donovan stomped on his chest, breaking his ribs and piercing his lungs and heart.

Two swift kicks, one to the head and one to the stomach, and Senturi was gone. He'd breathe for a few minutes more, but the internal bleeding and damage would kill him soon enough.

Donovan looked down at his friend. "I'm sorry. It's nothing personal," he said in case Senturi could still hear him. "I'm a node for the soldiers, not the Council. I'm not here to defend or follow orders. I'm here to conquer. To take. To have. This is my world," he explained. "I was going to share this with you, but you broke my trust. She was mine."

Senturi groaned. Blood bubbled from his mouth.

"Your mother on the Council will die quicker," Donovan promised. "I'll leave her for the decoherence to wash away. She won't feel anything but impending terror, and then there's silence." He knelt down by Senturi. "You know how I know? Because I have died so many times, death is all I know. The pain followed by the silence. Then I wake up and kill myself again. Every day."

Senturi's pulse stopped fluttering in his neck.

Donovan checked the man's wrist. "Dead. Welcome to silence."

He stood back up. There was no need to bury the body. The grass here was aggressive, and no one walked in the hills. They kept to their villages. Four hundred and thirteen buildings in every one. Every person had an assigned job, a designated place. Everyone was happy.

She had been happy here. Would have been happy to welcome him home. Now he needed to raid another iteration to find the red-haired woman again.

His timer chirped, warning him that the next portal was opening. The anomaly would take him to the tunnels running between Control and the civilian towers. Hopefully, there wouldn't be any industrious techs coming home late from work again.

He'd hate to ruin the afternoon with another murder.

CHAPTER 30

> "For too long we have defined a human as someone with a certain set of correct features or genes. In humanity's long and painful history, we have at times labeled people as subhuman because of their language, the color of their skin, or the illnesses that affect them. We have a dark past wherein we have savagely murdered each other over inconsequential differences. And while the age of mass murders may be over, we are still guilty of trying to define a human with terms of bigotry and hatred. Today, that ends. We will no longer let hate define humanity. Today, we accept a brighter future and a broader definition of brotherhood."
>
> ~ Senator Adam Sharp speaking at the signing of the Cayc Law I2—2070

Tuesday January 14, 2070
Florida District 8
Commonwealth of North America
Iteration 2

Ivy shifted uncomfortably on her bare, tiled floor as she tried to make sense of the files. She'd called up Dr.

Runiker to ask him about the Jane Doe she'd seen in October. He told her that the CBI had concluded the investigation, and the matter was closed.

But it wasn't.

Dr. Runiker had been willing to send over the autopsy reports. It was a silly thing. Senseless to look into it, really, because she wasn't sure she wanted the answer. But the two girls were so similar, Ivy couldn't let it go.

Ivy looked up at the poster on her wall of CBI Agent Samantha Lynn Rose, hero of the clone rights movement. The camera had caught her imperious glare and fierce determination, but the words she'd spoken meant more to Ivy than anything else. I AM NOT YOUR POSSESSION.

Maybe that's why she liked Miss MacKenzie so much. She'd said nearly the same thing. It didn't matter if the victims were clones, they were people first, and they ought to be treated as people.

She stretched before picking up the datpad, hoping against all rational hope that she'd find something she'd missed before.

But the facts were staring at her in black and white. The fingerprints matched. Jane Doe was Lexie Muñoz. That could only mean that the woman Dr. Troom was accused of killing had been a clone.

Ivy closed her eyes. Feeling like a traitor, she dialed the number Miss MacKenzie had given her.

"Tickseed Meadows," a cheerful, elderly voice answered after the first ring. "How can I help you reach enlightenment today?"

"Do you have a Rose there?"

"Lots of roses, honey. Do you want to buy a floral arrangement or a wedding set?"

"A Rose MacKenzie. Blond hair, contacts, puts on bronzer even though she's Latina? Short?" She couldn't think of anything else to say.

"Oh! The one with the dog. Of course. She's in the kitchen."

Ivy frowned but waited.

"Hello?" Miss Mackenzie sounded strange on the phone. "Who's this?"

"Ivy. Officer Clemens."

"Ivy!" She sounded like someone greeting an old friend, and part of Ivy wished she were. "What's up?"

"I was just going over some files, and I found something that raised some questions." She let the hint dangle, not sure how to ask how the other woman had gotten her hands on a classified case file.

"What'd ya find?"

"A fingerprint," Ivy said. "It's . . . maybe it's not enough."

"Anything helps."

Ivy sighed. "I'm going to be up for a few more hours looking this over. Do you think you can help me write up the report? I know I need to turn this evidence in. I just don't know what to say."

"I can do that," Miss MacKenzie said. "I'm just putting the finishing touches on some spaghetti sauce for my hosts. Want me to bring you something?" she asked in the same breath as, "Are you allergic to anything?"

Ivy shook her head. "No, I'm not. And you don't need to worry about me."

"Please, I bet your fridge has a couple of full-nutrition smoothies, granola bars, oatmeal, and maybe some skim milk. Go ahead, tell me I'm wrong."

She wasn't. "That's a good guess."

"Good ol' Shadow House food," she said. "I know the diet."

Ivy pulled the phone away from her ear and blinked at it in confusion. Had Rose MacKenzie just admitted to being a clone? Or was she saying she'd worked with Shadows before? Reflex made her curl up on herself. "Um . . ."

"It's not what you think," the other woman said as if she was reading Ivy's thoughts. "One of my best friends was raised as a Shadow. Her gene donor was killed in a car wreck, and poof! That was it. She was a free woman. Crazy stuff."

"That's what happened to me!" Ivy blurted out.

"It's not that uncommon, really," Miss MacKenzie said casually. "So, spaghetti or no spaghetti?"

Ivy smiled and relaxed. "I'm fine, thank you. You don't need to worry about me. I'll see you soon."

"Later, gator." The phone clicked off with nothing more.

It was nearly an hour before Ivy realized that she hadn't given Miss MacKenzie directions to her apartment, and by then, the doorbell was ringing.

Sam shifted from foot to foot and cursed the existence of fire ants. Blah, blah, blah, all God's creations were beautiful! The world was excellent! The Psalmist had never met fire ants, or there would be a Bible verse that read, "Ye, and the ants of fire, they are abominations before God and ought to be burned."

Maribel insisted that poisoning them was not a natural, harmonic way to coexist. But neither was waking up with seventeen welts on her feet because the ants liked the taste of her lotion.

Sam rang the doorbell again and debated whether investing in boots would be a good idea. Probably, because when she got Henry out, they'd be building the machine in the swamp.

I miss Australia.

The door swung open to a surprised Ivy. "Miss Mackenzie, I didn't realize I'd given you directions."

Dang it! She'd slipped. Time to fake it. "I took a wild guess on what government Shadow housing might look like, then came to the only door with a light on in the window. Nine o'clock is the usual bedtime at the Shadow Houses, right? It can be a tough habit to break."

She held out the organic, hand-woven hemp bag full of goodies from Tickseed Meadow and hoped Ivy wouldn't question her logic.

Ivy took the bag and held the door open. "It's not hard to change your body clock when you work the graveyard shift for two years straight."

"That would do it," Sam agreed.

Ivy was looking in the bag with a face of resigned horror.

"I know what you said, but when I told Maribel I

was going to visit a friend, she insisted. I cook when I'm stressed, and I guess they're running out of cupboard space. Yesterday, the local soup kitchen took a donation of two hundred homemade cookies because Tickseed Meadow needed their fridge back."

"Oh," Ivy said in a tiny, defeated voice.

"It all freezes," Sam offered. "Or you could throw it out. I promise not to be offended. It's your body, and you get to choose what goes into it."

Ivy smirked. "You really have spent time around clones."

"A few," Sam said with a nod. "Actually, probably more than I ever realized. The difference between you and me is negligible."

"I have a clone marker."

"That doesn't make you any less human." She smiled and tried not to bite her lips in anticipation. "Where's this mystery fingerprint?"

Ivy took the bag of food and stuffed it into the mostly empty fridge before coming back to the living room floor covered in papers. "It's not a mystery print. It's Lexie's. On the Jane Doe's body from District 18 in October." She held out the file. "It's clone-on-donor violence."

"You don't know that," Sam said as she sat down to read through the autopsy. "Do you know if . . . oh. There it is." She sucked air in through her teeth. "I was hoping they hadn't found that."

"Found what?" Ivy asked, sitting down beside her.

Sam pointed out the tiny circular patterns on Lexie's bones. "This."

"The little Zen circles you hate."

"Yes they are." Sam put the file down and stared into space. "That complicates things."

"How?"

"It means I made a mistake." Henry had already built the time machine. History was wrong, and people were dying. She could feel the first push of tears behind her eyes. The bitterness and frustration of the past month threatened to crush her.

Sam choked it down, letting anger burn through the other emotions until there was nothing but fury.

Ivy scooted a little closer. "Are you okay?"

"I'm not, but I will be. Thank you for asking."

"Your voice sounds very . . . flat," Ivy said.

"Only because screaming won't help." Sam sighed. She patted Ivy's knee. "Your report?"

"It's going to get someone in trouble." Ivy looked at the ground. "I hate doing this. We've fought so hard for rights, for the chance to be human, and I'm going to betray one of us. It doesn't matter that she's a killer. All I can see is clone."

Sam shook her head. "Lexie didn't have a Shadow. I checked. I double-checked two hours ago when they found her body. The MO is the same. So, even if something had happened with a clone, the Shadow couldn't have been the killer. Lexie wasn't much larger than me."

It was Ivy's turn to shake her head in confusion. "But, I saw her body. I saw her."

"You saw *someone*."

"With the same fingerprints? That's impossible."

"Obviously not." Sam flipped through the rest of the files, then frowned. "There was a fingerprint found on one of the bodies?"

"Oh, yeah, the investigator didn't say anything about it, but it belongs to an Agent MacKenzie. He's a . . ." Her sentence trailed off. "Miss MacKenzie?"

"Hmm?"

"You have a funny look on your face."

Sam shook her head. "Just a strange thought. Don't think anything of it." Mac wouldn't have hurt anyone. The fingerprint had been dismissed as a protocol error—Mac forgot to put on his gloves. But what if things had gone differently? What if Mac in another iteration had fallen not into depression but into rages?

She looked at the victims again. A pattern started to form. "The killer had training."

Ivy peeked over her shoulder. "How do you know?"

"Look." Sam pointed at the left shoulders. "There's a rhythm here. The same set of moves every time. A punch to stun the victim, a kick to the left shoulder to keep them down, two more well-placed kicks."

"Is it enough to find the killer?"

Sam shut her eyes tight. "That's going to be a problem. Ivy, I know this is going to sound like a very bad idea, but you weren't officially on these cases, right?"

"Right." Her voice was soft, almost beaten.

"I'm going to strongly recommend you not write a report." Sam looked at her, hoping and praying she could sway Ivy to her point of view.

Ivy looked appalled at the thought. "This is new evidence!"

"This"—Sam tapped the files—"is a death warrant. You haven't seen this before, but I have. I was in the wrong place at the wrong time, and I wound up in a very bad situation. The people responsible for letting the killer loose are way over your pay grade and mine. The CBI has specialists for this."

"So we contact them," Ivy said. "We give them this information."

Sam shook her head. "You can't explain it."

"You can."

"I signed a nondisclosure agreement. If anyone in that organization thinks I talked, I will lose all freedoms. They will lock me in the deepest, darkest hole they can find in the penal system, and I won't even have a trial. I don't know what they'd do to you."

Ivy frowned. "What if I hinted at the right people that I might know something."

"No. Don't. If it ever comes up. If anything similar crosses your desk, and the CBI loops you in, act shocked. Act surprised. Protest. It'll keep you alive."

"But . . ." She looked at the lineup of the victims' faces. "How do we stop this from happening if we can't get the CBI involved?"

Sam pressed her lips together. "I do something really stupid that I hope I won't regret, and I go after them."

"I'll go with you," Ivy offered.

Sam smiled. "I wish I could let you, but it would

mean uprooting you and dragging you across the country. Possibly out of the country. You've got a future here."

With a resigned sigh Ivy looked at the floor. "No, I don't."

"Call it a hunch," Sam said. "Better times are coming. Bigger cases."

Ivy looked at her. "This is a really bad idea."

"Sometimes those are the only ones that work." Sam gave her a sideways hug. "Do you want to do breakfast tomorrow before I take off?"

"I can't," Ivy said sadly. "I have to get to work early. Will you call, when it's over, and everything is okay?" Ivy asked.

"Yeah," Sam lied. "I can do that."

CHAPTER 31

"A lie becomes truth if it is spoken enough."

~ from *The Handbook of Modern Politics*
by Feror Delgado I3—2067

Day 201/365
Year 5 of Progress
(July 20, 2069)
Central Command
Third Continent
Prime Reality

"How could this happen?" Donovan asked, as Emir handed him the black band to wrap around his arm. "Commander Rose was always so cautious. For her to miss a jump is unthinkable."

Emir's face was set in a permanent scowl. "You are certain you gave her the proper coordinates?"

"Yes, sir," Donovan lied. He secured the band in place. "I gave Senturi the new jump location, and he was in contact with Commander Rose the whole time."

"Senturi didn't come back either."

Donovan tilted his head to the side, pretending to think. "I can't think of a less likely pair of coconspirators, sir."

The scowl turned to a sneer. "You aren't kept around for your brains, Captain. Rose didn't agree with Senturi's politics, but they were a team. I'm not sure if the concept has ever crossed your mind."

Donovan's hands fisted at his sides.

Emir opened his office door without noticing. "Prepare your team for another jump in three days. This whole day was a fiasco."

"But the iteration is gone," Donovan said. "We've regained prominence."

Emir looked at the ceiling. "Captain, if I ever come to you for advice, please do me the courtesy of taking me directly to the medic for a full mental evaluation. No. The iteration didn't collapse. No. We are not in the Prime position. We're rapidly slipping away from dominance. We are missing a node!" he shouted. "Do you know what that means? No, of course you don't. You're an infantile man whose only focus is on his own base need for approval from underlings."

"You should learn respect, Doctor," Donovan said. "Before anyone else realizes that the iteration that is the Prime is the iteration where you are dead.

The old man looked at him, and Donovan saw death in the man's eyes. "Don't test me, Captain. I don't need you to survive, but you still need me."

Donovan walked out, fear running down his spine like icy water. He'd seen Emir play vicious little games.

He knew all the rumors about dead rivals and people who existed and were then erased from history. But he'd always thought that Emir had someone else do the dirty work. Now, he wasn't so sure.

He looked over his shoulder, wondering if he ought to have left Emir behind and let Rose return.

CHAPTER 32

> *"If one is ruled by destiny, then every choice one makes is pre-scribed into the foundation of the universe. It presupposes that the individual has no choice. Destiny is finite. It is only through the belief that the individual choices we make determine our future that one can grasp the infinite and the divine."*
>
> ~ **Treatise on the Divinity of Science**
> **by Lara M. Rushell I3—2071**

Monday January 20, 2070
Florida District 8
Commonwealth of North America
Iteration 2

Sam leaned against the hood of her rental car while Bosco hung his head out the window, panting in the chilly sixty-degree weather. A sizable puddle of drool had collected in the pothole by the car. He whined, and Sam reached out to scratch his ear. "Wait for it. Henry should be out in a few minutes."

Ten minutes later, Henry appeared, walking through

the glass-lined hall leading out of the correctional facility. He'd grown a scraggly beard and was wearing a pair of slacks with a white undershirt. Probably the same clothes he'd been arrested in. The desk clerk scanned him out, handed him a receipt for something—possibly his shoes since he was shuffling in prison slippers—and he stumbled to the door.

He stepped outside with a bitter glare at the clear, afternoon sky.

"Henry!" Sam waved her hand.

His shoulders slumped, and he shuffled across the broken parking lot. "I told Devon I'd pay the gas." He stopped a few feet from the car. "Agent Rose?"

"In the flesh." Sam put on her friendliest smile.

He stepped backward. "I really was hoping my roommate would pick me up."

"In the car, Henry. We need to talk."

"Do I have a choice?" he asked as he skulked closer to the car. "This is about the machine, isn't it?"

Bosco's tail thrummed on the roof of the car. He leaned out, trying to lick Henry.

"Ni-nice dog. Agent Rose, I'm sorry. I'm tired, and I'm . . ." He let out a deflated sigh. Shaking his head, he said, "This is too much. I'm going to the apartment, buying the plane tickets, and flying home to Palawan. It doesn't have the kind of physics research the Commonwealth has. It doesn't have much except for views, but it's home, and it's safe. I can let things calm down. Maybe get a job somewhere else. Start over." He shot an angry look at her. "Did you have to tell them about Krystal?"

Sam waited for him to finish whatever it was he was ranting about, resting her elbows on the roof the car. When he was done, she asked, "Do you believe in destiny?"

Troom frowned at her in derision. "What?"

"Do you believe in destiny? That you have no choice in what the future holds? That every action is set in stone, even before it happens?"

"No. That's utter nonsense. You can only believe in destiny if you don't believe in science. It's nonsensical. Ridiculous. Why do you ask?"

Sam snapped her fingers and pointed to the rear seat. "Bosco, *trô lai.*"

Bosco climbed into the backseat and lay down.

"You are destined to die in nine weeks. I know, because five years ago, I was the agent called to the lab to identify your body."

Henry opened the car door and sat inside. "Nine weeks in the future was five years in your past?"

"Yes." She dropped into the driver's seat, shutting the door behind her. "Want to close the door, so I can turn on the AC?"

He shut it. "You're talking about time travel."

"Yes."

Henry buckled his seat belt. "Dr. Emir never achieved time travel."

She was glad he caught on quick. "Oh, he did. He just didn't know what he had." She turned on the car and drove toward A1A. "The Emir you worked with didn't fully understand what he'd created. He thought he could send messages to the past, to warn himself about upcoming events."

"To warn the government," Henry corrected primly.

She shrugged. "Either way, he meant to send messages. His machine didn't work like that."

"I know!" Henry huffed and crossed his arms across his chest. "One of my biggest regrets is that he never got to see that dream come true. He worked so hard for it. It kills me he couldn't have it."

"Oh, he got it," Sam said. "That's what killed *him*."

"Huh?"

"The machine doesn't connect a single stream of time—it connects with alternate versions of reality. In some realities, Emir is alive and well. In some, I'm a psychopathic husband-napper. In some, things are really terrible. And, probably, in some of them, things are really great."

He held up a hand. "Go back to the bit where Emir fulfilled his dream, and it killed him."

"Another Emir from another reality killed our Emir," she grumbled. "Well, technically, he convinced Marrins to kill our Emir by promising Marrins a chance to go back in time and stop the nationhood vote. But then he betrayed Marrins and left us for dead. Except now he's back, I think, and someone's kidnapped Mac."

"Mac?" His expression had grown more and more confused as she spoke, and it was clear he had latched onto the last piece of information to formulate the first question he could think of.

Henry shifted in his seat. "What are you doing here?"

"I need you to finish rebuilding Emir's machine. You started it, didn't you?"

He looked out the window.

"Henry . . ." Sam drawled his voice as if she were talking to a rebellious child. "Lying doesn't work. I've been to your future. I know you have."

"I could have built it in that iteration of time and not this time," he said. "Emir explained the probability fan to me. If you were moving around the flow of time, you could have diverged multiple times. You probably did." His confused frown turned to a glare. "You probably broke time."

"I accept that," Sam said with forced cheerfulness. "Regardless, I need to get Mac back. And I need you to help me. So let's make this easy; tell me what you need to finish the machine, and I'll get it for you."

"I need the core Dr. Emir used on the original machine. It's a rare material, and you can't legally source it in the Commonwealth. Not even for research. The best I can do will probably lead to an explosion."

Sam nodded to his feet. "Check my purse, the zipper pocket."

"Okay . . ." He reached down and opened her purse. A pale glow illuminated it. "Is that . . . is that what I think it is?"

"Yes."

"How?"

Sam glanced at him, then turned her attention

back to the road. "Don't ask. Check the outer pocket. There's a notebook there."

"This is mine," Henry said. He turned through the pages. "This is not mine. It looks identical, but the dates here are wrong. I didn't journal in prison. I never did half of this. What is this math back here?"

"Calculations that allow you to target where the portals can open. Which leads me to project two."

"Wait, what was project one?"

Her palms were sweaty on the car wheel. "I need you to rebuild the machine and program in coordinates that will allow me to enter the timeline Mac is trapped in, so I can get him out. Having something to help me get back out would be great, but I'm not sure we can do that. But, something you said made me think about this case I'm working. You said you tested the machine, and little dust devils popped up?"

"More like sand fountains. You could recreate the effect with sound waves or magnets. Sand grains are very responsive."

Sam nodded. "Look at the back of your notebook. I tucked a map in there. Tell me what you see?"

Henry unfolded the paper. "Lots of red dots."

"Look for a pattern."

"Can I draw on this?"

"Sure, the stylus is—"

"—in your purse. I figured." He started connecting the dots. "It's rings. A spiral pattern. But if you were looking for concentric rings, this would be the intercept points where a moving pattern would overlap."

Sam blinked.

"Think of throwing a rock into a pond. The kinetic energy from the rock produces concentric rings that ripple through the water. Now, throw multiple rocks in a neat line, each landing a little closer to shore than the last. There's a ring around each one, but they overlap, interacting."

She nodded. "That fits."

"What do you think is happening?"

"I think someone is using those fountains of energy to cross over from somewhere undetected. You were traveling, so the machine was traveling. Once you held still, a cluster formed around here, but at different points."

"Oh," Henry said. "So the person is using a different door each time."

"If we have those points, though, it's just math. We can calculate backward and find where they came from. Right?" She stopped for a red light and looked at Henry. "Am I right?"

He shrugged. "I need to look at the maps, but, in theory it sounds good."

"I need to be right. If I'm wrong, the price is going to be too high."

CHAPTER 33

> "I'll believe my enemy is dead when I see their corpse
> in the ground."
>
> ~ old American proverb I2—2053

Day 205/365
Year 5 of Progress
(July 24, 2069)
Central Command
Third Continent
Prime Reality

With a vicious kick, the door to Locker 666 crumpled outward. Rose unfolded herself from the locker, black dust billowing around her like the birth of an avenging goddess. Nemesis in all her glory would have laid down her sword and bowed at Rose's feet.

Growling, Rose strode into the main hall and headed for the control center. Everyone moved. Techs scuttled to the side. Operatives and agents stepped back. Her furious steps echoed through the building like the drums of doom.

The gene lock slowed her down for only a moment, then she threw open the door.

Emir was stepping through the portal. She calmed herself, moderately mollified. At least she'd returned before Donovan had a chance to abandon her in that wayward iteration. He would pay for that. Prime only needed one Warrior, and they had MacKenzie.

She put her hands on her hips as she watched Emir turn with a little smile. He was coaxing someone through the portal, pulling her out of the light.

A woman with a mass of unruly black hair tripped through, falling in a gangly sprawl like a washed-up jellyfish.

Emir left the woman there as he walked to office with a smug smile.

Ire building like the rage of a volcano, Rose stormed down to the landing platform. "Who are you?"

The woman looked up, and Rose took an involuntary step backward. There was a bruise on her cheek, and far too much weight on her, but it was her other self. Another Rose from another iteration. The audacity and hubris—

"Rose?" Emir stopped and stared in horror.

It was worse than she'd thought. He'd brought an iteration of her home and not known the difference.

"What is the meaning of this?" he demanded.

"It means you missed. You brought one of their nodes home with you." She pulled her gun, not entirely sure if she wanted to shoot Emir or the sniveling other-her first.

The woman surged to her feet, ramming Rose in the chest with her head, then danced through the portal as it snapped closed.

Rose turned to Emir. "What were you thinking?"

"I thought you were testing security measures!" He held his hands up in a gesture of surrender. "You were complaining that the anomalies weren't secure. When you didn't come back, I assumed you were trying to make a point. The rogue iteration didn't collapse, so I went to find you."

"I was missing because Donovan changed the jump location, and no one told me! I spent four days in that hellhole waiting for a convergence point. I ate things growing on trees and, and . . ." She didn't know how to describe the meat cylinder wrapped in stale bread that someone had offered her when she stumbled into a group gathering. Her only excuse for eating it was that she'd been delirious from hunger and dehydration. "I had to break back into the facility to use the machine and escape. You are lucky that it didn't collapse as scheduled."

Emir descended the stairs slowly. "Donovan didn't give you our new location?"

"He did not." She was wary of the fury on his face.

"He told me differently." His tone grew cool. "He gave the location to Senturi, and Senturi was meant to relay it to you."

"He lied."

Emir took a deep breath. "He risked an einselected node in an act of hubris." He turned to one of the scrub-clad techs who was watching the drama unfold with wide eyes. "Sound an alarm. Lock down the building. No, the whole city. I want Captain Donovan found and brought to me immediately."

"If he was planning a coup," Rose said, "he couldn't have worked alone. He would need support from the ruling party."

Emir's eyes narrowed. "Senturi didn't return. " He sighed and rubbed the bridge of his nose. "I thought they could be trusted past the decoherence. I wanted to let them run things a little longer, but they have forced my hand.

"Commander, it is time for the culling to begin."

Donovan saw red. For a time, he wasn't in his right mind. He came back to himself washing blood out of deep gouges in his hands and forearms. There was probably a dented recycler somewhere in the building. He splashed cold water on his face, then stared at the mirror.

Rose was back.

The rogue iteration hadn't collapsed. If anything, it had grown stronger with Rose's presence. The entangling spiral had cut away, and for a few brief moments, the universe had breathed a sigh of relief. Donovan had gone to Rose's memorial service, said all the proper things, gone through all the right gestures even as Emir raged.

Then the rogue iteration had plummeted down to the baseline, inverting the probability fan.

It had felt like dying. Lying in his bed, sweat-soaked sheets tightening around him like a noose, he'd dreamt of every possible death and woke gasping for air. The command center had been in a panic. Emir vanished for nearly an hour, and when he returned, the probability fan had collapsed to just the two iterations, and Rose had returned.

Men he'd trained with for nearly a decade were avoiding him. Even the non-nodes had felt the shock as the iteration had lost dominance. Emir's standing had grown overnight. No one was willing to experience that again. If that was a taste of decoherence, then he knew what hell felt like.

Donovan dried his face and dressed with a singular focus. With a vicious tug, he secured his boots.

It was time to attack.

Mac rubbed a hand over the two-day beard on his chin.

He wasn't sleeping at night, not well. Every time he rolled over, Sam was missing. She was gone, and the nightmares were back. This morning he'd woken up choking and spat blood into the sink after biting his cheek to keep from screaming. It didn't matter that someone had shelved him in an abandoned cubicle down an empty hallway with nothing more than a cot and a three-legged stool. Showing weakness here would be like dumping blood in the water. The sharks were always looking for a meal. They didn't need an invitation.

Mac jumped at the sound of sirens followed by the insistent tattoo of someone's hammering on his door.

"Wh—?"

Donovan pushed inside before Mac could finish the word. The other man slammed the door shut and glared at Mac.

"What?"

"Rose is back." Dark circles under his eyes and sunken cheeks said Donovan was circling an abyss.

"That's nice," he said. Unfortunate, because it had looked like Emir was close to caving, but it meant he'd finally get out of this fishbowl of a room he'd been locked in.

Donovan started pacing. "I'm leaving."

"Good-bye?" Mac wondered if he should break it to Donovan that he didn't care what happened. The world would probably be a better place without him. Easier for Mac if nothing else.

Pivoting, Donovan glared at him. "Rose needs to die."

Mac shook his head and shrugged.

"She promised you she'd get you back to your iteration, but it will never happen," Donovan said. "Emir would never let it happen. Rose is lying to you."

"It's time travel," Mac said. "I'll figure out a way home."

"In thirty-six hours, there won't be a home for you to go to. The rogue iteration, your iteration, is in a death spiral. They can't survive much longer without you. Once it dies, you can't jump back in time to when it existed. It ceases to have ever existed."

Mac's gut clenched in fear.

"I need to leave." Donovan's face warmed with cruel emotion. A smile as sick and sadistic as any murderer's grew on his face. "My next return window is in thirteen hours. If Rose is dead when I arrive, I'll get you home. Your iteration will have a fighting chance at survival. If she's alive, I'll kill you. But not before I sort through time and find your wife and kill her. You get to pick who dies, MacKenzie.

"Choose a Rose."

CHAPTER 34

> *"I made one choice, then another. They fell like dominoes, each as inevitable as the last, pushed by the gravity of inevitability until I no longer had any choice, I was only falling into the future. Ever falling."*
>
> ~ excerpt from *Everfall*, a work of fiction by Del Eya Monsien I2—2063

Monday March 3, 2070
Florida District 8
Commonwealth of North America
Iteration 2

"And what did I say about the cemetery?" Sam grilled Nealie for what seemed the millionth time as he roasted a tarpon fillet over the campfire.

"Go with Connor, talk with my dad, don't pick up hitchhikers or strangers." He flipped the fish, and Bosco whined. "What are you expecting me to see, miss?"

She'd never figured out how Nealie met Donovan

or Gant. "Just . . . be careful. There are mean people out there."

"I'll keep an eye on him," Connor promised.

"Even at the college?" Sam pressed the point.

Connor nodded. "Watch him, keep an eye on Henry, and if I see an Officer Clemens, I'm supposed to treat her with respect."

"Good." Sam nodded. "That's all I need."

A car driving along the dirt road to the camp scared up a flock of barn swallows that nested under the eaves of the derelict building they'd been using. Sam had a tent in the back that she'd moved into after Maribel tried to drag her into a sweat lodge. It probably was only a few degrees cooler than the lodge in the middle of the day, but it made her untraceable. The last thing she needed right now was for Ivy to stop by Tickseed Meadows looking for her.

She and Bosco had been there more than a week before she realized it was the same building she would eventually chase Gant to before arresting him as his mind shattered. Gant's future was likely hers. She knew the risk was there once she crossed over into the other iteration.

A half-forgotten prayer to St. Jude skipped across her mind, and she crossed herself.

"You okay?" Connor asked.

Sam shook her head. "Probably not, but I don't have many choices left."

On the far side of the hedge, a cloud of dust heralded Henry's arrival. He pushed through the indigo bushes and waved.

Sam waved back in welcome. "How was work?"

"Awful." He sat down next to Nealie. "Not because of Krystal. I don't know how you did it, but they've swept the whole thing under the rug."

"I might have hinted that Krystal was an undercover agent working to infiltrate radical groups who posed a threat to national security." She shrugged. "There's no proof she wasn't."

Henry raised an eyebrow. "And, being suspected of murder? I expected that to come up at least once."

"You stayed silent because you didn't want to put Krystal at risk," Sam said. "Making you look very noble and patriotic."

"You used to be worse at lying," Henry said.

"I used to be a normal person," Sam said. She tossed a twig in the campfire. "Why was work so awful?"

"I couldn't sleep last night. I keep having these car-wreck dreams. This morning, I was up at three with a sore neck, half-convinced there was a piece of glass in my eye. My roommate would probably think I was crazy if he'd been home to see me stumbling around."

"It's memories from the other iterations," Sam said.

"I know, I read the journal you brought back." Henry took his satchel and pulled out both copies of his private journal from his bag. "This is the weirdest thing I've ever seen."

Sam smiled and held up her plate for Nealie. "You say that six times a day, Troom. Find some new material. How is everything tracking?"

"Good." He grimaced and shook his head. "Not

good good, but everything is still lining up. The dreams are all the same. The timeline doesn't seem to be damaged by your arrival."

She hmmphed in annoyance. "I'm trying to change the timeline. I'm not giving you all this information because I want you two to go kill yourselves again."

"I don't kill myself," Nealie said. "You said someone else kills me. I don't have suicidal tendencies." He smiled proudly.

"Right." Sam looked to Connor for help.

"She doesn't want you to get killed. That's why she's telling us this. If you don't listen, then you're a fool, and you got yourself killed," Connor said. He flipped hoe cake on another cast-iron griddle and swore as the wind picked it up and threw it in the dust.

Sam laughed. "Bosco, *tân công*."

The dog leapt up and attacked the hoe cake with enthusiasm.

"Good boy, Bosco. Good boy!" Sam rubbed his ear and gave him a bite of her carefully deboned fish. "Henry, did you ever come up with a theory of what will happen to Bosco if he crosses over?"

Henry shrugged. "Without experimenting, all I have is guesses."

"And?"

"And, nothing bad should happen. You're stepping between places, like stepping from one slat on a bridge to the next. There's a gap, there's a risk that the next slat is rotted and will crumble, but physically we're not talking about breaking you into atoms and reassembling you. Your physical integrity remains intact throughout the process."

Nealie and Connor shared the confused look they always had when Henry started talking about advanced physics.

"What about mentally? A crazy mastiff is never a good thing," Sam said.

Henry shook his head as if he could rattle the ideas into place. "This is just a hypothesis, you understand."

Sam made a hurry-up motion with her hand.

"From everything you've provided me with, it looks like the people who experienced the most dissonance were those who were fully aware of the changes. For the Gant gentleman you told me about, he faced extreme cognitive dissonance between what he expected as the outcome of events and the actual reality he faced. For me—or the possible iteration of myself—I was experiencing the psychological fallout of the collapse of other iterations. A form of psychological radiation poisoning almost.

"With you here to explain what was happening, though, I'm able to alleviate most of the dissonant anguish. The nightmares are nightmarish," he translated for the pirates, "but I can put them in context and stay sane." Henry looked at Sam. "I think that the last time you did this, you must have opted not to tell us what was going on."

"Mac and I debated that a lot," Sam said. "Whether or not telling people about the future would change things. Whether we had a right to interfere. I was always pro-change. Mac felt that we needed to let our past selves have their own lives." She twisted the ring on her finger. "Did you, by any chance, have a chance to check to see if the history I remember still existed?"

Henry nodded and smiled. "Everything up to your arrival in the Commonwealth was the same as you remembered. There's a slight possibility that the captain of the freighter you came in on was arrested or banned, but you didn't know, so I couldn't verify."

"But Young Me and Young Mac are where they should be?" She hadn't had a way to check after she'd moved here.

"Right down to the same apartment and phone numbers," Henry said. "Even your old passwords worked."

"I knew that, but remind me to change my passwords," Sam said. She wiped her hand on her well-worn jeans, gifts Nealie and Connor had picked up at their favorite thrift shop. After a few weeks in the mangal swamps, Sam found she wasn't all that picky about where food or clothes came from. "All right, Doctor, are we ready to test your machine?"

Henry pulled out his phone and checked the time. "Eleven minutes until our first window. Are you ready to be our first temporalnaut. Tempusnaut?"

"Naut is a Greek word," Sam said. "So, I'd be the first *foranaut*? A Time Voyager." She chuckled at their expressions. "Mac and I had a lot of free time in Australia to look these things up. Time traveler just doesn't sound as exciting. And I don't want to be a time tourist."

"Tourists are awful," Nealie and Connor agreed in unison.

Henry stood up. "Do you have plans for getting back? I mean, a window picked or something?"

"Ideally, I'd return somewhere in the near future, after my younger self escapes. Realistically, it probably won't be back to this time. We have no idea how my travel will affect all of this. For all I know, the iterations will wind up so distant that I'll be stuck back in 2030 or something." That would be awful, but if Mac were there, they'd survive. They always had.

"You might get stuck in another iteration," Henry warned. "I can leave the machine running."

"There were windows before this," Sam said, "and I'll sleep so much easier if there isn't a machine here creating a bridge between iterations for Gant and Donovan to cross."

"No," Sam said, even as she nodded and petted Bosco's head. "I don't mind getting stuck in another iteration, not if I have Mac with me. If there's an emergency, I trust my younger self can handle it. After all, I did when I was her age. Come on, let's get this over and done with. I'm getting homesick, and it's a long boat ride back to Australia."

Henry and Connor set up the final machine as Sam rechecked her packed bag, stuffed an extra bag of dog treats in it for Bosco, and helped Nealie put out the fire.

He watched her with a slightly hurt expression.

"Something you wanted to say?"

"I just . . . wish you could stay," Nealie said. "You're

real nice. Camp's not going to be the same without you."

"Thanks. For what it's worth, I'm glad I got to know you. Before this, you were just one of Edwin's stories from the swamp. Marshmallows and pirates." She sighed and fought back the tear stinging her eye. Edwin . . . she hadn't thought about him in nearly five years, and now she wished she could get a note to him, tell him not to worry. Or a note to herself telling her to get Ivy to the Academy. She snuffled.

"Sam?" Nealie touched her shoulder. "You okay?"

She wiped her nose on the sleeve of her long T-shirt. "Yeah. I'm fine. There's just a ton I want to do here, and I can't. I've got friends here. I miss 'em. They don't even know I'm gone, and I miss them." She shook herself. "I'm here, but it's not really me, you see? The Agent Sam Rose walking around in town doesn't have my memories. She doesn't have my experience. I'm worried she's going to get it wrong and ruin everything."

Bosco bumped her knee.

"Don't travel in time, Nealie. It only messes with your head."

He nodded. "I'll do that, miss. No time traveling. I'll stay right here."

"Good choice."

"Rose!" Henry waved his arm. "You have forty-five seconds until your window opens!"

She picked her pack up. "Đến đây, Bosco. Let's go. Is it calibrated?"

Henry nodded. "This is set to take you to the same

iteration you saw when you rescued me, and it matches the iteration the killer is coming from." He took a deep breath. "Be careful. I can't guarantee you won't walk in on the killer, and you're his type." Henry shook his head. "I wish I knew how to get you home."

"You destroy this machine and let me worry about getting myself home," Sam said.

The machine hummed as a dark purple light appeared and began spinning. The whirling vortex turned lilac, then topaz blue, then blinding white.

Sam gave the boys one last smile. "Don't wait up for me." She stepped through the vortex, Bosco trotting along beside her.

CHAPTER 35

> "We expect decoherence to affect everyone. Even non-nodal citizens will notice the changes. Many will feel anxious, uneasy, or experience night terrors. We recommend everyone be issued the proper medication needed to ease these worries until the new Prime iteration settles in, and the fan once again reaches an expansion point."
>
> ~ memo from Central Command I1—2070

Date Unknown
Location Unknown

Grit blasted Sam's face. Sand and dust blinded her, tearing across her bare arms and slicing at her throat. Choking, she pulled her sweater from the bag and wrapped it around her face. "Bosco?"

The dog whined.

She pulled his leash closer, grabbed his collar, and walked forward. Now she knew how she was going to die. Right here. Carved like a mountain by the wind until she was nothing but bone. She pulled her arms into her T-shirt and prayed. "I'm sorry, Bosco. It wasn't meant to be like this." Where, in the name of all that was good, were they? Birmingham didn't have deserts. There was not this much pollution anywhere in the South. It was like walking into a demolition zone, only it wasn't stopping.

Swinging her pack around front, she pulled out a sweater to cover her arms and a thin scarf to wrap around her head. Bosco's whimpers grew louder, and she wrapped him up, too, although he fought her on the socks.

"*Dùng lai*, Bosco." He stilled obediently. "No chewing until we find some shelter. Heel."

Bosco pressed against her leg.

Left arm stretched out in front of her, Sam did the Stingray Shuffle forward. Feet scooting but never lifting off the ground, it was meant to kick rays out of the way in the water since stepping on one meant a toxic dart to the leg. Now she did it so she didn't trip over anything. Her visibility was zero.

Even as she walked, she calculated the odds of survival. She'd learned from Los Angeles. Her pack had enough food for two weeks, water for one, but the bottle collected moisture from the air. They'd be able to stay alive if the weather didn't kill them—which wasn't a given. There was no way she'd be able to set up the small tent Nealie had given her in this wind.

The toe of her boot struck something hard. Bending down, she rolled her sleeve up enough to touch the surface, praying it wouldn't be anything organic. It felt rough, like concrete or broken rock. She covered her hand again and felt around for more lumps. There was a small pile, then something smooth. Running the side of her covered hand against it she tried to get an idea of the shape. She didn't want to get excited, but it felt doorish. Smooth, tall, rectangular.

She led Bosco through the rubble and explored the smooth surface more. It was metal, dented in a few places, but solid enough. Even if it was just the carcass of a car, it meant shelter.

There was a whine from Bosco, a muffled yap, and the reassuring sound of creaking hinges. Bosco pulled her out of the dust storm into utter darkness. The door banged shut behind them.

"Good work, Bosco."

He grumbled in complaint.

"I know." She reached into her bag and found the flashlight. With a click, their hiding place was illuminated. A poster of a woman holding a tube of toothpaste smiled cheerfully back at Sam from behind a layer of oily filth. "That's . . . not what I was expecting."

She unwrapped Bosco, washed off his scraped paws, and once they were ready to walk again, she took a better look as Bosco lay by the door. There was a long tunnel of sorts, metal on one side and rubble on the other. It looked like a bus stop almost, a nice bus station. "This must have been the high-rent district."

The dog wuffled in response.

"I'm saying it still is." She shook her head. "You know, if things weren't like they were, I think I could have enjoyed this. Traveling between all the possible worlds. It's a bit like archeology."

Bosco curled his tail under his legs.

"It can't be this bad in every iteration." But what a terrifying thought it was. She tested the stairs with a little run, then came back to Bosco. "There are tunnels down there."

He didn't look impressed.

"The air smells better."

Still nothing.

"Come on, Bosco. Mac might be down there! I mean, where else could people be living in this hellscape? Obviously, something triggered a nuclear winter or a worldwide storm, or we're in a test region for a tornado-control machine. Don't look at me like that. I've seen shows about this. Okay, they were spec-fic horror movies, but anything is possible, right?" Landing in the middle of a testing region for storm control did defy reason a little. The portal was supposed to open near the other machine. Since up wasn't an option, the portal had to be down. All she had to do was follow the tunnels until she found another human being.

She hit her hand on her thigh. "Up, Bosco. Dên đây. Let's go find Mac."

With a snarl, Bosco stood, shook the dust off, and followed her down the steps.

"It is not the end of the world," she promised, but her hands were shaking. This couldn't be the end, not after everything she'd gone through. This was supposed to be easy. Step in, grab Mac, flee for the far edges of the country, or alternate Australia, or even back home if it was possible.

Up ahead, voices rose in argument. Sam shut off the flashlight and pulled Bosco to the side as she crouched down.

"Where's Senturi?" an angry man demanded. "He promised to take us with him."

"That's his own problem. If I see him, I'll let him know." The second voice was deep, also male, and vaguely familiar.

"My people are waiting," the angry one said, his voice growing louder as they drew closer.

Sam touched her palm to Bosco's nose, signaling him to stay silent.

Two men walked past with headlamps on that barely illuminated the space in front of them. "I'm just saying, if you want our help, there has to be some in return," the angry man said.

"There will be," the other replied. "Now, do your job."

They turned a corner, and the voices dimmed.

Sam was still debating whether to follow them or not when a door slammed, and one set of footsteps started walking toward her. She waited until the man passed, then stood and turned on her flashlight.

The man turned. "What in the fragging sixth hell? Who are you?"

He was shorter than average, covered in a heavy canvas coat that looked like it might have been a Vietnam War-era tent stolen from a museum, and a heavy leather cap that covered his neck.

"Who am I? *What* are you?" Sam asked. "Is there a quarantine? Plague?" She held out a helpless hand to his clothes. "Diesel-punk convention?"

"I'm a survivor." he said with an exasperated yell.

"Of what?"

"Where have you been your entire life? This place was bombed until you couldn't buy bread if you fragged the mayor." His face was the cragged, aging face of a man of indeterminate race hidden behind dirt and grease He looked at Bosco and licked his lips like a man in a desert sighting water.

"Don't look at my dog like that," Sam said. "What city is this?"

"Birmingham." He choked and coughed, spat something black onto the dirt floor. "I don't know what it's like in the Shadow Prime, but show some respect. You're in my place now. No how do you do? No manners?"

Sam shrugged, feeling a bit guilty and very overwhelmed. "Sorry. Hello. How are you? What is the Shadow Prime?" She hadn't formed a fully-fleshed-out idea of what she expected to encounter on this side of the portal, but it wouldn't have been this. Somehow, she'd figured it would be closer to home. More trees, maybe with better tech or a different government. This level of destruction wouldn't have crossed her mind even if she'd extrapolated the worst-case scenario for the old countries not forming the Commonwealth.

He pointed at the dog. "Where'd you get that?"

"This is Bosco," Sam said, petting him for comfort.

"He's a boerboel. Very well trained." She stopped, tilting her head in thought. "Why did you ask where I'd found him? Don't you have pets?"

The man grimaced. "Not anymore." He leaned against a shadowy wall. "I had one as a kid. A beagle." He shook his head. "It was hard enough keeping myself alive during the wars. I couldn't keep a dog, too. You have a name?"

"CBI Agent Sam Rose from the Commonwealth of North America. And you are?"

"Jaycob Landon." Landon stepped closer, cold eyes boring into her. "*Samantha* Rose? The commander and the Paladin?"

"That might be a version of me," she admitted cautiously. "But I'm not responsible for anything she's done."

He snorted in disbelief. "Yeah. Who are you here to kill?"

"No one. I'm here to find my husband." Sam wasn't sure if she was appalled or amused when Landon looked her up and down with a masculine gaze.

He shrugged. "Not really my type, but I won't say no. I mean, when Senturi said he could smuggle people out to the new iteration, he said there was a bit of a gender imbalance. Not a lot of men. But you should have waited for us to cross over."

"I already *have* a husband," Sam said "He was kidnapped by someone in this iteration. I'm here to take him back. It sounds like you're leaving, too."

"That's the agreement." Landon turned and shuffled into the darkness. "You coming, Agent? I don't care one way or the other if you want to go back into the storm. But if you want to go for a walk, let me keep the dog. He looks friendly enough."

Bosco bumped her knee and barked. He was bright enough that someone had said they liked him, and friendly people often gave him treats. Bosco was not above begging.

Sam sighed. "We're coming." Going back outside wasn't an option.

Which left her with what, she wondered? A future living in the ruins of Birmingham?

Wasting away from some disease in the water or from radiation poisoning?

Her and Mac's fifth anniversary was coming up. They had been planning on finding someone to watch Bosco and sail down to see Antarctica. She had tomatoes to harvest at home. Friends who would miss her eventually.

She sighed again.

Landon turned on a flashlight and shined it directly in her face. "You don't look like what I expected. Senturi made it sound like everyone in the Shadow Prime was real serene. Docile, he said. You look angrier than I expected. Like you could handle a fight."

"I can," Sam said. "I don't know what the Shadow Prime is or who Senturi is. Sorry. You work for him?"

Landon shrugged. "With him. Sort of. His squad caught me raiding the food stores in the towers a year or so back. I took a beating for it, wound up press-ganged into the infantry. But I'm smarter than a grunt.

Worked my way up, and as soon as they gave me enough freedom, I skedaddled. Thought it was over until a few months back, when Senturi hunted me down.

"Offered to get me and ten people I picked out of here if I manned a stationary landing site. Two, one here and one in the control tower. Senturi used the mobile sites more often, but this one was static jumping between here and the new world." He looked at Sam. "I thought maybe the jump had gone wrong."

She shook her head. "Sorry. Henry—Dr. Troom—he used the Fountain Variance Calculations to pick a location near a big city. We tried to find a place where someone stepping out of a glowing portal wouldn't be noticed."

"A park?" Landon guessed.

"A known drug alley where everyone would be high." Sam shrugged. "In my world, the security in that area is more or less ignored. There have to be a few blind spots for undercover agents to meet their handlers, and most the drugs are legal. It's a Vagrant Walk."

He flicked the beam of light to the floor. Pieces of asphalt appeared.

Bosco walked up to Landon, straining at the leash, and put one giant paw on the man's thigh.

"He's hungry," Sam said. "He only just ate a fish three minutes before we came, but you know how dogs are."

Landon patted his head and pushed Bosco away.

"Not sure we have much to offer. Why'd you bring the dog?"

"I was afraid that if I left him, I'd never see him again. There's only a fifty-fifty chance I'll get my husband back. Leaving Bosco would be too much. Plus, he keeps me safe."

Landon glanced sideways at the dog and nodded. "The main substation is this way. Not far now." He turned and walked on.

"What happened here?" Sam asked, as they passed a pile of shattered glass and rusting metal.

"Emir happened. Him and the world government," Landon said. "Anyone who didn't agree with their terms fast enough was eliminated. EMP bombs, regular bombs, street sweeps with snipers and assault rifles. I wasn't here then. But I moved here. Kept getting pushed out of everywhere 'cause I have a record."

"As what?"

He shrugged one shoulder as if it didn't matter. "A bit of everything small time. Carjacking was what got me, but I did a bit of hacking, bit of grifting. Wasn't born rich but didn't want to die poor. I should have gone to jail, but the hard-line judge I was supposed to get was sick. So I got this real nice old lady with a soft spot for bad boys, I guess. I was a lab rat for a new rehab program. Instead of jail, I went to be a locksmith's apprentice. Wound up designing custom locks. It was lucrative for a few years. Until the whole Manifest Destiny of Time and Forward Progression of Humanity projects changed everything. There's no custom anything anymore. No luxuries. No . . ." He waved his hand over his head. "You know, whatever. We're all the same. That's why we all want to leave."

"Makes sense to me," Sam said.

Landon nodded. "Everything's hyperregulated here. Makes all those old communist governments look like Little League soccer games. Down in the tunnels, things are . . ." He laughed. "They're worse. Much worse. No running water or food allotments or medicine. But we're free."

"I read a book once that said true freedom was the freedom to die alone."

"Sounds like a terrible book."

"I think it was meant to be satire."

Landon stopped and leaned against a section of the cement wall that looked no different than the rest. It swung open in silence to show a squalid room illuminated by tallow lamplight. "Welcome to my little piece of hell. *Mi cuchitril es su casucha.*" He must have seen despair on her face because he shrugged with an apologetic grimace. "It's temporary. All tunnel homes are, but this one is really temporary. Soon as Senturi gets back, we're leaving for the new world. Big fields, small towns, lots of food, quiet women."

Sam gave him a look of feminist disgust. "Quiet women?"

Landon raised a shoulder. "The only women around here would kill you as soon as look at you! Quiet sounds less fatal is all. I'm not judging. Just saying."

"In my experience, quiet women tend to be better

at hiding the bodies. You sure they aren't the reason there's such a gender imbalance there?"

He grimaced. "You are full of nightmares. Cupboard over there has a bit of water and some antiseptic wipes. Better take care of the dog first. I'll go see if I can find a spare bit of rations." There was a quiet pause, then he shook his head. "Hide their bodies," he muttered as he stomped down a narrow hall. "Flaming praying mantis woman."

Sam stroked Bosco's head and looked around the hovel. The first winter in Australia, Mac and Sam had driven to Coober Pedy in South Australia and spent a week in the famous underground town. In Coober Pedy, the walls were carved and smoothed by years of wear. Bright lights and colorful characters had made it a fun, vivid, and very memorable place.

This was Coober Pedy's depressed, goth cousin. The walls were covered in soot. Every single item in the room from the three-legged chair to the leaning shelf was in disrepair. It was DIY upcycled trash without the upcycling or joy.

Grimacing, she patted Bosco in apology and led him to the cupboard Landon had indicated. "Sorry, puppy." Gingerly, she reached for the cupboard door, ready to jump back if it fell off. Instead it stuck, the faux wood warped by the abuse it had suffered. She tugged hard, and it opened to reveal a hodgepodge of half-empty bottles and a yellowing piece of gauze.

"I hope you weren't expecting something fancy," Landon said from behind her.

Sam spun, hand dropping to the truncheon she carried concealed in her pocket.

Landon was holding a chipped ceramic bowl with muddy water and a rectangle covered in green plastic that might be a granola bar. "For the dog," he said, lifting the bowl. "For you." He held out the green rectangle. "It's city rations. Senturi brought us two boxes a week back. Should be enough to get us through another four days, even with you around. Fifteen hundred calories and all your daily nutrients."

Sam turned it over in her hand. "This is what people eat?"

"Mostly."

It was awful. She hadn't even opened the package yet, and she knew it was awful. In her mind, she started calculating how many people she could smuggle back to her reality without risking overpopulation. There was the whole duplicate problem she and Mac faced with their younger selves. And, of course, there was the risk of insanity like Gant had suffered when he was cut off from the Federated States of Mexico.

But if she established a little colony?

In Australia, or maybe New Zealand? There was lots of land in New Zealand. Or Kansas, even. Practically no one lived in Kansas.

Landon raised his eyebrows. "You okay? You zoned out there for a moment."

"I was trying to calculate the grocery bill if I invited you and all your friends over for a proper meal. Maybe a seafood pasta with squid."

He shook his head. "I don't eat things that might try to eat me back. Besides, this is coming to an end. We've seen pictures of the new place. I've got a house picked out."

"This"—she held the ration bar up to eye level—"is an abomination. This can't be healthy."

"Vat-grown seaweed is the only thing that grows anymore. There's too much dust in the atmosphere for plants. Too many toxins in the oceans. They say it's because of overpopulation, but me? I think we just got greedy." He pulled out a wobbly, three-legged stool and sat down. "Your place is better than this, is it?"

She shrugged. "Every place has its problems, but it's better looking than this. We don't have the overpopulation problem. There was a plague."

Landon sat and watched her while she cleaned off Bosco.

Sam looked up at him. "Are you expecting me to do something interesting?"

"Was wondering what to do with you, is all. How were you planning to find this husband of yours?"

"Well, that plan hinged on me having access to computers and mass transit. I thought I'd call around, find Emir, and go harass him until I found Mac. But, since I'm guessing you didn't see a surly guy with a weird accent and a good tan come through"—she looked at Landon, who shook his head—"I'm guessing Mac came in at the other jump point you mentioned. So I'll go there."

"That's in Central Command. The Ministry of Defense has soldiers and trainees in two buildings, and there's sixteen towers for civilians. Maybe a quarter of a million people when I lived there. Maybe a bit more."

"In sixteen buildings?"

"Eighteen." His smile was bitter. "Security is tight. Everything's gene locked, so you either bribe someone who has access or you threaten them." Landon leaned forward. "You're not very threatening."

Sam leaned forward. "But I have great genes."

CHAPTER 36

"All the world is a stage, and someone just stole my spotlight."

~ Comedian Willado Shakesbeer at the
Florida Renaissance Festival 12—2068

Wednesday March 19, 2070
Florida District 8
Commonwealth of North America
Iteration 2

Ivy stepped in front of the poster of Agent Rose as she lined up her gear. The Hello Kitty pocketknife, her flashlight, that she was thinking of naming Skullcrusher, and the semi-illegal phone Miss MacKenzie had given to her when she went back to California. In case she needed to call, Miss MacKenzie had said. She wasn't comfortable taking the gun with her. It was hidden behind her nightstand, and if she had it her way, it would stay there until she grew old and died.

Technically, the Caye Law allowed her to own a

phone just like it allowed her to own an apartment. But most of the major phone providers required a gene scan for their accounts, and clones—being the duplicate of someone else's priority genetic code–couldn't have a gene scan unless their genetic donor created and controlled an account with them.

Jenna Mills, Ivy's original owner, was dead, but her genetic code was on file with all the good carriers. The one Miss MacKenzie had provided was some rugged-looking knockoff of a designer brand. It was heavy as a half brick and probably counted as a lethal weapon in most of the country. She fixed a lanyard around it and stuck it in her pocket.

Miss MacKenzie wasn't likely to ever call, no one called Ivy, but she'd take any improvised weapon she could find.

Her work phone rang, and she turned on the speaker as she tied her boots. "This is Officer Clemens."

"This is Dispatch Operator Bogomil. We have a report of a dead body floating in the water south of Twenty-seventh Avenue Park."

"That's great . . . why aren't you calling a patrol car?"

"I did, they told me to have a drone take care of it. A drunk swimming into a riptide is a waste of an officer's time. That's a direct quote."

Drone. Of course. She ground her teeth together. Taking a deep breath, she looked at the angry-eyed poster. What would Agent Rose do? Silly question. Agent Rose would handle it. Agent Rose could handle anything. "I'll be there in fifteen minutes."

"Better make it ten," Bogomil said. "The news crews got a tip-off, too, and we want a sheet over the drunk before they get there."

"Is there an ambulance on its way?"

"Yes, ma'am. I told them you'd meet them there."

She took the "ma'am" with a smile. At least some people were willing to treat her like a human being. "On my way."

The park at the corner of 27th and A1A was nothing more than a parking lot with a few amenities, so the locals had a place to pee between building sand castles and being chased by sharks. At least that's what the locals liked to tell the tourists. New Smyrna Beach enjoyed a relatively idiot-free existence.

She parked next to the tennis courts and the ambulance before hiking up over the boardwalk protecting the dunes. A red flag waved in the breeze, warning everyone to stay out of the water because of riptides.

Apparently, someone hadn't gotten that message.

Two EMTs were carrying a covered body while a nervous retiree and his tiny dog looked on.

"Are you the one who called the police?" Ivy asked.

"Oh." He startled, and the tiny fuzzball on a leash yapped. "Yes. Sorry. John Watson. I live over there." He gestured across the street to a set of apartments undergoing renovation. "Sherlock and I were out for our morning constitutional."

The dog yapped.

"John Watson . . . and Sherlock the dog?"

He shrugged with an apologetic little smile. "I can't help what my parents named me, and playing to type doesn't hurt when I'm looking to meet new gentlemen friends. A little tea and polish impresses boys who've ever only known overly muscled surfers."

Watson was wearing stained khaki shorts with an equally stained shirt from the Riptide Surf Shop that had a bright pink silhouette of a woman surfing over their motto: CURLS AND GIRLS! Far be it from her to say that mismatched socks with flip-flops and a hole in the pocket didn't look polished.

Sherlock stepped forward and sniffed her shoe.

"Right," Ivy said, nudging the dog aside. "You were out for your morning walk, and you saw the person on the beach."

He shrugged. "Sherlock and I usually walk down to The Wind Chaser for breakfast. They've got a very nice staff, and the kitchen boy always brings Sherlock his own sausage and water."

"What time do you usually have breakfast?" Ivy asked as she pulled out her pen.

"We leave at seven, and toast and tea is served at quarter after promptly. Earl Grey. Hot." He smiled as if he were anticipating a laugh.

Ivy raised her eyebrows.

Watson rolled his eyes dramatically and folded hairy arms over his stained surf shirt. He huffed.

"I'm sorry," Ivy said.

"You need to catch up on your classics, young lady."

"Officer." Her smile dropped a few degrees of warmth. "Breakfast at seven fifteen. When did you start walking back?"

He gave her a pouty little frown. "Sherlock and I walk along the avenue to see Shakespeare at eight every morning. He's Mrs. Hawkins parrot." Again, he waited as if she should know who he was talking about. "Jamie Hawkins? She runs the Treasure Chest. On Orange Street." Brown eyes bored into her. "Do you not shop? At all?"

"No. I really don't. At all." She dropped her smile entirely. The city didn't pay her enough to go shopping unless she ran out of socks. "At eight you talked to Shakespeare."

"Mrs. Hawkins is doing inventory this week, so he has to stay home. I talked to him through the window. Then we continued on our way home."

"How long did you talk to the parrot?" She hated herself for asking that question.

Watson shrugged. "Maybe five minutes. He's not a very eloquent old bird. Then Sherlock and I wandered onto the beach."

"That's illegal," Sam said. "The whole coast is pet-free."

"We were chasing a plastic bag!"

Which sounded unlikely. New Smyrna businesses didn't offer plastic bags anymore, except for the recycled ones that felt like satin and cost half her day's wages. "Right, you chased the bag."

"And saved a turtle!" Watson said vehemently. "The

poor idiots will eat anything. Not the brightest crackers in the drawer."

"Uh-huh. And then?"

"Since we were already there, I decided to collect the rest of the trash that washed up with the tide. I blame the cruise ships, personally. Full of tourists, and where does their trash go? Straight overboard! Every time! Like a drag queen on Halloween!"

Since tourists were the major cause of every problem in New Smyrna, from pollution to the lack of school funding, Ivy zoned out while Watson ranted. When he said "body," she tuned back in.

"I thought it was a sea turtle," he said. "It's a little early in the season for them to arrive, but with the way the weather's been the past few years, who could blame them for arriving early. I blame—"

"Tourists," Ivy said. "Back to the body."

"It was rolled up in some sea grass. We went over, and there he is. Dressed and everything!" Watson sounded offended that the deceased was dressed.

Ivy's shoulders slumped in defeat. "Did you check for a pulse?"

Watson's eyes went wide. "Ewww! His neck was sliced open! I wasn't touching that."

"Sliced?" Ivy stared at him, trying to process the information. "I thought he was drunk."

"He might have been," Watson said placidly, "but that's not what killed him. Someone took a chain saw to that boy's throat."

As it turned out, it wasn't a chain saw. Something thin had choked him, then the crabs and fish had helped muddy the crime scene by trying to eat the deceased. Ivy followed the ambulance to the CBI building and escorted the victim up the public elevator in full view of the local WIC office, where a little boy watched with wide eyes. The poor kid would probably grow up to write cheesy horror movies.

The CBI morgue was usually locked down when they dropped someone off—District 8 didn't have its own ME–but there was someone there today. He was a handsome man, slightly older than she preferred, but with an easy smile. It didn't quite reach his hazel eyes.

"Officer Clemens," she said by way of introduction.

"Agent MacKenzie."

She couldn't hide the surprise. "MacKenzie?"

He froze and looked a little wary. "Whatever you heard, it's not that bad."

"No, it was just that I met a Miss Mackenzie a few months ago. Missus, technically. From California. Her name was Rose . . ." She trailed off, realizing she sounded like an idiot. "Oh, I'm sorry. It's just not the most common name here. It's funny running into two MacKenzies in such a short time. Rose was real nice."

His frown wasn't encouraging. "You mean Agent Rose?"

"Oh! No." Ivy smiled and told herself not to fangirl like Rosie Girl. "Rose MacKenzie. She came out to work a case, and I helped her." *Time to shut up.* She'd been in a very gray area verging on illegal with Miss

MacKenzie. Half those records were Eyes Only, and her security clearance was still lower than a meter maid's.

He laughed. "Right. Sorry. My partner is Agent Rose and . . ." He shook his head and laughed again. "I'll have to tell her that one. She'll get a kick out of it. Last August, she introduced us as MacKenzie Rose. Took half the day before the clerk helping us out realized her name was Sam Rose."

Ivy pressed her lips together and rocked back on her heels. *Agent Samantha L. Rose!* She felt light-headed.

"Hey, the phones aren't hooked up here, and my cell battery is low. Would you mind running to the CBI office and grabbing Sam?"

"Sure!" Ivy said in a squeaky voice that sounded like she'd swallowed helium. "No problem." She stepped backward. "Not a problem at all."

She was going to meet Agent Rose!

In the hall, she stopped to check her reflection in the glass of a Realtor's office. Her hair was pinned back neatly, just like Agent Rose's. She'd never figured out makeup, or how or why she was supposed to hide her freckles, and now she was suddenly conscious of them in a way she'd never been before.

Touching her nose, she wondered if Agent Rose liked freckles.

No.

Deep breath.

Agent Rose was a clone. Like her. She would understand.

By the time she reached the CBI office, she had her game face on. Calm, composed, and utterly in control. Exactly like her hero. She stepped into the room, swept it with a haughty glance, and caught on the eager smile of a ginger giant perched behind a ridiculously small desk.

"Hello, ma'am. I'm Junior Agent Dan Edwin. Can I help you today?" He reminded Ivy of the Irish setter that had gotten loose at last year's dog show: energetic, eager to please, and too large for Ivy's safety.

She had an insane urge to throw a ball to see if the junior agent would chase after it. She shook the image of a large red-haired puppy running down the hall from her head.

"I'm Officer Clemens from the local precinct. I rode in with a murder victim we found down on the beach. Agent MacKenzie upstairs asked if I could see if Agent Rose was available." There, cool and calm as the Pacific.

"Oh! We haven't fixed the phone since the rats got into it." He stood up and towered over the room. Everything around him shrunk.

Ivy sat down from the shock, bouncing on the little office chair.

Edwin smiled, sidled across the room with an apologetic hunch, and knocked on the door.

A voice Ivy had only ever heard in news recordings came from the other room. "Yes?"

Edwin ducked inside and closed the door behind him.

Ivy's hands started to sweat. Her face was going numb. She started counting breaths, five in, six out. Agent Rose was only one room away!

The door opened, and Ivy popped to her feet.

"Next of kin?" Agent Rose said as she stepped out of the office.

She looked exactly like her poster: crisp white blouse, navy blazer and skirt, black hair in a flawless, shining bun, and just enough mascara to capture the attention while maintaining a I-Woke-Up-Like-This freshness.

Ivy's knees wobbled.

Agent Rose looked at her expectantly.

"This is Officer Clemens, ma'am," Edwin said with a cheerful smile.

Agent Rose nodded. "You have a corpse for us?"

"Yes, ma'am. He washed up with the tide this morning, and I escorted him to the morgue. An Agent MacKenzie asked me to come ask if you'd be available to view it."

Her smile was humorless but patient. "Well, if I didn't find him a body to play with soon, he'd get bored. Edwin, I'm going to go see our new customer." She turned to Ivy with a much friendlier smile. "Can you fill me in on the details as we walk to the morgue, or is the chief expecting you back before lunch?"

"No one will miss me," Ivy said. She hurried after Agent Rose, almost stepping on her heels.

Agent Rose paused at the elevator and turned with another polite smile.

Ivy made a note to practice her smiles so she could put so much meaning into the look.

"First DOA case, Officer?"

"Yes, ma'am! My first real case." She was hyperventilating.

They stepped into the elevator, and Ivy could smell her soap. She was going to faint from happiness.

"And they're letting you handle it alone?"

"Oh, yes. I've been with the force for ten years now, as a drone. I'm a clone." Ivy squeezed her hands together. They were clones together. Doing something important. *Together*. It was the happiest moment of her life. "I've always wanted to meet you," she blurted out. "You're amazing. A clone in the CBI. That's amazing. All of us look up to you."

Agent Rose sighed and squinched her eyes shut. When she started rubbing her temples, Ivy realized something was wrong.

"Um . . ."

Agent Rose shook her head. "It's not your fault. The rumors were all over the place. But . . ."

Ivy held her breath, not sure what was going on.

"But I'm not a clone. I don't have a clone. I do not support cloning or the harvesting of clone organs." She looked sideways at Ivy as the elevator pulled to a stop. "I'm sorry."

Ivy felt her world crashing down around her. "B-but, what about all the reports from this summer? Everyone said the bureau was covering up the fact that a clone was working as an agent."

"There was a cover-up, but it didn't involve clones." Her tone was chilling.

"Not even the Chimes girl?"

With a sigh, Agent Rose said, "Melody had a Shadow, but that clone was never involved with the case."

Ivy felt hollow. All those hopes and dreams of becoming someone real . . . "I'm sorry to have brought it up, ma'am." She wasn't even sure if the agent heard it, as her voice sounded so small to her own ears.

"Don't be. It doesn't bother me," Agent Rose said. "I supported the Caye Law, and I support the integration of clones and Shadows into society. Your humanity isn't based on how you were born."

"I hope so," Ivy whispered. Taking a deep breath, she rolled her shoulders back and put her game face back on. Agent Rose was still a hero of the clone rights movement. It wasn't her fault she'd come from a uterus instead of a test tube. Still . . . a small part of Ivy wilted. There was no more guiding star in the midnight sky. No road out of the drone life she was trapped in.

"Stop hoping and start proving," Agent Rose ordered as she keyed in the password for the morgue. "Tell me about our John Doe."

Yes, ma'am. Ivy snapped to attention. "A little before eight, Mr. John Watson called 911 to report a dead body. Originally, everyone thought it was a drunk who went swimming. There are a ton of bars and hotels there, and the riptides have been bad for the past few days."

Agent MacKenzie pushed a rolling chair out of the small office attached to the tiny morgue. "Hello."

"You have a new body for me?" Agent Rose asked.

"No, yours is perfect, but I do have a wonderful homicide that Officer Clemens brought us." He smiled at Rose, and Ivy blushed.

Agent Rose didn't seem to notice his flirtation. "You two met already?"

Ivy nodded.

"We don't usually have an ME," Agent Rose said, "but Mac's here on vacation. Trying to avoid the snowy weather in Chicago."

"Oh." Ivy didn't ask why a vacationing ME was in the morgue working. That was CBI business.

He smiled. "Henry Troom is a friend of mine. I was planning to come down for a conference anyway. When he was arrested I was worried. He caught a lucky break, but I thought it would be a good idea to check on him." Ivy could tell the explanation was for her, but his eyes were on Agent Rose the whole time.

Ivy studied her boots. She'd bet lunch Henry Troom wasn't the only person this guy had come to District 8 to check on.

"How'd the John Doe die?" Agent Rose asked. "Drowning? Alcohol poisoning? Blow dart?"

"All three, actually," Agent MacKenzie said with a smile.

Ivy stared at him. "But, I thought—"

He laughed. "Sorry, just joking. He was garroted—strangled from behind by something, I'm guessing a plastic rope or knotted bag. Something that was probably readily available. It certainly wasn't a professional hit."

"What?" Only one case came to mind that matched the description, and that had been a public-relations nightmare. "There was a similar case a few years back. Accidental drowning after a fishing line tangled around a boy's neck. Could it have been something like that?"

Agent MacKenzie stared at her for a moment longer than was comfortable. If he told her she was an idiot and needed to hand in her badge, she probably would. There was something about his stillness that triggered a primeval impulse to flee.

"I think it is very unlikely that this is accidental. John Doe is in his early twenties, has no ID on him, no fingerprints on file, and doesn't match any known missing-person report in the district. He died midday—between eleven and two I'd say—of asphyxiation when someone wrapped something around his throat and pulled back, choking him. There's subcutaneous bruising on his back where someone propped a knee to hold him steady. I need to do an autopsy to be sure, but I'm guessing he wasn't in the water when this happened."

"You said plastic," Ivy said. "What makes you think the killer used that?"

"No fibers yet." He shrugged. "A metal garrote would have cut into the skin, a fabric like a scarf would have left trace, maybe even a dye. There may be some when we do a microscan, but as smooth and as wide as the markings are, it looks like plastic to me. Just a hunch."

"How long was he in the water?" Agent Rose was taking notes on a datpad.

Ivy pulled out her notebook and started taking notes, too.

"Two hours, tops. And, you'll like this." He pulled up an image on the screen showing the John Doe's wrists. "See the red marks? Like his wrists were bound, but someone cut whatever was holding him off before the body was dumped."

"Trying to make it look accidental?" Ivy suggested. The only time she'd seen bondage marks were on one of the domestic violence cases several years before.

"This would only look like an accidental death if you'd never worked a homicide before," Mac said.

"Mac," Agent Rose said with an exasperated tone, "how many people in this district do you think have ever seen a murder before?"

"We don't get many," Ivy said. "A few domestic violence calls, and two years ago during the heat wave, two old ladies started a fight at a shuffleboard match. Someone got hit with a stick, and someone else threw a puck for revenge. But other than that, it's quiet here."

"There was the Lexie Muñoz case," Agent Rose said. "Petrilli took that. They said I had too many ties to Henry to be professional."

Mac sneered. "Petrilli doesn't know you well."

"None of them do."

Ivy cleared her throat. "New Smyrna Beach did an assist on the Lexie Muñoz case. But the newspapers buried it hard. Two people from out of town . . ." She trailed off. The killer still wasn't in custody, which meant Miss MacKenzie hadn't caught up with him yet. And that was definitely not something she had the clearance to talk about with the CBI.

MacKenzie frowned. "Right." Another shrug. "It's still pretty hard to make strangulation look like an accident."

"But accidents happen," she said. "A guy goes out for a swim, gets tangled in the swimming line, manages to keep his head above water as he tries to untangle himself but it cuts off his air supply, and he dies."

Both agents were studying her like a bug that tried to salsa dance. She shrugged helplessly. "It's happened before. Last time was in 2067 during a minitriathlon at the beach. Run a mile, bike a mile, swim a mile. Cory Andrews was a seventeen-year-old high-school junior and in the lead until he swam into a fishing line. The crew on the rescue boat got to him in minutes, but he was already unconscious.

"After that, the mayor ran on a campaign to clean up the beaches. It was all over the news during fishing season or whenever the vote to up the cost of fishing licenses comes up."

Agent Rose grimaced. "So, there's a chance someone could have tried to copycat the accident? Wonderful."

"I wouldn't look at local suspects first," Mac said. "Whoever did this didn't check the tide tables to make sure the body was washed out to sea."

A perfectly shaped eyebrow rose over Agent Rose's brown eyes. "Unprofessional. Opportunistic. Maybe accidental? A kidnapping gone wrong?"

"Maybe," Agent MacKenzie said. "The guy was

wearing a university T-shirt from one of their intercollegiate teams. I figured he's probably a student, so I'm checking the class lists now. I should have a name and address within the hour."

Agent Rose nodded.

Agent MacKenzie leaned his chair back and put his hands behind his head. "Sam, this isn't a casual killing. It takes a lot of force to choke someone with a plastic bag. You don't do that to a random stranger."

Ivy said, "Maybe it was a robbery. Maybe he had something the killer wanted. I mean, I know it's too early to connect the two, but that home invasion at Basilwood Apartments last week was violent, too. And all they wanted was Dr. Troom's computer." Henry had called her first, but she'd been pushed off the case. "Maybe it's the weather. It seems like the town is attracting crazies lately.

Agent Rose tilted her head to her shoulder and back. "And Henry. If he hadn't been at work, who knows what would have happened."

"Who would want anything to do with Henry?" Agent MacKenzie asked. "He's a nice guy, but it's not like he's still working under a defense contract—" He snapped his mouth shut with an audible click.

Agent Rose was giving him a look that said volumes in a language Ivy didn't know. They were remembering something, a shared something, that was making the pieces fall into place for them.

"It's not likely," Agent Rose said.

"Bet you a dollar?" MacKenzie challenged her. He stood up.

Agent Rose folded her arms. "We'll see. Get the autopsy done and get me this kid's name."

He held up a hand in surrender and dragged his chair in the direction of his office. "As you wish."

"Officer Clemens?"

"Yes, ma'am?"

"Will the chief object to your working this case? It won't be glamorous, but this is a quiet district with few resources, and I need someone to check the beach. I don't want to start a manhunt if this really is just a tragic accident with a fishing line."

"I won't be missed." She was starting to realize just how much she said that, and wondered if it might be a self-fulfilling prophecy.

As if wondering that herself, Agent Rose raised an eyebrow. "I'm sure you would be. Make sure to check in at the precinct and report back here before calling it a day. Even if you find nothing, that matters."

"Yes, ma'am." Ivy nodded a quick good-bye to Agent Rose and hurried out the door.

Her hero wasn't everything she wanted her to be, but then again, heroes probably never were. Agent Rose was still an excellent agent, and it seemed like she was helping open a new path for Ivy.

CHAPTER 37

> *"As decoherence approaches, the future becomes a sharp point, the sword upon which dreams die."*
>
> ~ excerpt from the writings of the
> rebel poet Loi Liling I1—2069

Day 206/365
Year 5 of Progress
(July 25, 2069)
Central Command
Third Continent
Prime Reality

Several years ago, when Mac had gotten into reading apocalypse literature, Sam had tried a few. Breann Zander's *Absent Bridge* about a gear-fueled sorceress fighting genetically altered humans in the wastelands of the Outback had left her bored although the movie was good. What she had liked was *Death by the Cottonwood* by Myra Lejean.

The book opened in a dusty, dark city surrounded

by a storm, and even if it was really the protagonist's depression-driven nightmare, that's all Sam could think of when she saw what was left of Birmingham. How had Lejean put it?

Shrouds of darkening clouds spun around the city, quickly coiling like the hangman's noose around the dead man's throat. Buildings rose sharply, cutting into the sky and making it bleed black rain...

Perhaps the author had been traveling through iterations when she wrote it. Or maybe she'd been a node and dreamt of it. Either way, the description was spine-tinglingly accurate.

Broken towers, the tombstones of a forgotten civilization, stretched skyward as an ugly brown cloud of pollution circled. In time, Sam had no doubt, the toxins would win. Everyone here was living in a toxic crypt of their own making.

Landon clucked his tongue. "Like the view?"

"My Birmingham is beautiful. Called the city of dreams." The first Muslim-American president was raised there. Sanaa Mian quoted Martin Luther King Jr. more than the Constitution. She'd come and gone before Sam was old enough to pay attention, but even in the Commonwealth, Birmingham was known as The City of Dreams. "How can anyone be happy here?"

"You have a better option?"

She hesitated. Taking them all with her wasn't feasible but abandoning them hurt. "Maybe." Maybe she could work out a trade deal. Give this iteration samples of the pollution-absorbing algae and trees that had been developed in Mexico in 2058. Offhand, she didn't remember the name of the inventor, only that he'd been born with a genetic disease and survived in such a way that there were at least three biopics about him.

"We'll think of something."

Landon sneered at her, at the landscape, at life in general.

Sam licked her lips. "You said there's a door there?"

"Somewhere in the city," Landon said with a nod. "Me and mine, we don't go out there much. Not anymore. I used to have some contacts." He shook his head with a closed-off expression. "Last few months, things have gone sour. No more convoys out. Not much communication. Used to be that when we raided the stores, someone came for us. Now they act like nothing happened."

"Why?"

He shook his head. "Something about a decoherence, whatever that means. There were posters up last time I was there. Might be a social movement."

"Who actually runs things?"

"Central Command." Landon pointed to a distant peak of a tower. "That is 156 floors, goes nearly a mile underground, and the base is big."

Sam looked at him in confusion.

Landon shrugged. "I've seen bits and pieces, but rumor says it takes all day to walk across."

"Probably only if you walk slow. It's, what, ten miles from here? Maybe a bit more?"

"Thirteen."

"Right, so unless it's lopsided, or this area touches the base, it's not that big. It might be a couple of city blocks wide." But it wasn't likely if this Birmingham was like hers. Alabama had a complex underground water system. The limestone sometimes gave way, creating sinkholes. It wasn't a stretch to imagine a densely populated building digging down to access the water, but they couldn't get far if they wanted to keep the building standing.

A thought came to her. "What kind of security do they have?"

"See the clouds?"

"Yeah."

"That's the security. If the wind doesn't get you, the air will. Nothing travels far unless they use the tunnels."

"Which should mean the tunnels are heavily guarded."

"By who?" Landon laughed. "Central Command doesn't think about tunnels. They don't go below the top levels unless there's an emergency. The people, they're starving. Everyone's on rations. Everyone's scared."

She would be, too, if she were planning on staying in this hellscape. "How do you even function?"

"Like people."

"This is . . . anarchy. There should be solutions."

"Yeah, the little door to another world," Landon said. "If you're one of the elite, you can leave anytime you want, do anything you want, and come back here."

Sam nodded. "Vacation in another reality. It's not an original idea, but why not." Somewhere in the murky depths of time, a young Emir must have been a very tortured individual. Only someone with an obsessive need for control would make a machine to change history. "All right, million-dollar-question time: Can you get me in?"

"Sure can," Landon said with a smile. "I even have a way for you to get to the top."

"Oh?"

He pulled a chunky square computer from the satchel tied to his thigh. "Here." He pushed a series of buttons, and Sam's face appeared.

It wasn't exactly her face. The woman glaring at her was a good thirty pounds lighter, a bit paler, and had a thin white scar on her chin. "So she is here."

"Yup. Commander Samantha Rose of Central Command. She's a bit of a celebrity," Landon admitted. "When the program first went into effect five years ago, she was on all the news feeds. Convinced people to move to the big cities. Said everyone was safer if they packed themselves together and took action for a better future."

She could see a twisted version of herself saying that. Especially a young, idealistic version. "I'm just shooting from the hip here, but I'd guess she has government ties."

"Her father is a bigwig in the world government. Lead orator or something like that. Not a voting member of the Council, but he has influence."

"And he's charismatic." Was charismatic in her history—right up until he decided to start abusing painkillers. An old twinge of guilt stabbed her like a rusty knife jabbing an old scar. He'd made his choices. She'd made hers. The first time she'd gone to his rescue. The second, she realized he would let her drown to save himself, and so she'd let go.

Landon was watching her. "Problems?"

"Memories."

"Nothing good?"

"Plenty of good ones, but that one was bad." She sighed. "What's your plan for getting Commander Rose out of the way?"

"Taser," Landon said. "Ever heard of one?"

"Yup, I even know how to use it."

"That's the plan."

"Tase her and stuff her in a closet?" Sam raised an eyebrow. "That's not going to give me much time."

He shrugged. "I'm going in with you. I can smuggle her out."

Jane Doe's broken face rose up in Sam's memory. "What would you do with her?"

"Nothing worse than I did to you." He frowned with a defensive curl of his lip. "I treated you just fine. You shouldn't have any complaints. I fed you."

"True."

"Senturi was on Commander Rose's team. If anyone can find him, she can."

"And then you get to escape to this happily-ever-after he promised you."

Landon had the good grace to look embarrassed. "I'm not saying it's heaven, but it sounds a sight better than this. Sunshine. Fields with grass. You can't tell me it's better if I stay here."

"No I can't," she said. "When do we leave?"

"Soon as the sun starts to set. It's too hot during the day. But once it's down, it's just you, me, the dog, and lots of walking."

Bosco wagged his tail with joy.

CHAPTER 38

> *"As decoherence approaches, the future becomes a sharp point, the sword upon which dreams die."*
>
> ~ excerpt from the writings of the
> rebel poet Loi Liling I1—2069

Saturday March 22, 2070
Florida District 8
Commonwealth of North America
Iteration 2

Ivy pulled her car to the side of the road and leaned her head against the steering wheel. One hastily heated portion of the spaghetti pulled from the freezer. and a shot of an Extra Energy Lime drink did not make up for having been awake for nearly twenty hours.

"Patroller?" the dispatcher's voice floated through the car like a ghost.

"This is Officer Clemens. I'm in the armpit of nowhere following lead 391. Sending GPS coordinates now."

"GPS coordinates received, Officer," the dispatcher said. "Check-in scheduled for twenty minutes from now."

"Check-in scheduled," Ivy agreed. "Exiting the car now." She slammed the door shut on the dispatcher's response. Missing person's cases were the worst. She didn't know if Devon Bradet was trying to get attention, or if he'd just snapped in the wake of Hurricane Troom's life, but this was ridiculous. She was in the ball sack of nowhere, and Bradet was probably sleeping off his tantrum at a friend's house.

Ivy pulled her windbreaker over the thin body armor she'd been issued and looked out over the palmettos framed by moonlight and stars. There was worse weather for a manhunt than 60 percent humidity and low seventies with a sea breeze.

Stretching and yawning, she rubbed her eyes. There was no way someone cruising along A1A at fifty miles an hour had seen anything specific enough to send a real officer out here. Purple shirt, maybe maroon? *Right*. At best, the driver had seen a white guy walking along and called it in hoping to get some of the reward money. What she was probably going to find was a guy planning to do some fishing in Ponce Inlet who looked nothing like Bradet and didn't want her around.

Which meant she was going to go wander through Mosquito Central with a flashlight for the next twenty minutes, like it or not. Flicking her flashlight on, she started humming Top 40 songs in a desperate bid to stay awake.

She was mumbling the high note of the chorus "Clone It If You Want to Keep It" when she reached the mile marker where the tipster said they'd seen Bradet. Sure enough, it was dead center in the bridge. Exactly where a fisherman would stop to drop a line before dawn.

Kicking some gravel aside, she tried to see anything that would convince dispatch the lead had found them a fisherman. A faded candy wrapper, a torn flip-flop, but nothing that indicated someone had set down a bucket or gutted a fish here. Maybe the driver had seen a drunk.

Or nothing at all.

Yawning again, she shined her flashlight down the far side of the bridge. It arced across the water and caught on the squared lines of a man-made building. She checked her watch: seventeen minutes to check-in.

No one with half a brain would sleep under the bridge with the fire ants and rotting fish, but a pickled drunk might. And the old road leading off into the mangroves would be her first pick if she wanted to hide a body out here. Under the bridge, the crabs and ants would pick a body clean in days.

She walked down the slope of the bridge. Dropping over the side into the soft sand, she was swarmed by midges and the smell of rotting bycatch. Pulling her jacket over her nose, she shined her light around the sand. There was nothing but some sea grass marking the high-tide line and ghost crabs scuttling away from her intrusive presence.

With a glance at her watch, she looked up toward the old road. It curved west behind a copse of fiddlewood shrubs to a broken wooden sign where the faded words SPRUCE CREEK were still legible. Back in, what—'64? '65? Something like that—there'd been rumors of the Spruce Creek Cannibal. Ol' Crazy Ivan, a Shadow who had gone mad, run off to the swamps to live off fish guts, and ate tourists.

Nine minutes to check-in.

Crazy Ivan versus Crazy Ivy . . . she touched the phone in her pocket and wished Miss MacKenzie were around. It would be nice to have a partner right about now. She looked up the gravel hillside to the bridge. It was less than a half-mile sprint back to the car. A scraped knee was a risk, but she ran every day, and if she couldn't get away from an imaginary, aging, homeless clone, she didn't deserve her badge.

Stretching a knot out of her neck, she walked toward the old bait shack. The roof was missing and so was one wall, but the words BAIT AND CHIPS were still visible on the broken sign. Spiderwebs made a maze of the dried winter stalks of grass and decaying wooden poles that were probably meant to define the original parking lot.

An abandoned airboat listed at the edge of the water, rusted, but it looked like it still had an engine. It was worth checking out.

With one last sweep of her flashlight, she climbed back up the hill for check-in. She was climbing over the bridge rail when she heard something in the distance. Maybe just an echo or a frog jumping onto the old boat.

Frowning at the darkness, she waited.

A flock of roosting birds took off a half mile north along the old road.

She ran to the car as the dispatch line lit up.

"Patroller?"

"This is Officer Clemens," Ivy said. "I've checked under the bridge."

"Nothing there?" dispatch asked.

"Nothing but bycatch." She hesitated. "There's an old shack around the bend. A bait shop. I'm going to walk down the road a bit to see if there are signs that anyone was here."

"Check-in in twenty," dispatch said.

"Check-in in twenty," Ivy agreed. "But it shouldn't take that long." Back in her air-conditioned apartment, there was a soft blanket and a firm mattress waiting for her. Reaching into the car's open window, she grabbed her water bottle and took a swig.

The night was unnaturally silent. The cicadas had fallen still, and even the bats had fled.

Ivy tightened her grip on the flashlight. One of her first instructors had said a good flashlight was a solid investment. Solid was the key word. Hers weighed over two pounds. Right now, it was the only protection she had from whatever was out there.

Dry grass, yellowed by drought and made brittle under the winter sun, crackled under her feet. Every step sounded like a cacophonous march.

Something thudded. At the very edge of hearing, she got the cadence of a human voice.

She shined the light into the carcass of the bait shack but saw nothing except the bones of a memory. Turning quietly, she surveyed the rest of the wreckage. Dilapidated wooden parking columns, a weed-choked path to the landing, and the boat. It wasn't nearly as old as the rest of these ruins.

"Hello?" Ivy said to the darkness, furious with herself that her voice wavered. She squared her shoulders. "This is Officer Clemens of the New Smyrna PD. If you're out there, show yourself." A cricket chirped. "Please?"

A muffled thud, and in the silver spill of moonlight, the airboat rocked ever so slightly.

Skidding across the loose gravel of the old parking lot, she ran to the boat. "Hello?"

A thump this time, as if someone was kicking.

"Hold on," Ivy ordered the mysterious occupant. Procedure said one officer should stay to help a trapped or injured person, the other should call it in. But she didn't have a partner.

She gritted her teeth and swallowed her curse. Raging against the department's policy of using her like a robot rather than a person wouldn't do any good. She clipped her flashlight to her belt, pulled out the phone Miss MacKenzie had given her, and with it pressed between her ear and shoulder, she climbed onto the unstable vessel.

"If this is an emergency," a recorded voice told her, "please dial 911."

Ivy rolled her eyes and slid one cautious foot across the warped floorboards of the boat. It looked deeper than it should have. Almost as if . . . her foot sank between rotting boards and caught in a hidden compartment.

Lucky her, she'd found a smuggler's old boat. They'd built the floor up to hide contraband from the Coast Guard.

"If this is a medical emergency," the synthesized voice said, "please press two."

She took the phone from her ear, hit two, and let it ring.

The gear box at the far end of the boat rattled. If there was a cat trapped in there, she'd never hear the end of it. Or a gator . . . a momma gator wouldn't climb up on a boat to nest, would it? She was pretty sure she wouldn't.

With a quick tug, she pulled her leg free. She looked over the side and considered climbing back out, but the gear box hung over water, and she was not going wading in the swamps in the dark. That's how tourists went missing.

"This is New Smyrna medical dispatch," a familiar voice said. "My name is Jill, can I have yours?"

"Jill, it's Officer Clemens. I'm away from my car but at my last check-in location." More or less. "I may have found a body."

"May have?" Jill sounded unimpressed.

"I haven't gotten the box open yet."

Jill sighed. "Look, you're wasting time. Is there a medical emergency?"

Ivy took the last slippery step and threw the box open. An unpleasant cocktail of smells of urine and sweat overpowered the stench of rotting fish. Ivy grabbed her flashlight, switched it back on, and shined the beam into the wide eyes of a bedraggled man wearing a torn T-shirt. "Yes! Oh, son of clone, yes. Get an ambulance to my location, stat." She choked on bile. No one should look that dead while still alive.

"O-officer Clemens?" Jill stuttered.

Ivy put the phone on speaker and looked at the mangled person in front of her. "Devon Bradet?" The left side of his face was swollen, lips cracked and bleeding, and his arm broken in at least two places.

He managed to nod.

She reached down and pulled the duct tape off his mouth. "Jill, I've found Devon Bradet. I need an ambulance and a backup unit to my location ASAP. Tell them to put their lights on and not stop for donuts."

"Understood. Units dispatched to your location. They should be there in ten minutes."

Right, and the Statue of Liberty was in Cancun. "Acknowledged." She shut off her phone and leaned down to pull Bradet out of his makeshift coffin.

Bradet struggled to keep his balance. He weighed more than she, but she was able to prop him up like a crutch.

"Help is on the way, Mr. Bradet. Just . . ." The old boat tipped under their combined weight. "We're just going to ease off. Okay. Can you sit on the side and swing your legs over? I'll help you get down."

His good hand squeezed her shoulder as he swung a leg over to straddle the boat edge. "They're near." It was a grunt.

"Near? Who's near?" Fear clutched her like a nightmare monster, squeezing her heart and freezing her lungs. "Help is near," she said, forcing every ounce of confidence into the words.

He wasn't unconscious, and she'd check his pulse when they got off this death trap, but she was pretty sure he hadn't lost too much blood. Bradet had gone missing the previous evening, so at most he'd gone all day without food or water. It had been nearly seventy degrees all day, but he was conscious, which meant he hadn't been in the locked box the whole time.

His grip tightened, and he swayed. "Kill me. Near. They'll kill me." The words slipped through his blood-cracked lips with a lisp.

"The people who did this to you are near? Who were they? Can you identify them?"

His head fell to his chest in a nod, but he said nothing.

"Okay, well, we don't need to worry about that right now," she lied. "I'm a police officer." An unarmed one. Even her Hello Kitty pocketknife was at home. She had the flashlight, the steel-toed boots she'd started wearing on patrol last year, and the self-defense moves she'd picked up at a YMCA class.

We are going to die.

She climbed over the side of the slowly collapsing boat and held up her hands for Bradet. "Go ahead and drop. I'll catch you."

If he'd been more alert, he would have realized he outweighed her by too much for her to catch him with ease. He didn't, and when he landed, Ivy fell back, twisting her leg enough to make her wince.

"Okay. Good. Can you stand up?" She pushed him back on his knees and took the chance to check his pulse. It was high but strong enough. There was probably internal bleeding.

Ivy pushed to her feet, dragging Bradet with her. "We are going to take ten steps to that old bench there."

In the shadows away from her flashlight, someone chuckled. All the hairs on the back of her neck stood on end.

"We're going to die," Bradet whispered. "They told me. They want Henry, but I can't find Henry. We're going to die."

Ivy patted his arm. Her hand came away sticky with blood. "Just . . . just be calm. Help is on the way." If the backup unit got here, and she was dead, she was going to haunt them.

The boat rocked forward, nearly falling on them.

"Hello, little girl," said a voice from the shadows.

Ivy's jaw tightened, and despite the surprise, her training and confidence had her stand up straight. Loudly, she called, "Hello? You're the big bad wolf, I presume. Is that how this story goes?" She tightened her grip on her flashlight. "My name is Officer Ivy Clemens," she said as she stood up. "Want to walk into the light and introduce yourself?"

A muscular man with buzz-cut hair and a wicked-looking fillet knife stepped up to the boat. "Name's Donovan, and I like killing cops."

"Wow. Great intro. You use that pickup line on all the girls?" Ivy smiled as her hand slipped to her phone. She turned the volume down and dialed 911. "Nice knife. Compensating for something, Donovan? You come out here to Spruce Creek to do a little late-night fishing? Using my buddy Bradet here as gator bait maybe?" Cold sweat beaded her forehead. *Stall. Stall. Stall. Help can't be more than five minutes away. Twenty if they stop for a snack.*

Donovan chuckled. "Why don't you come down here? Pretty girl like you, I'll make it quick. Slit your throat."

"Your people skills need work."

"Considering how much I dislike people, not so much." Donovan walked toward around the bow of the boat, moonlight shattering off the knife blade like broken glass.

Ivy pushed Bradet behind her. "I have a backup unit and an ambulance on the way. Don't be stupid. Put your knife down."

"You hear any sirens? See any lights? No? That means I'm taking *him,* and that ambulance is taking *you* to the morgue."

His first kick knocked her flat on her back. He followed up with his knife hand.

Ivy kicked back, arching her back and slamming both booted feet into his chest. Donovan staggered backward. She lunged at his legs, missed, and fell in the dirt.

Donovan dropped to his knees on her back, driving the air out of her. He chuckled as he pulled her braid from her throat. A heavy hand pushed her face down into the grass.

Ivy choked, tensing, and then hot blood splashed on her neck. The weight on her back lifted, and she pushed up, shaking. Rolling over, she saw a nightmare in the spotlight of her fallen flashlight; a body on the ground and Donovan standing over it.

"Bradet?"

A muffled scream made her turn. Bradet was standing where she'd left him.

Donovan was standing over the body holding a combat knife now.

And the body was . . . Donovan.

She scrambled to her feet. "What the hell?"

Donovan, the other one, stepped toward her. "I can help you." He was leaner than the first one, with a wild look in his eyes and dried blood on his hands.

She shook her head and stepped back, nearly tripping over her flashlight. It seemed dangerous to reach for it, but she did, grabbing her only weapon and shaking off the fire ants that came with it. The sharp stings of their bites were the only thing that convinced her she hadn't fallen asleep in the patrol car. "Who are you?"

"Donovan," the man said calmly, as she scooted back to Bradet.

"What, like a clone of him? Or was he a clone of you?"

"He was my other self."

"Okay." *Not okay.* "I'd rather deal with Crazy Ivan the Cannibal, but sure." She grabbed Bradet's wrist. "We're leaving. You just . . . stay. Or go. I-I don't care which."

Donovan walked toward her with slow, deliberate steps. "You're coming with me."

"No." Ivy shook her head, quick, jittery shakes. "I don't see that happening."

"You're the red-haired woman."

She took another step back. "I'm *a* red-haired woman. We're really not that uncommon."

"You're mine."

"Oh. Oh, hell no." Here she was on familiar ground. "I am no one's property. Not yours. Not Jenna's. No one's."

Donovan reached to grab her, and she brought her flashlight down on his head. Hard.

He dropped to his knees. She stomped on his hand, driving it into the tide-dampened ground. Her knee caught his nose. For good measure, she hit him over the head again.

"Run," she told Bradet, pushing him toward the road.

"Can't . . . can't run." He swayed as he spoke.

Ivy grabbed his arm and put it over her shoulder, half carrying him, half propping him up. "We're leaving. Now."

Donovan wasn't unconscious, just stunned. In another minute, he'd have adrenaline enough to work through the broken nose and come after her.

Bradet fell down in front of her. Ivy picked him up by the armpits, dragging him into a standing position. "Up the hill. It's not much. My car is right there on the highway." But it was "much." He was heavy, a good thirty pounds more than she weighed, and barely walking.

He turned to look at Donovan scrambling to get up. "He's going to kill us."

"If he tries, I'll hit him again." She brandished her flashlight like a sword, but her legs were trembling. As if to echo that sentiment, the beam of light quivered, blinked, and faded, leaving them alone in the moonlight.

"We're going to die," Bradet repeated in a quiet whisper.

"You're in shock," Ivy said. She glanced over her shoulder. Donovan was watching them, the shadows of night making his face a harsh mask, but he wasn't following.

They reached the crest of the small hill.

Bradet sagged against her.

Ivy looked up and down the road. "I don't . . . never mind. Just across the bridge. There's a little gravel parking lot. And backup is coming." Backup had probably stopped for burgers and fries at Kelli's Kajun Kitchen, and she was going to give them hell about it.

Headlights flared up ahead. For the briefest moment, she hoped it was backup; then she saw the license plate. It was her car. Someone had stolen her car and was approaching at a reckless speed.

At the last second, she pulled Bradet to the relative safety of the guardrail. Nothing but a hand span of cement between them and the inky inlet below. Ivy looked down at the dark water. In his condition, Bradet couldn't swim. If they jumped, he'd die, and she'd be back down with Donovan.

The car's tires squealed on the asphalt as the driver turned sharply. It rushed toward them, then stopped, with screeching tires and the smell of burning rubber. The window rolled down, and a man leaned forward. "Hello."

Ivy's jaw clenched in anger. "That's. My. Car."

The driver looked casually at the lit dashboard and the torn-out dispatch radio. "It needs repairs."

"Get out. I'll make sure you get the mechanic's bill." She stepped in front of Bradet.

"That's not how I work."

"You are under arrest."

The driver shook his head.

Bradet screamed, and there was a sudden draft of chilly night air behind her where he had been. She turned to see Donovan stalking toward them. Bradet crouched on the ground beside her.

The man in the car tilted his head. "That's not my partner."

"Your partner have a fillet knife?"

He nodded.

"He's dead. This is the other Donovan."

The man in the car grunted. "Give me that one"—he stabbed a finger at Bradet—"and I'll run that one over for you." He pointed at the approaching Donovan. "Life for a life."

"I am Officer Clemens of the New Smyrna Police Department. You are under arrest. He is under arrest. Bradet may be under arrest. I haven't decided yet, but I think I can charge him with Loitering with Intent to Annoy. You are all under arrest!" she shouted.

"It's only a law if you can enforce it," the man said. "And you can't." He lifted a strange gun from the seat behind him. *"Vaya con Dios, Oficial Clemens."*

Sirens screamed as backup rounded the corner and sped toward them.

Ivy glared at the man in her stolen car. "Pull that trigger, and you won't have time to get away." Donovan, or whoever he was, was already running back to the swamp. "Go ahead."

The man in the car snarled, then stomped on the gas.

She had no doubt the car would be dumped in the next town. But, for now, she let it go. Crouching down beside Bradet, she squeezed his hand. "See that? The ambulance is here. All you have to do is keep breathing. Just keep breathing. It's all going to be okay."

Even if nothing about this makes any sense.

CHAPTER 39

"What would the Borgias do?"

~ engraved on a family crest created in
during the Neo Renaissance I3—2061

Day 206/365
Year 5 of Progress
(July 25, 2069)
Central Command
Third Continent
Prime Reality

She was shaking again. Even the sleeping pills couldn't stop her nightmares. Every time she slept, she dreamt of dying. The memory of her death haunted her waking hours. Colored every shadow.

The only thing that offered her a respite was running, burning all her energy until she collapsed into the cold bed at night. With the gym closed as part of lockdown, she'd taken to running in the empty service tunnels under Central Command. Her footsteps echoed, a steady cadence completely at odds with her racing heart. *It will soon be over*, she repeated to herself. *It will soon be over. It will soon be over.*

Decoherence is coming.

If she could just hold on to her sanity for a few more days, everything she'd done would be worth it. The deaths, the lies, the losses.

She slowed, stopping at one of the old watering fountains to take a drink. The water wasn't as well filtered on this level, and it tasted of rotten eggs, but she found she didn't care. Not about the water, or Donovan, or even Emir. She stared at the brick walls painted white and let her fears soak into the stones.

Shadows flickered down the empty tunnels. A flash of light was followed by the tread of heavy boot steps.

Donovan turned the corner, blood dripping from his nose.

"What happened to you?" Rose demanded, terror rushing back like the recoil of a gun on her shoulder. Fear of invasion and erasure pumped her with adrenaline until the world snapped into sharp focus.

Donovan looked up, and it seemed like he wasn't seeing her at all. His gaze roved through the shadows, catching on the lines of the brick and the shine of the water dispenser. "She's mine!" The shout bounced off the walls.

"Who's yours?" Rose took a step forward before realizing he'd fallen into the abyss he'd always teetered on the edge of. "Captain, report to the infirmary." Her voice cracked with fear.

Donovan charged her, raging forward with his fists leading.

Rose ducked under his initial punch, stuck her leg out and tripped him. That ruined his momentum but didn't knock any sense into him.

Donovan came back, twisting and rising up with a fist aimed at her torso.

Rose took the blow on her shoulder and drove her fist into his gut.

It didn't slow him down. Donovan lashed out with a left hook, a textbook response straight out of their training drills. He always had been stupid.

Catching his arm, Rose pulled, using Donovan's own momentum to throw him into the wall. "I will kill you," she warned. "I might not want to, but I will."

"You ruined it! She's dead. Senturi is dead. This is your fault!" He pushed off the wall, trying to tackle her.

Rose stepped to the side and used her boot to send him sprawling onto the floor, where his head bounced. She took off her belt and tied his hands behind his back while he was still stunned. "You're not in your right mind. I'm going to get the guards. If you're still here when I get back, I'll tell Emir this was pressure brought on by decoherence. If you try to escape or come after me, I'll tell him exactly what you said." She peered at his hands. There was more than his blood there.

Kicking him in the back so his kidneys would remember her threat, she stood. "Think very hard, Captain. Is this really how you want to die?"

With a heavy sigh, she turned... only to see herself watching the tableau with a curiously blank expression.

Rose blinked, shaking her head. She had the nauseating sensation of being in two places at once. Memories that weren't quite hers buffeted her. And then she saw the dog.

"You're Commander Rose?" her other self asked.

"What are you doing here?" The other iterations didn't know about decoherence. All non-Prime threats had been removed. And if this was decoherence... it was wrong. She wasn't supposed to feel like multiple people. She wasn't supposed to feel anything.

Her other self smiled. "I'm here to pick up my husband. I may arrest someone in connection to a series of killings, but I consider that a secondary goal." The woman leaned to the side to look around her. "That man on the ground, what size shoe would you say he'd wear?"

"What?" Rose clutched her stomach as a wave of nausea twisted her insides. Drinking the water down here had been a poor choice.

"Doesn't matter," the other-Rose said with a shrug. "He fits the description of my murder suspect. If he's alive when I'm done, I'll arrest him. If he's not, then I'm just picking up Mac and leaving."

Rose shook her head as she fought the pain. "You can't. He's our node." She hesitated and shook her head again, growing angry. *This is not how I die.* "You should be dead. I collapsed your iteration. I collapsed all the iterations. This morning, the machine was showing only one line." Emir had told her so himself.

He'd sworn it was over.

"Is that what you were trying to do, destroy us?" her other self asked. "You're not very good at it, are you? This makes, what, three attempts? Four? Maybe you should have outsourced to the Marines. You know, for when it absolutely, positively has to be destroyed overnight?" There was a lilt in her voice, a sense of dark humor that stole the foundation of Rose's hate.

"What are we doing?" The memories were growing. Rose stepped back. Maybe the water was poisoned. That would make sense. Fatigue, dehydration, and chemicals in the water were conspiring to make her hallucinate.

The dog stepped forward.

"Why do you have an animal?"

"Because I like dogs, and leaving him with my neighbors seemed like a bad idea since I wasn't sure I'd get back to my iteration," her other self said. "I couldn't leave Bosco alone."

"That's not right." Rose felt dizzy and confused. "You can't just step through like this. You can't change anything. You're a reject. A rogue. Impossible." She shook her head. "You're wrong. Everything you do is wrong." She grabbed her head. It hurt. Everything hurt.

Her other self shrugged. "Next time I go to confession, I'll be sure to mention this." She raised her splat gun with a smile.

"You can't!"
But she did.

Sam watched as Landon caught the other-Sam. Bosco sniffed her, then sat down in disinterest.

"Bit heavier than I was expecting," Landon huffed. "Now what?"

"He needs to be secured for transfer. She needs to be hidden for a day or two. I'll need her uniform and any ID cards or keys she has. Do you think she brought a day planner?"

"To go jogging?" He sounded skeptical.

She untwisted Bosco's leash from her wrist and went to help Landon move the unconscious other-Sam. "I can hope, right? I'm going in with no information about this building, no idea of the layout, and no clue where my husband is. If he were here, he'd kill me."

Landon looked up sharply.

"It's an expression. He wouldn't actually kill me. He'd just be very frustrated with my choices right now."

"He wouldn't be wrong."

"Of course not. But, then again, if he were here, I wouldn't be hunting him down. Would I?"

"Suppose not."

They hefted the other-Sam to a metal sledge that they'd found in the corridor.

Sam rubbed dirt off her hands as she walked over

the man her other self had beaten and tied up. He was glaring. "Donovan? I thought I recognized you."

"I am going to kill you." His words were calm and cold. It was a fact in his mind, not a guess.

She squatted down as Bosco trotted over to stand guard. "How many women who looked like us did you kill?" she asked. "Lexie Muñoz is the only one I can tie you to right now—there were witnesses—but I bet my badge your boot fits my other victims."

"They were nothing. You are nothing." His pupils were dilated to pinpoints of darkness. Wherever Donovan was, it wasn't reality.

"Where's Mac?" Sam asked.

Donovan squirmed, trying to stand. With a scream of inarticulate rage, he spat at her.

Sam stood up, wiping the spittle off her cheek. "The urge to kick him in the face is really quite strong," she told Landon.

"It's going to be a pain pushing her back. With him on there?" Landon shook his head. "Do they need to live?"

"I'm generally opposed to murdering people."

"It'd be easier is all I'm saying."

"Very pragmatic." She frowned down at the sleeping Commander Rose. "Do you still have that Taser?"

Landon nodded. "You want to go first?"

"At this point, it's like shooting a rabid dog," she said over Donovan's shouts of protest.

"So you want the real gun?" Landon said, reaching for his pack.

Sam shook her head. "No, just tase him. I do not have time to hide a body."

"Why hide it?" Landon asked as he pulled the Taser and shot Donovan in the leg. "Soon as the next opening comes, me and mine are leaving for the Shadow Prime. You're leaving. So who would track us down?"

"Dead bodies get noticed." Sam nodded to Donovan's hands as she reached for his legs. "You leave one lying around long enough, it's bound to cause trouble."

They carried Donovan over to the sledge and dropped him beside the other-Sam, his feet dragging on the ground.

Landon shook his head. "Wouldn't get noticed before we get gone is all I'm saying."

"You're going to push the same button to haul them out as you're going to push to haul yourself out," Sam said. "The extra weight won't slow you down. Now, I need her uniform, I think." Shooing Landon around the corner, she unlaced the commander's boots, stripped her down to her base layer of jogging shorts and tank top, then switched clothes with her. The uniform was heavy. How the other-Sam had run comfortably in it she wasn't sure. But it fitted, and that, she told herself, was the main thing. "Oh!" She reached down and grabbed Melody Chimes's truncheon from her pocket. The faded Auburn sticker gave her hope.

"You can come back out," she called to Landon.

He turned the corner, did a double take, then frowned. "Your hair is wrong."

Sam pulled hers into a high bun on her head. "How's this look?"

"Anyone who knows this lady well is going to know you aren't her. Not once you get close."

"As long as they don't notice until I'm close enough to knock them out, it doesn't matter. I still have me splat gun. I could use it." *Could* being the operative word. If she could get away with not hurting anyone else, she would. "And I have Bosco."

Landon didn't look convinced. "How many of those little magic bullets you got? Besides, that dog may look fierce, but he's not vicious."

"The splat gun has nine bullets left."

He nodded. "So, I'll expect you to come running with a fully armed battalion chasing you?"

"It will only be because they want to remind me of their love."

Landon's eyes went wide as his lips rolled into his mouth and vanished. After a long moment, he asked, "Is everyone in your reality this crazy?"

"Nah. I'm one of the normal ones."

"Is that supposed to reassure me? 'Cause it doesn't."

"Don't worry about it," Sam said. She realized she was using the voice she usually reserved for tourists and felt a little guilty. With a little placating smile, she said, "Everything's going to be fine. If all goes well, I won't even bother you again. You can jump to the Shadow Prime. I can go back to my life. It'll be great." She rubbed her neck. She had a headache building and an uncanny sense of déjà vu about this whole place.

He grunted and shook his head. "Fine. Help me load him up?" He nodded to the cursing Donovan.

"Tase him first," Sam said. "Otherwise, he's likely to bite."

Five minutes later, both the unconscious other-Sam and Donovan were loaded up.

"I'll get them to the rail line, load them there, and the auto transport can haul them the rest of the way."

"Be careful with them," Sam warned. "I don't trust either of them farther than I can throw them."

"One of them is you!"

Sam nodded. "I know, that's why I don't trust her. I fight like a mongoose when I'm cornered."

In Florida—her first time through 2070—Sam had found a warehouse full of paintings done by Dr. Emir. As Mac walked into Emir's private office in the Prime, he realized this was the parallel. The paintings weren't all the same. There were more cities and fewer depictions of Sam, but the thought behind it was the same. Emir had tried to capture the memory of the worlds he'd destroyed in his conquest of time.

Emir watched him as he walked a circuit around the room before coming to the oversized desk Emir hid behind. The doctor steepled his fingers together. "What do you think?"

"What a waste," Mac said.

Emir cocked his head to the side. "Of paint? Of time?"

"Of life. Of possibility. Look," Mac pointed to a painting of a glass-and-steel building shaped like a ship's sails. "Where was that? Who created it? What happened to the architect and the builders? To all the people who worked or lived there? They're gone, aren't they? Lives wasted. Because of you."

"There can only be one iteration of each person," Emir said.

"Why?"

The doctor blinked in surprise. "It is a matter of logic."

"Of hubris," Mac argued. "I know two variations of the same person can share a timeline because I've been living side by side with my younger self for five years. We shared an apartment for a few days. Neither of us imploded."

"It isn't safe," Emir said. "All these worlds were flawed."

"All worlds are flawed. That's why I'm here, isn't it? Because something's gone wrong in your perfect world?" It was supposition only. The command tower had been quiet for the past twelve hours. The cantina had been empty when he'd gone for food. Jane was missing. Everything about the situation said trouble with a capital T. Emir's summons was all the confirmation he needed that the Prime had just gone to hell in a handbasket.

Emir turned at his desk. "We reached decoherence this morning. These pieces of art are all that remain of those worlds. My memories have become imaginings."

The spark of hope that had kept him going was extinguished with one thought: Sam was gone.

Mac couldn't cry. He couldn't even find a nameable emotion. Only a coldness that swallowed him whole and left him empty.

The last time he'd felt like this, he'd been carrying a dead soldier across his back in the deserts of Afghanistan. Then, all that mattered was putting one foot in front of the other as he tried to outrun death. Now there was nowhere to run. His eye twitched.

"You shouldn't have said that."

"I shouldn't have warned you?" Emir's patronizing grin seemed to mock him. "You would have wanted to know. The decoherence was softer than I imagined. The iterations ran parallel for several hours this morning until they showed up as a thick black line on my machines. There's no more probability fan. We only have one choice, and that is to go forward as we are, with what we have right now."

Mac's hands became white-knuckled fists. It didn't matter what happened. He was going to kill Jane for this. Donovan, too, if he had the chance. Emir. It didn't matter. They'd taken him away from Sam. They'd destroyed the life he'd worked so hard to put back together.

Emir's explanations became white noise.

Memories of Jane Doe's broken body slipped through his mind like a mission briefing. A hit here. A boot there. It all fit.

The dehydration and abuse he'd seen on her corpse wasn't from imprisonment as he'd assumed, it was from living here. This iteration had leached the very marrow from her bones. Now they were weak enough for him to snap them with icy precision. Only, this time, she wouldn't be buried in Alabama District 3 because she had destroyed it.

Humanity better pray there was a probability fan Emir couldn't see, some rogue iteration spinning off by itself, because he was about to burn this one to the ground.

Donovan rolled sideways as the auto transport rattled away from him. He stayed still, hoping no one noticed, and as the auto transport turned a corner, he stood up. He was torn, for a moment, between chasing after the unconscious Rose and the man guiding the sledge, or going back to Central Command. The need to treat his injuries won out. There'd always be another Rose to kill.

Especially today.

His head was still ringing when he had returned from the rogue iteration to the Prime, but he swore he'd seen two Roses after the commander tied him up.

Gripping the belt strap between his teeth, he pulled it loose, freeing his hands.

At a steady jog, he could reach the lower levels of the command tower in good time. He knew the tunnels better than anyone. Knew where the old medical bays were, where the supplies were. From there, he could plan his assault.

It took him less than an hour to clean up, take a few stimulants to clear his head, then he was ready to deal with humans again. He ran a hand over his short hair and looked in the mirror. A little worse for the wear, but he'd looked rougher after a hard day in training. Soldiers weren't meant to look clean cut. Not if they were fighting men.

Donovan pushed a heavy shelf to one side and pulled out a metal wall panel. When he'd brought the old comm kit down here, he'd meant to use it for listening in on Emir's plans. But he'd also given Senturi permission to use it to contact the Council as needed. He punched in the code from memory.

Gray waves appeared on the screen, then the tight face of an older woman. "Who are you?"

"Captain Donovan, reporting in for Senturi."

She nodded, iron-gray curls catching the light. "Is he ready for us?"

"Yes." The lie slipped off his tongue with ease.

"Do we have the coordinates?"

"As soon as we have the control room, coordinates will be provided." The second door in the badlands worked well for getting in and out of the Shadow Prime, but he needed to find the red-haired woman. He swayed on his feet, the memory of his dead-self holding her mixing with the memory of the same woman trying to cave in his skull as he rescued her from himself.

"Captain?" the Councilwoman asked. "Are you in good health?"

He wasn't, but that was not for her to know. "Yes, ma'am. When will your troops arrive?"

"They are in place and will breach the command tower in eight minutes."

"I'll go meet them," Donovan said.

"To the Council goes the victory," the woman said as she signed off.

"And the power." He remembered that line from training. Wiping away fresh blood from his nose, he stared at the metal walls of the medical bay. In retrospect, he should have waited to kill Senturi. It would have made retaking the control tower easier.

He shook his head and went to the stairs.

Decoherence was coming—it was the ache in his bones and the confusion in his mind—and there was much to do before the probability fan closed completely.

"Right or left?" Sam asked Bosco. They'd been following signs of habitation—stairs, open doors, litter—and she was fairly certain they were near the top of the tower. But she'd stopped counting floors after thirty.

He sniffed at a door that looked no different to her than the other dozen doors they'd passed.

"Okay, doors are good." She waved the stolen ID in front of the lock, and it swung open revealing six rows of heavily armed SWAT with weapons. There was a moment of stunned silence from both parties, then Sam dodged to the side and hit the lock again. Someone had called in reinforcements.

"Wrong door. Bosco, *chay*."

They skidded around the corner as gunfire sprayed down the hall.

"I told Landon dead bodies would cause trouble. They weren't even dead!" She opened another lock, slammed the doors behind her, and searched desperately for something to barricade it with. The hall was as empty and sterile as an abandoned hospital. "St. Jude, St. Samantha, help. Oh, golly, Bosco. Why did we leave home?"

He sniffed at the door and growled.

Sam snapped her finger and took off running, looking for a side hall or an exit. Anything that would get her away from the police.

Up ahead, a door swung open and slammed shut. Unbelievably, MacKenzie—or at least *some* version of MacKenzie—turned to her.

The rattle of gunfire swallowed her cry.

MacKenzie walked toward her, eyes burning with fury.

"Mac." He didn't recognize her. She wasn't even sure it was her Mac. "Bosco, *tân công*."

The sound of gunfire drew Mac into the hall. He saw Rose running toward him, face full of fear. He was going to push her back at the attackers. Drag them both into the hail of bullets.

Then Bosco knocked him to the ground.

The dog licked his face.

"Off, Bosco, off. You're crushing me."

"Oh my . . ." Sam shook her head in stunned belief. "It *is* you. I found you," she said, as she choked on tears.

Mac held up a hand, and she helped him up.

"Sorry. You looked very not yourself." She ran her hands across his face. "Mac . . ."

There was so much more she wanted to say, but a percussion grenade went off in the distance. She took a deep breath. "I love you. It's good to see you again. Where is the exit of this insane place? There's a SWAT team after me, which is really overkill considering I only knocked out two people."

"What are you doing here?" Mac demanded, grabbing her arm and pulling her away from the sounds of fighting.

"Rescuing you—kind of." She smiled apologetically. "The SWAT team was not planned. I was going to try to sneak in and out."

Emir stepped into the hall, looking around in confusion. "MacKenzie, Rose, what is the meaning of this?"

Sam looked up at Mac, then back at Emir. She shrugged. "There seems to be some technical problems with this evening's entertainment." It was a joke from a TV show she liked, and it went straight over Emir's head.

With a frown, Emir stormed back into his fortress of an office.

"He's going to call for help or come back with a weapon," Mac predicted. "We need to get out of here. The jump room is down this hall. Do you have a key?"

Sam held up Jane's ID. "I borrowed this when I showed up. She's alive, if you're wondering."

"I really don't care." He took the lead, unlocked the jump room, and pulled Sam close as the heavy doors silenced the coup outside.

She was here.

She was *here*.

With him. Gently, he tilted her head back and kissed her, claiming her. Reassuring himself that she was alive and his Sam. Tears stung his eyes and blurred his vision. "You're here."

"I am." She ran a hand through his hair. "I love you."

"I love you, and nothing else matters."

A look of panic suffused her face. "Oh, no. Other things matter. Like the fact that we are leaving, Linsey Eric MacKenzie. I don't care how much this little military-complex life appeals to you. I have eaten the food here. We're not staying."

He laughed. "I don't like it here."

"Oh, thank you. Thank you. Thank you. Thank you." She sighed with relief and smiled. "I saw all the uniforms and everything and thought you would probably fit in."

"I do fit in, but that doesn't mean I want to stay here. There's no beaches. The beds are awful. And you're so right about the food." He shook his head in disgust.

She nodded. "Okay. Do you need to pack anything? Bring a souvenir gun or whatever it is husbands pick up on vacation?"

He brushed her cheek with his thumb. "No. I'm good."

Bosco rubbed against his leg. "You brought the dog?"

"I didn't want to leave him alone if we didn't make it back to the right iteration."

"According to Emir, there are no more iterations."

Sam grimaced. "There was when I left last night." Her face suffused with horror. "Did I kill us? Do you think I caused the collapse by jumping over?"

"I don't care. Emir and Jane kept saying that after decoherence, there was an expansion. I'm willing to believe in that. Come here. I think you can get this machine to work," he said as he walked to the inner door and jiggled it. "Locked."

"Try the swipe card."

The light glowed red.

"Wait," Mac said, "This is a hand-scan door. You have to do it. Um, left hand. Jane always used her left hand here."

Sam reached out her left hand. "It's warm." With a muffled click, the door slid open. "It worked!"

"Of course it did. There are two more doors, and a lock on the machine itself. Left hand for all of them." He checked the corridor behind them, made sure Bosco got through, and forced the door shut. This wasn't a defensible position, and getting caught was out of the question. He looked around, lifting the chairs to see if they were heavy enough to work as weapons if Emir woke up and came after them.

"Here," Sam said with a put-upon sigh as she held out her backpack.

He unzipped it. "Ah, honey, you brought my gun."

"And my splat gun." She unlocked the inner door to the main jump room with the spiraling floor. A dull, purple light filled the room with a sickly glow. "And there is my least favorite piece of technology."

Mac gently pushed her through the door. "Right now it's my favorite. Start it up."

"Do you know how to set where we're going?"

"The last time Jane's team used it, they said there was a convergence—our iteration and theirs are spiraling around each other." He shrugged. "At least we'll be at home."

"But when?"

"Does it matter?"

Sam looked at him, then at the door locking behind them. "Guess not." She held up her hand. "Here we go. Open sesame." She scanned her hand as she'd done on the locks.

The light glowed green, the portal began to swirl faster, and a red light flared on the lock.

"Um . . . Mac . . . it just rejected me."

"Try it again." His heartbeat sped up like the rhythm of soldiers running. Even through the thick walls, he could hear the percussion of the fight. "I think someone is using grenades."

"Not helpful!" Sam said. She scanned it again and shook her head. "It's saying something about 83 percent match?" She looked at him in confusion. "Mac, how can I only be 83 percent me?"

"Maybe this one scans more than genes?"

"But Jane and I are identical. Right? According to Emir's theory, that's what all the parallel evolution was. Same diseases. Same life history. Same broken bones. Same DNA."

His mind raced through a mental file of Sam's life history. He looked up. "The baby."

"What baby?"

"You were pregnant."

"This is not the time to discuss the miscarriage," Sam said angrily.

"I'm sorry, but that's why you aren't identical. That's where you diverged. You married me, and you were pregnant. You're a chimera now."

"What?" She shook her head. "I love being compared to a mythological creature as much as the next girl, but you're gibbering, Mac. I need you to focus."

He shook his head. "During pregnancy, the genes can go both ways. The baby's genes can pass to the mother, making her a mix of her own DNA and her child's."

"And her husband's." Sam grimaced. "That's just weird."

Mac nodded in agreement. "But that's why. Probably. Maybe. This could also be a trap."

Sam gave him a frustrated look. "We should leave. We can go hide out somewhere. Come back another day."

The building shook under them.

"We'll have to fight our way out," Mac said, hefting

the handgun for reassurance. He checked the magazine for ammunition.

Sam rolled her eyes. "It's loaded, but the safety is on."

"Carrying a loaded gun? I've corrupted you."

"Focus, MacKenzie, give me exits," Sam ordered as she pressed her hand against the lock.

"There's a service lift, two stairwells, and the main lift that they're coming from."

"Stairs, then. The lift will be a kill box in a few minutes."

He could have kissed her for that. "What would I do without you?"

"Probably get yourself killed." She pushed him. "Move, MacKenzie. I am not dying in this iteration." She clicked her tongue to grab Bosco's attention, and they ran for the stairs.

Donovan stepped into chaos. Sirens were blaring, people were running, and a medical team was swarming Emir's office. He went to the jump room, following the soldiers in riot gear. Someone had tried to break in.

How MacKenzie had gotten through the locks, he didn't know, but it didn't matter. The machines here had what he wanted.

His computer terminal still accepted his access codes. Emir was so fragging arrogant, he hadn't even considered what would happen if a node led a coup. Even if he'd used small words, it wasn't likely that Emir would have understood.

A machine angrily spat out papers with a wildly oscillating sine wave. Expansion and decoherence chasing each other. If this measured the heartbeat of the universe, the universe was having a heart attack.

Donovan tossed the synthpaper to the side.

Right now, he needed to open a gate to the red-haired woman.

He'd knew where she was. His wife. The perfect woman. With cinnamon freckles and red hair that curled in the humidity . . .

It was going to be a complicated relationship. He could see that. Most relationships fell short of the literary ideal, but that didn't matter. He could explain why his other self had attacked her. There would be questions, but in the end, all she would remember is that he had saved her.

In a few years, they'd be laughing about how they met. Because she loved him.

She had to.

Working quickly, he pulled up the necessary programs to calculate the exit coordinates. Arranging for a portal to open near the Council was difficult. It would require opening multiple portals, with numerous anomalies. The results would be catastrophic in some areas. Already, the computer was warning him of tsunami risks and earthquakes.

Shock waves would obliterate Central Command.

The idea made him smile.

With a quick, light touch, he dismissed the warnings. And then he smiled.

The doors to the control room cracked open, glass spilled in with the sounds of heavy fighting.

"Donovan!" Emir stormed into the room. "What are you doing?"

"I'm doing what nodes are meant to do. Making a choice. Opening the portal."

The machines screamed a warning as the portal turned white.

"Decoherence is here," Emir screeched. "You must stay!"

Decoherence was here. Which was exactly why he had to leave.

The worlds were collapsing. Darkness was closing in, and Donovan stepped into the light, leaving the chaos of destruction behind him.

CHAPTER 40

> *"EXPANSION (n): a period of time when new iterations form and new realities begin to solidify"*
>
> ~ excerpt from *Definitions of Time*
> by Emmanuela Pine, I1

Tuesday April 1, 2070
Florida District 8
Commonwealth of North America
Iteration 2

Director Alexander Loren, head of the CBI in Florida, closed his office door on the lunchtime silence, head filled with the dire predictions of Agent Rose. There was pressure from above to keep a lid on things. To make sure—

The click of his swivel chair turning at the desk made him turn around.

A woman with black hair peppered with white was waiting for him. At his desk. In *his* chair.

"Who are you?"

"The Ghost of Christmas Future," she said. "A future that won't happen unless you listen very closely." She stood, and the sunlight angling through the plastic blind caught her profile in just the right way.

"Agent Rose?"

Her smile was cryptic. "A number of years ago, yes. I was a CBI agent. Not the best or the brightest, but I daresay no one ever questioned my drive. I don't know when to stop. It's one of my defining features."

"You were?" Loren looked at the door. "I saw you leave twenty minutes ago."

"And twenty years ago. Yes. A younger me. A . . . hmm . . . what would be the best way to describe that young Sam? She's a seed, a glorious vessel of potential and drive. You, on the other hand, are something of a dam. A big, fat rock in the road." She moved toward him with the sinuous grace of a snake. "You're a problem, Director Loren."

"Get out of my office this minute, or I will have security arrest you."

One dark eyebrow rose as her lips twitched into the faintest of smiles. "Director, how do you think you can stop me? You don't know where I'm from or when. You are playing with the biggest weapon since the atom bomb, and you're treating it like a Frisbee."

"Ma'am, all this information is classified."

"Sir," she said mockingly, "I wrote the book on that ticking time bomb you're about to detonate. I'm the one who keeps you from going up in a pile of smoke and stupidity."

Loren frowned at her.

"You're not a dumb man, Alex. You didn't become director by playing Yes Man. So, go sit at your desk. The files are there. If you make the right choice, we all live past Thursday. Make the wrong one, and . . ." She shrugged. "I'm here. According to the theory of decoherence and expansion, that means you will make the right choice. Doesn't that give you a warm, fuzzy feeling of accomplishment?"

"I'm calling security."

"Great, tell them to stand here for a decade or two and wait for me." The woman touched something on her wrist and contracted, winking away in a sliver of white light.

For several minutes, Director Loren stood there, watching the empty space with a skeptical frown as he debated going down to the medical section for a quick physical. It sounded like a stress-induced hallucination. But he'd seen the files.

He knew about Emir's machine. And he could smell the faint traces of a floral perfume mixing with the stale-coffee smell of the office.

Lips curving into a snarl, he stalked toward his desk. After a quick sweep for bugs or explosives, he sat gingerly in the chair and reached for his phone.

"Agent Edwin, how may I help you today?"

"Agent Edwin, this is Director Loren. Is Agent Rose in her office?"

"No, sir, she called to say she was driving back about forty minutes ago. Do you want me to patch you through to her car?"

"That won't be necessary. Thank you." Loren hung up the phone.

On his desk, amid the clutter of this latest debacle, was a fresh manila folder with a datpad code and honest-to-goodness wood-pulped paper. He flipped it open with one finger and skimmed the opening paragraph. The words dragged him onward, down the page, and to the end of the thirty-page document.

He closed the folder and pushed it away, not yet ready to make the choices he was being asked to make.

CHAPTER 41

> *"There is only life you should take; your own. Take it forward. Take control. Choose your path and follow your passion until your heart is full."*
>
> ~ from the teaching of Soyala Méihuâ I4—2067

Sunday May 19, 2069
Alabama District 3
Commonwealth of North America
Rogue Iteration

In front of Donovan, the beauties of paradise unfolded. Trees, insects singing in the bushes, flowers, and summer. He opened his arms wide and turned his head up to take in the breathtaking vista of the million stars.

It was a shame Senturi had never lived to see this, but, then again, Senturi wouldn't have fitted into this new world he was creating.

He'd pieced it together slowly, the whole reason the other iteration wasn't collapsing. It hadn't made sense until he realized he was the reason the other iteration survived everything. He was here before Emir, or Rose, or MacKenzie even. He was here at the beginning of the decoherence and the end.

For a moment, he luxuriated in being the center of the universe. If this was how Emir felt all the time, he understood the man's obsession with control. But it wasn't done yet. There were still a few things to do.

If he'd calculated the temporal cyclone correctly, there was a road nearby, and on it, an old man in a truck.

It took a few minutes to find the road, neatly paved with tidy reflective squares sticking up every meter to help drivers navigate the darkness. Donovan stood on the side and waited.

On schedule, the truck appeared as a set of lights on the horizon.

Donovan waved his hand, and the truck slowed to a stop.

The window rolled down. "Hey there, you lost?"

"A little," Donovan lied.

"Where's your car? I can give it a jump."

"Actually, Mr. Robbins, I was hoping I could give you something."

The bushy gray eyebrows on his dark face jumped up in surprise. "You know me?"

"Through a friend of a friend. Someone who said you weren't a fan of the way the country was being run. Someone who said that, for a price, you wouldn't mind taking the night off."

His face wrinkled in a deeply creased frown. "I'm no terrorist, Mr. . . ."

"Call me Donovan. And I'm not a terrorist. I'm an opportunist. Call in sick, give me your phone, and I will give you this." He pulled the money he'd stolen on one of his trips to this iteration out of his pocket. Several of the Rose look-alikes he'd found had been carrying significant amounts of cash. Tips, usually, but cashed-out wages weren't uncommon, either.

He'd been saving them, not sure why, until now. He was going to buy the future.

Mordicai Robbins's eyebrows moved so far up his head, they threatened to encroach on the few wisps still clinging to his balding dome. "Where'd you get that?"

"Donations from concerned citizens. You aren't alone, Mr. Robbins. You aren't the only one who thinks this"—he caught himself from saying iteration—"that this country needs to change. Let me help you be a hero, Mr. Robbins."

"All that for my phone?"

"And a phone call to work telling them you're sick." Donovan held the cash toward the open window. "You take a few days' minivacation, and when you're done, the whole world will be a better place."

Robbins shut off the car. "Sure thing. I could use a break." He dialed his phone. "Hey, Melody, it's ol' Mordicai. Look, honey, I hate to do this, but my back's acting up something awful. Can't seem to get this kink out. You mind if I call Kinsley? She can come on in in my place." He paused, a small smile growing on his face. "Sure thing. Yeah, sweetie. I'll take some aspirin. You be good, you hear? Okay. See you next weekend."

He turned off the phone and gave Donovan a stern look. "That little girl at the lab, Melody Chimes, you leave her alone. Got it? She's good people even though her daddy's got money."

"I won't touch her," Donovan promised. "I won't even go to the lab except for recon. No one will know I was there."

Robbins nodded. "Okay. Toss the cash on the seat. I'll toss you the phone. You sure you don't want a ride?"

"Someone else is picking me up." Donovan reached in the window and dropped the cash on what he guessed from his limited experience was a very nice leather seat. "This is a nice truck."

"Vintage," Robbins said. "I'm a collector." He picked up the cash and flipped through it. "And this is going to give my '47 Akadeem a nice new fuel injector. Thank you, kindly, Mr. Donovan. You have yourself a blessed day, you hear?"

Donovan caught the phone that was tossed to him and smiled as the old man drove away with music pouring out of the truck's rolled-down windows. This was going to be a beautiful life.

He dialed the contact number from memory.

"Agent Marrins," a gruff voice said. "Who's this and why the hell are you calling me this late? There better be a dead body. And not a clone this time."

Donovan looked up. He could all but see the stars aligning. "Agent Marrins, I'm a friend. I want what you want."

"Sleep? Good. Than hang the hell up."

"I want the Commonwealth to end."

There was a poignant silence on the other end of the line.

"I want you to have everything you deserve." A smarter man would have questioned that. Con artists made their livings selling people dreams that disappeared in the morning light. But he'd met Marrins, and the senior agent was not a smart man. He was a greedy, venal, piece of intertemporal flotsam.

"What exactly are you proposing?" Marrins asked.

"What if I told you there was a way to step back in time? Go back to before the Commonwealth formed and stop the vote for unification from ever happening. I could give you dates, names, a list of the things you would need to change to give yourself a better future."

Marrins snorted.

"Right now you're being outshone by a scrawny girl with more money than sense."

"Ain't that the damn truth," Marrins muttered.

"Your staff is made up of what?"

"A girl and a drunk. Gez can't focus for more 'an two minutes straight and probably drinks the pickling juice down in the morgue. Half a wonder he ain't dead yet."

"You could have more. A better career. A better life. With what I'm offering, you could be king." He strung the words out like a fishing line with a tiny, silver hook at the end.

Marrins laughed. "For just a bit a money, I'm sure. You want my life savings, son? It's forty dollars and some change. I ain't never had much mind for putting things away for the future. Or you think I have some stocks to cash out?"

Now Donovan remembered why shooting people was so much easier. And why he'd never run point as an undercover operative in another iteration. He was better at menacing people than talking.

"Agent Marrins—"

A sudden wind snatched his words away. A light was growing in the trees.

Someone was coming for him.

"Agent Marrins, in a few days you'll receive a very urgent call from a man named Dr. Emir."

"Who's he?"

"Here, no one of importance. A scientist. But you'll receive a second call, from another Emir, and that one you must listen to. He is going to offer you proof that the device in Novikov-Veltman Nova Laboratories can change time. When he does, take the offer. And bring your gun. You'll need it."

The light was growing brighter.

Marrins chuckled again. "You're a funny man. Everyone knows CBI agents don't carry weapons that can use lethal force."

"You have one stashed in your office," Donovan said, rushing his words as he grew desperate. "This phone belongs to a guard named Mordicai Robbins. He knows about tonight. About what's happening. He thinks like you, and he'll help you."

He hung up on Marrins's protests. A two-person hit team stepped through the portal. He tossed the phone into the long grass by the road and turned south toward the laboratory.

They were not taking the future from him.

"Where the heck are we?" Sam asked as she looked around. A portal had opened in front of them as they'd run down the stairs, and since an unknown world was better than one with bullets flying and buildings shaking, they'd stepped through.

"*When* is a better question," Mac said. "We need to find a building. Unless you have a phone on you."

"I didn't bring one. Seemed like a security risk." The silly things were too easy to track. She wasn't the tech-savvy one, but even she could pull up most tech's GPS info in under ten minutes. Mac could do it in seconds.

They did not need that kind of surveillance.

She patted her leg. "Bosco."

He ran obediently to her side, and Sam unclipped his leash. "Bosco, *tìm thấy*."

With one thunderous bark, he plowed ahead through the scrub.

"I guess we go that way," Mac said.

She looked around at the long, dry grass.

Mac searched the darkness, too. "You get a feeling like this place is familiar?"

"It smells like magnolias and summer," she said. "Like Alabama."

"That's what I thought, too. It feels like going home."

"This is certainly the adventurous route," Sam said. Despite herself, she was smiling. Exhausted, dehydrated, bruised . . . but they were home. Somewhere near here was a cozy old house with wooden floors and a giant kitchen table worn by loving memories. There was Miss Azalea and her fried chicken, Bri, and Hoss.

"Hoss!"

"What?" Mac looked around in confusion.

"We might be near Hoss!"

"No, Sam."

"What? Bosco would like a friend."

"We could easily be in post-Gant Alabama with Hoss dead and us listed as wanted fugitives."

"Pessimist," she grumbled.

"You still love me," Mac said. "I can see lights up ahead. There's a house or a building."

"A recharge station would be best. They'd have food, and we could probably borrow a car."

"Of course, if we landed after we stole the machine, then we'll be on camera and likely to be arrested," Mac pointed out.

"Hopefully our younger selves were smart enough to head to Australia, making this irrelevant." A disturbing thought occurred to her. "We can't be stuck in a time loop. Can we? Is that a thing?"

Mac shrugged. "According to what they said in the Prime, none of this is possible. Our iteration should have collapsed when they killed Emir. Or when you left. Or, there were half a dozen other reasons why that Prime was going to survive and the rest of the iterations were doomed. I think this proves Emir was very, very wrong."

"Fantastic. So we could get stuck in a time loop. Just what I always wanted." She sighed. "I wonder who the patron saint of time travelers is."

Mac laughed. "If you're really good, maybe you can claim the title."

"I'd need to do a miracle."

"We're alive . . ."

Mac stopped walking. "I know that building."

Sam had to stand on her tiptoes to see over the crest of the hill and past the scrub to the building. "That's Emir's lab. Makes sense. Every portal needs to open near another portal. At least we know they'll have a phone available. What are the chances we'll not run into anyone we know?"

"Statistically, the odds are in our favor," Mac said.

But Sam knew with a dark certainty that their luck had run out. She could all but feel the weight of time pushing her forward. Rushing toward her inevitable death.

Donovan looked the building over. This is where Emir had died, but there was no sign of the police from this iteration. He stepped closer to the glass and peered into the dimly illuminated lobby. A tree planted by the door of the glass atrium shuddered in the breeze of the temperature controls. The room was empty except for a single young woman, black hair twisted up, bent over a book . . . she was no guard.

He smashed his fist into the glass.

The girl looked up. "Hey! This is a private laboratory! You can't be in here." She approached him with nothing more than a truncheon and a glare on her delicate face.

"You should run. I don't usually kill girls who look like you, but I will."

"Sir, this is a private facility. The police are on their way. I'm going to need you to sit down and wait until they arrive."

His first punch knocked her to the floor, cracking her skull on the tile. The truncheon she'd held rolled away under the desk. He listened for alarms or sirens and heard nothing. She'd been bluffing.

Donovan looked down as the girl's eyes opened wide in shock and pain. She looked everywhere, her desperation palpable and intoxicating.

"I told you to run. You should have. I'm a bit shattered. It's seeing yourself die that does it. Nodes are supposed to be stronger," he confessed, "but I'm not. So I go for walks. Long walks. Sometimes I get lucky and find someone who looks like her."

The girl's face wrinkled in pain and agonized confusion.

"You don't look like her, but you got in my way. Sorry 'bout that." He stomped his boot down on her face as hard as he could, crushing her nose into her skull and ending her terror.

The first thing he was going to do when he found

his red-haired woman would be to explain to her how fragile she was. She needed him near her at all times. During the day, she'd stay safe at home while he went to work. He'd make sure she understood. Leaving the house had gotten her husband killed the last time, and she didn't want that.

She wouldn't want that at all. Because she loved him.

He wiped the blood of his boots off on the dead girl's green shirt, then walked over to her desk. A textbook with pictures of paintings lay open. He pushed them aside and pulled up the computer's main screen.

Sunday May 19, 2069.

That wouldn't work at all. He'd seen the red-haired woman in this iteration in 2070. She had to be within a few hundred miles of the machine, but he wasn't going to wait another year for her to appear. She belonged to him. They were happy together. He needed—

Donovan turned at the sound of voices.

"And someone's here." That was MacKenzie.

"I've got a really bad feeling about this, Mac."

Donovan's nostrils flared as he heard Rose's voice. The cadence was wrong, but it was her. She'd followed him. She wasn't dead.

He watched MacKenzie shoulder the door open. The other man swore at the sight of the girl on the floor, and looked up too late.

Donovan was already running down the hall to the jump room. They weren't taking him back to Prime.

Sam ran to Melody, but Mac pulled her back.

"We can't touch. We can't disturb anything here. And we can't stay here. Melody's body was flung back in time. We either need to get to the machine or get out of range before Donovan turns it on."

A square tile lifted up and floated to the body.

"Cleaning bots," Sam said. "Why didn't we think of that the first time? There was no blood because the cleaning bots tidied everything up. Melody must not have triggered the alarm."

"No alarm, no police, and no reason for the bot to leave a foreign liquid on the floor." Mac said. "The bots were fried, so we didn't have any logs to check."

"Because of a power outage. We thought that came before the break-in, but it must be coming."

"Or not be coming at all. Things are definitely changing."

Bosco barked angrily.

"Our cleaning bot has friends," Sam said. "Gotta love security bots."

MacKenzie swore as the dark gray cylinders vacated their charging spots on the wall and moved toward them. "We need to leave."

Sam knew the hall. She'd walked through the rubble the morning after this incident. It hadn't happened yet, though. "Mac . . ." Sam stood on tiptoe and kissed him. "In case this doesn't work out. I'm sorry about dragging you into this. I love you."

He kissed her back. "We'll be fine. Stay here while I take care of Donovan."

She crossed herself as he went, hoping no one else died tonight. Except for Donovan. She was not going to cry any tears if he wound up dead. If they'd arrived ten minutes earlier, Melody Chimes could have lived to finish college.

She let out a sharp whistle, and Bosco appeared, trotting through the trailing security bots, who were trying to figure out what he was. "Bosco," she said, pointing at the lead bot, "pee."

Tongue lolling out of his mouth, he lifted a leg and peed on the bot.

The others went crazy. It was a flaw in the programming. If the module leader was incapacitated, they fell apart like a hill of ants on acid. Circuits fried, the bots started stabbing each other, and when the cleaning bots came in, there was a merry war.

"Sam!" Mac shouted.

Sam snapped her fingers to call Bosco over. "We're here."

Emir's workroom was empty. The machine quiet.

"What happened?" Sam asked. "Where's Donovan?"

"I don't know. I searched the place. There are no exits, and the machine wasn't on."

Sam walked in and kicked the door shut behind Bosco.

Mac peered around her, looking out through the lab windows, which were about to be blown to smithereens. "What did you do?"

"Security bots in medical research facilities have a limited AI, but they can detect hazardous materials. They self-destruct if they sense ammonia or urea. Call it a fatal flaw." She smiled at him. "Don't worry, the cleaning bots will pick up everything. By morning, it will be nothing but fried bots and no organic trace materials for the crime lab."

"That is a major design flaw," Mac said, his horrified look turning to a grin as a security bot was flipped over by a cleaner and squirted with cleaning solvent.

"They get recalled in September." Sam looked around. "I kind of want to leave myself a note."

"Don't," Mac warned. He pointed at something on the screen. "Here, what's this?"

"Donovan was doing calculations," Sam said, scrolling down the screen. "These are similar to the Fountain Variance Calculations Henry did to get me to the Prime. When the iterations run too close together, there's, um, basically friction sparks, I guess? Little bursts of energy that create side portals. Henry figured out how to calculate where they were and which iteration they would lead to. Donovan must be looking to use one near here."

Bosco bumped Sam's leg and whined.

She looked around. "Mac?"

"What?" He was walking toward the other computer station. "We've almost got this figured out."

"Where's the light coming from?" None of the overhead lights were on, but the room was glowing. Lit up and bright as day. Or as bright as a portal.

Warm air circled her legs. "Mac?" He was across the lab. A few meters, but now it felt like miles.

He looked up in horror.

"Come back!" Sam screamed.

Mac was already running, closing the distance . . .

"Mac!" Her scream was swallowed by the portal, giant and terrifying. He was a shadow, a blue-gray figure on an expanding horizon. All around her was the white-hot fury of a portal collapsing and moving everything but her.

CHAPTER 42

"You only have one chance to get today right."

~ Elosia Travkin I3—2061

Wednesday April 2, 2070
Florida District 8
Commonwealth of North America
Iteration 2

Ivy was almost certain she'd been sent to the abandoned town of Eldora to get her out of the way.

Agent Rose's house had been attacked. Agent MacKenzie was injured, there was a dog in the hospital, and Gant and Donovan were still tearing a trail through the quietest district in Florida. If the bodies were any indication, they'd been steadily working their way south. Killing a college student for his car and laptop, then breaking into the apartment of Henry Troom and Devon Bradet, then assaulting a biker outside the Gator Trap . . . that had seemed to break the chain of attacks. Something there had changed things, but repeated visits—all which involved Agent Edwin trying to get her to eat a fried-gator sandwich—hadn't turned up anything useful.

Gant was obsessed. Donovan was angry. Together, the pair became a nigh-on unstoppable force.

Half of Florida's CBI agents were in town now. They were fussing over Agent Rose and edging the police out. Ivy knew there were things she wasn't allowed to know, things too classified for the CBI to share with the local police, but she wished they weren't so obvious about it.

It felt deliberately insulting.

She tugged at her half-broken radio and hoped it worked. "Dispatch, this is Officer Clemens. I am pulling into the second parking area on River Road going south. There's a light there."

Probably a fisherman coming in late. She'd write a fine and continue driving the loop down to River Trace Lane, east on Eldora Road, then south on A1A to South Road, and back north on the mazing stretch of River Road. Again.

"Acknowledged," the dispatch said, voice cracking as the radio Gant had broken lost its connection again. "Check-in—" The voice was cut off.

Ivy stuffed the radio back down in its patch and checked the charge on her phone: thirty percent and no signal. *Of course.* She was in a ghost town. Having cellphone service was probably listed under "unnecessary human encroachment on wild habitat" because the local protestors thought sea turtles were confused by cellphone towers.

Cursing protestors, tourists, and people in general, she grabbed her flashlight and the gun Miss MacKenzie had given her months ago from under her seat. One close call with these bastards was enough. There was playing by the rules, and there was being smart. And when it came to tromping around abandoned buildings in the swamps, she'd learned her lesson.

Anyone who jumped out at her tonight was getting a warning shot in the kneecaps.

Exiting the car, she took a moment to soak in the beauty of the night. Over the inland estuaries, the clouds were grumbling and spitting lightning. Here, she stood outside the storm. The stars were bright and clear in the black sky. Tree frogs were singing to welcome the first warm week as the harbinger of spring. The scent of magnolia blossoms mixed with the brine of the brackish river and aroma of sea grass from the dunes on the other side of A1A. It was the perfect night for a stroll on the beach.

Too bad she was on the riverside looking for fish guts and drunks.

Ivy sighed and flicked on her flashlight. The parking lot had two older cars that had been abandoned the year before and still not towed. Eventually, someone was going to break them down for parts and save the city a few hundred dollars. Or maybe they'd get washed away in the next hurricane.

She pointed her light at the water. Then, realizing that finding a light with a light wasn't going to work, she turned it off. A crescent moon spilled silver moonbeams over gentle waves. A bat swooped past her ear, clicking.

New Smyrna Beach was a gentle glow on the northern horizon. The next nearest city to the south was Port Canaveral, and she was certain there wasn't a launch scheduled from the space center. Which left only bioluminescent algae or humans as the cause of the glow that had attracted her attention, and it was the wrong season for glowing blue waves.

She gave up on the idea of stealth. "Hello?" Her voice carried over the water and was lost in the mangals.

"Hello." The voice that floated back through the darkness filled her with terror.

Ivy pulled the strange gun out of the shoulder holster. "Donovan?"

"I came back for you. Even though you ran away." He stepped out of the shadow of a palm tree. In the moonlight, he was a broken man made of a sharp, jagged darkness and ghostly-pale skin.

She stepped back as her heart rate sped up. "You are under arrest."

"No. I'm not. You can't arrest me. You can't hurt me. You belong with me. *To* me. This is my future."

He fell backward on the ground, and Ivy stared for a long, breathless moment before realizing she'd raised the gun and fired.

In the silence, the radio in her car crackled. She needed to check in. In a daze, she walked back to the car. "This is Officer Clemens checking in."

"You find anything?" dispatch asked.

Ivy stared at the body lying on the sand, waves lapping his shoes as the tide came up. "I've found Donovan. He . . . he attacked me. I shot him." She lifted the gun so the starlight sparkled on the barrel. "He's dead."

"We have an ambulance en route," dispatch said. "Were you injured?"

"No. No, I'm fine." She dropped the gun on the seat and sat down. Clones couldn't kill in self-defense. All she could hope for was that the court believed she was human."

CHAPTER 43

"You only have one chance to get today right."
~ **Elosia Travkin I3—2061**

Thursday April 3, 2070
Fort Benning, Georgia
Commonwealth of North America
Iteration 2/ The Nova Prime

Director Loren watched the live feed of Agent Rose's exit with a frown. Agent MacKenzie had gone with her, just as the file said.

Now he was waiting for the second event. Or for death. He wasn't sure what that would look like. How it would feel if he suddenly ceased to exist because this iteration failed. The notes hadn't been helpful.

It was a quarter to five in the morning, and he was losing hope. The machine was crippled. The silence of the facility was daunting. But better the sepulcher silence than the screams of people dying because he told them to hold the line against the impossible.

He must have drifted off to sleep because a barking dog jolted him awake. The sun was barely warming the horizon, which meant it couldn't be much past seven. Loren stretched, stood, and opened the door.

There, two frazzled agents and a dog were trying to open the barricaded door. "Agent Rose."

She turned slowly. "Director Loren?"

"You look worse than when I last saw you."

"Which was when, sir?" She stepped closer. This Rose was older, a little beaten, and perhaps a little more fragile-looking. She wasn't yet the cold woman he'd seen in his office, and she wasn't the young woman he'd seen rush through the portal a few hours earlier.

With an enigmatic smile, he pointed two fingers at Agent MacKenzie and Agent Rose. "You two, into my office."

The dog followed after, looking cheerful despite the hunted looks of the two agents.

"Cute dog. Is this Hoss?" Loren asked as he held the door open for them.

The dog licked his hand and went to sit beside Rose.

"Hoss was shot, sir. I picked up Bosco five years ago in Australia." She opened her mouth. Shut it. Shook her head. "Sir, I don't think I can explain."

"We could try," MacKenzie offered. "You just won't like what we have to say."

"I'm aware of that," Loren said, retaking his seat. "Two days ago, a woman broke into my office leaving a file and a mild threat. I let things play out. And you did exactly as she predicted, Agent Rose. You left the bureau and broke into a government facility."

Agent Rose winced. "It seemed like the only choice at the time, sir. I'm fairly certain I'd make it again."

"You did," he confirmed. "Both of you went through the portal. It's damaged. I'm told it might not be repairable, but it was enough to tether you. Which leaves us with two problems."

"Whether or not to arrest us?" Rose guessed.

Loren nodded. "And what to do with Hoss. You, that is the Agent Rose who just left, gave custody of Hoss to Agent MacKenzie, who left a timed note to me telling me to take care of the dog."

"Hoss!" Agent Rose smiled for the first time. "I'll take him back." She caught herself. "That is, if you aren't arresting us."

"We have a house in Australia," MacKenzie said suddenly. "We could go back there. We're legal citizens. We'll tell the neighbors we had a vacation, and that will be the end of it. No more intrusions. No more questions. It wouldn't hurt anyone."

"He has a point," Rose said with an eager nod. "We both resigned. If you don't tell anyone we came here, then there's no reason to arrest us." Her smile was pathetically optimistic.

Loren leaned back in his chair. "Australia sounds nice."

"The house is in Cannonvale," Rose said. "You could visit if international tensions ever eased up."

He shook his head. "I can't let you go. Not back to Australia, at least. Your resignations are denied."

"What?" Rose demanded, standing up. "Do you

know what hell I've just been through? They kidnapped my husband. They ruined my life. I am done playing nice. I am going home, with my husband and my dog. I already saved everyone from their mass stupidity. *Twice.* That's my lifetime limit."

Loren laughed.

Rose's shoulders sagged. "Why are you laughing?"

"You said almost the same thing when you came to the office two days ago. You said we were about to go up in a pile of smoke and stupidity."

She looked at MacKenzie, then back at him with a shrug. "Well, I wasn't wrong. You almost did."

MacKenzie tugged on her hand, and she sat back down.

"Love, I think what Director Loren might be suggesting isn't returning to Australia or being arrested." The quiet man raised an eyebrow. "You have something else in mind?"

"A new assignment," Loren said. "For a new branch of the CBI. We haven't named it yet, but Dr. Troom is willing to work with us."

"Henry survived?" Rose sounded a little surprised. "I was worried about how his run-in with Gant would go."

Loren raised an eyebrow. It would be very interesting to hear what history these two remembered. "Dr. Troom survived. Gant is in jail. Donovan, Gant's companion, was shot last night while attacking a police officer named Ivy Clemens. The CBI agent in charge, that would be you, Rose, ruled it an accidental misfire on the part of Donovan. Officer Clemens isn't facing consequences."

"I know her," Rose said. "She's a smart woman. The force is lucky to have her, and the bureau would be better if we could steal her away."

"Yes." He drummed his fingers on the table as a theory formed. "You don't know where she got a gun, do you? She's a clone, and it's a very strange weapon."

Rose's face suddenly became still and expressionless as glass. "I can't imagine where that weapon came from, sir."

"You're a very bad liar, Agent."

"It's been a very long day, sir. A long series of bad days, even."

He smiled. "I'll get to the point then. You're being reassigned, effectively immediately. I'm not giving you a choice."

"Where are you going to set up the labs to test and control this?" MacKenzie asked. "There's no safe place in the Commonwealth. The MIA is explosive. And it's an open invitation for trouble. We're better without it."

"We're opening a new lab in the interior of Alaska," Loren said. "There's nothing but tundra for hundreds of miles. Anyone who wants to try invading can deal with the arctic weather."

Rose shook her head. "Absolutely not."

"It's not a bad idea," MacKenzie argued. "They can't injure anyone this way."

"It's a terrible idea! Alaska is not Airlie Beach. It's

not Cannonvale. It's not warm." Her words had the cadence of a familiar argument.

"We can arrange for you to have a home in Hawaii, on one of the smaller islands," Loren said. "I've already looked into it."

Rose kept shaking her head. "Our stuff is in Australia. My good wedding ring is there!"

He considered the problem. "I can offer to work on our relations with Australia?" Loren shrugged. "That's the best I have at the moment."

"I'll get you another ring," MacKenzie said, reaching for her hand.

Loren hid a smug smile. He'd guessed right. The bureau could be a demanding mistress, but sometimes the demands built strong couples. Friends or lovers, it didn't matter. He'd built both kinds of relationships over the years, and it was gratifying to see that the two people he needed on the upcoming project were already committed to each other.

"Take it as a win, Sam," MacKenzie said in a soft voice. "We're alive. We're together. We have jobs. This beats anything else that could have happened. We can't just go back to Australia and pretend nothing happened. You couldn't leave the CBI alone when we were there, and things were calm. Let's take this, run with it. We can make it work."

She sighed. "Fine. I hate this idea, but fine." She glared at Loren. "Are you coming to freeze to death with us?"

Loren sighed. "Sadly, yes. My family and I will be relocating up there in about two months. The bureau wouldn't let me recommend starting a new branch unless I was willing to take full responsibility for it. I considered the limited range of options and decided I could handle this. After all, retirement is only four years away."

Sam let Mac take Bosco's leash as they walked into the Georgia sunshine. "I think my car is still parked somewhere nearby. We can go find some food. Check in to a hotel and get some sleep."

"And you still have the place in Florida."

"You still have the one in Chicago," she said. She closed her eyes as her brain sprinted ahead of her, gathering problems. She groaned. "Two weeks to pack isn't enough. I don't even know if I want to go back to the Florida apartment."

"We ought to at least check in on everyone."

Sam wrinkled her nose. "Let's save that for later in the week. I need to read my emails before I try to talk to Brileigh, or this whole operation is going to be declassified faster than you can say 'gossip.'" She leaned on Mac's shoulder. "Don't hate me, but I think I'm going to miss the tourists. Cannonvale was boring, but it was a good kind of boring. You know? Nothing we did changed the future of the world. I like easy choices like that."

Mac wrapped his arms around her and kissed her forehead. "I know. But we'll be okay. We've been through worse."

She smiled up at him. "There's one big question that you haven't thought of yet."

"Oh? What's that?" Mac asked as he stole a kiss.

"Where are we having the wedding?"

ACKNOWLEDGMENTS

No book is ever written in a vacuum, so I'd like to thank the people who made writing this possible. To be beloved husband and ever-patient children, thank you for supporting me. I couldn't chase my dreams if I didn't have you for backup. To my parents for reading to me, supplying me with books, and having a family crest that mentions the Borgias. Amy Laurens and Derek Hawkins, thank you for listening to me rave, rant, cry, and whinge more than a grown woman should. Jason Nelson, thank you for keeping that scene on your hard drive and emailing it to me eleventy-billion times. Thea van Diepen and Stephanie McGee, thank you for adding your lyrical gifts and poetry to the book. To my editor, David Pomerico, and my agent, Marlene Stringer, thank you for believing in my crazy world and giving me a chance. Last by not least, thank you, dear reader, for spending time with me and my books.

ABOUT THE AUTHOR

LIANA BROOKS lives in Alaska with her husband, four kids, and a giant mastiff puppy. When she isn't writing, she enjoys hiking the Chugach Range, climbing glaciers, and watching whales. You can find Liana on the web at www.lianabrooks.com, on Twitter as @LianaBrooks, or on Facebook as ByLianaBrooks.

Discover great authors, exclusive offers, and more at hc.com.